PRAISE FOR TAHOE HIT

"I'M ADDICTED TODD BORG'S INTRICATE, FAST-PACED
MYSTERIES..." — *Cathy Cole, Kittling: Books*

"ANOTHER TENSION-FILLED SIGNATURE BOOK, with twists,
turns, and surprises by master storyteller TODD BORG — *Silver Reviews*

PRAISE FOR TAHOE DEEP

"A SMART, INTRIGUING MYSTERY...A SUPERIOR ENTRY"
— *Kirkus Reviews*

"JAW-DROPPING INVESTIGATIVE SKILLS... DEEP, THOUGHTFUL
AND COMPLEX" — *Gloria Sinibaldi, Tahoe Mountain News*

PRAISE FOR TAHOE SKYDROP

"ANOTHER IMPRESSIVE CASE FEATURING A DETECTIVE WHO
REMAINS NOT ONLY DOGGED, BUT ALSO REFLECTIVE."
— *Kirkus Reviews*
"A SURPRISE TWIST WILL GIVE YOU AN EXTRA JOLT...a great addition to the Owen McKenna series." — Gloria Sinibaldi, Tahoe Mountain News

PRAISE FOR TAHOE PAYBACK

"AN ENGROSSING WHODUNIT" — *Kirkus Reviews*

"ANOTHER GREAT TODD BORG THRILLER — *Book Dilettante*

"FAST PACED, ABSORBING, MEMORABLE" — *Kittling: Books*
Borg's Tahoe Mystery series chosen by Kittling: Books as *ONE OF THE TEN BEST MYSTERY SERIES*

PRAISE FOR TAHOE DARK

"ONCE AGAIN, BORG HITS ALL THE RIGHT NOTES FOR FANS
OF CLASSIC DETECTIVE FICTION in the mold of Dashiell Hammett,
Raymond Chandler, Ross Macdonald, and Robert B. Parker."
— *Kirkus Reviews*

"TAHOE DARK IS PACKED WITH ACTION AND TWISTS. THE
SURPRISES JUST KEEP ON COMING...THE FINAL SCENE IS AN-
OTHER TODD BORG MASTERPIECE." — *Silver's Reviews*

"I LOVE TODD BORG'S BOOKS...There is the usual great twist ending in Tahoe Trap that I never would have guessed" – *JBronder Reviews*

"THE PLOTS ARE HIGH OCTANE AND THE ACTION IS FASTER THAN A CHEETAH ON SPEED" – *Cathy Cole, Kittling: Books*

PRAISE FOR TAHOE HIJACK

"BEGINNING TO READ TAHOE HIJACK IS LIKE FLOOR-BOARDING A RACE CAR... RATING: A+"
- Cathy Cole, Kittling: Books

"A THRILLING READ... any reader will find the pages of his thrillers impossible to stop turning"
- Caleb Cage, The Nevada Review

"THE BOOK CLIMAXES WITH A TWIST THE READER DOESN'T SEE COMING, WORTHY OF MICHAEL CONNELLY"
- Heather Gould, Tahoe Mountain News

"I HAD TO HOLD MY BREATH DURING THE LAST PART OF THIS FAST-PACED THRILLER" *- Harvee Lau, Book Dilettante*

PRAISE FOR TAHOE HEAT

"IN TAHOE HEAT, BORG MASTERFULLY WRITES A SEQUENCE OF EVENTS SO INTENSE THAT IT BELONGS IN AN EARLY TOM CLANCY NOVEL"
- Caleb Cage, Nevada Review

"TAHOE HEAT IS A RIVETING THRILLER"
- John Burroughs, Midwest Book Review

"WILL KEEP READERS TURNING THE PAGES AS OWEN RACES TO CATCH A VICIOUS KILLER"
- Barbara Bibel, Booklist

"THE READER CAN'T HELP BUT ROOT FOR McKENNA AS THE BIG, GENEROUS, IRISH-BLOODED, STREET-WISE-YET-BOOK-SMART FORMER COP"
- Taylor Flynn, Tahoe Mountain News

Titles by Todd Borg

TAHOE JADE

by

Todd Borg

THRILLER PRESS

Thriller Press First Edition, August 2021

TAHOE JADE
Copyright © 2021 by Todd Borg

This novel is a work of fiction. Any references to real locales, establishments, organizations, or events are intended only to give the fiction a sense of verisimilitude. All other names, places, characters and incidents portrayed in this book are the product of the author's imagination.

Library of Congress Control Number: 2021937104

ISBN: 978-1-931296-29-8

Cover design and map by Keith Carlson

Manufactured in the United States of America

For Kit

ACKNOWLEDGMENTS

I can't heap enough praise on my editors, Liz Johnston, Eric Berglund, Christel Hall, and my wife Kit. Great editors make the difference between a book with good potential and a good book.

And check out the nuance and impact of the TAHOE JADE cover by Keith Carlson. It makes me think of carved jade, and the Pony Express, and the long rich history of Lake Tahoe. Just beautiful.

I hope this story is worth all the great help I received.

Thanks again to all.

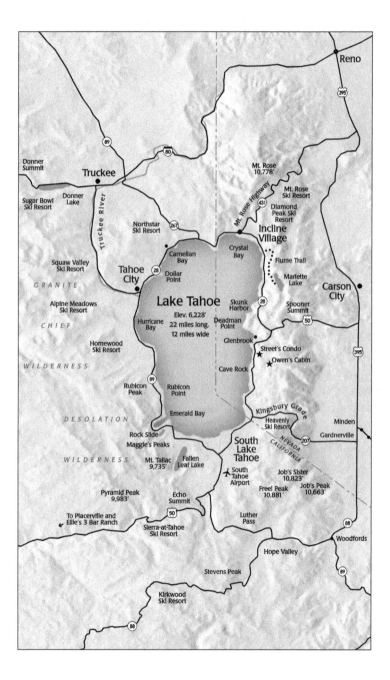

PROLOGUE

October 5th, 1861
Buckland Pony Express Station, Silver Springs, Nevada

"You the new kid?" the stock tender said to Jimmy Wilson as he helped Jimmy saddle up his mount. "Couple things you should know right up front. First, never mind what you mighta heard. Not that many riders have died. 'Course, this could be your big day. Maybe you get smoked or eat a arrow or somethin'. No point in stressin' 'bout it. Second, forget your dream o' glory. Ever' new rider think they gonna sweet-talk their way through a Paiute attack, or maybe swim 'cross a flooded river. Some think they gonna set a new speed record for their course. Get that crap outta your head right now. Git to your station without losin' the mail is the job. You see Paiute warriors, best you turn 'round and high-tail it back to your last station. The station keeper'll set you up on a different route. Come to a flood in a monsoon storm? Don't try to be no hero. You'll lose the mail and your life. The closest station will give you a roof 'til the monsoon dies down. And no matter what, don't be thinkin' 'bout trying to be fastest. It's just a simple fact you won't do the ride near fast as Pony Bob. That's okay. He's the best. Ever' body gotta start as a beginner. At least you'll have good weather over the first half of your route."

"Pony Bob..." Jimmy said. "That's Robert Haslam."

"Yep. Best rider in the Pony Express. Holds all the records. Distance and speed. One time, he rode three hundred sixty mile in thirty-six hour. Another, he rode a hundred twenty mile nonstop after he took a arrow through the mouth. Arrow took out three of his teeth and set his cheeks flappin' and sprayin' blood, 'n he still rode. No one gonna match Pony Bob."

"He didn't ride all that on the same horse, though," Jimmy said.

"'Course not," the tender scoffed. "We always put riders on a fresh horse ever' ten mile or so."

"I don't think I could ride a hundred miles non-stop, fresh horse or not," Jimmy said. "I'd have to take a break or two. This route to Friday's Station at Lake Tahoe isn't that far, is it?"

"No. Friday's Station more like eighty mile from here." The tender gave Jimmy a hard, appraising look. Maybe he saw dismay. "Don't worry, you'll do okay. You built just like Pony Bob. You guys're all skinny and little. Wiry strong. Like jockeys. No doubt you can make time. Difference with Pony Bob is he always rode like he was on a race course. Don't try it. Push your horse too hard, he'll miss his footing in a ravine and break a leg. And then where'll you be? Paiute target practice."

Jimmy frowned. He figured the stock tender just wanted to impress him with stories of Pony Bob. Maybe it was a standard way to motivate new riders, talking about their finest rider.

"How do you know I'll have good weather?" Jimmy asked as he tightened the saddle's cinch strap. He was worried about the weather, about the fierce Paiute Indians, about getting a late start. And he was stressed that he would probably have to ride the most mountainous section – the mountains that went up to Lake Tahoe – in the dark.

"I only know the weather for the first half of your ride." The stock tender pointed west. "See that distant mountain peak to the west? That's near Virginia City, where they discovered silver a couple years ago. When the air's clear from here to there, the weather'll be good even farther west, pro'bly through to Carson City. Can't say for Lake Tahoe up in the mountains past that. That dark gray sky in the distance? Look like a cloud bank from here. This time of year, any cloud that dark usually mean a snowstorm up at the lake."

Jimmy made a solemn nod. "I remember the big flat valley south of Carson City. But I wasn't much more than a little kid the only time I rode up the mountains to the lake. All I remember is it went straight up forever. Any tips for finding the route out of the valley?"

The stock tender shrugged. "Never been there myself. Got no interest in a place where it snow yards instead of inches. But there's lots of miners coming in from California on the other side. They went there for gold ten years ago. Now they're comin' back to Virginia City for silver. I heard they come through ever' pass in the mountains, like ants streamin' up and over somethin' in the way. You'll probably see a well-worn trail."

The stock tender lifted up the mochila. It was a type of knapsack with pockets for mail in each corner. The pockets each had little padlocks so the mail couldn't be tampered with. The man slung the mochila over the saddle horn and attached the straps.

Jimmy put his foot in the stirrup and swung his other leg up and over the horse's back.

The stock tender pointed at the mochila. "Set the mochila so your thighs go over these two rear corners."

Jimmy shifted and got the mochila in place.

The horse was a small mare, 14 and a half or 15 hands, a mustang, maybe 4 or 5 years old. Probably saddle broke in the last few months. Very frisky. She seemed to bounce on her front hooves. But Jimmy had practically grown up on horseback. He felt comfortable as the mustang spun back and forth like a crazy compass needle, then reared a bit, jerked, and bounced. A spirited horse was no problem for Jimmy.

"I's worried when Pony Bob blew out his bum ankle," the stock tender said. "Hard to find a replacement. But it look like you know what you're doin'."

"Well, you're stuck with me, anyway," Jimmy said. "I'll get the mail to Friday's Station in Tahoe. You can count on that."

The stock tender gave Wilson another long look. "I'll believe that when you come back tomorrow with the east-bound mail."

"One more thing," Jimmy Wilson said. "I've heard scary stuff about the Paiute. But I've never seen any. Are they as bad as people say?"

The stock tender tipped his head left then right as if

stretching his neck. He rubbed the back of his neck, squeezing the muscles. It seemed to Jimmy that the stock man was trying to think of the right words.

The man started to talk, hesitated, started again. "The Paiute are – what's the word – all 'bout honor. Problem is, Paiute girls are real pretty. And some of the white miners have taken them for real bad stuff. There's pro'bly no single thing that makes a Paiute warrior as crazy as that. Same for any fathers, I guess, civilized or not. So the whole justice thing for Paiute make sense when you think about it. Anyway, if they suspect you be one of the bad whites, best get your ass back to the last station you were at."

Jimmy nodded. He gave his horse some rein, squeezed with his legs, clicked his tongue, and the mustang shot off into an instant gallop.

The desert trail was smooth, the curves gentle, and Jimmy made excellent time. The scents of sagebrush mixed with his horse's sweat and the leather saddle, and the dry desert dust that was as much a part of the breeze as the air itself. This was a world that Jimmy Wilson knew well. He felt comfortable.

The 190 Pony Express stations were set up at roughly ten-mile intervals all the way from St. Joseph, Missouri to Sacramento, California. At each station, the riders would switch to fresh horses and continue on to the next station. It was a continuous relay, with riders going both west and east, switching horses every ten miles. After riding eight or ten horses and covering 90 or 100 miles, the rider handed off the mochila mail pouch to another rider. With two riders carrying the mochila each day, the mail moved 1900 miles from Missouri to California in only ten days.

Every day, a new batch of mail headed west from Missouri and east from California, which meant there were always ten mochilas of mail heading west and ten heading east.

At the next station, ten miles to the west, Jimmy switched to a fresh horse, a gelding paint. He repeated that process at each station. As Jimmy rode, he scanned the horizon in all directions, watching for Paiute warriors. But he lucked out. He was alone on the desert.

After he'd galloped 40 miles, he was sore. It was hard to imagine he was only halfway to Friday's Station at Lake Tahoe. Despite the soreness, he had no doubt he'd make it. But the idea of turning around and galloping back 80 miles the next day was intimidating.

Jimmy Wilson picked up his eighth and last horse, another mustang mare, chestnut-colored, at the Genoa Station in Carson Valley. Genoa was tucked in against the mountainside several miles south of Carson City. Jimmy Wilson continued south on his fresh horse, looking for the place where the trail turned off to climb 3000 vertical feet up the Carson Range and into the Lake Tahoe Basin.

He came to a Y in the dirt trail and took the right fork. The trail was well worn but eroded into large ruts from past rains. The trail immediately started climbing. The fresh mustang from Genoa Station took the trail fast, as if running up the mountain were no different for her than running on the flat. Jimmy had to slow her down to a trot to safely navigate the twisting, rutted trail in the dim light.

The mountain above was covered with sagebrush on its lower half. Its upper portion was capped with forest. In the growing twilight, it looked ominous, the trees dark and forbidding. The top of the mountain was covered with a deep purple-gray blanket of clouds. In minutes, Jimmy was well above the valley floor.

To his side, Jimmy could see down below from where he'd come. There was a flickering from a campfire. Squinting in the gathering dark, he sensed a hut in the style built by the Washoe Indians. Near the fire were three or four figures. Even though Jimmy was riding away from them, it was reassuring to see them because the Washoe were peaceful and more accepting of white men than the Paiute who, when accosted or when their daughters were kidnapped, fought back ferociously.

Jimmy's comfort at seeing the Washoe evaporated when thick snow suddenly fell like a blanket from the sky.

Jimmy had seen snow back when he moved as a child from Texas to the Nebraska Territory. But that snow was usually gentle and dry, like falling bits of cotton.

This heavy snow was something he'd never seen before. It came down in giant clusters of flakes. He pulled down his hat so the brim would block some of the snow, and he lifted his kerchief up over his nose and mouth. The snow was so heavy it was hard to breathe. The valley below him disappeared. The trees above him lost all shape. They were merely a layer of darkness.

The trail quickly turned white, which made it more visible in the growing darkness. But it also made it slick. Jimmy gave his horse free rein, letting her pick and choose her footing.

Like all animals, horses understand trails as the easiest route through any territory. With no guidance from Jimmy, the mustang followed the white path up into the dark. Occasionally, she would slip and scramble to regain footing. But the sharp leading edge of her hooves were good at gripping on slippery surfaces.

Once, all four of the mustang's hooves slid backward. Jimmy leaned forward, trying to lower his center of gravity and help stabilize her balance. Jimmy was ready to slide off to lighten her load. But the horse skittered off the trail, then made a small leap forward, three hooves sliding. She regained her footing and then continued to climb the trail.

Jimmy marveled at her composure. He'd grown up riding larger, more sedate horses. They would have never made it up this mountainside. But this mustang didn't even huff. The mare was used to such trails and such weather.

After a couple of hours of climbing into the snowstorm, the trail crested the top of the pass. Jimmy knew the valley floor was far below and behind him. But all he could see looking down or up were dark purple clouds and snow.

Jimmy knew it was more dangerous riding down a slippery trail than it was riding up. Yet when the trail pitched down, it wasn't nearly as steep. The west side of the mountain was relatively gentle compared to the steep east side.

Jimmy let the mustang pick her way. The horse needed no input from her rider. The horse slipped in several places but always regained her footing. The snow grew deeper at a fast rate.

Soon they were riding through a foot of snow. Not much later, a foot and a half. But the horse didn't seem to mind. And as they lost elevation, the intensity of the snow lessened.

When the trail leveled out, Jimmy knew he was close to the level of Lake Tahoe. It wouldn't be long before the trail approached Friday's Station, the final stop on his 80-mile ride.

He'd hand off the mochila to the next rider, unsaddle and stable the mare, and head to the bunkhouse for dinner and a long sleep on one of the cots.

Jimmy saw a light shining dimly through the falling snow. He was relieved to think he was close to his destination.

Except the light was moving. As he got closer, he saw it was a kerosene lantern swinging back and forth. A signal for a rider. The lantern grew brighter in the storm.

Jimmy slowed his horse.

"Stop your horse," a man called out in the rough voice of someone who'd smoked heavily for decades. "Hazard ahead."

Jimmy came to a stop. A single dark figure stood in the trail. Jimmy couldn't see the man's face under his big fur hat.

"I'm Jimmy Wilson doing the Pony Express run in place of Pony Bob. I need to get to Friday's Station."

"I figured as much. Friday's Station is only a quarter mile. But the creek is just ahead. And a tree is down across the bridge. If you help me, I think we can move the tree."

Jimmy dismounted. "Let's have a look."

The man gestured. "Just up this way. Careful. The bank of the creek is steep. And this snow is treacherous." The man took a step back, politely allowing Jimmy to step ahead. "Take a look. You know best what your horse can handle."

As Jimmy walked by, the lantern light shined up at the man's face. He was older than most any miner. 50 years at least. Maybe 60. Gray hair sprouted in tufts from under the edge of his fur-skin cap. Gray whiskers speckled his cheeks. He'd been unshaven for many days. The man smelled sour, like a bear. His lips caved inward, indicating no teeth.

Hopefully, he could still help Jimmy move the tree.

Jimmy walked forward, squinting his eyes, looking through

the curtain of falling snow. He saw no tree.

When the Pony Express rider walked past him, the old man swung a rock at the back of the rider's head. It made a soft, squishy thud. The rider fell to the ground, a muffled movement that was silenced by the insulation of snow.

The old man walked back to the Pony Express horse. He lifted the shield on his lantern and blew out the flame. After it had cooled for a minute, he tied the lantern to the saddle. With significant effort, he got his foot up in the stirrup, swung his leg over the horse, lifted the reins, and rode off.

It wouldn't be long before the snow covered the dead man and his tracks. They might not find the rider's body for a day. If the snow kept up, they might not find it until the following spring.

An hour later, the old man had watered the mustang mare at another creek and headed to the barn where he'd made his camp. The mustang whinnied, knowing by scent that another horse was near.

The man dismounted and walked the horse into the rickety structure that was only used in the summer by some sheepherders who'd long since driven their sheep to the west, down out of snow country. He would head that way himself the next morning.

After the mustang and his own horse greeted each other, he put the mustang into a stall with hay the herders had left. The stall was next to the one where the man's horse stood. The two horses lifted their heads over the stall wall that separated them and sniffed each other. The man took off the mustang's saddle and bridle and hung them over the stall wall. The tack was clearly marked as belonging to the Pony Express. The mustang was branded as well, but it was less obvious. The man would be able to sell the mustang for a good price when he got down to the Central Valley in California.

The man lit a lantern, built a fire in the wood stove, and warmed up his dinner. After eating and drinking half a flask of whiskey, he sat down and forced open the little padlocks of the mochila.

There were many letters of various sizes. They bore a range of Pony Express stamps. He went through them all, tearing them open, slipping his fingertips into the envelopes, looking for money. He found some bills and some coins, but nothing significant.

He put the money in his inside jacket pocket and buttoned the flap. As he returned the letters to the mochila, he noticed that one of the letters seemed different from the others. He pulled it out of the group.

The envelope was somewhat larger than most of the other letters. The paper was thick and looked expensive. The writing was with a dip pen in an elegant style.

In the center of the envelope was the address. The man had very limited reading skills. But he could make out most of the words.

> To the Honorable Leland Stanford
> Governor Elect of the State of California
> Sacramento, California

At the upper left corner was the return address.

> President Abraham Lincoln
> The White House
> Pennsylvania Avenue
> Washington

Having already checked the envelope for money and found none, the old man had no interest in the letter, even if he'd been able to read like an educated man. He knew presidents were supposed to be important. But the work a president did had no bearing on miners and grifters like the old man. Nevertheless, the man realized he could possibly sell the letter to a book-learned person.

He stuffed the envelope with its letter into the same jacket pocket where he'd put the money. He draped the mochila over the same stall wall on which he'd hung the Pony Express saddle and gear. Maybe someone would find the opened letters and send them on their way. The man closed the door to the wood stove, climbed into his bedroll, and went to sleep.

In the morning, the old man took the halter off his mount, put it on the mustang, and tied a rope to the halter ring. His bridle and saddle went back on his horse, and he rode away from the old barn, the mustang in tow.

Although the snow had stopped falling, it was windy, the air biting at exposed skin. The cold front that came through had dropped another two feet of snow. A fluffy white blanket, more than three feet thick, covered the world. The sky was rose-pink, and wisps of clouds swirled. The old man rode west, looking for the trail that climbed up the Sierra crest before heading down the long west slope to the valley where palm trees grew. The horses trudged through the snow without complaint. In lieu of a trail to follow, they accepted the man's direction.

The forest looked different than the man remembered. The landmarks were covered in white, the forest contours reshaped in unfamiliar ways. But the man could see the brightness of the sun shining through the thin clouds, and thus he knew the general direction. If he headed toward the mountains to the west, he'd eventually find a pass through them. Twice, and then three times, his horse came up against unseen obstacles and suddenly stopped. Each time, they proved to be downed trees, obscured by the white that covered them.

The man came to an opening in the forest. The vast blue plate of Lake Tahoe was only a half mile to the north. On the lake's western side was the familiar wall of mountains that separated Tahoe from the long slope that headed down to the warm country of California. Between the lake and mountains was a meadow area. If he went to the meadow, his travel would be much easier. No more buried trees would block his route through the snow.

The meadow led directly to where the mountains rose up. Once he got to the base of the mountains, he could travel along them until he found a trail that would climb up to a pass.

Of course, the man knew about avalanche hazards, especially after a snowfall like that of the previous night. It was the man's expertise about threats like avalanches that had allowed him to thrive in a mountainous environment that others found so threatening. The man would stay well out from the wall of rock. No avalanche would bury him.

It took just a few minutes to reach the meadow. The lake shore was close. They could travel along the shore. But windwhipped waves threw freezing spray toward the man and horses. It would be better on the meadow. As the man directed his horse onto the large field of white, the horse balked.

"C'mon, hawsey boy," the man said. "Ain't nothin' hiding in the grass under this snow. No snake gonna jump up and scare you." The man shook the reins. His horse stomped his left front hoof but otherwise didn't move. The man noticed that the line that went from his saddle horn back to the Pony Express mustang was taut. He turned to look behind him.

The mustang didn't want to come, either.

"Trust me, hawsey boy. Ain't no bear or cougar in this meadow. An' we're too far from the mountain to get buried by no avalanche. No need to worry."

He gave the reins another shake, clicked his tongue, gave the horse a strong squeeze with his legs, and said, "GIT!"

His horse took fast steps into the snow-covered meadow grass, and the mustang came along behind.

Except it wasn't a meadow. A layer of ice had formed on a pond that lay back from the shore of Lake Tahoe. The ice was just strong enough to hold the snow.

But the horses broke through the ice and plunged into icy water. The man's horse jerked with surprise and made a bucking movement as it struggled to turn back to firm ground.

The old man was tossed off his horse. He landed on his back in the snow. Now that the ice was broken, the snow blanket where the man lay sagged down into the water. The snow immediately turned to slush, and the man became instantly soaked in ice water.

The man struggled to find his footing, to turn over and stand up. But the slush was like cement, holding him in position. The man flailed his arms and kicked with his feet. But the cold sapped his energy in seconds. The man was astounded to realize that his body was quickly made numb by the ice water. Soon, he no longer had control of his muscles. With his heavy clothes soaked and laden with icy slush, the man slowly sank beneath the surface as the two horses climbed free from the pond and trotted away.

ONE

September 1st
Present day
Lake Tahoe

After I finished my morning coffee, I called my girlfriend Street Casey and got her voicemail. I left a message saying I was tired of all work and no play and would she and Blondie like to join Spot and me for a walk on the beach or something.

Spot and I headed down the mountain and stopped at Street's condo in case she was in.

Street opened her door as we pulled up. Blondie was a blur racing toward the Jeep as I opened my door. Just as I got out, Blondie leaped up and hit the rear door with her front paws.

"Easy, girl. His Largeness doesn't instantaneously teleport out of the Jeep. I have to open the door for him."

Blondie raced around in an excited circle.

Inside the Jeep, Spot was wagging with anticipation, his tail thwacking back and forth between the front and rear seat backs.

I got the door open. Blondie wisely jumped to the side as he leaped out. 45 pounds of small yellow lab versus 170 pounds of Harlequin Great Dane would make a poor result if they had a direct collision. They shot off into the woods, Spot chasing but not catching her.

I walked over to Street, who was holding a bicycle helmet. I bent down to give her a kiss and hug. "What is this outfit?" I asked. "Parachute pants for biking? But I didn't bring my bike. And matching shoes? But they don't look like what I've seen cyclists wear." I reached down to touch the padded gloves and wrist guards that hung from a miniature carabiner attached to her waist band. "Maybe this is a disco outfit? But I thought disco went out in the eighties."

"This isn't for disco dancing!" She lightly slugged my shoulder.

"Well, you look good in these threads, whatever they are. But of course, you'd look good in a horse blanket."

"This is parkour gear. Maybe you'd like to try the sport."

"What's parkour?"

"It's kind of a cousin to running an obstacle course, but with an unusual approach to obstacles, and you do it at hyperspeed. If you want, we could practice on one of the boulder fields near Mr. Toad's. It's marvelous for physical conditioning."

I thought of what I remembered from Mr. Toad's Wild Ride, the Tahoe mountain bike version, not the Disneyland ride. "And you do it on a mountain bike?"

"No, parkour is running, not riding. And I don't go where the mountain bikers come flying down the trail. But nearby. I just go there for the boulders."

"So parkour is the sport of running through boulders?"

"You run through any kind of obstacles. The emphasis is on using the obstacles to help you go through them or over them or around them. You use your hands for support while pivoting and vaulting."

"I've sort of jogged in boulders," I said. "I thought it was kind of like skiing moguls. You go from boulder top to boulder top. But I couldn't call what I did a run."

"Parkour is much more intense than jogging. You might jump from the top of a boulder to another. But it's more likely that you'd be down among the boulders snaking through them at full speed. And it's as useful in an urban alley as it is in a boulder field."

A thought came to me. "Like in a Jackie Chan movie and he's escaping the bad guys? He doesn't just run down the alley. He vaults over dumpsters, swings from fire escape ladders, rolls over piles of debris, and when he gets to the end of the alley, he leaps up and plants his foot on the right wall, then ricochets to the end wall and then over to the left wall."

Street was nodding. Grinning. "Yes, exactly! And when Jackie Chan goes up a wall like that, it's called a tic tac climb, running up a corner wall with his shoes gripping the surface. And each leap brings him a little higher until he can cat-leap to the top of the wall, swing himself up and over, and drop down the other side to escape. That's classic parkour. Of course, most of us mere mortals can't do anything like Jackie Chan."

"Why the funny name?" I asked.

"Parkour? It comes from French military training. They look at any daunting landscape, natural or urban, and get through it ultra fast."

"I think I've seen this on YouTube. Only it was called free running."

"Free running's more about showmanship. Parkour combined with dance and flips to dazzle an audience. Hard-core parkour participants don't go for show. They just go for speed."

I gestured at her outfit. "And these are the clothes to wear for it."

She nodded. "You're welcome to come with me. Of course, you're not wearing appropriate protective gear for parkour."

"Have you ever seen me wear a uniform? I quit that when I quit the SFPD. Before I met you."

Street nodded. "I recall your sarcastic lecture about people and their sports-specific outfits. Like a person can't have fun unless they've got the right clothes."

"Sorry. I know my comments can be very rude. I just react when someone goes over the top with it."

Street grinned. "Like the guy you knew who wore a special outfit for trimming his bushes."

"Yeah." I laughed, remembering. "There was an actual bush-trimming logo on the collar of his shirt and on his gloves and on the back of his bush-trimming shoes. They were part of the bush-trimming tools brand. That's his business, and more power to him if it gives him a bush-trimming thrill. But I confess to being privately amused."

"You probably think a guy could trim bushes while wearing

only blue jeans and a t-shirt, and cheap hardware-store gloves." Street grinned.

"Yeah, I probably do," I said, trying not to laugh. "But with you, I assume form follows function. You're not just wearing those clothes because they look good. You're wearing them because they help you parkour your way over a boulder field."

"Right. Mostly, it's about safety. The main thing about these clothes is tough fabric that's loose enough to allow freedom of movement."

"Like disco," I said. I started singing a line I remembered from the Bee Gees song How Deep Is Your Love.

"No, stop, stop, stop!" Street protested. "I'll have that song stuck in my brain and it'll cause a parkour accident."

The dogs came running back. They were panting with vigor. Blondie ran up to Street, who bent down and pet her. Street turned and looked at something on the ground that caught her eye. It was a yellow rubber duck, a bathtub toy.

Street turned to me. "Watch, I'll show you a trick. I've taught Blondie how to put her toys away." Street opened her front door wide. Then she walked over to the rubber duck. "Blondie, you forgot your toy in the dirt. Come here." Blondie looked up at Street with the loving rescue-dog devotion we'd come to expect.

Street lowered her hand and pointed at the duck. "Blondie, put the duck away."

Blondie looked at the duck, then lifted her head to look at Street again.

Street pointed at the duck and then pointed toward the open door. "Put it away."

Blondie picked up the duck and trotted into Street's condo. I stepped over to the doorway to watch. Blondie went across the living room, dropped the duck into her toy box, then came back out to look up at Street, who bent down and praised her lavishly.

"Largeness," I said. "Are you paying attention?" Spot looked at me and made a slow, tentative wag. "Your dog friend here is a candidate for a Rhodes Scholarship. You could learn something if you paid attention."

Spot walked over and picked up a stick that was large enough to qualify as a small log. He lay down on the grass patch near Street's door, crossed his front paw over it to hold it in place, and began chewing it up into splinters.

Street watched him. "That's what Spot does with his toys?" Street said.

"Right. And even if he did know how to put his toys away, he wouldn't."

"The recalcitrant street-smart kid," Street said, "who has no use for book learning."

"Not unless the book delivers treats."

"I was going to do a morning workout. Then I have to get ready for the trip to Bend, Oregon."

"That's right. The entomologist convention to talk about insects. What did you call it? Bug papers and bug panels. When do you leave?"

"I catch the flight from Reno to Portland later this afternoon. Then I'm riding with some other scientists to Bend. We'll have two days of presentations, and then I'll be back. You want to join me for a workout before I leave?"

So we squeezed the Rhodes Scholar dog and the recalcitrant street-smart dog into the back of the Jeep, drove to South Lake Tahoe, headed southwest out Pioneer Trail, and parked where there was an access trail into the forest. The dogs trotted into the trees while Street and I hiked to a large boulder field near the bottom of Mr. Toad's Wild Ride.

"You want to give it a try?" Street said as she pulled on her gloves and wrist guards.

"You first," I said. "Show me how it's done."

"Of course, I'm just an amateur," she said as she took several running steps, hit a small boulder without slowing down, leaped to a taller boulder, banked left and arced through the air, landed on the ground with lots of forward motion, put her gloved hand out and placed it on a tree stump, did a little twisting vault, landed next to a house-sized boulder, spun around it, and disappeared.

I took some running steps, jumped up onto a boulder, and teetered, nearly losing my balance. Holding my arms out for balance, I bent my knees and carefully jumped back down to the ground. Safe. Uninjured. Ever competent.

After a minute, Street appeared in the distance, running toward me, slaloming around boulders, careening here and there, hurdling a downed log, vaulting up onto a flat-topped rock more like a table than a boulder, then made a leap that brought her arcing through the air as she lifted her arms up and out like a gymnast doing an official dismount. She landed just four feet in front of me with her feet together and arms coming down at her side, perfectly balanced.

She looked svelte and beautiful, breathing heavily and smiling broadly.

"I guess the uniform really helps, huh?" I said.

Her eyes narrowed. "Yeah, it's a super hero thing. Put on the uniform, you can win the gold medal. Did you give it a try?"

"Yeah, it was great. Fast and furious. I only had one scary moment as I made a tricky descent while moving like a fighter jet. I thought I'd have to absorb the shock with a somersault on the ground. But my innate balance saved me, and I came to a stop with no injuries."

Street made a slight smile. "Shall we do a run together?"

"Group parkour? Sounds great," I said, a bit worried but then relieved as my phone rang.

I pulled it out and hit the button. "Owen McKenna," I said.

"Thank you for answering. The first thing you need to know is I'm not crazy!" A woman's voice. She sounded very stressed. "Please don't hang up. Please hear me out. I'm not crazy!"

TWO

"Got it," I said to the woman on the phone. "You're not crazy." I walked over to a boulder and sat down on it.

"No, I mean it," the woman said. "If you ask around, you could probably find people who will say I'm paranoid. And maybe I am." The woman's breathing was as heavy as if she'd been out running a parkour course. "Maybe I'm something of a hypochondriac. But I'm not crazy. What's happened is not a figment of my imagination!"

The woman's voice was getting louder as she spoke. I'd never had a stranger begin a conversation by shouting at me.

"Please, stay calm. Let's back up a bit. Take a deep breath, hold it a bit, then tell me, please, what is your name?"

I heard more breathing. "Jade," she said. "Jade Jaso."

"Jade," I repeated. It sounded unusual to me, but I was the first to recognize that I'm not familiar with name trends.

"It's after my mother. She was Chinese and part of a long line of women going back many generations. All named Jade."

"And your last name again, please?"

"Jaso. My father was Billy Jaso. The first non-Chinese man to marry into the line of my female ancestors. So I'm the first who's only half Chinese. But my mother still gave me the name Jade."

"Jade Jaso. Cool name," I said, trying to make calm conversation.

"Jaso is Basque. Maybe you've heard of the Basque country. It's an area in Northern Spain."

"I once had a client who was Basque," I said, thinking of Paco Ipar, the ten year-old-kid who was targeted in a crime of medical theft. "Jade, what is your phone number?"

She told me, saying the digits too fast for me to remember them.

"I'm sorry, I missed that. Can you please repeat that more slowly?"

She did. Her voice was still much louder than necessary, but answering the simplest of questions had made her a bit less strident.

I repeated the number, speaking aloud, visualizing the numerals, a trick to remember them. I saw Street mouthing them, no doubt to remember them as well.

"Where do you live?" I said.

"I'm on the South Shore. Do you know Christmas Valley?"

"Near Echo Summit?"

"Right. There's two roads that go out Christmas Valley. The first one is Highway Eighty-nine toward Luther Pass. The second is South Upper Truckee Road. It turns off Highway Fifty at the bottom of Echo Summit."

"I remember," I said. "That's how you get to Meyer's Grade, the old road over Echo Summit."

"Yes, of course." She said it with a voice so brusque it was as if she were trying to get me to hang up on her. But she gradually became less stressed. "If you drive past Meyer's Grade heading south you come to the Celio Ranch."

"The old ranch from back before the Civil War," I said. "They raised cattle. They were around when the Pony Express had Yank's Station in Meyers."

"Right. Our land is near the Celio Ranch. We're the Jaso Ranch. You can't see it from the road. There's no sign. There's a narrow drive that goes in to the west, then turns south. My great grandfather sold off most of the ranch back in the nineteen fifties. The remaining property is a narrow north-south strip, sixty acres, right up against the mountain. You've no doubt driven up Highway Fifty to Echo Summit, right? It's probably the most traveled road in and out of Tahoe."

"Sure," I said, trying to ignore the snarky flavor to her comment.

"The summit is a thousand feet straight up above us. If you stop in one of those little pullouts up on the cliff road and look down, you're looking down at me."

"Are you in the ranching business?"

"Used to be, but no longer. Too many rules. Even private parcels are constrained by strict rules. Grazing requirements, corral location, water runoff issues, water table depth, topography, every little thing is monitored and regulated to help protect the clarity of Lake Tahoe. Fortunately, private people can still have horses if you don't attract attention. I've got three horses left. Who knows when they'll be outlawed too."

"I'm curious. First you used the plural 'our' to describe your ranch. Then you used the singular 'I,'" I said.

I heard her inhale deeply as if to calm herself.

"I'm still getting used to it. The ranch was me and my dad. I've lived here most of my thirty-one years. Then Dad died in a fall three months ago. He was an older father. Had me when he was forty-five. I'm still trying to adjust. It's been a nightmare. He was my world. And before you ask the question, no, I'm not a weirdo geek who lives in the family basement. I've just always loved my life here with my dad and our horses and the beautiful mountains."

"Do you have a job outside of the ranch?"

She hesitated. "I took early retirement from the fire department in Sacramento. It suited me to come back here after my firefighting career. And it suited my dad. We always got along well. I do most of the cooking and take care of tax filings and such. I also take care of the horses. Dad does most of the ranch maintenance, barn and fencing repairs and such. Wait, what am I saying? It's been months since he died, and I'm still speaking in present tense instead of past tense." I heard her breath catch with emotion. "Anyway, I'm pretty good with tools, and I'm very strong. But putting in fence posts and strapping up rails is not an easy job for a small woman, no matter how strong."

She now seemed calm enough that I could ask about her reason for calling.

"What can I help you with, Jade?"

I immediately heard her breathing again.

"My life was threatened last night. It was terrifying. I don't know what to do!"

"What was the threat?"

"I got a call on my cell phone. It didn't ring because I was in my barn, which has a metal roof, so I don't get cell reception there. The call went to voicemail. When I came out of the barn, the phone made the beep that means I missed a call. The time stamp showed the call had come two minutes earlier."

"You were threatened in the voicemail?"

"Yes. A man's voice. He said he was coming for me at my house and I had ten minutes left to live. Naturally, I couldn't really think after that. I just jumped in my pickup and left. When I got a good distance away, I parked in a place where I couldn't be easily seen, and I called nine, one, one and reported the call and my address. When the cops came down the street, I followed them into my drive. I played them the voicemail. They searched the house and the barn. They didn't find anything. I didn't know what to do. I was panicked. So I went and stayed at a motel. This morning, I came back to my house. Someone had been inside. Things had been moved. I'm scared to death. I don't dare go more than a few feet from my truck so I can make a fast escape. The cops said I should call again if anything else happens. So I did that when I got to my house this morning. The cops came back and looked around again. One cop said he could refer me to a private investigator, and he gave me your name and number."

"Who was that cop?"

"Let me pull out his card." There was a short pause. "It was Sergeant Bains from the El Dorado Sheriff's Office."

"Bains is a good guy," I said. My comment was a small reassurance to the woman and a reminder of sorts to myself that I should consider the woman's case legitimate. Bains wouldn't have given her my name if he didn't think her concerns had merit.

"Now I'm back at my house," she said. "But what do you do when someone threatens to kill you?"

THREE

I didn't have a good answer to Jade's question about what to do when your life is threatened. "Did the cops have suggestions?"

"Nothing useful. They asked for the caller's number, but there was no caller ID on the voicemail. They asked if I recognized the voice of the caller. When I told them no, they said there wasn't much they could do. They told me they would need some specific evidence that could be linked to the person making the threat."

"Can you think of anyone who might want to hurt you?"

"Maybe someone from my old job."

"Could any of them have been the caller? Disguising their voice?"

"No. I'm good at recognizing voices."

"Why would someone from your old job have bad feelings about you?"

"A guy died. They blame me. I'll tell you about it when you get here."

"I haven't said I was coming there."

"What do you mean?" The woman sounded exasperated and nearly hysterical. "Are you so busy you can't help someone in danger?!"

I understood that the woman was very stressed. But I automatically resist when someone is very pushy and presumes what I might or might not do.

"First, I have some more questions," I finally said.

"What? Ask!"

"I need you to be calm if I am to help you."

"I am calm!"

Now it was my turn to take some deep breaths.

I said, "Is it possible the voicemail was meant for someone else and maybe they dialed you by mistake?"

"No. I know because the caller mentioned Barry, the guy who died. He was a firefighter."

"Okay, that certainly identifies the call as directed at you. But could the voicemail have been a tentative threat? A kind of bluster?" I asked.

"You mean like a pretend threat? No. This is real. I'm under siege, here! This threat is tormenting me. I'm scared to death that someone will break into my house when I'm here and cut my throat or something!"

"Is there somewhere else you can stay?"

"No."

"Is there someone you can ask to come and stay with you?"

"No."

Because she answered both questions so quickly, it was obvious that she hadn't thought about it. She simply didn't want to consider it. She had decided that I would somehow help instead.

I took another breath. "Have you talked to your friends? Maybe one of them could help."

Jade went silent on the phone. After a long pause, she said, "I don't have any friends. No one would help me except my neighbor Andrew, and he's leaving Tahoe on some kind of religious journey."

"When does he leave?"

"He's joining a Buddhist temple in China, and he has to be there a week from yesterday. I think he said he leaves in two days."

"Have you talked to him about this situation?"

"I mentioned it. But I don't want to distract him from his mission. It's very important to him. He calls it his most important life marker. Whatever that means. Anyway..." She stopped talking.

"Anyway what?" I said.

"Nothing. Forget I said it."

"Jade, I can't help you if you're unwilling to answer questions about your problem."

I heard her breathing.

She said, "He thinks I'm paranoid and that it makes me imagine things."

"Earlier, you said you were maybe a little paranoid. Like you think it too."

"Yes, but my paranoia isn't delusional. I'm not imagining things. It's more that I'm hyper aware of how things can go badly. I've had several situations in the past where I suspected bad stuff was going on, and it later turned out that I was right."

"Is Andrew a sensible guy? Does he often say things that make sense to you?"

"I know what you're doing. You're trying to force me to acknowledge that if he's right about other things, he might be right about this. Well, that doesn't work. You'll know, too, when you hear the voicemail." She paused. "Hold on. I hear a sound outside. I'm walking over to look out the window."

"That's fine," I said, waiting for her response to the sound she'd heard.

I recognized her statements as part of a familiar pattern. When people believe something strongly, no amount of contrary evidence will sway them. If anything, opposing information just makes them dig in deeper. 'Maybe I've been wrong in the past,' they'll say. 'But this time I know I'm right.'

I'd also learned that wide-ranging paranoia was self-fulfilling. If you worry about everything going wrong, then whenever something does go wrong, as inevitably happens, it seems to prove that your suspicions were right because you had worried about it. Never mind all the other things that didn't go wrong.

After the silence stretched out, I said, "Do you still hear the sound?"

"No. There's nothing there." She didn't elaborate.

"Do you want to call me back later?"

"No."

"Then what is it you'd like me to do?" I asked.

"I want you to come out here. Listen to the voicemail. Look around and… Do whatever private investigators do. Check my house and barn. I'd also like protection. I'll pay your going rate to stay here at night. Then, if either of us hears something, you could investigate."

"I don't do bodyguard work."

"Why not?"

"Because it's not my strength. I'm a detective, not a guard. I'm not expensive relative to my investigating skills. But I would be expensive for guard work. You could hire a guard service for less. I know some off-duty cops looking to moonlight. I can give you some recommendations. You could stay in a hotel for the next week, and I'll come during the day."

"Not with my horses. I have to be here to take care of them. I can only be gone for two days, max. The automatic waterers are reliable. But plumbing sometimes breaks down. Any longer than two days and one of my neighbors would have to fill in. But that mostly comes down to Andrew. And now with him about to leave, that option is gone. So, no, I can't accept that. If you won't work as a bodyguard, then I'll hire you to do your investigation thing. Just do it at night so I can get some sleep. At the very least, you can come out to the ranch and see for yourself what's involved. Maybe something that wouldn't stand out to me or the cops would be noticeable to your trained eye."

My normal inclination to say yes to all requests was absent. It felt like working for Jade Jaso would be a big mistake. But I couldn't say no just because the woman seemed like she was somewhat out of control.

"Hold on a minute," I said. I covered my phone and talked to Street. "The woman on the phone lives nearby. Would it be okay with you if we stopped by her place to talk?"

"Of course, hon."

"Thanks." I uncovered my phone. "Jade, I'm with my girlfriend, and we have our dogs. However, we're not far away. Okay if we stop by now?"

"Yes. I've got nothing else to do but my chores. Chores and worry."

She told me where to look for the two reflectors on the tree that highlighted the address number. She explained that the drive was just a trail through the forest, easy to miss, and that the first house I would come to after I turned onto the trail belonged to Andrew and Sam Garden.

"Sam is Andrew's grandfather. They live together. Andrew is helping Sam the same way I helped my dad." As Jade said the words, it sounded like her voice choked with emotion. "Anyway, their house is a small brown cabin with a detached garage. Very tidy like in a magazine on cute country cabins. Just past them, the drive curves through some trees. Go another fifty yards and you'll see our barn and the corral. Our house is right behind it. My house. Not so tidy as you will soon notice."

"Be there in a bit," I said and clicked off.

I whistled in the manner that meant treats were waiting. The dogs charged out of the forest a minute later.

We got the dogs in the back of the Jeep and headed out. As we drove, I told Street what I could remember from my conversation with Jade Jaso.

FOUR

We took Highway 50 toward Echo Summit and crossed the bridge that went over the Upper Truckee River. A few hundred yards farther, just where the road pitches up to climb toward the pass, we turned south on South Upper Truckee Road.

It's a gently-winding neighborhood road that stretches south several miles toward where the headwaters of the Upper Truckee River tumble out of the high country near Steven's Peak, the 10,000-foot mountain that dominates the landscape to the south. Although fall was approaching and the summer had been relatively hot, the north side of Steven's Peak still had snowfields left over from the previous winter.

We came to the historic Celio Ranch with its classic buildings from the 1850s. Not far past it were the reflectors Jade Jaso had told me to watch for.

The driveway in from the road was just as she described it, a two-path dirt trail. It looked like a place to hike or drive a 4-wheel-drive pickup, nothing more. It snaked through trees, went over embedded cobbles, crossed a shallow ravine where snowmelt flowed in the spring, and headed back to where the mountain rose cliff-like up to the Echo Summit pass above.

The tidy house that Jade described where Andrew Garden and his grandfather Sam lived was on the left. The lap siding was painted beige, and the trim was red. The front door was red as well, a charming country look.

Parked on the dirt drive was an old green Toyota pickup with a topper over the back. The tailgate was open revealing yard tools as well as a chop saw.

A young man was outside raking up pine needles and small Lodgepole Pine cones. He was dumping the piles into large plastic trash cans. As we approached, he bent over to pick up the trophy-sized cones produced by Jeffrey pines and the even larger cones from a huge Sugar Pine that towered above the cabin. Tourists often pick up the latter, which are the largest in the world and grow up to two feet long. Locals pick them up as fire starter for their wood stoves. Because they burn so well, removing them from around houses also helps maintain defensible space.

I slowed to a stop, waved, and rolled down my window.

The man leaned his rake against a tree and approached. He walked with a kind of hesitation in his stride. It wasn't as if he were limping or had a physical problem. It was more like the walk of a person who didn't have physical confidence.

"Afternoon," I said. "I'm Owen McKenna, and this is Street Casey. Jade Jaso asked us to stop by. I'm hoping this is the correct drive?"

"It is," he said carefully. Up close he looked like he was in his mid-twenties.

"Are you her neighbor Andrew?"

"Andrew Garden, yes." His manner was cordial but not especially friendly. Which was probably just right for a neighbor coming upon strangers in a neighborhood where at least one owner was under threat.

Andrew pointed down the drive. "You'll see her place just after you follow the curve through those trees." He turned back to stare into the back of the Jeep. "Yellow Labs I'm familiar with. But that other guy... He's a big dude."

"Great Dane," I said.

"Jade has horses. I wonder if they'll be spooked?" More caution. Another good neighborly trait.

"I haven't had that happen with other horses. But we'll keep the dogs in the Jeep until Jade says otherwise."

"You must be the detective. She talked about calling you to look into the voicemail she got."

A woman appeared in the trees. She was walking a small terrier on a leash. Or perhaps he was walking her. He strained at the leash like a sled dog, pulling hard, all four paws digging into the dirt. Lagging behind the woman and dog was a young boy. He was pudgy and looked sullen. He carried a 4-foot stick and used it to hit each tree as he walked past it.

I realized there was a trail that I hadn't seen at first. It's one of the great features of Tahoe, trails everywhere, good for hiking, mountain biking, and walking dogs.

"Hey, Andrew," the woman called out.

He turned toward her and nodded. "Hi Amy."

She went on past. The terrier arced out to her side and was now pulling toward us. He'd seen our dogs in the Jeep, and he longed to join them. Amy leaned away from the terrier to resist his pull and continued to drag him forward. As she went by, he ended up behind her, trying to go backward.

"Little Bear, stop it!" Amy shouted at him. She continued into the forest, dragging him.

"Looks like the woman's dog is a handful," I said to Andrew.

"Drives her crazy," he said. "The dog is the opposite of the boy, who mostly just plays video games. Amy says walking a terrier is like having a nuclear reactor on a leash. Energy about to explode in every direction."

I nodded. "Interesting description," I said.

"Amy's a physicist. Used to work at the Diablo Canyon nuclear power plant in SoCal. She says she got tired of the perfect coastal weather and wanted to ski. So she moved to Tahoe."

"Some of us think Tahoe has perfect weather."

"If you like to shovel snow," Andrew said with a disapproving tone. He looked down the drive toward where I imagined Jade Jaso's house was. "How do you catch a phone terrorist?" he asked.

"There's no easy way. Have you seen anyone you don't know poking around the area? Or unfamiliar vehicles in the neighborhood?"

He shook his head. "No. I try to be aware because Jade gets stressed easily."

"Is there something about Jade that would draw someone's ire?"

"I'm not really... You should probably ask Jade that."

The man seemed like he'd be a good source of information, so I wanted to keep him talking. "She told me on the phone that you think she's paranoid."

He took a moment before he responded. "Let's just say that Jade is naturally tense. Life hasn't been easy for her. So she tends to jump to negative conclusions."

"It sounds like you've known her a long time."

"All my life," he said. "We have a lot in common. We both grew up here, we both lost our mothers when we were very young, and we both still live next door to each other. Jade worked in Sacramento for several years. But we're both back to our homesteads now."

"If I have other questions after I talk to her, is it okay to stop and talk to you?"

"Of course. However, I'm leaving in two days and will be gone a couple of months, maybe longer."

I remembered that Jade had mentioned that he was going on some kind of religious journey. "Work?" I asked. "Or vacation?"

"Neither, really. I'm heading to a Buddhist retreat in Guangdong, China. It's a kind of spiritual quest. Most people don't understand it, so I've stopped trying to explain."

"Going to study the four noble truths?" I said.

The man gave me a big smile. "Oh, wow, you've studied Buddhism? That's very cool."

"No, I confess I haven't. But back when I was with the San Francisco Police Department, we had a cop who was into Buddhism, and he would always mention the four noble truths. It's the only thing I know."

"It's nice when anyone in this country cares enough to notice. The U.S. doesn't have an official national religion. But we might as well acknowledge that Christianity fills that role. Studying the four noble truths doesn't really fit in here."

"You're probably right." I made a little wave, Andrew nodded, and we drove off.

A short distance later, a barn appeared. To one side was a

large horse trailer and a silver Dodge Ram pickup. On the other side was a fenced, circular corral that was 60 or more feet in diameter. The corral was joined to the barn by a rectangular area, also fenced. In the rectangle was a V-shaped hayrack into which hay was dropped from the barn's hayloft above. The horses could pull it out through spaces in the hayrack. There were two horses eating the hay. Both were small, one brown with three white socks, the other nearly black with no socks. The horses were focused on the hay and paid no attention to us as we drove up.

A third horse was out in the circular corral standing at the part of the fence that was closest to us. The horse's head was over the top rail of the fence. The horse was large and gorgeous with a golden yellow coat and cream-colored mane and tail. Unlike the two smaller horses, the large one stared at us as we drove up. Its ears were turned toward us. I stopped, and we got out.

"My God," Street said. "That palomino mare is amazing. She's huge. Looks like a thoroughbred."

"How can a palomino be a thoroughbred? I thought they were two different kinds of horses. Like different dog breeds."

"I don't know the genetic details. But I remember that palomino is a color thing and thoroughbred is a breed thing."

"You learned that when you worked at the dude ranch in Jackson, Wyoming?" I said.

"Yeah. After my sophomore year at Berkeley. One of the best experiences of my life." Street was focused on the horse at the fence. "I remember that the science of palomino coloring is similar to red hair in people. Roughly one percent of people get the genes to have red hair. They can be white people from Ireland or black people from Papua, New Guinea."

I pointed at the horses eating hay. "The smaller horses are sort of plain compared to the palomino."

Street looked at them for a moment. "Those geldings look like mustangs."

"The wild horses in the Nevada deserts," I said.

"Yeah. Other states, too."

I glanced at the Jeep. "Our hounds are looking at the horses.

I hope Jade Jaso is okay with them meeting each other."

"Remember that bio-tech case," Street said, "when we went horseback riding?"

"Every moment," I said. "We were trying to find the wild mustang named Heat, the mustang that was lost in Tahoe's forests."

"Spot came with us then," Street said. "He wasn't afraid of the horses, and they weren't afraid of him. So I'm guessing that these horses wouldn't be afraid of him, either."

I saw movement off to the side. The front door of a ranch house opened. The house was small and plain. But above the door were two dramatic lights. They looked like glass sculptures the size and shape of partially deflated basketballs.

A woman appeared. She walked toward us. She was quite short, maybe 5 feet, with straight, shiny black hair cut off in a hard edge at her jaw line. She wore jeans and a blue, long-sleeved shirt. She had the shirt sleeves rolled up exposing thick forearms. And while she was wearing tall, tan cowboy boots with decorative stitching, the bulge of her calf muscles was still obvious. Her shoulders were heavy with muscle, but she had no belly fat. She was a mesomorph, muscles being her predominant flesh. But the primary characteristic of the woman wasn't her athletic build but her tension, a piano-string tightness that made her seem to quiver with agitation. As she walked, the sun glinted off an unusual necklace. Two of them. Reflective metal tags. I'd seen them before. Military dog tags. So Jade was in the military. Or her father. She'd said on the phone that he recently died.

I waved. As she approached, we saw what looked like a recent severe wound on her left hand. Her thumb and first two fingers were missing. The last two fingers were at an odd angle, the ring finger projecting down, the little finger projecting up and out. The skin was taut and puffy red, and covered with surgical stitch marks. It appeared that the three missing fingers had been violently torn off, the remaining two had been badly wounded, and the surgeons had struggled to save what they could. There were thick cords of gray scar tissue along the back of her hand. From the damage and the awkward way she held her hand, it made me wonder if the jury was still out on whether the rest of the hand would have to be amputated at a future date.

"Hi Jade," I said as she got close. "I'm Owen McKenna." I started to reach out to shake, then hesitated.

She reached out her right hand. "Shaking is fine. It's only my left hand that's bad. Right hand is good."

We shook. Her hand was small with medium thick fingers and dry skin and a no-nonsense grip. Her strength was obvious. She could probably crush walnuts without any tools. "And this is Street Casey," I said.

They nodded at each other.

"Thank you for coming," Jade said. Her countenance was as serious as if she'd been in a war. "I'm sorry I sounded harsh on the phone."

"It's okay." I gestured toward the corral. "We were just admiring your horses."

She nodded. "The two hay hogs are Cyrano and de Bergerac." She looked toward the palomino. "And my beauty queen is Anne Gregory."

I saw Street break into a large smile. Jade Jaso noticed Street's smile. Jade made a tentative grin, her lips sealed.

"What am I missing?" I said.

Street answered. "The poem by William Butler Yeats. 'For Anne Gregory.'" Street looked at Jade. "Tell me if I'm remembering this correctly. In the poem the narrator is talking to a young woman with dramatic blonde hair and says that no one but God could love her for herself and not her yellow hair."

Jade Jaso made a tiny nod. She watched Street with what I thought was a look of appraisal.

"Meaning..." I said.

Street said, "I think Yeats meant that beauty corrupts an observer's perception. That those who are beautiful go through life with undeniable advantages and possibly a few disadvantages as well. We can't see really beautiful creatures without being distracted by their beauty. Certainly this gorgeous horse must distract all judgment. She is spectacular, no doubt about it. But the disadvantage is that observers might fail to notice the horse's achievements and only think of her beauty."

Street turned back to Jade. "Did I get that right?"

"Yes. Perfect."

"The opposite of Cyrano de Bergerac," Street said.

Jade nodded. "Edmond Rostand was a contemporary of Yeats, although French. Rostand's play was the opposite side of Yeat's poem, just as they lived on opposite sides of the English Channel. I thought it okay to split the name, Cyrano for one horse and de Bergerac for the other. Good names for homely horses. People glance at Cyrano and de Bergerac and just see plain, small geldings. People always focus on Anne Gregory and gush about how graceful and gorgeous she is." Jade Jaso made a little grimace with her teeth, what seemed to me an unconscious self-awareness. "But the larger story is that Anne Gregory is an amazing horse to ride. Of course, any poet would think I've committed blasphemy, naming a horse Anne Gregory. But the name fits nevertheless."

"Now I remember," I said, the vague memory coming back to me. "Cyrano de Bergerac was the homely guy with the big nose."

"You've seen the play?" Jaso raised her eyebrows, a hopeful look on her face.

"Sorry, I have to confess I only saw the Steve Martin movie. I think it was called Roxanne."

Jaso made a knowing nod. But perhaps she would look past my lack of education and realize that movies that are purely about entertainment can still introduce people to important themes.

I said, "I remember that Cyrano was overlooked by the beautiful girl because he was homely. She only had eyes for the beautiful man. But Cyrano eventually proved his worth to her by his ability with words and his devotion."

Jaso nodded. She looked at me with a certain reserve. She wasn't going to accept my value unless I proved it to her.

I said, "Let's get to the reason you called."

Jade nodded. "I'll play you the voicemail." She pulled out

her phone, thumb-tapped the screen a few times, then held the phone out toward us. The male voice was rough, the words halting and the cadence awkward. It sounded like the man was reading.

"I know you killed Barry by pushin' him down that light shaft. He was worth ten of you. Twenty of you. I know where you live. You got a few minutes left to live. Ten at the outside. I ain't decided yet how you'll die. Maybe I'll light you on fire an' drop you off a mountain so you know what it feels like. Burnt, then crushed. Get ready."

FIVE

The voicemail death threat clicked off.

"That's very disturbing," I said.

"I'm so sorry, Jade," Street said.

We looked at each other while the gravity of the situation made its impression.

"Before we go any further, I'd like to get a copy of that voicemail. Is there a way to email it to my phone?"

Jade looked blank. "I'm not tech-savvy."

"Me neither."

"The easiest way," Street said, "might just be for her to play it again while your phone is on record."

I handed Street my phone. She pressed buttons. Jade played the voicemail. The second time around was just as horrible.

Street held out my phone so I could see the face. "When you want to listen to the recording, do these steps." She moved her finger slowly so I could follow. "Press here. Then here. The final step is this."

"Thanks." I slid my phone into my pocket.

"And the threat's not the end of it," Jade said.

"Because your house was burglarized last night," I said.

"Right. While I was staying at the motel."

"How did the person break in?" I said.

"He didn't physically break in. The door wasn't kicked in, if that's what you mean. But someone came inside. I'm sure I locked the door before I left, so the intruder must have had a way to pick the lock. Unless they had a key. But I've never given anyone a key. And I never knew my dad to do that, either."

"What was the evidence of the burglary?"

"Drawers had been opened, stuff moved. Even the frozen food in the freezer had been shifted. Someone was looking for something."

"What was taken?"

"Nothing that I know of."

"Are you sure that it happened last night? Could it have been before that? Some time when you left the house unlocked?"

She paused. "When I go out to the barn to take care of the horses, I certainly don't lock the house. I'm right here. It would be very ballsy for someone to come in while I'm in the barn. But as I think about yesterday evening, I didn't open the freezer. It was when I opened the freezer this morning and saw that stuff had been moved around that I checked drawers and such. So I suppose it's possible that the person came in during the day yesterday, and I didn't notice until this morning."

"You said the cops came again this morning?"

"Yes. They came first thing. They were prompt, and I was glad for that. But they looked around and couldn't find anything. Just like before, they wanted to see specific evidence. I showed them the stuff that had been moved. But they said that wasn't enough for them to go on. What do they expect? Do they think a burglar is going to leave a business card?!" Jade radiated tension.

"Let me be sure I understand the timeline. Yesterday afternoon, the threat on your voicemail came in while you were in the barn, which has a metal roof and doesn't let cell signals in. When you came out of the barn, you got the voicemail message. You immediately drove your pickup out to the street, dialed nine, one, one, and then waited. Sergeant Bains came, looked around, didn't find anything, and left. So you went and stayed at a motel."

Jade Jaso nodded at me.

"Then this morning you came back to the house and saw that things had been moved. So you called the cops again. They came out and looked around like before."

"Right."

"Did they have any advice?" I asked.

"They suggested I get webcams installed in the house and the barn. So I called a burglar alarm service. First they told me

I'd have to upgrade my internet connection. Then they said they'd monitor my house and grounds from their company. I told them no way would I want someone watching inside my private spaces. They said I don't have to worry about privacy issues. That they're totally secure. But that made me think of when my bank assured me that their computers were secure, and then two weeks later they were hacked, and a hundred fifty million of their customers' records and passwords were stolen. These companies promise great security. But it's all just B.S. I also read about a guy who worked at an alarm company, and he sold insider information to a burglary crime ring." The woman was raising her voice again, venting.

"That would be frustrating," I agreed.

Jade said, "Before I called you, I called the cops back and told them that the webcam idea required a new internet connection and that it couldn't happen anytime soon. The cop on the phone said the only other thing would be to hire a full-time guard or get a guard dog. But then he said I should check with my homeowner's insurance company, because they might cancel me if I get a guard dog because of liability. So what am I to do? The stress never ends!" Jade sounded plaintive and pleading.

I looked over at a group of lawn chairs near a stone fire pit. "Let's sit and talk this over."

Jade looked frustrated. "I need protection, not talk!"

Street saw my look and understood my desire. "Owen and I have been out running. We'd like to rest for a bit." Street walked toward the chairs and sat down. I turned to follow and gestured for Jade to come along.

We three sat. Jade on the edge of one chair, elbows on her knees, one foot bouncing with nervousness.

I looked across toward the corral. "Did you grow up with horses?" I asked.

"Most of my life, yes. I've always been an introvert. After my mom died when I was little, I had anxiety attacks and shut myself in my room. Dad knew I was smitten with horses. We already had a pony and a quarter horse. So he took me to horse events in an effort to get me focused on other things besides mom. The rodeo in Reno. Harness racing at Cal-Expo in Sacramento. One day, he took me to the Bay Area to see the thoroughbreds race at Golden Gate Fields racetrack."

"The one just off Interstate Eighty near Berkeley," Street said.

"Yeah. The afternoon we spent there was one of the greatest of my life. Just me and my dad, the jockeys, and those gorgeous animals. Two years ago, it was through some horse people Dad knew at Golden Gate Fields that he learned about Anne Gregory and bought her for me."

I looked over at the palomino. "Was she a racehorse?"

"Apparently, not. Her owner was always in trouble with the law. I remember his name. Dell Davis. Gambling debts. Financial scams. He called himself an auteur. My dad told me he was one of those hucksters who was always focused on some big scheme but was too disorganized to even be an effective crook."

The realization that Jade's horse had come from a crook made me wonder if there was a connection to the death threat. "When you say 'auteur,'" I said, "do you mean movies?"

"Yeah. Dell Davis was sent to prison for targeting old people and selling them phony shares in a movie he was supposedly making. The movie was supposed to be about horse racing, and he dazzled potential investors with videos of Anne Gregory and told them she was going to be in the movie. He told people that his movie would return one hundred dollars for every dollar invested. The minimum buy-in was ten thousand dollars."

I did the math in my head. "At a hundred to one, a ten-thousand-dollar investment would return a million dollars if true."

Jade nodded. "I never got the details, but Dad said lots of people invested. And once someone was interested in investing, Dell would supposedly let them in on a private side investment that was reserved for just a select few investors who were passionate about horses."

"Let me guess," I said, looking at Anne Gregory. "Shares in the amazing palomino race horse."

"That was exactly it! She was so beautiful that people lost

their common sense and fell for it."

Street said, "I'm guessing her name must have been different back then. Dell Davis doesn't sound like the kind of guy who would know poetry."

"Right. AG's original name was Dixie. Dell Davis said they were a team. Dell and Dixie Davis. Imagine that. And people gave him money."

"But he was caught," I said.

Jade nodded. "He was ordered to pay restitution to his victims, but the money was already gone. And once in prison, he could no longer pay the boarding fees at the farm where Anne Gregory was stabled. California has an equine lien foreclosure process that allowed the boarding company to sell the horse. So Dad bought her for me. Of course, I changed her name to something more appropriate. I don't think she minded."

Jade stood up. "Come over and meet her." She walked to the corral, opened a gate, and held it as we walked through. Jade shut the gate, walked to Anne Gregory and stood beneath her neck. Jade reached her arms up as if to encircle the horse's neck, although she wasn't tall enough, nor were her arms long enough. "I bet you could have been a good racehorse, huh, baby?" It was the first time I'd heard Jade sound relaxed and gentle.

Anne Gregory made the slightest rumbling sound, very low in pitch, her breath barely audible.

Jade said, "I'm so worried that Dell Davis will try to get her back. He sent a letter from prison, telling my Dad that it wasn't legal the way he bought her. Davis said he was going to take her back the moment he was out of prison. Now I've heard he's been paroled. I'm scared to death for my baby."

"Is there any basis for Dell Davis to think your ownership of her is illegal?"

"No! We checked it every which way with a lawyer."

"Then you should be fine. With legal change of ownership and the former owner disgraced with his past record, it would be hard for him to get any traction pursuing the matter." I said it partly to ease her concern, but mostly because it was true.

"I hope you're right." Jade ran her hands down Anne

Gregory's cheeks. "If I lost my girl, I'd lose my purpose."

Street took my hand and pulled me toward Anne Gregory. "Let's meet the beauty queen." We both held our hands out for the palomino to sniff. Street gently drew her hand down Anne Gregory's head, from ears to nose. I followed Street's lead.

The horse tossed her head up and down, the gorgeous yellow mane ruffling.

I looked around at the corral and the grounds. "I'd like to start by having you show me what the intruder moved in the night."

Jaso said, "Then let's start with the barn. But first, would you like to let your dogs out to run? They look cooped up."

"They'd love it," I said.

"They don't charge horses, do they? The Yellow Lab doesn't concern me. The horses are used to smaller dogs. But I'm concerned about the Dane."

"No problem. He's been around horses. He'll just sniff noses and then probably be more interested in the other barn scents."

She nodded.

We went back out of the corral. I opened the rear door of the Jeep. I took hold of Spot's collar as he stepped out. Blondie ran out behind him. I introduced Spot to Jade as Blondie trotted in widening circles.

Jade turned sideways to Spot in the classic manner of showing interest but no threat, a technique to prevent dogs from feeling threatened. It was a valuable approach if the dog was potentially aggressive, and it showed that Jade knew dogs. Of course, Jade didn't know that Spot was a couch lounger who thought all the world was fun and organized for his exclusive pleasure. Jade didn't withdraw as Spot lifted his head and sniffed her chin, which was no reach for him. Then she stepped next to him and rubbed his neck, then gently fingered the faux-diamond in his ear.

"An ear stud. He's a fashion model." Unlike everyone else who noticed his jewelry, Jade didn't say it with enthusiasm. But she sounded pleasant.

"You know dogs," I said.

"I grew up with a Border Collie named Emily. She lived to be sixteen. She was the same age as me. So I felt like we were sweet-sixteen sisters before she died. After she died, I was bereft."

"Border collies are the world's smartest dog, right?" I said.

"Emily certainly thought so," Jade said.

We went up to the fence where Anne Gregory stood just on the other side. The horse reached her head over the top rail. Spot looked at me and then stepped toward the horse. They sniffed noses. He wagged.

Jade walked us back through the corral gate and shut it behind us. Anne Gregory walked toward us, tossing her beautiful head, the creamy mane waving in the breeze. I stopped and held Spot's collar. The horse made another deep-throated sound, not very loud. The sound was pulsing yet very gentle.

"She made that sound a little bit ago. What do you call that?" I asked.

"That's nickering," Jade said. "It means just what it sounds like. 'Welcome. I'm pleased to see you. You make me happy.'"

"What about the high-pitched call I sometimes hear horses make? Is that what's called whinnying?"

"Yes. And if it's really loud, we call it neighing. It's a loud vibrato call to other horses in the neighborhood. It means, 'Hello, out there! Anybody around? Speak up. Announce your presence.'"

Jade pet Blondie. A small flock of tiny birds raced past us, like a tangle of energy. They performed acrobatics, swooped up and down, then flew off.

"Mountain Chickadees are the best," Jade said. "So enthusiastic, even as we head toward winter. They stay in Tahoe all winter, through all the snowstorms, through all the stress of weather that seems as if it's trying to kill them. The birds give me hope."

Street had been looking at Anne Gregory. She turned toward Jade and said, "Hope is the thing with feathers?"

It made no sense to me.

Jade stared at Street. "If you're accepting applications for friendship, I'd like to submit one."

I turned to Spot. "Hey Largeness, let's you and me go find a world we know about." I walked him toward the barn.

"Emily Dickinson," Street called after me. "Practically her most famous poem."

"No doubt," I called back behind me. I turned toward Spot who was trotting ahead of me. "Hope and feathers," I muttered to Spot. "Of course, anyone but me would know that." Blondie ran S-turns in front of us.

I walked Spot over to Cyrano and de Bergerac. They both turned their heads to look at Spot. They kept chewing, hay protruding from the sides of their mouths.

I pet their necks. They turned back to the hayrack. Spot walked around the hayrack, then trotted back toward Anne Gregory. The appeal of a yellow-haired beauty.

"The barn door is over on this side," Jade said as she and Street walked toward us.

We all walked around to the end of the building. The barn entrance was a double door. Each half was swung open. The opening was wide enough to drive in a big vehicle like a horse trailer. Above the door were two more of the fancy lights, these much larger than the others. They were made of colored glass, translucent enough to let light shine through but not clear enough to see through.

The center section of the barn floor was like the outdoor corral, made of dirt, not very soft but not hard, either. The sides of the barn had floors made of dark gray concrete or something similar that could presumably be hosed down.

On the left side of the barn was a tack room. The door was standing open, and I could see saddles and bridles and other gear. There were wall hooks and a closet rod with various clothes and jackets. A shelf held boots. The room did not discriminate between horse gear and human gear. The room had a solid steel door lined with weather stripping. It would probably keep out weather, but, more importantly, it was probably designed to keep out rodents.

The upper part of the barn was a loft area filled with bales of hay. The loft had a half-door that was positioned above the hayrack outside. I had no idea how the bales of hay were brought up into the loft. But I could see that they were dropped out of the upper door into the hayrack.

On one side of the room were four horse stalls. The walls were made of horizontal 1-by-6 lumber nailed onto the vertical studs. The horizontal boards had spaces between them so one could see through the walls. Maybe that was so humans could check on the horses. Or maybe it was so the horses could check on each other. Each stall had a large door with a small window that looked out into the central area of the barn. In the stalls were thick black rubber mats that were hung up. Probably they could be hosed off and then laid down to give the horses a more comfortable surface to stand on.

"I can show you what was moved," Jade called out. "Come into my dad's glass shop."

Her mention of it made me think of the glass sculptures I'd seen hanging above the house door and the barn door.

I walked through another door. It was a large room. The most prominent feature was a large box about four feet wide and six feet tall. It appeared to be made of fire brick. In the center was a heavy door about two feet square. I realized I was looking at a blast furnace for heating glass.

Near the furnace were two large workbenches made of steel. They had smooth steel tops. Fire proof even when subjected to molten glass.

I reached over to the furnace. Feeling no heat, I lifted the big latch and swung open the door. The inside was pitch black. Spot appeared at my side, sniffing out what must be unusual scents.

"How hot do these things get?" I asked.

"Two thousand five hundred degrees," Jade said. "But it's my understanding that most glass work is done around two thousand degrees."

"Toasty," I said.

"It takes over twenty-four hours for the furnace to get hot enough to use and even longer to cool. I've spent my whole life being afraid of that furnace. Dad showed me how just bringing something combustible near the open door makes it burst into flames."

Spot moved off to inspect other scents.

"Your dad was a sculptor who made glass lights?" Street said.

"Yeah. He was good at it. Sold a lot of work even though he didn't care much about sales. He mostly just liked making functional art. And he liked that glass came from the earth. He showed me once. He put a mixture of stuff in a ceramic bowl. I think it was sand and limestone and ash of some kind. Then he heated it up. When he pulled it out of the furnace it was glowing yellow, and it was liquid."

"Alchemy," Street said.

"Yes. And very scary. And when it cooled, it was glass." She walked over to a set of bins on one wall. "This is what I found that had been moved." She pointed to tubes of colored glass in the bins. Green, yellow, blue, and pink. There were some that were striped like candy canes. Each tube was about a foot long and an inch in diameter. "These are the glass stock a blower uses. You heat them in the furnace and then turn them into whatever shape you want."

"By blowing air?" I said.

"Blowing air is one way. But glass sculpture is made with many techniques."

"These tubes were moved?"

"Yeah."

"How do you know?"

"Dad always sorted them by color. I never touched them after he died. But when I walked in here this morning, I saw that the colors were somewhat mixed. Someone had pulled some out and put them back in a different place."

"How many people have touched these tubes?"

"You're thinking about fingerprints," Jade said. "I already wondered that. When Dad was alive, people would come and visit. He'd show them his shop, and everybody would pull out tubes and look at them. People are curious, and the colored tubes are pretty. So these have been handled by many people."

I looked around the shop. There was a set of bins with electrical supplies, light sockets, wire nuts, and two large spindles of wire. "Anything else moved?"

"Just inside the house."

She led us back across the corral and into the house.

The inside of the house was cozy and small and unremarkable, more like college dorm rooms than a nest that's been decorated and furnished with care. There were prints of paintings on the wall, held up by tacks. There was a framed photo of Anne Gregory looking fabulous. There was an eclectic grouping of furniture, a wood-burning stove in the corner, a bunch of poetry books in a book case.

Jade opened the freezer and pointed. "Everything in here was moved as if someone had lifted stuff out to see if anything had been hidden underneath." She walked over and pointed to a footlocker that served as a low table in front of an old couch. "We keep some blankets and pillows in here. It had all been moved and stuffed back in."

"Did the police look for fingerprints?"

"Yes. But they said there was nothing. Whoever was in the house wore gloves." She went back to the bedrooms. There were two of them, separated by a small bathroom. She pointed. "My room's this one."

I leaned in the doorway and saw a small bed and dresser.

She moved down the short hallway. "My dad's room is that one. The clothes in his closet were pushed to the side. And the clothes in his dresser were moved as well. Same for his desk. Everything moved around."

"You think someone did that last night?"

"Maybe, maybe not. I hadn't looked in my dad's room since the night before I got the death threat."

We went back to the living room. Without asking permission, I sat down on the couch. Often, talking to a person inside their home made it more difficult for them to have a psychological barrier.

"The death threat message mentioned someone who died. Someone named Barry. Tell me about him."

Jade's face grew pink. She started to talk. Hesitated. Began again. "I was a firefighter in Sacramento. Eight months ago, we were called out on a warehouse fire. It was as ugly as fires get. I was on the roof trying to help people get down the fire escape. There was a partial collapse of the cubby where the internal stairway came up to the roof, and flaming timbers fell. One trapped me and crushed my hand. One of the guys from our firehouse fell into a light shaft and died. His name was Barry. Some people thought I was responsible. There were accusations that I disobeyed an order from the Battalion Chief. The reality was that the roar of the fire was so loud that I never heard anything on my radio."

"Did you lose your job?"

"Because of my injury, yes. I can't be a firefighter with a ruined hand." She looked at it, turning it back and forth. It looked very painful. "So I moved back up the mountain to live with Dad and the horses and try to start a new life."

"Can you think of a reason why the threatening voice would say you killed Barry?"

Jade looked off, then shut her eyes. "Barry and I didn't get along."

"Was there a specific reason? Or did you just not have compatible chemistry?"

Jade's breathing was heavy. Whatever the reason, it was traumatic. "We just didn't see things the same way. In firefighting, you have to be close with the others. You have to be willing to work with them and help them and save their lives no matter what horrible situation you find yourself in. But with Barry…" She stopped.

We waited, neither of us interrupting. I thought of speaking, of prodding her. But I realized she was in a delicate place. I'd seen what happens when someone feels backed into a corner.

Jade sat motionless. Tears rolled down her cheeks, but otherwise there was no communication of her thoughts.

"We can talk about it later," I eventually said. "The things that were moved in the house and in the barn, obviously someone was looking for something specific. Can you think about anything in particular that someone might have been looking for?"

Jade shook her head slowly. "No."

"Think about the guy who died in the fire. Barry. Can you think of any possible connection between him and something that might be hidden in your house or barn?"

"No. The idea seems ridiculous." Jade's brusque attitude was back.

I saw Street look at the time and remembered her trip to Bend. "We need to head off to another commitment," I said. "I can come back tomorrow. Does late morning work for you?"

Jade looked very worried. "I'll deal with the horses, then go back to the motel tonight and come back here to meet you."

I thought I should know her location. "What motel will you be at?"

"I've got some of their cards." She pulled one out of her pocket and handed it to me.

SIX

O n the way back to the East Shore I talked to Street.
      "What do you think?"

Street frowned. "I think that poor woman is under great stress. There is the voicemail threat, of course. And losing her father. But there is obviously something else about her previous career, the guy named Barry who died, her work as a firefighter, her horrific injury, the warehouse fire. It's loaded with emotion. Figure out that stuff and you may learn why she got the voicemail threat."

We rode in silence the rest of the way to her condo. After I parked, I stood on her doorstep.

"What's the focus of this entomology conference in Bend?"

"It's a pretty routine discussion of how climate change has impacted insects," she said. "Most people would find it excruciatingly boring."

"I wouldn't. When the day comes when all the trees near people's houses have died because global warming and the resulting dryness allowed the bark beetles to kill the trees, the subject will seem a bit more germane to your life. And when those dead trees burn up along with the houses, the boring preoccupations of scientists will start to seem relevant."

"Wow, you could be a poster boy for the science of entomology. Would you like to run for president of our trade group?"

I laughed. "It's very tempting to think of spending more time with entomologists, especially if they're all as cute and sexy and, most of all, as smart as you."

"I take it that's a no?"

"Correct. A no thanks. I've already got a job." I stepped closer and hugged her and ran my hands down her body. "Sure you don't want a ride to the airport?"

"No. I'm fine driving myself. And that way I have a ride home when I fly back to Reno. But you'll still take Blondie and show her a good time?"

"Of course. Beer and popcorn at the log cabin. She won't think about you once."

"Thanks." We kissed and hugged hard and long, then said goodbye.

I was sad as always when I drove the dogs up the mountain. Street was my heart and soul, and, while I was comfortable being alone, there was always a nagging emptiness when she went off on work travel.

Jade was in the corral when I drove up with Spot and Blondie the next morning. She held a long line that went to a halter on Anne Gregory. The horse was trotting in a big counter-clockwise circle around Jade. Cyrano and de Bergerac were over at the hayrack, eating, ignoring Jade and Anne Gregory.

I walked up to the corral fence. "What is this?" I called out.

"This is longeing." She pronounced it like lunging. "But it's spelled differently." She recited the letters. "A longe line is used for training horses. They walk or trot or even canter in a circle. It's an easy way for a horse and trainer to fine-tune technique." She held the longe line with her good hand. Tucked under the arm with her damaged hand was a long, thin rod. "This is the longeing whip."

"That sounds and looks scary," I said.

"There's no whipping involved. There should be a different name for it. The whip is just used to touch the horse and communicate when to move."

"Ah. Good." I looked back at the Jeep. "Okay if I let the dogs out?"

"Of course."

I opened the rear door, and the dogs ran toward the barn. None of the horses seemed alarmed at the sudden motion.

Jade kept at her longeing. Anne Gregory periodically sped

up to what I figured must be the canter mode. Then the horse would slow to a trot. I couldn't see that Jade did anything differently to control the horse's speed. It must have been a very subtle change in the way she held the line.

"How does Anne Gregory know what speed to go?" I asked.

"The trainer and the horse develop a working relationship. Style, technique, and voice commands versus movement commands. Horses are very sensitive and hyper-aware. While many riders can simply hop on many different horses and ride, if you want horses to perform well, they need practice and training and an understanding of the individual rider's approach."

Anne Gregory seemed to trot flawlessly around the longeing circle.

"Is it okay for us to talk while you're training?"

"Sure."

"I was thinking about your background, which of course includes your father. Can I ask you about him?"

"Of course."

"You said he died three months ago. How did that happen?"

Jade didn't immediately reply. Maybe she was taken aback that I would quickly dive into such a sensitive subject. Jade kept Anne Gregory trotting in the big circle. Jade slowly rotated in position. Eventually, she talked.

"Near the end of every warm summer day, Dad carried a bucket of water out to a young fir tree that he'd damaged a few months before. He'd driven the pickup with a load of pine needles over to our composting pile. When he backed up to turn around, he hit the tree. He hadn't crushed it, but it had been pushed down and over so it was listing to the side. Dad felt so bad about that. He'd propped it up, positioning some dirt and rocks to hold it in place. He also thought he'd probably damaged the roots and it was no longer able to get enough water. So every evening, he poured water around the base of the tree.

"One night, as dusk was falling, we were inside. We'd eaten dinner and were reading. Dad suddenly remembered that he'd fetched another couple of rocks to help hold the tree upright but had left his water bucket out there. The wind was coming up, and Dad didn't want the plastic bucket to blow away. So he took his flashlight and went out to get the bucket.

"I was reading and didn't immediately notice that it had been some time and he hadn't come back. So I went out to check."

Jade sounded choked up.

I waited. Anne Gregory trotted round and round while Jade rotated.

"I saw his flashlight shining on the ground. I found him lying nearby. He was breathing but unconscious. There was blood on the side of his head. I realized he'd tripped and fallen and hit his head on a rock. I called nine, one, one. They came and rushed him away to the hospital. I waited there for hours while they worked on him. At four in the morning, the doctor told me Dad had died from brain trauma. Bleeding on the brain."

I said, "I'm very sorry, Jade."

She was silent for a long time.

"My dad was a Vietnam vet. A fighter pilot. One of the Bien Hoa Buzzards. The Five Hundred and Tenth Tactical Fighter Squadron had been activated in Vietnam in nineteen sixty-five. Dad flew F-One Hundreds with them in sixty-six and sixty-seven. He came back to a country that barely tolerated the soldiers and pilots who had merely followed orders from the previous generation. He didn't talk about it much, but the pain was always there. He used to say that 'LBJ and Congress sent us to die in Vietnam based on a phony story about an attack in the Gulf Of Tonkin.' He would always raise his voice at that. Dad never got over the fact that old men used a lie to send young men to war."

This time the silence was longer.

"I haven't recovered from his death," Jade said. "I still can't believe that a robust man who flew F-One Hundreds on bombing missions in a war could trip and fall and die an accidental death. Life is so unfair."

"Your father was a good guy," I said, hoping to keep her

talking.

"The best. He stayed with the Air Force for twenty-five years. Then he retired and married my mom. When she died, he raised me by himself. Doted on me. Read to me in bed every night, made my brown bag school lunches every single day of my life. And every day he'd put in a surprise. All the way through to high school graduation. When it was time to eat at school, I'd find my sandwich and apple and chips and cookie, and then there'd be a little folded paper, taped shut. Inside would be a little heart-shaped note that said, 'I love you,' or a crude drawing of a flower and it would say, 'I picked a daisy just for you.' One time when I was worried about a test I had to take, his surprise was two new pencils, sharpened to fine points and a note that said, 'You'll do great.'"

"Wow, he sounds amazing." It was a sincere statement coming from me. I never had a dad who I knew.

Jade nodded. She was still rotating, facing Anne Gregory as the horse traced circles.

"One day, a Friday when it happened to be my birthday, he kept me home from school. He'd packed food and clothes. We saddled up his horse and my Shetland pony. When I asked what we were doing, he said we were disappearing for my birthday. And so we rode up into the mountains for a weekend horse-camping trip. One of the greatest experiences of my life. Campfires at night, roasting marshmallows, watching the stars, studying the birds with binoculars. Jumping into ice cold lakes for a swim. After that, we disappeared many times over the years. And when his arthritis and knee problems got too bad to ride, I still disappeared by myself. Especially after the warehouse fire and the loss of my fingers. Impromptu disappearing is a great way to clear your brain of anger and stress. I've been thinking about it since the death threat."

On the far side of the corral, the dogs appeared and ran into the barn.

"I've even thought about organizing horseback trips. I'd call it Disappearing and Rebuilding on Horseback. For women who've..." She paused. Started again. "Women who've struggled to find a way through trauma."

"A very good idea." I watched her work with Anne Gregory. It seemed a strong connection, each trusting the other. "Jade, have you seen anyone unusual in the area?"

She shook her head.

"I'd like to ask your neighbors. Can you direct me?"

"Andrew is good to ask. But you've already spoken to him. His grandfather Sam is getting dementia. So we can't know if the things he says are real or not. Amy lives down the street, first house on the left, but she doesn't like me, so she won't be helpful."

"Why doesn't she like you?"

Jade made another one of her invisible communications to Anne Gregory, and the horse came to a stop.

"Because I'm not normal. I don't gossip. I do hard physical labor. I read poetry. And I don't do girly stuff."

"What is girly stuff?"

"Putting on makeup, and caring about my nails, and shopping for girly clothes, and talking about men, and fussing about my hair, and worrying about how I look, and reading romance novels and women's magazines." She paused, her frown severe. "I'd probably have a more fun life if I could've been a girly girl. But I'm sorry, that's not me. I'm a tough girl. Always have been." She walked up to Anne Gregory and unclipped the longe line from the horse's halter. She picked up an unusual brush from one of the fence posts and began rubbing Anne Gregory down.

"Are there any other neighbors I should talk to?"

"Just Sorin, I suppose. Sorin Lupu. He's Romanian, which is cool. But he's weird. He has some kind of sun allergy. If the sun hits his skin, he breaks out in a bad rash. Don't get me wrong. I don't have a problem with a sun allergy or a rash. But I think the rash is what makes him act weird. He's so self-conscious, he can't just be normal. Everything is awkward all the time. He's definitely out on the edge of the normal spectrum."

I thought Jade was near the edge of that same spectrum. "Might that be at all similar to the way you're a tough girl?"

She seemed to think about it. "Yeah, I suppose it is. I should do a better job of trying to see through his awkwardness. But it's hard to find a connection when he talks about strange stuff all the time."

That piqued my curiosity. It was almost a cliché that when cops interview neighbors of a serial killer, they say, 'He seemed like such a nice guy. But he was always talking about strange stuff.'

"What kind of strange stuff?" I asked.

"A wide range of subjects that make no sense to me. The last one was something called the philosophy of the mind."

"Is he a philosopher?"

"I don't think so. He's more like some kind of mathematician. That's so far from horses and poetry. It's probably why it's so hard for me to talk to him."

She was working the brush down Anne Gregory's front legs. "I will say his smile is a dream. Not that I've ever seen it more than two or three times."

I stood at the fence and watched as Jade finished brushing Anne Gregory.

There was a soft sound. I turned and was startled to see Andrew Garden at the fence next to me.

"Oh, you surprised me," I said. "I didn't hear you coming."

"Sorry. It's a bad habit I have. I was bullied as a child. So I keep my back to the wall and walk softly. Now, as an adult, I guess I need to do a better job of announcing my approach. Like when mountain bikers come behind you on the trail. If they don't have a little bell, they need to say, 'Approaching on your left,' or something. I should get a bell."

I nodded.

"I have to go shower, Owen," Jade called out. "Maybe you could talk to Andrew?"

"Sure. I need to leave soon anyway."

"Another motel night for me?" she said.

"Might make sense," I said.

Jade turned and walked toward her house, her disappointment obvious.

SEVEN

Andrew and I leaned against the corral fence and talked. "Sorry, I didn't mean to interrupt you and Jade," he said. "It's been awhile, and I wanted to check and make sure she was okay."

"She was just showing me the longeing routine with Anne Gregory."

"An amazing horse," Andrew said.

"Must be exciting, going off to a Buddhist temple."

Andrew nodded. "It sounds like a big deal. But the reality is that it's more like a retreat for westerners who are looking for spiritual guidance. I'm sort of a classic neophyte and don't really know much about what I'm getting into."

"Will you learn to meditate or just study Buddhism?"

"Both, I think. There's about two dozen of us from the U.S. and Canada. We check into what's called a Theravada school and study the Four Noble Truths. We'll be confined to the temple school, cut off from our social life. Very little or no talking. No travel. No contact with people back in the States."

"Quite a major deprivation for most, I would think."

"Yes. That's what gets me most excited about it." As he said it, Andrew's voice revealed his excitement. "I just keep thinking that my life to this point has been risk free. I take no physical risks. But more important, I take no mental risks. Every day of my life is the same old process. I work the same old job, I interact with the same people, customers and suppliers. I play the same video games, watch the same shows, listen to the same music, eat the same food. But when I get off the plane in China, I will temporarily end my current life. And when I get into the temple school, it will complete my transition to an alien world I know nothing about."

"How long does this last?"

"I signed up for one month. If I do a good job of learning, they will allow me to stay a second month. If I continue to succeed, I can stay additional months. But most people don't stay more than a month or two. The process of becoming a monk and moving down the path to liberation is tough, and there is a high fallout rate. So who knows how long I stay."

"You quit your job to do this?"

"More of a sabbatical. I've been working as a handyman independent contractor for ten years. It's time for me to try something different from home repair."

"Is the temple school expensive?"

"No. That's what's great about it. The monthly fee is reasonable, and it covers room, board, and instruction. I could probably afford to stay three months if I wanted. And if you integrate well, they move you toward some of the work the monks do, and you eventually earn your way."

"You might end up as a Buddhist monk?"

Andrew Garden grinned. "You never know." His excitement was obvious. "Of course, I might not want to stay a long time. I'd miss my grandfather. Jade, too, for that matter."

The way he spoke, it sounded as if just the thought made him wistful.

"Are you and Jade close?"

He shrugged, suddenly seeming a little embarrassed. "I probably feel closer to her than she does to me. After an entire lifetime of living near each other, being close but, you know, not really, it's like that novel… What's it called? Love in the Time of Cholera."

"I don't know it."

Andrew squinted, his eyes seeming to wrinkle with emotion. "I suppose if a person knows love and loneliness, then you know the main range of human feeling. Does that make sense?"

"I think so," I said. "I'm lucky. I found a woman who is my center."

"You are lucky indeed," he said.

"When do you leave?"

"Tomorrow afternoon."

"I'll be back here tomorrow. Maybe I'll see you before you go."

"'Til then," he said. I called the dogs, and we got into the Jeep. As we drove away, we passed Andrew as he walked back to his cabin.

EIGHT

When I got to my office, I let Spot and Blondie in, then called my ER friend Doc Lee and asked if the El Dorado County coroner was still using the same pathologist to examine bodies for cause of death.

"Pretty much," he said. "Unless it's a slam dunk, then we don't bother her at all."

"What's a slam dunk example?"

"If a guy's under doctor's care for some deadly condition, lung cancer or something, and he croaks from that condition, we don't need confirmation for cause of death. It's obvious. The doctor fills out the form."

"Croaks?" I said.

"You spend twelve years learning to be a doc, you learn lots of descriptive words."

"Right. What about croaking from an accident? Like falls?"

"Any sudden or accidental deaths usually get looked at," he said.

"Do you remember a man named Billy Jaso? Late seventies. Fell and hit his head on his ranch in Christmas Valley. Three months ago."

"No. But you should call Doc Train, see if Train can 'splain."

"You could be a rapper," I said.

"Nope. I ain't got the look or the chutzpah. But I've got rapper wheels."

"The black Porsche, I agree. Train's been the county's go-to pathologist for a few months now, right?"

"Yeah," he said. "Call her and see if she knows your body."

"Maybe you could call and get me an intro and ask her to take my call?" I said. "Otherwise, I probably won't get through."

"Sure," he said. "Better yet, I can maybe have her call you."

"How does that work?"

"She owes me for doc stuff."

"Sounds like something I don't want to know about."

"Something like that," Doc Lee said.

We said goodbye. My phone rang five minutes later.

I answered, "Owen McKenna."

"I'm Doctor Benicia Train. Doctor Lee asked me to call you about a case."

"Thank you very much for calling. I'm investigating the death of a local man named Billy Jaso. He fell and hit his head at his ranch in Christmas Valley. Does that sound familiar?"

"It does. Let me pull it up on the screen."

I waited, drank some coffee, waited some more.

The woman spoke. "I ruled it an accidental death. He hit his head on a rock. He died from complications related to intracranial hemorrhage."

"Is that common when someone falls and hits their head?"

"Yes. In this case, his head struck a sharp rock. The rock punctured his skull. I found a small chunk of granite buried in his brain tissue. The bleeding produced enough back pressure to seal up the tissue from the inside."

"Like a flap valve in a toilet tank," I said. "The back pressure closes it tight."

"Wha...? Um, well, that's an unusual metaphor for a brain injury. But I suppose it works."

"Is it possible that his death wasn't an accident?"

She went silent.

"Attributing accidental cause seems to be the most logical explanation for how he was injured," I said. "But consider this, please. If someone hit him with a rock or pushed him from behind, couldn't the same thing have happened?"

"Sure. But there were no marks or contusions on the body, nor any other indication to support that. To get a cranial puncture like his would require a hard, focused blow. It looks very much like he fell, hit his head on a sharp rock, and died."

"Such is the nature of an accidental death, right?" I said. "A person can swerve a car, crash, and die in an accident. Maybe they swerved because they weren't paying attention to the curve in the road. Or maybe they swerved because another person ran out in the road. If the person who ran out was trying to cause the crash, the death still looks like an accident, even though it might be murder."

She didn't respond for a moment. "From what I was told, no one was there when Mr. Jaso fell. But I suppose many accidental deaths could be, well, not as accidental as they seem."

"Do you recall any notable aspects of the death?"

"I remember what seemed notable at the time. While the damage to his skull and brain was significant, the nature of it was unusual."

"Can you elaborate?"

"People often die from head trauma suffered in falls. But they rarely puncture their skull on rocks. It is, of course, certainly possible and even likely in certain environments. But it isn't common."

"What is common?"

"When a person hits their head hard enough, they fracture their skulls. They split their skin and bleed. They suffer internal bleeding. But a skull puncture like a hole is unusual."

"When you do get a puncture, what is the normal cause?"

"Gunshot wounds. Stab wounds. Knives, scissors, screwdrivers, things like that."

"Yet this was a rock."

"Right," she said. "And there was a piece of granite inside his brain."

"So he fell, hit his head on a sharp piece of granite, and a piece of the rock broke off inside his skull."

"Yes."

"You were able to identify the piece as granite. No other material was present."

"Correct. Mind you, I'm just a normal doctor, and I only have standard diagnostic imaging and other tools available to me. Those of us who work in the real world don't have the fancy stuff you see on TV shows. In fact, many things you see on TV are pure fiction. But we still try hard to work with our tools. And we usually get a pretty clear idea of what happened to cause a death."

"Granite in the man's skull sounds quite clear." I thanked her for her time and hung up.

NINE

The next morning, I was up early. Street was in Bend, Oregon talking bugs, so I had nothing to do to occupy my time other than helping a former firefighter in distress.

After our morning walk in the forest above Lake Tahoe, I let Spot and Blondie into the Jeep and headed back through South Lake Tahoe and out to Jade Jaso's ranch.

When I drove down the dirt track through the forest and came around the last turn before the Jaso barn, I saw movement in the corral. I slowed to a crawl.

Jade Jaso was riding Anne Gregory at a slow gallop. They were making a gradual turn, going counterclockwise around the corral. Their turn brought them around in front of the barn. They seemed to straighten out as they approached a wide obstacle in their path, what looked like a white, horizontal, vinyl fencing rail about 12 feet long. The rail was propped up on supports like sawhorses. It sat about 3 feet above the ground. Anne Gregory maintained a constant speed. As horse and rider approached the rail, the horse jumped over the rail as smoothly as if it had not been there at all.

Spot had reached his head forward from the back seat so that his head was next to mine. He stared ahead. He seemed as focused on the action as I was.

"Whoa, see that, Spot? Could you do that?" Spot's body was oscillating a bit, indicating that he was wagging. Blondie was next to him in the back seat. I had the sense she was more interested in watching Spot than Anne Gregory.

I didn't want to startle Jade or her mount, so I didn't pull forward. Instead, I eased to a stop.

Jade was slowing her horse. She came to a stop, and dismounted. It was a long jump-slide to the ground from her stirrups. Her cowboy boots hit the dirt hard enough to kick up a cloud of dust. She let go of the reins and walked toward the rail they'd just jumped over. As Jade turned, she saw us. She raised an arm high and beckoned us toward them.

I drove slowly toward them. Jade lifted up on each end of the rail, raising it a foot or so. She walked back to Anne Gregory. I was curious about how it would work, a woman so short getting up on a horse so tall. I stopped well back from the corral fence and watched.

Jade stepped to the left side of Anne Gregory. The left stirrup appeared substantially higher than Jade could reach with her left foot. She reached up to a black bag that was attached to the side and rear of the saddle. She lifted a flap and pulled out a piece of heavy webbing that had a stirrup on the end. The stirrup hung down much lower than the normal stirrup. It was still a reach, but Jade got her right foot into the booster stirrup and, pulling on the saddle leather for help, straightened her right leg and stood up. Her right foot in the booster stirrup swayed in space beneath Anne Gregory's belly. Jade was now able to put her left foot into the standard stirrup and then swing up into the saddle. Once sitting, she raised the booster stirrup, coiling the webbing, and stowed it back in the black bag.

Jade started Anne Gregory forward, moving at a trot, then speeding up.

I was pleased that she didn't let my appearance interrupt her workout. It was intriguing to watch a thousand-pound animal do its training exercises.

Jade kept Anne Gregory running in a smaller circle than before, passing to the inside of the jumping rail.

On the second path around the circle, she moved Anne Gregory out to a larger-diameter path and headed toward the jump which was now about 4 feet off the ground. Once again, the horse was as smooth and competent as she was beautiful. She didn't break stride as she seemed to float up and over the jump.

Jade had a look of pleasure on her face, almost a Mona Lisa smile as she came toward us. Bouncing at the hollow of her throat were the dog tags. She stopped the horse at the fence and dismounted.

I opened the doors of the Jeep, and Spot and Blondie ran out.

"That was very cool," I said.

Jade took off her helmet, reached over the fence, and pet Spot, who was still wagging with enthusiasm.

"I don't know how to even ask the obvious questions," I said. "Is Anne Gregory a specialty jumping horse? Or do all horses know how to jump?"

"She's a thoroughbred who is most comfortable simply galloping fast. But she's also a competent jumper. When I got her, she came with an English saddle. It's perfect for jumping, so I'm having fun with that. We have western saddles for Cyrano and de Bergerac."

"You told me about getting Anne Gregory from the farm that boarded her. When did you get your other horses?"

"About four years ago, Dad bought Cyrano and de Bergerac as a pair that had always been together. They came from a ranch in Carson Valley."

"I've only done the smallest amount of riding. But it was on a western saddle. The English saddle you're riding is quite different. There's no saddle horn to hang onto."

Jade looked embarrassed for me. Her reaction made me realize that the purpose of a saddle horn was obviously not for holding when one was riding.

"At first," she said, "I didn't think I'd like an English saddle because I'd grown up with a western saddle that I used when I rode as a kid. Dad rode a quarter horse, and we had a Shetland pony that I rode. We had matching saddles, large and small. But now I've switched. This saddle has worked well for most purposes. And I've learned to do some jumping with it. It moves your weight forward, which helps the horse because you're over the horse's center of balance instead of farther to the rear on the horse's back. I've used this saddle for all my trail rides. I've come to really like it."

"What about your other horses, Cyrano and de Bergerac?

Are they jumpers?"

Jade made a sound that was vaguely like a chuckle. "Not really. Partly, they don't have the conformation of good jumpers. Despite their small size, they're all about brute strength and endurance, not grace. You need grace to be a good jumper. But even though de Bergerac lacks grace, he'll jump if he has to. But I have to make certain he understands there is no alternative. Cyrano, however, will go to any length to do a runout."

Jade must have seen the confusion on my face.

"A runout is when a horse runs around a jump. Cyrano will crash through brush or leap into deep water if he has to. Anything to avoid a jump."

"Is that because he doesn't know how to jump? Or is he afraid of it?"

"It's more fear than anything. I think all horses know how to jump, but good luck getting Cyrano to do it. My guess is that at some point early on, he made a jump only to find himself landing on something scary. Rattlesnakes or something."

"So there's a psychology to getting horses to do what you want."

"Absolutely."

I reached across the fence and patted Anne Gregory's cheek. "What does a horse like Cyrano do if you try to force him to jump?"

"If he can't do a runout, he simply refuses to jump. He'll do a quick stop."

I looked over at Cyrano and de Bergerac, who were both eating hay at the hayrack just as they had been the last time I'd seen them.

"That sounds dangerous," I said.

"It is. Horses can stop really fast. If you launch head first off a horse at thirty miles an hour, you can break lots of bones."

I ran my hand down Anne Gregory's neck. "Did you stay at the motel last night?"

Jade nodded.

"Everything seem okay here when you got home?"

Another nod. "Maybe the voicemail threat was just about

scaring me. Like the person was agitated about his friend Barry dying. It could be he called to yell at me just to blow off steam." She looked down at the ground. "Maybe I was too quick to assume that the threat was literal."

"Could be," I said. "But I'd still vary your schedule. Stay at the motel. Or a different motel. Be unpredictable."

I looked back down the drive. "Andrew told me he's leaving this afternoon." I didn't know if it mattered to Jade.

"Yeah, I'm worried about that. His grandfather Sam will still be here. And, of course, the other neighbors are around and would possibly see if a trespasser is exploring the woods. But I'm uneasy."

"Will you be talking to Andrew?"

She shrugged. "Maybe. We're not buddies. He's nice. I'm nice. Well, cordial at least. But we don't have any reason for a big goodbye." She started loosening the cinch strap on Anne Gregory's saddle.

"I understand. I wanted to talk to him again before he left. I thought now might be good."

"Help yourself," Jade said, no warmth in her voice.

TEN

I left the dogs to hang out with Jade while I walked down the rutted drive. I found Andrew on his front deck. He had a large pack set out on the picnic table. There were some piles of clothes and supplies. He was staring at the pack and the piles as if making judgments about how much room he had and what he'd have to leave behind.

I walked up. "Tough to pack for a trip to the other side of the world."

He looked at me and nodded.

"I'm curious," I said. "How does a guy who grew up in Tahoe get interested in Buddhism? California's Chinese are mostly in the Bay Area."

Andrew shrugged. "I guess it ultimately came from growing up with Jade's dad Billy as my closest neighbor. I don't know if you're aware, but Billy Jaso was Basque. The Basque are Europe's most ancient culture. Their language is unlike anything else in the world."

"I know a little about the Basque, the people who live in the mountains between Spain and France. But I don't know about any connection to Buddhism."

"Billy often talked about how the Basque believe in animism."

"What exactly is that?"

Andrew frowned. "I'm not sure how to describe it. I think animism is basically about how all things, animals, plants, and even rocks, have a kind of spiritual quality. A soul. Billy made it sound almost romantic. That none of us are alone. That we're surrounded by the elements of nature and those elements are all connected."

"Similar to some Native American beliefs?"

"I think so, yeah. Billy told me about flying bombing missions during the Vietnam war. I looked up Vietnam because I didn't know anything about it. I ended up reading about Buddhism, which is the main religion in Vietnam. It turns out that Buddhists are into animism just like the Basque. And they're on the opposite side of the world! So that got me thinking there really was something to this animism stuff. The more I read, the more I was intrigued. I found out about this Buddhist temple where you can go to stay for a time and study. It's kind of like a working vacation for Buddhism. So I applied and was accepted. I'm very excited." He looked at his watch. "I have to leave in less than an hour if I want to make it to the airport in time."

"That's cool. I hope you learn lots and have a great time."

He grinned. "Thank you. I'm sure I will."

"What does your grandfather think of your trip?"

Andrew's face went from happy to concerned. "I'm a little worried about it. I don't think Sam's completely comprehending it. He's...I hate to think it, but he's getting a little dementia. He's taken to talking in rhymes and such. Especially when he's uncomfortable. It's very strange. The doctor says that certain kinds of dementia produce bursts of creativity unlike anything from earlier in the person's life."

"Is your grandfather comfortable about you going on a long trip?"

"I've talked to him about it, and he says it will be a good experience for me. But I think he's putting on a good face. I've wondered if the stress of having me leave is accelerating his dementia. Sometimes you can't get a straight answer out of him. He's off in this other world. At least, he doesn't drive anymore, so I don't have to worry about him getting in an accident."

"How will he get his groceries and such when you're gone?"

"He calls the local market and they deliver. Not long ago, I heard him on the phone placing his order. I heard him say, 'Deliver the food. I pay the bill. I eat the food. I eat my fill.' It stuck in my mind because it was so... out there."

Andrew made a little shake of his head. "I've given them advance payment for four months worth of food. I've set up all the other bills on auto pay. I don't have much money, but Sam got a reverse mortgage on this cabin several years ago. That, plus his social security, covers the basic expenses. He should be fine. And he makes a point of saying he'll be fine. But, frankly, he makes too much of a point of saying that. So it has me a bit worried. But he also says that he's aware that his forgetfulness is only going to get worse. He's adamant that I go and do this travel now while he can still take care of himself. He says I only need to come back to put him in a rest home or something."

"Do you have other friends or family checking in with him?"

"It's just him and me. The only other person close to us beside Jade is Sorin Lupu, who lives down the road a half mile. He said he'll stop in and check on Sam every few days. Frankly, Sorin is a little strange, so I hope my grandfather doesn't need his help." Andrew pointed through the forest. "Down the road five or six houses, on the left. Brown house, white trim."

"Sorin Lupu," I repeated to make sure I heard him correctly. "There's a name."

"Yeah. He's Romanian. He says it means sun wolf. Which is a little ironic because he has some kind of skin condition where sunshine makes him break out in a rash. He can't come out in the sun without white sun block covering his face. He always wears one of those hats with the long brim and the wide flap that hangs down over his ears and neck. Wears gloves, too, even in the summer. Anyway, he's lived here now for seven or eight years. So he might be good to talk to."

"Is he friends with Jade?"

"I don't know that they're friends. But they talk. He comes down the trail, especially in the evening when the sun goes behind the mountain. I've seen him by her corral, leaning on the fence, talking to her about her horses. He seems to know horses some. Anyway, Grandpa Sam has Sorin's number in case anything comes up. But at Sam's age, who knows if he'll remember where Sorin's number is written down?"

"How old is Sam?"

"He's either eighty-eight or eighty-nine."

"There a question about it?"

Andrew nodded. "The other day, I said, 'Grandpa Sam, you must know your own age.' And he said, 'I do. Eighty-eight or eighty-nine. Take your pick, take your time.'"

"An example of him talking in rhymes."

"Yeah. I'd think it was fun if I weren't worried he's losing his mind. Anyway, Sam's made it clear that he's okay with me going. He says a person can tell when their end is getting close. It's a morbid subject and I don't bring it up. But he does. He says he's leaving me the house. But the reverse mortgage has already used up most of the equity, so I won't really have anything to speak of. Of course, it's his house. He can do what he wants with it. And I don't begrudge him that." Andrew looked across at his piled clothes and gear. "I better get back to this packing. My Uber ride is coming to pick me up soon."

"Got it. Thanks for talking, and I hope you have a great time at the Buddhist temple."

We shook hands, and I walked back to where I'd parked at Jade's ranch.

I spent another hour talking to Jade, mostly about memories of her father and their great experiences "disappearing" on horseback. When she seemed comfortable, I told her I had errands to run the next day, and that I'd be back after that. I called the dogs and left.

ELEVEN

The next day, I got to the Jaso ranch in the late afternoon. I could see Anne Gregory through one of the open barn windows. The other horses were out of sight. Probably in the barn as well.

I knocked on the side of the barn door before I walked into the big space.

"Owen McKenna calling," I said so I wouldn't startle anyone, human or horses.

"In the tack room," Jade called out.

I walked in. The horses were in three separate stalls. I could see Jade through the open tack room door, scooping grain from a metal storage can into a bucket.

"Time for their dinner?"

"Yes. They love grain, and Anne Gregory is a bit bossy. So I have to separate them. Otherwise AG chases the other horses away and eats all the grain."

Jade carried the grain bucket out and began pouring it onto feeding trays in each horse stall. "I've read that elephants and dolphins are more cooperative," she said. "They try to be sure that everyone in their social group gets enough to eat. I don't know how true that is. But it certainly doesn't apply to horses. If a mountain lion comes around, a stallion will protect his harem physically, but none of the herd actively shares food supply."

"Same with dogs. You have to monitor to keep things fair."

When Jade was done divvying up the grain, we walked out to the corral. Jade stood near the fence, put a boot up on the lowest rail and leaned on the top rail. The lowering sun shined on her damaged hand, making the skin grafts seem extra pink. One of her remaining fingers stuck out at a greater angle than I'd realized before. She didn't just lose three fingers, the remaining two were damaged as well, one dramatically. Lines of stitches curved across her hand, as noticeable as train tracks from up in a plane.

I stood next to her and leaned on the fence.

"Anything new?" I asked. "Phone messages? Emails? Visitors to the ranch?"

"No. Andrew called yesterday afternoon after he'd boarded his plane but before it took off. He wanted to thank me in advance for keeping an eye on Sam. I think the reality of him leaving Sam finally soaked in as he left. It made him insecure. He's got neighbor Sorin checking in on Sam. But Sorin's, well, not the most reassuring person to put in charge of your grandfather's care."

"Isn't he reliable?"

"He probably is. In fact, he's probably a good guy in every respect. He just doesn't telegraph comfort. I can't seem to have a normal neighborly friendship with him. Everything is so awkward."

She looked off toward the barn. She reached up with her damaged hand and used the little finger to brush some hair from her eye. It gave me a surprising jolt, seeing Jade's pink, scarred, disfigured hand doing something that I'd seen countless women do with normal hands.

"You look ill-at-ease," I said.

"I shouldn't complain. I have food and a roof over my head and beautiful horses. I have much of what other people in the world would think is a dream life."

"Dreams can be shattered. It's okay to complain after what you've been through."

Jade turned her head and looked up at me. Her forehead was creased by an intense frown. But it didn't seem like it was a frown of disagreement, more a sign of concentration on what we were saying.

We had a quiet moment. Jade looked toward Anne Gregory who had walked out into the corral and tossed her head. I felt a kind of psychological pull from the horse. I'd ridden a little when Street and I searched for the lost mustang in Tahoe, and I'd watched a lot of Westerns. But something about Anne Gregory was captivating. Perhaps it was the same connection that drew humans to horses from the beginning.

The high-pitched call of a raptor brought me out of my reverie. Jade and I both looked toward the sky. We saw a soaring bird very high.

"Is that an Osprey?" I asked.

"I think so. When I was a little girl, I remember my mom telling me about Fishing Hawks in China. That's what they call Osprey. Osprey are noble. Monogamous. While the female tends the nest, the male protects the nest and brings the food for both the female and the chicks. When I grew up and studied poetry, I learned that Chinese poets wrote about Fishing Hawks over two thousand years ago."

"Osprey were important to the Chinese," I said, stating the obvious because I was interested, and I wanted Jade to keep talking about it.

"Very important," she said, completing my thought. "Buddhism celebrates the Osprey as the king of birds. Some call the Osprey the White Eagle." She looked up at the sky. "I've seen Osprey fly over this ranch, way up high like that one that just went by. Probably on their way to the lakes in the high country of Meiss Meadows or Caples Lake by Kirkwood. All they eat is fish."

I looked up, following her gaze.

"My father always helped my mother raise me. When she went into the hospital for surgery, he took over everything. When the surgery didn't work and my mother died, my dad became the king of fathers. He taught me to hike and ride horses. He even taught me to fish."

"Just like the male Osprey," I said. "Maybe Andrew Garden will learn about Ospreys as he learns about Buddhism."

Jade nodded. She reached up and touched the military tags hanging at her neck.

"Your father's dog tags?" I said.

She nodded once, slow and solemn. "It reassures me to have them close. In the night when I can't sleep, I get some comfort from touching them."

After a long silence, I said, "I just stopped by to check in," I said. "I need to go get some dinner. But I'll be back in the morning, say, nine o'clock. Are you comfortable with that?"

Another nod. "Are you staying at the same motel?"

"Yes."

I made a little wave as I left.

The next morning as I drove to see Jade Jaso, I came to a roadwork slowdown near the airport, which delayed me ten minutes. While I'd learned that Jade was a naturally-stressed individual, I didn't worry about a ten-minute delay.

When I pulled into the drive that wound back to Jade's house, there was a greater sense of quiet than before. I remembered that Andrew Garden had left for his Buddhist retreat two days before. But his grandfather Sam was still supposed to be home. Inside, no doubt, coping with Andrew's absence and the coming, inscrutable absence of his own mind.

Spot and Blondie had their heads out the windows, watching the Garden house as I cruised past. I went around the curve, through the thick trees, and pulled into the parking area near the corral and barn.

Even though I'd been delayed, I figured Jade would be there, tending, as she had been every day, to her horses. Except that Jade's pickup was gone.

TWELVE

When I saw that Jade's truck was missing, my first thought was maybe she'd forgotten that I was coming in the morning. She could be running a quick errand and planning to return any minute. Or she could have pulled her truck into the barn. Anne Gregory was not at the fence. Cyrano and de Bergerac were not at the hayrack. Were the horses in the barn as well?

I parked and let Spot and Blondie out. They trotted around the area in meandering figure-eights while I walked into the barn. The barn was empty and seemed more cavernous than before. I looked out the end windows of the barn and saw forest where before the view had been of Jade's horse trailer.

I looked in Billy Jaso's glass shop. I went back outside and walked around the barn. There were some vague footprints in the dirt where the horse trailer had been parked. But dusty, dry dirt doesn't take impressions well. I couldn't even distinguish between human footprints and horse hoofprints.

The house doors were shut, front and back. I knocked but got no response. I tried the doorknobs. Locked. But the blinds weren't lowered. I cupped my hands at the windows and peered in. Dishes sat on the counter, a serving spoon sticking out of a cook pot on the stove. The glass coffee pot was out of the coffee maker. It still had a little coffee in it.

On the table was a coffee mug with a teaspoon sticking out of it. There was a partial bowl of what looked like brown rice. A fork was in the bowl. Another bowl had what looked like wilted spinach, baby carrots, cherry tomatoes.

I couldn't be sure, but not many people eat brown rice and salad for breakfast. Which suggested that Jade was interrupted during last night's dinner. She managed to lock the doors but not much else as she loaded her horses into the trailer and left.

Did she leave voluntarily? Maybe. There were no obvious signs of a physical struggle. But she hadn't planned to leave so suddenly, as evidenced by the half-eaten dinner and the unwashed dishes.

I walked back out to the parking area and looked at the dirt. By studying the area where Jade's horse trailer was parked, I could make out the vague tire tracks as it rolled away. They made a gradual curve into the compacted, two-track dirt drive that went out to the street. What little was recognizable of the trailer tracks grew too faint to see as it entered the two-track drive.

I went back and studied the point where the trailer track transitioned from vague tire marks to no marks. I moved around, squatted down, checking from multiple angles like a golfer checking the green before hitting the putt.

After making a circle around the area, I saw that the tracks didn't make sense. I changed directions and went around again. This time, I began to see something that made me very uncomfortable.

I was pretty sure that, as the trailer tracks merged into the hard dirt drive, another set of tracks came over them from a different direction. The implication was that after the horse trailer had pulled onto the dirt drive, another vehicle pulled out and followed.

Probably, Jade drove her pickup and all three horses were in the trailer. So who drove after her? And was that person a friend?

I doubted that. A friend would at least let Jade finish her dinner and pick up her dishes. A friend might even wash the dishes for her.

The likeliest reason for Jade abandoning her dinner was that someone was forcing her to hurry. Load the horses in the trailer and leave. The person making the demands was probably the person who followed her out of the drive. Maybe the person following Jade was talking to her on his cell phone, telling her where to drive.

The realization that she probably hadn't "disappeared" of her own volition but had been forced to leave hit me hard.

I should have seen it coming. I should never have allowed myself to wonder if the voicemail threat had merely been bluster. I knew from my law enforcement background that all threats represent serious risk. I'd screwed up big time, and now Jade was gone. I was the so-called expert on the scene. It was up to me to judge the risks and act appropriately. No amount of defensive explanations took away the simple fact that I was the culpable party. She was gone, and it was my fault. I deserved more blame than anyone except the person threatening her. I'd made major mistakes in the past, but this was up near the top of the list.

It took me a moment to force my thoughts away from self-recrimination and focus on what I needed to do next.

I pulled out my phone, went through my contact list, and found the personal number of Sergeant Bains of the El Dorado County Sheriff's Office. Jade had told me that she'd met him and he was the one who gave her my number.

"Hey, McKenna, long time," he answered. "How's Street? How's the hound?"

"Good and good," I said. I was about to explain the reason for my call when he said, "Do you remain in contact with Glenda Gorman?"

"Yeah your intended amour is still turning heads with her moxie and trenchant journalism."

"That wasn't what turned my head," he said. "Although I'm sure they were present. Sure wish she would reconsider me."

"You and a lot of other guys. I'm calling with bad news. I'm at Jade Jaso's Ranch in Christmas Valley, and it looks like she's been taken."

"What's that mean?"

"I came to meet her a few minutes ago and found her and her horses gone." I gave Bains my idea of what might have happened.

"Be there in a few," he said and clicked off.

While I waited, I walked the perimeter of the house and barn and did a loose grid search of the area. I was looking for clues but had no idea what form they might take. Mostly, my mind wandered to all the ways I'd misjudged the situation. I'd found nothing of interest when Bains pulled up. I held out my hand to make sure he stopped before he came to the tire tracks.

"Sarge," I said when he got out.

He nodded at me. "McKenna." Bains is like an advertisement model for a career in law enforcement. Or anything for that matter. He's 6-2, square-jawed with a jutting, dimpled chin, blondish with a little cowlick at one o'clock on his hairline, dark eyebrows over blue eyes, wide shoulders, narrow waist. He looked sharp in his uniform.

Spot trotted up. Bains rubbed him. Blondie hung back.

"Any ideas?" he said as he looked around.

"Looking through the windows, you can see her half-eaten dinner. Dishes left out."

"A sudden interruption last night," he said.

"All three horses are gone, as is her pickup and horse trailer." I walked over and pointed at the ground. "I believe these tracks are from the horse trailer. These other tracks come over them."

Bains looked back and forth. "So Jade put her horses in the trailer and hooked it up to her pickup. When she pulled out, another driver followed behind."

"Right. But none of the tracks reveals tread pattern. I've done a loose grid search but found nothing."

"I'll get my tech people to go over the house and contents. My new woman, Kelly Maven, has a great eye for this stuff. She can find a human eyelash on a shaggy dog. She came up from the Contra Costa County Sheriff's Office in the Bay Area. Loves mountain biking in the Sierra. Their loss, our gain." He stepped back as if to survey the scene from a broader perspective.

"Come look in the windows," I said.

We walked over to the house. I pointed out the unfinished meal and the dishes in disarray.

"This looks like a possible kidnapping to me," Bains said. "You concur?"

I thought about it. "Except for the fact that she probably loaded her horses in the trailer herself, and she probably drove her own pickup out of here."

"If you don't call it kidnapping, then what? A carjacking? A horsejacking?"

"Looks like it," I said. "Which makes it FBI territory. You want to call Agent Ramos? Or should I?"

"I've got to talk to him anyway," Bains said. "I'll let him know. He can call you for particulars if I miss anything. I'll get Kelly and crew out here to take a close look."

"Thanks."

"Hey, McKenna. I know that look. This could turn out to be a real sad thing. But you didn't cause it." He shook his head at me. "Don't beat yourself up about it."

"Right."

THIRTEEN

B ains left.

It's hard to canvas a neighborhood in a vehicle, pulling from one driveway to the next and repeating the process. So I left the Jeep at Jade's house and walked. My first stop was at the cabin where Andrew and Sam Garden lived.

Spot is always a good conversational lubricant. But his size sometimes unnerves people, so I took him by his collar. Blondie trotted next to us, heeling even though she hadn't been asked.

The green Toyota was still in the drive, where it would probably remain until Andrew Garden returned from the Buddhist temple in China. Andrew had said that his grandfather Sam didn't drive. No doubt the garage was filled with other stuff.

I walked up and knocked on the door. There was no answer. I knocked again. After a minute, I stepped over to one of the windows, cupped my hands to the glass, and peered in. No lights. No movement.

"You hold the floor, I'll get the door," a voice said. It took me a moment to realize the voice was outside. I turned. An old man was coming through the trees on the trail where I'd previously seen the neighbor named Amy walking her terrier and young boy. The man carried a walking stick in each hand. They were like ski poles, metallic blue with rubber tips. He walked at a good pace even though he took care to place his feet carefully.

"Hello. I'm Owen McKenna," I said as he approached. "I met your grandson Andrew a few days ago. You must be Sam Garden."

"Yep. Sam Garden, if you'll pardon. Strolling Sam's got sand in his garden."

He came up the steps slowly, carefully. He was slight of build and probably stayed thin from lots of walking. The man had more hair on his eyebrows and ears than on his head. The rims of his ears were furred, like little white arched caterpillars. His eyebrows were white tooth brushes. Under the eyebrows were bloodshot eyes, as if the owner was permanently sad. The old man looked at Spot, who probably outweighed him by 30 pounds.

"That dog's a Dane. You could lean on him like a cane."

I realized that Sam Garden was wearing thin slippers.

"Do you always wear your slippers when you go hiking?"

He frowned at me, then looked down at his feet. "Sam the missing memory man. Slippers Sam who lost his shoes, memory's gone, that's the news."

I remembered that Andrew had said his grandfather's approaching dementia was making him talk in creative rhymes.

"Okay if we talk a little?" I asked.

"Talk is cheap when memory's empty. Thoughtful Sam lost his thoughts."

There were two metal chairs on the small deck. "Shall we sit on your porch?"

Sam Garden stepped over to one of the chairs and sat down. He kept hold of his walking sticks, his arms held out to his sides, poles planted on the deck. He looked like a skier crouched low in a big mogul field, planting his ski poles to navigate a complicated landscape.

"Andrew told me you'll order your groceries delivered while he's studying Buddhism in China."

"Eat your fruit, eat your vegetables, but save room for cookies."

I looked at Sam as he stared off at the trees. Clearly, his mind was organized differently from those of other people. But his memory wasn't empty. Somewhere in those gray cells was an enormously creative word artist. I thought the news about Jade going missing might be upsetting. So I started on a different subject.

"I wonder what you can tell me about Billy Jaso."

"Best of man, the Jaso clan. Understands Chinese, talks Basque, don't even try, it's a task."

"Was he a good friend?"

The old man didn't say a word. He just nodded, and his red eyes teared up.

So much for not upsetting him. I let him sit for a minute.

I said, "Sam, I'm wondering if Billy Jaso had secrets."

He seemed to think about it. "Secret treasure by any measure. Don't let pressure ruin the pleasure."

"What kind of treasure was it?"

Sam lowered his voice. "Secret treasure's a secret." He looked down again at his slippers. "No clues for lost shoes. Wonder where I put them." He stood up, leaning on the walking poles, and turned toward the front door.

"Would you like help finding your shoes?"

He didn't answer. He reached for the door and turned the knob. It was unlocked. I wouldn't be surprised if he hadn't locked it in a decade. He walked inside. I followed.

Sam used his walking poles in the kitchen and the living room, no concern about the rubber points leaving marks on the glossy varnished wooden floor. Sam sat down on an easy chair. He still held the walking poles. His eyes went to his hands and the pole grips. He looked surprised. "Found the poles, that's my goal."

I walked the perimeter of the living room looking for wayward shoes. Next, I looked in the two bedrooms. One was messy with clothes everywhere like a teenage cliché, but piled in groups using some kind of organization that wasn't immediately apparent. Like Sam's mind. Two piles seemed to be about lights and darks. For laundry? Two others seemed to be about what part of the body they were for, one group with shirts and sweaters, one with pants and socks.

The other room was hyper neat. Even the loose items on the desk were lined up in a row. I guessed that the neat room was Andrew's for the simple reason that he seemed like the kind of guy who would have neatened it up before he left on his travels. In front of the bed were two worn and scuffed shoes.

Like someone sat on the bed to put them on, then forgot.

"I think I found your shoes," I called toward Sam in the living room. I looked around the room.

The old man appeared in the doorway. "Someone put my shoes here. Shoes like clues. Like history, it's a mystery. Maybe it was Anders."

I handed him the shoes. "Anders?"

Sam Garden seemed confused.

"You mean Andrew?" I said.

"Names are a game."

"Sam, I stopped by because Jade Jaso was going to meet me. But she's gone. Her horses are gone, too. Have you seen her?"

He frowned, then looked up as if suddenly remembering. "Gone, gone, hasn't been long. Left last night, didn't seem right."

"She drove off with her horses in the trailer. Was there anyone else? Any other vehicle?"

"She had an escort, a mean fellow, not at all mellow. His truck was yellow."

"Why do you say he was mean? Did you see them up close?"

"The way he leaned toward her. The way he preened toward her. Stabbed his finger, shook his fist."

"How did you see them if they were driving?"

Sam didn't answer. He looked confused.

"Do you have any idea where they went?"

Sam's eyes went wide like there was a ghost standing ten feet away. He slowly shook his head.

I tried to coax him. "What were you going to say, Sam?"

He stayed silent, his scared eyes moving back and forth just a little as if looking at the ghost's eyes. Left eye, right eye.

"Is it okay if I stop by and visit the next time I come 'round?"

Sam was silent. He appeared to be still staring at a ghost.

I walked to the door as if to leave, then waited to see if Sam had another comment. Spot was just outside. Blondie was down off the deck, waiting.

Sam still didn't speak, so I left.

I walked out to South Upper Truckee road. The closest houses were to the south, so we headed that direction. The first house was a small blue ranch design, probably two bedroom and one bath. One-car garage. No sign of people. I knocked, waited, knocked again. No response.

Same for the second house, a cute little red cottage with two small gable dormers in the roof indicating some type of attic room. No garage.

Because it was August, the busiest tourist month, one might expect vacationers to fill every house in the Tahoe Basin. But there are many people who like to keep their Tahoe cabins to themselves and not rent them out. Those lodgings are usually vacant more often than not.

The third house I came to was across the street. It was the common, newer, two-story box design stained dark brown, with the main portion of the front being a garage, above which sits the master bedroom. Spot and I walked up the long wide stairs to the entry. Blondie waited at the bottom. I pressed the bell.

An immediate frantic, high-pitched barking came from inside the house.

I still held Spot's collar. I pulled him back a step so we didn't crowd anyone who might open the door. Spot's nose was on alert, lifted up high, nostrils flexing. An aroma like lasagna was pronounced and enticing.

The door opened. The pudgy boy I'd seen on the trail a few days before stood there without speaking, his eyes huge and fixated on Spot. On the floor nearby was a wire kennel containing the terrier that the boy's mother had called Little Bear. The terrier barked and jumped and barked some more, a piercing, irritating sound that made me want to plug my ears.

"Hey, dude," I said in a loud voice that the kid probably couldn't hear over the barking dog. "My dog's name is Spot. You can pet him if you want."

Spot pulled at his collar, reaching his nose forward and down toward the terrier. I held on tight.

The kid left the door standing open as he turned, ran up

the indoor steps to the living and kitchen level, and shrieked, "Mom!"

"What, hon?"

"There's a giant dog!"

"Sweetie, don't get so bent out of shape. You've seen big dogs before." Then she shouted, "LITTLE BEAR, SHUT UP!"

As if the woman were a saint performing miracles, the terrier stopped barking.

The kid came pounding back down the steps. He stood there and stared at Spot.

Spot glanced up at me, then looked again at the kid, then at the terrier in its kennel, and wagged.

Footsteps came across the living room. I saw feet in slippers and then blue jeans descend the steps and come down into my view. It was Amy, who'd been walking the terrier when I was talking to Andrew Garden.

"Oh, my," the woman's voice said. "You're right, Kenny. That is a giant dog."

"Morning," I said. "The dog is Spot," I repeated, "and he's friendly. My name's Owen McKenna. I saw you on the trail near Andrew and Sam's house. I'm a private investigator. I'm inquiring about your neighbor, Jade Jaso."

"Oh? What's she gotten all cracked up about now?" The woman's eyes went from crinkly friendly to squinty and suspicious. She tipped her head in a manner that suggested disapproval. The tilt also made the light illuminate the black roots at the base of her blonde hair.

"Jade seems to be missing. Along with her three horses. They're all gone."

"So? Nothing surprising about a tempestuous woman like her going missing." Her tone made it clear that she couldn't care less.

"Any idea of where she might have gone? Have you seen her or her horses?"

"Haven't seen her, don't care."

"May I ask why you seem disapproving about her?"

The woman took her time trying to decide how to answer

me. "I don't really know what to say. Jade's never been friendly. Until recently, she'd spent years working for the fire department in Sacramento. It was just Billy at the house. Those were better times."

"Did you know Billy well?"

"Well enough to be really sad when he died. He was such a nice guy. Always friendly, always solicitous. One time when our snowblower broke, he came by in his tractor with the big scoop and cleared our drive and our neighbor's, too. The opposite of Jade. She is so hard. So many edges. Then, several months back, Jade moved back home to live with daddy. Hurt her hand on the job, I was told. Clearly, there was something wrong with her. A couple of times, she came down the street making so much noise. And that was before Billy died."

"What kind of noise did she make?"

"Hollering. Wailing. Like she's in agony. My husband is a physical therapist. He said she probably has PTSD. He said there's medications that keep people from hollering, but obviously she's avoiding doctors or something." The woman paused. "She's half Chinese, you know. Same as being all Chinese in my book."

"Right. Does that have something to do with doctors? Or wailing in agony?"

The woman looked at me like I might be an enemy. "She's just, you know, different."

"If you were to guess where she would go with all three horses, where would you think of?"

"She could go anywhere. She's very athletic. Very strong. I've seen her ride. It reminds me of watching a ski racer. Carving turns, left and right. And just like ski racers, she's not sensible at all. A total risk taker. But I guess that fits with working for the fire department. So there's no place that would be off limits." The woman glanced up at the 2000-foot wall of mountains that comprised the east side of Christmas Valley. "I know some riders go up to the Tahoe Rim Trail. I've heard the high country around Tahoe is popular with horse types."

"Do you have an idea of why she might go to the Rim Trail?"

"I don't know. To get away from people, probably. Jade isn't a people person. In fact, I think she's the opposite. What's that called? Sounds like a miserable-dope."

"Misanthrope?"

"Yeah."

"If she went up to the Rim Trail, how would she go?"

The woman shrugged. "I have no idea."

"Is there anyone in the neighborhood who might have additional information?"

She pointed across and down the street. "You could ask the guy over at that house." She pointed through the trees to a brown rambler with white trim, probably the house that Andrew Garden had mentioned to me. "He's always bothering Jade. Probably one of the things that makes her so crazy. The guy has a weird name. Sorn Lupus or something like that. And he talks about weird stuff. I heard him talking to Andrew Garden one day. Something about a Chinese room. The Chinese are taking over."

"Andrew Garden mentioned Sorin. Said he had a sun allergy?"

"Allergy?" the woman scoffed. "I guess you can call it whatever you want. To me he's just weird. Weirder than his name. I call him the shadow because he only comes out at night. I don't know why he would be sensitive to sun. His skin is quite dark."

"Thank you, I'll go see him." I turned to her son. "Kenny, you want to pet Spot?"

Kenny looked up at his mother.

The woman nodded. "It's okay. The man and his dog both seem nice." She spoke with positive words, but she had ice in her voice.

Kenny stepped over the threshold. His head was the same height as Spot's. I held tight on Spot's collar so his scent curiosity wouldn't cause him to stick his nose in the boy's face.

Kenny reached his hand out very slowly, ready to jerk it back as if he were about to touch a wire that might electrocute him. His hand hovered in the air.

I put my other hand on Spot's head. "Right here," I said. "He'd like you to pet him right here."

Kenny moved his hand closer. His arm came near Spot's nose. Spot sniffed him. The boy jerked away. Tried again, then once more. His arm was just long enough to reach past Spot's face and touch his head between his ears. Eventually, Kenny put his palm on the top of Spot's head. Made a little motion. Spot wagged. The kid pulled his hand back. Looked up at his mother, his grin beaming as bright as a ray of sunlight.

"Mom! I want a big dog!"

"No, you don't, Kenny."

"Thanks for your help," I said to the woman. I pulled on Spot's collar and we walked down the steps.

"Mom, I want a giant dog!" the boy said again behind us.

"C'mon, Kenny. Inside, you go. You need to pick up your room."

"Mom, I want to see that dog eat! I bet he eats a lot!"

She pulled him inside and shut the door.

I walked away, wondering what made her so angry. Maybe it was because she wished she were a natural blonde and resented that she had to use chemicals to achieve the look. Or maybe it was because her natural hair was dark enough to be Chinese.

FOURTEEN

I walked a hundred yards down to the brown house with white trim, the house I understood was the home of the Romanian named Sorin Lupu, the man multiple people disparaged for being strange, awkward, and having some kind of sun allergy. There was a small generic compact car on the street in front of the house, which had no driveway or garage. I walked across a thick mat of pine needles peppered with a thousand cones and knocked on the door.

The door opened. The man inside saw Spot, gasped, shut the door most of the way, and looked at me through a two-inch gap.

"Sorry, does my dog bother you?"

"I'm afraid of dogs. Can you put him in your car?"

"Sorry, I walked. How about I step back with him?" I moved far away from the door. "Is that okay? He's very calm and friendly. We can talk from this distance."

"Sorry, but I was bitten when I was a child. Even my neighbor Amy has this little terrier who isn't much bigger than a bag of groceries. But he has big teeth. He scares me. No, I would be very afraid to be near your giant dog."

"I understand. I'll hold tight to his collar."

He opened the door a little farther. "Your dog is magnificent looking, I'll say that."

The man was tall and excessively thin. He was in his mid-forties like me. His face was covered in white sunblock. And he wore a black, hooded sweatshirt with the hood half on, half off. He looked vaguely like the grim reaper. He wore blue jeans. His black hair was as smooth and thick and wavy as that of a shampoo model.

"Are you Sorin Lupu?"

"Yes. What can I help you with?" He had a slight accent.

"My name's Owen McKenna. I'm a private investigator."

"Good to meet you."

"Several days ago, I was hired by Jade Jaso to look into a threat she received. Last evening, she went missing."

"What does that mean, 'went missing?'" He looked worried.

"I was supposed to meet her at her house this morning, but she was gone. Her horses are gone, as well."

The man's eyes widened with alarm.

I continued, "I'm canvassing the neighborhood to see if anyone has seen anyone or heard anything unusual."

"I don't understand how she wouldn't be there. Jade is very reliable. If she said she was going to be there to meet you, she would be there unless she canceled first. She would have called you."

I didn't immediately reply. I've learned that when people feel an uncomfortable silence, they often fill the space with words.

"But if she suddenly went away, her horses would still be there, right?"

"I would think so, yes," I said.

Lupu's frown deepened. "This is scary to me. Did you ask the Gardens? Sam is almost always there. He would have seen someone come and go. Of course, he's getting a little foggy. But Andrew is also there a lot."

"Andrew headed off to a monastery a couple of days ago," I said.

"Oh, that's right. The Buddhist temple in China."

"You know about that?" I watched the man's posture. There was no body language that telegraphed anything unusual.

"Nothing about that temple, no," Lupu said. "But Andrew's been talking about it for a few months or more. How unfortunate that Jade goes away right after he left. He isn't there to watch over her."

"When Jade called me, she made a point of telling me she wasn't crazy. Does that suggest she needs watching over?"

Sorin Lupu looked down and then to the side. It was a look

I'd seen from suspects who I thought were guilty.

"I don't know what Jade needs," he said. "I wish I did. I'd like nothing more than to help her."

"Are you close to her?"

He shook his head. "I wish I were." He made a momentary smile, just a flash before it stopped. A stop-motion picture of how he'd feel if he could be close to Jade. I remembered that Jade had described Sorin as a strange guy with a skin condition who nevertheless had a dream smile.

"You like her?" I said.

He hesitated. "A lot, yes. Jade is… She has a compelling personality. Lots of opinions. She's not the easiest person to talk to. But she's really smart. Espresso witty. I've been totally drawn into her world of poetry ever since I met her."

"I met Anne Gregory," I said, as if that explained that I understood him and his awareness of the role of poetry in Jade's life.

"Precisely," he said. "You cannot be uninterested."

"Espresso witty is a great phrase," I said.

"From 'Virgin Mule', a poem by Andrei Codrescu, one of Romania's most famous poets."

"You know poets?"

"Not like Jade," he said. "She's the one who introduced me to Codrescu. Anyway, she's probably too young and too smart for me. At some core level she knows it. She looks right through me. Like I'm just another mule in Codrescu's metaphor about people being like unthinking herd animals." He seemed very sad as he said it. Or maybe he was clever and scheming, creating a character presentation that would influence my perception.

"Can you think of anything that would help my search for her? Strangers that have come through the neighborhood? Things Jade might have said?"

Lupu shook his head.

"Your neighbor Andrew said you know horses."

"I know a little about horses. I grew up with them in Romania. Horses are one of the things I miss most from my country. It's probably why I like to be around Jade's horses."

"Have you ridden horses in Tahoe?"

"No. I would like to. I imagine being up in the mountains, taking in the views from horseback. That would be a spectacular experience."

"Jade told me that when she feels too much pressure, she sometimes disappears on her horse. She saddles up Anne Gregory and heads up into the mountains. Are you familiar with that?"

"Da. She told me that as well."

"Da?"

"Oh, sorry. It's Romanian for 'yes.' I slip in and out of the two languages when I'm preoccupied."

"Any idea where Jade goes when she disappears?"

"No. How strange that she's gone. But didn't you just say her horses are gone, too? That doesn't fit. She would have let us neighbors know." He looked embarrassed. "With Andrew Garden gone, she would have told his grandfather. And, either way, if she expected you to come by, she would have told you she was leaving. Even in her most distracted poet-focused mind wanderings, she would keep to her commitments."

"Jade said that someone broke into her house and moved things as if searching for valuables. Can you think of anything she ever said about valuables?"

Was Sorin Lupu too quick to shake his head? "No," he said with conviction. "Jade and her father Billy have the ranch. And it's probably worth a great deal of money. But I never got the sense she had anything else. I suppose Billy might have had something and not told Jade about it. So that could fit your question."

"Then another question, please. For several years, Jade worked for the fire department in Sacramento. She was injured in a fire, quit, and moved back to Tahoe. Do you know anything about those circumstances?"

"Only that she lost her fingers in that fire. It was a terrible thing. But I can't see how that would lead to her disappearing."

FIFTEEN

The next morning, Spot, Blondie, and I drove once again to Jade's ranch. The dogs ran around like they'd come to their favorite vacation ranch, although I noticed they explored the barn and corral very much as if they were looking for Anne Gregory and the other horses.

I looked around to see if I could find any sign that would suggest Jade had returned, even if for just a short visit.

There was nothing.

I loaded the dogs in the Jeep and headed up Echo Summit and then down to Sacramento to visit the fire station where Jade had worked.

When we got to Sacramento, it was already 2 p.m.

As if he had set an alarm clock, Spot woke up and pushed himself up to a sitting position on the back seat, butt on the seat, front legs on the floor, leaning against the seatback. One glance in the rearview mirror and I could see that he was groggy. He yawned so wide it made me think of the chasm leading down in Jules Verne's Journey To The Center Of The Earth. Blondie was awake and alert, watching Spot as much as she looked out the window.

"Can't work on an empty stomach," I said as I pulled off the freeway and came to a stop at the bottom of the exit ramp. Spot must have figured out my meaning as he leaned forward and stuck his cold, wet nose on the back of my neck. "Where to go," I mumbled, trying to remember the address of the fire station. While the light was still red, I reached over to the passenger seat and flipped through some sheets on the legal pad to find the address I'd written down.

There it was. North and east of our exit.

"So, Largeness and Blondie girl, if we are efficient, we could find some grub in a location proximate to where the missing maiden was last employed." Sacramento has 24 fire stations. The one I wanted was a few miles away. As I got close, I saw some fast food restaurants.

"Decision time," I said. "In the past, Largeness, you and I have derived enjoyable sustenance at Taco Bell. However, it comes with the caveat that we must agree to never tell Street that we dined on fast food. We don't want her to decide that our moral character is lacking, right? If she asks where we ate, we'll plead memory loss, but with the comment that we probably ate a black bean salad with sprouts and some other cow food at a mom-and-pop vegetarian restaurant with a hand-painted sandwich sign out front." I pulled into the Taco Bell restaurant. "Good?" I said.

His nose went back to my neck. Blondie was standing on the seat, looking out toward the restaurant, her tail wagging.

Fifteen minutes later, I brought out a large tray of burritos – Spot's favorite – and tacos – my favorite.

One minute later, Spot was done, and Blondie was finishing her last few bites. Five minutes later, I too was done. I took the dogs over to an outdoor faucet at the back of the restaurant. They each turned their heads a little sideways and drank from the flow while I finished my coffee. A quarter hour after that, I was parked out front of the fire station.

I walked up to the station. Two of the three tall garage doors were up. One fire truck was pulled outside, and young firefighters, three male and one female, were hosing it down and polishing the brightwork, making it shine like the other truck that was fully under the roof. They all wore navy pants and white short-sleeved shirts with collars. All had short hair. No tattoos were visible.

I nodded at them as I walked up.

The woman gave me a significant look. It wasn't the look of someone who was interested in me. After all, I was twenty years older, and I don't telegraph the cool attitude that permeates the firefighter culture and draws members to its ranks. Instead, her look was an assessment of whether or not I was one of those who have pejorative attitudes toward women in a job that was once the exclusive domain of men. I gave her a small nod that I hoped communicated that I had no prejudice against her.

"I'm looking for information about one of your former colleagues," I said.

One of the men paused his polishing and said, "Who?"

"Jade Jaso."

There was some kind of instant unspoken communication among them. They all looked guarded like when many song birds go silent when a raptor glides too close overhead.

"You'd, um, have to talk to GJ about that," he said.

"GJ?"

"Grant Jackman. Battalion Chief."

"Where do I find Mr. Jackman?"

He gestured with his rag. "I'd check in the office."

"Thanks." I walked over and stepped in through the main station door, which was held open by a swing-down door stop. Inside was a small entrance room with a high counter where one might leave a business card. There was an indoor window through which I could see an office. It contained a dented, gray, metal desk and matching metal file cabinets. Beyond the office area was a large break room. There were long tables with chairs, a fridge, a counter with two microwaves, a toaster oven, and three coffee makers. There was no regular stove with oven. Baking anything, whether lasagna or cookies, didn't fit with fire alarms and rushed exits.

I knocked on the wall and called back toward the rear of the station. "Hello? Anybody home?"

A burly guy wearing the same navy pants and white shirt came into view through a door on the far side of the break room. I don't think he had heard me. But he saw me now as he stopped in front of a wall calendar with a photo of an antique fire truck.

"Help you?"

"My name's Owen McKenna. I'm an investigator looking into the whereabouts of one of your former employees, a woman who's gone missing."

"What's her name?"

"Jade Jaso."

The man seemed to freeze in place. He didn't speak. But I could tell by the look on his face that he was actively thinking through potential responses.

"You should probably talk to the chief," he finally said.

"GJ, right? Is he here?"

"He... He's in a meeting." The way he said it, I thought it probably meant GJ was sleeping, a standard routine for people who worked 24-hour shifts.

"Any idea when he'll be free?"

"Let me see if I can find out." He walked through another door that probably led to the bunk room. He came out a minute later. "He'll actually be with you in a few minutes."

"Thanks."

The burly guy left. I waited. The bunk room door opened surprisingly soon considering that GJ may have been napping. Then again, the job required that a firefighter go from sleeping to driving a fire truck in less time than most of us take to brush our teeth.

The man was in his late thirties. He wore his dress blues, which suggested he was going to speak at a media conference or appear in a parade or maybe give a talk at a local school. Or attend a funeral. He looked like what one would see on the fire-station calendars that feature human models instead of trucks.

"I'm Grant," he said. "You had a question about Jade Jaso?"

"Yes, please. I'm an investigator working on a case involving her." I handed him my business card. "Jade Jaso hired me to look into some threatening events. Now it appears that she has disappeared. I'm hoping you can give me the names of people I can talk to, perhaps the firefighters who knew her best."

He made a slow shake of his head. "I'm sorry, I don't know. She's hasn't worked here for many months, and we haven't stayed in touch."

"Is there anyone here who has remained close to her?"

Another head shake. "Sorry, but I don't know of anyone here who is close to her."

"Did she make friends with anyone when she worked here?"

"I wouldn't know."

"Can you tell me how she came to not work here? Did she quit? Was she fired?"

"I'm not at liberty to say."

"Is there anything you can tell me about her that you are at liberty to say?"

He suddenly looked awkward, and his face colored a bit.

I breathed a sigh that was partly frustration and partly an attempt to make an impression. "I'm an ex-San Francisco PD Homicide Inspector. I understand the tightrope walk of bureaucratic rules and cover-your-ass answers that reduce liability and reveal nothing."

His skin flush darkened.

"Look," he said, "just between you and me, Jade Jaso didn't leave under the best of circumstances. There was some friction. I'm sure you understand that I'm reluctant to talk about it."

"Okay. I'll find out another way."

I walked out the open door. The young firefighters seemed to turn back to their task at once, as if they'd been hovering nearby listening. The woman picked up a trash can, hefted it to her side so that her hip took some of the weight, and started around the side of the station. She gave me a prolonged look and made a little jerk of her head as she walked away.

I got in the Jeep, drove to the next corner, turned, headed down the block, turned again. The woman was standing next to the dumpster, the trash can on the ground.

I pulled over to the curb and rolled down the passenger window.

She leaned toward the Jeep. "You got something to write on?"

I picked up my yellow pad, flipped over to a new page, and handed it to her.

She made a furtive glance behind her, pulled a pen out of her pocket, and wrote a phone number on the pad.

"My shift is over at four o'clock. Call this number after five.

My name is Yvette. I go by Vette."

She tossed the pad on the passenger seat and turned away without waiting for me to respond.

SIXTEEN

I looked at the time as Yvette walked away.

It was 3:30 p.m. I took Spot and Blondie to Discovery Park where the American River joins the larger Sacramento River. The American drains snowmelt from the Sierra. The water was low because the snow was mostly gone by the end of summer. The Sacramento drains snowmelt from Mt. Shasta 200 miles to the north, which, despite global warming, still has glaciers on its 14,000-foot slopes. The water is nearly always plentiful. The dogs ran along the water then up one of the levees. I followed. At the top I had a nice view of the river and trees and distant mountains and large homeless camps. They were messy tent cities with a varied collection of people. They ranged from the long-term unemployed who were mired in the swamp of drugs and alcohol to the not-so-long-term unemployed who had skills and a work ethic, but who had suffered bad luck and didn't have sufficient savings cushion for maintaining housing in tough times. And there were likely others who were employed but who still couldn't afford California rent.

The dogs and I explored those river-front areas where we saw the fewest people. As with so much of nature worldwide, if you take out the people, the birds and the trees and the river are beautiful and enticing.

At 5 p.m., I dialed the number the firefighter had written on my pad of paper.

"Hello?"

"Yvette? This is Owen McKenna calling about Jade Jaso. You gave me your number at the fire station."

"You are a cop, or what?"

"Ex-cop. Now a private investigator."

"You said Jade is missing?"

"Yeah. I'm looking for any information that might help me find her."

"Are you alone?" she asked.

"Just me and my dogs."

"I'm willing to talk to you if you agree not to tell anyone." She sounded anguished.

"Agreed. In my world, CIs are standard operating procedure."

"CIs..." she said.

"Confidential Informants."

"Okay. You know the Cal Expo racetrack?"

"Where they race horses? Yeah. I'm at Discovery Park, not too far from there."

"Meet me at the racetrack in, say, a half hour? I'll be on the southwest corner. There's a grassy rise near a parking area. They have evening training hours today. We can sit there while the harness racers train."

"It'll take me a bit," I said. "I've got a long walk. Better plan on forty-five minutes. See you soon." I hung up.

"Hey, Largeness, Blondie girl, care for some exercise? Only four miles along the river to see more horses."

The dogs seemed eager and energetic, which was reasonable considering they each still had a pile of burritos onboard.

We followed the winding path along the north side of the American River. I jogged. The dogs did a slow trot. Spot weaved off the trail here and there to explore scents, then trotted back to catch up. Blondie stayed close by. Ever since her former NFL football player owner had died and Street had adopted her, she was careful in the way that is common with adopted rescue dogs. She seemed especially wary of the homeless camps as we went by. Perhaps she smelled hints of despair and sadness.

I knew I was jogging at about a ten-minute-per-mile pace. After 40 minutes, we came to the Cal Expo State Fairgrounds. I took what I thought was an obvious fork in the trail, heading for the racetrack. But I came to a chain link fence. I followed the trail as it doubled back, then came to another fence. They didn't want to make it easy to get to the fairgrounds without buying a ticket. But I thought the racetrack didn't require a ticket when there wasn't a fair or a race. I kept trying various paths and eventually came to an unlocked gate.

The racetrack appeared in the near distance. Although the day was still bright, the banks of light over the track were turned on, giving the track the dramatic look of a big-time sports arena. There were a dozen or more horses pulling small, two-wheeled carts in which the driver sat. The horses were spread out over what seemed like a mile-long track. It didn't look like they were racing. There were no numbered jerseys as there would be during an official race. But all the drivers wore goggles over their eyes. The carts seemed perilously close to the rear hooves of the trotting horses. No doubt the hooves shot chunks of dirt up into the drivers' faces. The horses were going counterclockwise around the track. Some were doing what I thought was called a regular trot, hooves going back and forth in a pattern too quick to understand. But other horses had an unusual gait. It wasn't a trot, nor was it a gallop. But it was easy to see that the two left legs moved forward and back at the same time, and they alternated with the two right legs, which also moved together.

I saw the woman from the station standing at the corner of the grassy area. I held Spot's collar as I approached. "Hi Yvette, thanks for agreeing to meet me."

She ignored me. Instead she looked intensely at the dogs.

"Meet Spot and Blondie," I said.

"I saw your dogs in your Jeep." She bent over and pet Blondie, then turned to Spot. "This guy's a Great Dane, huh?"

"Yeah."

"Can I pet him?"

"He'll be upset if you don't."

I watched while Yvette pet Spot on his head, then rubbed his neck, then ran her hands along his chest, then bent over and hugged him. She made lots of talk, so gushing that Spot would have been embarrassed if he'd known all the words. But he merely wagged, continuously but slowly, happy to be the center of attention, something he'd learned to expect from the time he was a puppy.

Blondie watched from nearby. She'd grown accustomed to Spot being everyone's focus.

While Yvette gushed, I noticed she was physically similar to Jade. Not quite as short, and not quite as muscular, but definitely someone who could carry heavy hoses and ladders and maybe a victim who needed rescuing from a fire. Her hair was trimmed shorter than Jade's, and, though not coarse and black, it telegraphed the same attitude, that she was all about function and usefulness. Her physical presentation was shaped by her job. Like Jade, there was nothing frivolous about Yvette. She obviously had no interest in beauty touches like makeup or feminine hairstyles. But, again like Jade, her physical prowess had its own attractive quality. Health and fitness and strength and competence were compelling attributes no matter whether a person wore lip gloss or not.

She'd stopped hugging Spot and was now leaning on him. Spot had a dreamy, sleepy look about him.

"He looks contented, Yvette. I think he'd be very happy to go home with you."

"Vette," she corrected.

"Oh, sorry. You said that before and I spaced."

"Everyone does." She glanced over at the horses. "You want to sit on the grass where we can watch the horses?"

"Sure. Speaking of which, those horses are doing a striking kind of gait. Left legs together, then right legs together. Do you know what that is?"

"It's called pacing," she said as she got down on the grass. "It's a special kind of gait. Most horses don't do it. Or can't do it. I don't know which." She patted the grass next to her, reached up, and tugged down on Spot's collar. "C'mere, Spot. On the ground." It was a command, not a request, a trait I'd seen among cops back in the SFPD. Firefighters have the same top-down hierarchy, designed to get things done efficiently. No committee-type discussion necessary or allowed.

Not surprisingly, Spot did as told. Then he flopped over and lay his head on Vette's lap. He made a big sigh.

Vette pointed to the ground on her other side. "Blondie,

you lie here."

Blondie looked at her, then turned and looked at me as if for permission.

I pointed and said, "It's okay."

Blondie did as told.

Vette rubbed both of them.

I gestured toward the horses. "This is a cool place to watch the horses while talking."

"Yeah. Jade introduced me to this place. She liked to come here. It eased the anxiety of being away from her horses in Tahoe." Vette turned and gave me a searching look. "I can't believe she's gone missing."

I made a single nod. "She called me to investigate a threat she'd gotten. We spoke at some length a few times and planned to meet again. But when I went back, she was gone. Her horses were gone, too."

Vette made a look of alarm but also had a quality that suggested she wasn't surprised. "What was the threat?"

"It was on her voicemail. A death threat. I'm looking for any potential reasons why."

Vette took a deep breath, exhaled slowly, and said, "Maybe there's a connection. There was a guy at the station who threatened to kill her."

SEVENTEEN

"Was the person who threatened to kill Jade a firefighter?"

Jade nodded. "Yeah."

"Do you think it was just talk, or would he have gone ahead and harmed her or kidnapped her?"

"I think he would harm her. But he couldn't have kidnapped her."

"I don't understand. You said he could be the reason she went missing."

Vette nodded. "The reason, yes. But not the person who took her, if that's what happened. Because he's dead. He died in a fire."

"Was his name Barry?"

She nodded. "Barry Whaler. She told me what he said. He told her that if she gave him grief, he would push her off a roof. He said falls always looked like accidents, so it was important that she be nice."

"Did Jade think he was serious? Or joking?"

"She said the words were like a joke but that his tone was serious. It really bothered her."

"Could she have done something that might cause him to die in a fire because of that?"

She turned her head and looked at me hard and close. I felt like I could feel the pressure of her stare. It was a long time before she responded. "She could if she felt threatened."

"Jade played me the voicemail of the threat she got," I said. "The caller accused Jade of killing Barry."

"What?! Do you have a copy of that voicemail? I'd like to hear it."

I played it for her. I dialed up the volume so she could hear it over the racetrack noises.

The voice came out of my phone. "I know you killed Barry by pushin' him down that light shaft. He was worth ten of you. Twenty of you. I know where you live. You got a few minutes left to live. Ten at the outside. I ain't decided yet how you'll die. Maybe I'll light you on fire an' drop you off a mountain so you know what it feels like. Burnt, then crushed. Get ready." At the end of the recording, I turned my phone off.

Vette was shaking her head. "I can't believe it."

"Do you recognize the voice?"

"No. It's certainly no one at the fire station."

"Any idea of who it might be?"

She shook her head. "Did this caller go to Jade's house?"

"I don't know. She left and hid down the street right after she got the voicemail."

"And now she's missing." Vette looked shocked. "I guess there was no caller ID."

"Right. The way the caller spoke, almost tripping on the words, I think he was reading the message. So maybe the person making the threat got someone to read it for him."

"Someone Jade wouldn't know," Vette said.

"What can you tell me about Barry and Jade? About what led up to her leaving the fire department."

Vette took her hands off Spot and Blondie. She eased Spot's head out of her lap, brought her knees up, and wrapped her arms around her legs.

"From what I understand, Jade started at the fire department eight years ago. Barry started a year after that. I came three years later."

To fix it in my mind, I said, "Jade, then Barry, then you."

Vette nodded. "So Jade had seniority on Barry. Not that we operate on seniority. But Barry didn't like that. However, his major problem was that Jade did better than he did on the CPAT."

It took a moment to remember. "The Candidate Physical Ability Test. Hauling hoses up stairs and such."

She nodded, "Raising ladders, carrying heavy equipment,

breaking down doors, hauling a person out of a building, and all while wearing a fifty-pound vest. There's eight components to the test, so it sounds pretty serious. But it's actually not that hard to pass it in the required time if you're in decent shape and relatively strong. It's a pass/fail test. Something like seventy percent of women and ninety percent of men pass."

"Because it's pass/fail, and both Barry and Jade passed, then how did Barry think she did better?"

"Because it's timed. From what I've heard, Jade did the test a lot faster than several of the guys. Because Barry took the test after she took hers, and because some of the guys weren't wild about Barry, they kidded him about it. They still teased him even after I was hired."

"Serious taunting?" I said. "Or was it like the joking teasing that many firefighters and cops do?"

"I think it was jokey. The problem is Barry didn't. So when the guys would say something like, 'Dude, you deployed that hose slower than a girl,' he would get really upset. And he took it out on Jade."

"How?"

She took another deep breath. "He constantly gave her grief. Like, if something needed lifting, Barry'd say, 'That China girl Jade's so butch, let her lift it.' Or if someone had a problem or question about anything, he'd say, 'Go ask the China superwoman. She can leap off tall buildings.'"

"Obviously, there was no respect in the phrase."

"Oh, God no. It was a term of derision. He was always mocking. Jade tried hard to ignore him. We're supposed to work as a team and have each other's back. But constant needling can get under your skin. Sometimes, she couldn't take it anymore. One time he was mocking her in front of everyone, saying his routine about superwoman leaping tall buildings, when she came back at him. She said, 'I could push you off a tall building, that's for sure.'"

Vette suddenly stopped talking.

"How did Barry die?"

"We were on a multiple alarm, nine-story warehouse fire. It

was a terrible fire by every measure. The building had a confusing layout. It was night. The power was out. The building had none of the required emergency lights. There were multiple tenants, including one business on the top floor where employees worked the night shift. The other station hadn't gotten to the fire yet, while we were well underway. We had two engines but one less firefighter than was normal. And Jade and Barry started arguing."

Vette paused. "I think it was the arguing that clouded Jade's judgment. The building was fully involved, and the ladder on our old truck wasn't long enough to get the employees down from the top floor. And the top-floor business had boarded up the window that was the access point for the external fire escape stairs. So Jade and Barry were bringing the employees to an internal staircase and then up to the roof so they could go down the external fire escape. Jade was in charge. Later, it was determined that she didn't obey one of the IC's orders."

"The Incident Commander?" I said.

"Right. But she claimed – and I always believed her – that the fire was so loud that she didn't hear the command over her radio."

"What was the result?"

Vette looked off at the trotting horses. "They saved all the employees. Many of them later said that Jade and Barry were heroes, risking their lives to help the employees up to the roof and down the fire escape."

"And the other firefighters?"

"Everyone got out safe except Barry. He died."

"How?"

"Like the voicemail said. The warehouse had a light shaft. It was shooting flames like a chimney. Barry fell into it."

"From the roof."

Vette nodded. "Nine floors down into flames. The roof doorway cubby was near the light shaft. By the time they got the last of the employees down the escape, that doorway was on fire. Part of its wall was what collapsed and pinned Jade's arm and hand. She was trying to get her boot under the burning section to push it away and free her burning hand. Jade said that was when Barry fell. She thought he could have tripped. But people wondered."

"Anyone defend her?"

"We all did. We all held Jade in the highest regard. She's a woman of principles. She was the hardest working firefighter at the station. Even the guys would agree to that."

"Then why would anyone doubt her? Why would people wonder?"

"Because of the IC's command she didn't hear. And because of what she said earlier when Barry was mocking her."

"That she could push Barry off a building," I said.

"Right."

"Was there any evidence of wrongdoing on her part?"

"No. The fire investigator is a thorough, competent guy. But from what I heard, Barry's body was crushed and burned so badly that there was pretty much nothing left except the fire-proof fabric from his suit and his charred bones and teeth. There was no way to establish that the incident was anything other than a horrible accident."

She stared off toward the harness racers going round the track.

"Of the firefighters at your station, who was closest to Barry?"

Vette slowly shook her head. "I can't say anyone was close to him. None would have called him their friend. No one had beers with him after work or did anything social with him. He was simply an unlikable guy. A loner."

"What was Barry's relationship with GJ?"

"The battalion chief is the fairest guy you can imagine. He always treated Barry with respect. But I don't think he liked Barry. Actually, it would be more correct to say that I'm sure GJ didn't like Barry. No one liked Barry."

"No one? Did Barry have family?"

"Not that I know of. He didn't have any friends. There was only one guy who seemed to know Barry. The guy came by just once. It was just a few hours before the fire where Barry died.

The guy was… I don't like to say bad things about people. But he seemed like a real sick guy. A big sick guy who was twisted inside." As Vette said it, she looked up at the sky, then back at the horses.

"Do you know him?"

"No. And I only saw him that one time when he stopped by the station. I won't forget that day."

"Memorable character?"

"In all the wrong ways. The guy was real loud, and he talked to Barry about how they met the night before and how wasn't it a kick that they saw the China girl at the party. Then he said that they showed the China girl how real men do stuff. It was really terrible. GJ was nearby and overheard it. He looked disgusted. Then Jade walked in and saw Barry talking to the big guy. I thought she was going to puke. She went pale and made this choking sound. She was wracked with fear. The big guy said, 'What's the matter, China girl? I didn't make you happy last night? How would you even remember, you were so drunk.'" Vette made a little shiver.

"So Jade turned and ran out. The big guy pointed toward Jade and laughed. He said, 'There goes the China girl, running like a girl!' And Barry said, 'Trust me, she'll come back begging for more.'"

"I'm sorry to hear that, Vette. It sounds like they assaulted her at the party the night before."

"Yeah. She must have called the cops, because I later heard from a cop friend that they brought Barry in for questioning in the middle of the night."

"Did your cop friend say anything about the big guy?"

"No. He just mentioned Barry."

I was still holding my phone on which I'd played the voicemail threat. I gestured with it. "Do you think the big guy who came to the station could be the voice on the phone threat?"

"It doesn't sound like his voice. But he could be behind it. It seemed he has a negative attitude about women. Like the way Barry felt firefighting was not for women. Of course, Barry was unlikable, so what did I expect of some friend of his? But while

Barry was unpolished, his friend was revolting. A total yuck. He gave me the creeps. He absolutely could have been behind the threat to Jade."

Vette had been fingering a hangnail on her thumb. She bit it off and spit if off her tongue. Her nails were cut short and not very evenly, and the skin on her knuckles was dry. Her fingers weren't as thick as Jade's, but her hands looked very strong.

Vette said, "An assault would totally fit Jade's reaction of horror when she saw that man…" she stopped.

I waited.

"I got the idea that she'd bumped into Barry at a bar or a party, and he was with the big guy, and they both assaulted her."

"You think they gave her a date rape drug?" I said.

"That could be one way. Or they just took her someplace and forced themselves on her."

"Did you ask her about it?"

"Sort of. After the jerk left, I said, 'Hey, Jade, you okay? You wanna talk about it?' And Jade just shook her head. But she looked so ashamed and depressed. Really depressed. She sort of turned inward and barely said another word. A few hours later, we had the big fire, and Barry died."

"Did you get the friend's name?"

"No. I don't think Barry ever said it."

"Any chance you or any of the others took a photo of him?"

"No."

"What's he look like?"

"Real big. Muscular. Tats all over his arms. Short dark hair. One of those little pointy hair tufts coming off his bottom lip."

"Did you happen to notice what kind of vehicle the guy drove?"

"I did because he parked right in front of our garage doors, which is a no-no in our business. When a call comes in, we can't have any delays getting the trucks out. He had an old pickup, yellow paint. I remember that even though it had a little rust in places, it looked like the guy kept it washed and waxed. The glass was spotless, and the chrome sparkled. It had Nevada plates."

"Did Barry ever say anything about his friend? His name or where he lived?"

"No."

"Do the firefighters still talk about Barry or Jade?"

"No. Jade quit a long time ago. She turned in her resignation when she was still in the hospital. There was a lot of talk after those events. But very little recently."

"Is there a general consensus about how things turned out?"

"Yeah. Pretty much. I think most of the guys feel that Barry kept pushing Jade's emotional buttons, and that Jade's comment about pushing him off a roof was completely reasonable considering the circumstances. Of course, I think that's a no-brainer. Barry was a jerk, and all Jade did was try to survive under the assault of his constant harassment. Her comment about the roof was just a comment, nothing more. Barry's death was an accident. Nothing more."

"Was there any kind of official inquiry into the accident?"

"Every kind. You said you were a cop. When a cop dies on the job, the questions and inquiries must get pretty thick."

"Very," I said.

"Same with firefighters. We all had to make statements several times. We all had to answer lots of questions. There was a review board that went over our procedures like they were looking for a piece of dust in a dust warehouse. Jade got the worst of it. Constant Q and As from her hospital bed. Not because she'd had disagreements with Barry, but because she hadn't heard and obeyed the IC's order."

"What was the Incident Commander's order?"

"According to the IC, it was about pulling back and waiting for reinforcements. Of course, they didn't want to come down too hard on Jade because those top-floor employees said she saved their lives. But that doesn't relieve the need to have a command structure that works and is heard and is obeyed. Anyway, Jade always obeyed every order."

Vette looked off at the harness racers. She leaned forward,

reached out with both hands, and pet Spot on one side and Blondie on the other.

She said, "Everyone knows that firefighter morale is critical. You come down too hard on someone who saved lives, you take a toll on every firefighter. No one wants that. Nevertheless, Jade ended up quitting. We lost a very good firefighter when she walked away. Although, the reality is that you probably can't be a firefighter with a ruined hand."

"Was there any official disciplinary action? Or any legal action?"

"No. The Incident Command order that Jade didn't hear was attributed to too much ambient noise. As for legal action, Jade is not the kind of person who would pursue that. Nor would she allow anyone else to pursue that on her behalf. When she turned in her resignation, she told me that she was fully aware of the risks – all the risks – when she took the job. At Grant Jackman's suggestion, she accepted some kind of post-traumatic-stress stipend that the union had negotiated, a disability settlement, plus a little bit of accumulated retirement pay, and left."

After a minute, Vette said, "The job of a firefighter has too much tension. Throw a death into the mix, it gets hard to breathe." Vette's shoulder muscles flexed. "I don't think she was crushed by having Barry die. But having anyone – especially your fellow firefighters – wonder if you are partly responsible for the death, it would feel like your life caved in on you. Like an elephant was sitting on your chest."

We sat in silence for a moment. The harness racers cruised by in a hypnotic dance of flashing hooves and wind-blown manes.

Vette said, "Add to that whatever the dark crap was Jade had to deal with from Barry and his friend, it's just too much stress."

"Vette, before Jade went missing, she told me that one of her methods of coping was to disappear on her horse for a few days. Apparently, she leaves two of her three horses at her ranch with plenty of hay and water available. She packs camping gear on her third horse and heads up into the mountains."

Vette stroked Spot. "Do you think that's what happened?

Why she's missing?"

"That's what I'm wondering and why I'm asking. She knew I had agreed to look into the threat. Knowing that, do you think she would have left me hanging like this? Disappearing without giving me notice?"

Vette was shaking her head. "Not after asking you to help her. Absolutely not. If she felt that her life was boiling over and she had to make one of her getaways, she would have at least told you about it." Vette turned to look at me. "Did she take Anne Gregory?"

"She took all three horses. At least, all three are missing."

"Oh! That's… very uncomfortable. No note. No phone call. I don't like that at all."

We were silent again.

"Why did you approach me?" I asked. "Why not just stay silent like everyone else at the station?"

Vette thought about it. "I really like Jade. I looked up to her. We had a close connection of sorts. A lot of mutual respect. So when you came around and I realized that there were questions about Jade, I wanted to make things clear. I wanted you to know that Jade is a good and reliable and honorable person."

"I'm glad you went out of your way to talk to me."

Vette turned and looked at me. "I appreciate that you care about her. I don't know if anyone other than her father ever cared about her."

I sensed that she wanted to be done with the conversation.

"May I make one more request?"

She nodded.

"The pickup truck that Barry's friend drove… You said it was yellow and had Nevada plates. Do you remember the make?"

"No."

"Do you think you could recognize it if you saw it again?"

"Not in the sense of seeing a truck and being confident that it belonged to the guy. But I could probably tell if a truck was the same style."

"I'm thinking we could look at pictures of old pickups online and see if you recognize a model."

"Yeah, we could do that."

I pulled out my phone to search on pickups.

"Here, I can do it too."

Vette was much faster than me. She had pictures of pickups loading on her phone before I'd finished typing in 'old pickups' and clicking on images.

She swiped at her phone. Pictures of pickups slid up the screen. She stopped, angled her phone toward me, and pointed. "It was kind of like this."

"A Ford from the mid-eighties," I said.

She continued to swipe. I also managed to get a column of old Ford pickups on my phone. I found some more like the one she'd found.

Before I could ask Vette about them, she said, "This is it. Very close, anyway." She showed me. It was blue.

"Nineteen eighty-six," I said, reading the caption. "How sure are you?"

"I don't know how to answer that. Pretty sure."

"What if we found one that was yellow? Would that help?"

"Already on it," she said. She tapped, swiped, swiped again. "Here's one in yellow. Let me expand it." She looked at her phone up close, then held it at arm's length. "This is very much like the one he drove. It gives me a bad feeling just to look at it."

"An F-One Fifty. Maybe I can try to get the same one on my phone."

"It's faster and easier if I just email it to you," she said.

"Great." I gave her my email address.

She tapped. "There, done."

My phone beeped. I clicked on the email icon and had the picture.

Vette asked, "Are you going to look for this guy?"

"Yeah."

"Will you let me know when you find Jade?" She frowned. "You will find her, right?"

"Yes. And I'll let you know. I've got your phone and email." I handed her a card so she had my contact info. "Thanks very much, Vette. I appreciate your help."

EIGHTEEN

Vette pet Spot and Blondie goodbye and left. I stayed sitting on the grass at the Cal Expo racetrack. Because my private investigator resources don't include access to the Nevada state DMV, I emailed my buddy Sergeant Diamond Martinez the photo Vette had picked. I called Diamond on the phone.

"Am I interrupting?" I said.

"Sí. But the crimes in our idyllic Douglas County are so few, how could I not stop everything to aid a private cop whose work is… how would I describe it? Stay up late, sleep late, ski, sail, paddle, hike, and have an afternoon beer when the rest of us are working?"

"Yeah, this job is tough. It makes sense I take priority over anything else that comes across your desk. I'm calling to let you know I emailed you a mugshot, and I'm requesting that you put all your resources on it."

"I work for the Nevada taxpayers, so this would be at their expense."

"If you insist," I said. "In return, if I'm able to take one of your bad guys off the street, it will be at my expense."

"Magnanimous guy."

"Magnanimous," I repeated. "That's a lot of syllables to fit in my mouth."

"Good practice," he said. "This perp have a name?"

"Yeah. Nineteen eighty-six Ford F-One Fifty, yellow with some rust spots. A witness picked it out of a lineup."

"I'm assuming Nevada plates or you wouldn't call me."

"So I'm told."

"You got a human name that attaches to this ride?"

"No. But if you find a possible whose résumé includes sexual assault, consider that a likely."

"Understood."

"And please keep a lookout for Jade's pickup and horse trailer. I think I gave you that info."

"Got it." Diamond hung up before he heard my thanks.

I turned to Spot. "Hey, Largeness and Blondie, up for a four-mile stroll back to the Jeep?"

Spot lifted his head off the grass and looked at me droopy-eyed. Blondie was already looking alert and ready.

Three hours later, we were up the mountain and entering twilight. We stepped out of the Jeep onto frosty ground and into the cold air of early September at 7,200 feet. It was a good 40 degrees colder than the Central Valley air at the racetrack.

We went inside, and I scrounged up some food for the three of us. I'd just started a small fire in the wood stove and opened a beer when my cabin phone rang.

"Yeah?"

"I tried your cell, got your voicemail, remembered that you don't get reception in many places. Hard to beat an old-fashioned landline for reporting the goods on dirtballs."

"Yellow Ford pickup, nineteen eighty-six?" I said.

"Sí. There's eight of them in Nevada," Diamond said, "still paying the DMV fee. One belongs to a guy in Walker who just turned one hundred. He has no close family that I can figure. Another belongs to a woman in Vegas. Three of them are in Henderson. Some collector, apparently. Two of the eight trucks filed affidavits of non-operation. Of course, it doesn't mean no one's operating them. That leaves one that's registered to a Max Miller Donovan, a Reno resident. Of course, that's Washoe County, out of my realm to help you. His résumé features one felony battery conviction for which he paid two-and-two, which seems light to this cop considering he used a Louisville Slugger to make a guy's knee bend the wrong way."

"Two thousand fine and two years vacation at a state facility?"

"Yeah. He was also charged once with extortion and thrice

with sexual assault. But there were no convictions on the extortion or the sex assaults."

"Thrice?"

"Learning some Middle English to round out my education," Diamond said.

"Were the extortion and sex assault charges dismissed?" I asked.

"The sex charges were," Diamond said. "The extortion went to trial, but he was acquitted. A key witness refused to testify at the last moment. In all three sexual assault cases, the women reported a crime and later recanted."

"Coercive threats?"

"Something," Diamond said.

"My case with Jade Jaso, the missing horse woman, began with a threat on her voicemail. And there was an earlier threat at her work. She also experienced some kind of trauma outside of work – probably a sexual assault – that made her shaky scared. She reported it and the cops took a co-worker in for questioning. But her shakiness went into overdrive when she was at work and saw the guy who drove this truck."

"Lots of women don't report rape," Diamond said.

"This guy's address in your record?"

"You gonna rattle his crib?"

"Maybe," I said.

"Good. I'll email you his pic. You should know he's six-three, two-thirty. He looks like an angry beefcake. Neck is wider than his head."

"Maybe his head is just narrow. Could be he's got the brain case of a mule deer."

"Mule deer can kick," Diamond said.

"I'll be ready."

Diamond gave me the address for Max Miller Donovan.

When I got Diamond's email pic of Max Miller Donovan, he looked the way Diamond described him. I forwarded the photo to Vette and added the comment, 'Thanks for talking to me today. This guy is Max Miller Donovan. He came up on Nevada DMV records as an owner of a 1986 yellow Ford pickup. He has an arrest record that suggests he's the guy who assaulted Jade. If he doesn't look like the guy you remember, please let me know. Thanks.'

Before I went to bed, I called Street Casey. When she answered I heard the sounds of a busy restaurant, animated conversation, clinking of silverware, banging of dishes, a loud man and a loud woman having a vigorous disagreement, and a background country band with a lead voice that sounded like Garth Brooks.

I said, "Hey, babe."

"What? I can't hear you."

"You having a good time with the bugs?"

"The bugs are happy, yes. I better call you back from a quieter place."

"Okay. Tomorrow. I'm going to bed. I love you. Sleep tight."

We hung up.

NINETEEN

The next morning I walked the dogs in the forest with the world's greatest view, then loaded them into the Jeep.

Reno sits in a broad smooth valley that is shaped like a coffee cup saucer pushed down into a rippled fabric of mountains. I drove to the southeast side of the saucer. Nice smooth streets that led to rougher streets, which led to a gravel road that pitched up and dead-ended where a mountain came down. Maybe I'd driven past the boundary of the city. I couldn't tell. The address number for Max Miller Donovan was on a utility pole. The pole had an electric meter on it as if a builder had managed to get power brought in but got no further on the project. Set back from the pole about 80 feet was a fifth-wheel travel trailer facing down the slope. The pickup that had towed the trailer into position was gone. The front supports for the trailer were lowered to the maximum extent and pinned in place. Yet the slope of the lot was steep enough that the trailer was still out of level. Life inside would be a challenge. One would need grip tape under a coffee mug to keep it from sliding off the table. The person who'd set the trailer in position could have simply put concrete blocks under the supports. I wondered why not. Maybe the project was too complicated for the skills of a brute.

I parked, told Spot and Blondie to be good, and got out. The day was cool, but the sun was hot and there was no shade. Despite all the Jeep windows being down, I wouldn't be able to leave them for more than ten or fifteen minutes.

I walked up and knocked on the trailer door. As I expected, there was no answer. I knocked again, then walked around the trailer.

On the rear bumper of the trailer was a bumper sticker I'd seen variations of before.

My girl? Take her. My dog? I don't think so. My gun? Never!

The brilliant sentiments of great philosophers were breathtaking. Then again, it was probably a good burglar deterrent.

There was a weight bench in the dirt. The bar across the supports had three forty-fives and one twenty-five on each end. Including the bar, the total was probably 365 pounds. If he bench-pressed that more than a couple of times, he was no slouch. If he did three sets of six reps each, he could fill in at the local automotive garage if their hydraulic lift broke down.

Near the weight bench was a stand made of thick tubular steel bars. Hanging from the stand was a heavy bag suitable for boxing and kicking.

I peered in the trailer windows. The inside appeared neat and clean. Counters cleared off. No dirty dishes in the sink. Jacket hung up on a hook. No clothes lying on the floor or on the couch. There was a tiny, trailer-sized bedroom. The bed was neatly made.

At the far end of the trailer was a plastic garbage can with a white liner bag. It was filled with crushed Coors Light cans. I was walking past when something seemed unusual. I stopped and took a closer look. The cans all had bullet holes in them.

I continued around to the front where there was one more window to look in. It gave me a view of the dining table, which was bigger than the one in my own kitchen nook. There was an unusual vise attached to the table edge. There was also a cigar box-sized black plastic container with a skull-and-crossbones emblem on it. The box had been slid up against the back wall such that it was in partial shadow, and I couldn't read the words on it. Next to the box was a metal device with a rocker arm attached to it. On the wall was a tool rack with multiple unusual tools hanging from it.

Something about the items seemed familiar. I shaded my eyes at the window. Shifted a little to the side, moved back the other way. Then I remembered.

It was a custom ammo kit for hand-loading rounds. The vise

was a reloading press. The rocker arm was a precision scale. The specialized tools were for getting custom powder and bullets into cartridges.

Hand-loading enthusiasts sometimes do it to save money compared to buying their ammo in a store. But more often, the process is about producing higher performance ammo, sometimes called hot loads in the business.

In some situations, the handloader desires to create ammunition that can't be easily identified because it doesn't match commercially-produced ammo. When a forensic specialist compares powder residue patterns to known patterns, he or she comes up short. Law enforcement has less to work with when trying to find a criminal who uses hand-loaded ammo.

None of which made the trailer resident a criminal. Hand loading is legal in the United States and celebrated among some groups in Nevada.

"Looking for Max Donovan?" a high-pitched male voice called out from behind me.

I turned around. Across the gravel road was an older man walking a Rottweiler. Spot had his head out the window, watching the Rottweiler. Blondie was next to him but unable to squeeze her head out next to Spot's neck. Spot's tail was wagging. The Rottweiler was ignoring Spot. He just looked ahead up the road. Dogs have two common reactions when they encounter other dogs. One is to look toward the other with enthusiasm and, maybe, anticipation of play. The other is to look away as if to say, 'I'm not afraid of you, nor am I impressed by you.'

I nodded toward the man. "I see Mr. Donovan isn't around. Have you seen him recently?"

The man stopped walking. His dog stopped as well and stood facing up the road, putting just enough tension on the leash to keep it from slacking down to the gravel.

"You're law enforcement, huh? No, that wouldn't be right judging by your dog and the old Jeep. What are those marks in your fender? Bullet holes? You're probably a bounty hunter. Am I right?"

I couldn't recall ever being mistaken for a bounty hunter.

Maybe it had something to do with the man I was looking for.

"Let's just say I'm eager to talk to Mr. Donovan," I said.

"I'm guessing a federal warrant, huh? If there's anything I learned during my career at the prison is that federal types stay mum. That whole need-to-know, thing, right? Unless of course they want to impress you, then it's all, 'Outta my way or the ATF's gonna shake you upside down 'til your spleen falls out.'"

"When did you last see Mr. Donovan?"

"Your fee is ten percent of the bail, right?" he said, ignoring my question. "On a federal case, that could be big. I often wondered if I shoulda gone into the bail business. I'm good with numbers. But no matter now. Me 'n Roman, we got a good thing going. The pension is small, but the dog is big. Maybe not like yours. But Roman, he doesn't back down from anything, man or beast. Ain't that right, Roman?" The Rottweiler stood still.

"Any idea when Mr. Donovan will be back?"

The man shook his head. "Could be Max is off putting the hustle on a girl somewheres. Sometimes that uses up most of his day and night."

"He do that often?"

"Let's just say that Max thinks he's a real lady's man. He says they practically fall at his feet hoping to experience his magic. Magic is his word not mine."

"He have a regular girlfriend?"

The man made a little guffaw. "His style is the opposite of having a regular girlfriend. He keeps track somehow. He brags about it. Says he couldn't very well work on setting the world record if he had some permanent weight around his neck."

"Were those his words, too? Permanent weight?"

"Yup. That's the way Max talks."

"If you had to guess, when would he usually return? This evening? Late tonight?"

"A guess? I think he's gone for days. He's been talking about taking a horseback camping trip."

"He rides horses?"

"Sort of. He's part of a Pony Express re-enactment group.

They ride the same trails the Pony Express rode."

"He's a Pony Express buff?"

"Naw. He just goes to meetings to meet the ladies. I heard he rode once. But Max was just a monitor for them last year. Drove his pickup along behind the riders like a safety or something. I don't actually think he likes horses much. But he talked about some of the cowgirls who ride. Says they look hot in their jeans and cowboy boots. He's got a thing for cowboy boots. And they probably see he's a big handsome guy and they go all weak-kneed. I've learned, women fall for hair and height and a deep voice..." He stopped talking and made a little glance down at himself. "Maybe he does have magic. It's like the deer in these canyons. The most dramatic buck gets the girls. Never mind if the buck is a predator shithead who just wants to put another mark on his scorecard."

"Tell me about this horseback camping trip."

"Max is always talking about how to get rich. He heard about some treasure in the mountains. So he intends to find it."

"Where does he get horses for camping?"

"He said he had a go at a China girl in Sacramento. He said she had horses, and he decided he was going to take her and her horses for his own trip. It was a funny thing."

"How?"

"Just the way he called her a China girl. He said it with a sneer. He's got this thing about how the Chinese don't belong in this country."

"He's racist."

"No kidding. He thinks this country is for whites."

"And he applied that reasoning to the woman he called a China girl."

"Yeah. He didn't like her. But he still wanted to show her what a real American man is like."

It took my breath away and made me struggle to stay outwardly calm.

"You know the name of this Pony Express group or where they're located?"

"Nope." He shook his head.

"Guess?"

"They might be in Carson City. You probably know about the prison and the Mustang-training program. Lotta horse stuff around there. And the Pony Express rode through Carson City, so that would make sense."

"You know a lot about the Pony Express?"

Another head shake. "Nope, but anyone would know where they rode. They went through Dayton and Carson City and Genoa and Tahoe."

"Thanks for the info." I started walking toward the jeep.

"You gonna come back and haul Max in?"

"Maybe."

"You should know, it'd be a lotta work trying to get him to do what he doesn't want to do. He's into that mixed martial arts stuff. And you probably know about his guns."

"What about them?"

"Oh, man. He's a total gun porn freak."

"What's that? He likes women who like guns?"

The man looked at me with confusion on his face, like I was suddenly Rip Van Winkle awakening after a 20-year absence.

"Dude, I can't believe a bounty hunter is so out of it. Gun porn isn't about sex with girls," he said. "I mean, maybe he mixes guns and sex. But mostly, he just gets off on guns. Makes his own bullets. Plays with his guns all the time. Sometimes, I'll wake up to gunfire in the middle of the night. He'll be outside all alone, drunk and singing and shooting at that hill over there. He has a little ritual. Every time he drains a can of beer, he tosses it in the air and shoots at it. If he hits it, he's happy. If he misses, he gets pissed. He keeps tossing the can until he hits it. So you can imagine that after he's had ten or twelve beers, he misses more often and his anger gets cranked up."

The man gestured toward the mountain. "Sometimes he goes up there on the rise where you can look down at the freeway in the distance. He shoots at the big trucks. He says the trucks are so far away, he can't tell if he hits them. So he sometimes uses tracer bullets. It's like watching fireworks. Those little shooting stars arc down toward the trucks at night. 'Course, most of the truckers don't know what's happening. Probably no one gets hurt. But the trucks must get bullet holes, right? I sometimes wonder if some girl is at a store shopping for lingerie, and she finds a bullet in the lace. That would be something, wouldn't it?"

Maybe he wanted a response, but I didn't have one.

"One time I told him that those tracer bullets could probably start a wildfire, and I thought he was going to shoot me. He fired a round over my head and told me to git. So I got."

"What kind of guns does he have?"

"Well, I don't know specifically. But one of his rifles looks like a Remington. And there's a Winchester for sure. He's also got maybe three semi-auto pistols, at least one revolver, and a sawed-off that couldn't be more than twelve or fourteen inches. But his main toy is another rifle. It's so precious to him that he keeps it in a bag so no one can see it. But I'm guessing it's a Kel-Tec."

"If he won't let anyone see it, then how would you know what kind it is?"

"Because I was hiking up where he uses it, and I found an area with a bunch of shell casings. They weren't very scattered like with rifles that eject out the side. So I naturally thought of the Kel-Tec, which has a downward-ejecting model. The casings stay in a tighter group. Oh, and I should tell you, he must've gotten one of those conversion kits that make it full auto."

I made the logical guess. "Because it shoots multiple rounds per second?"

"Yeah. The guys at the prison call those rifles woodpeckers."

"I thought the conversion parts were extremely expensive ever since they made them illegal."

"Yeah, I 'spose. But that doesn't stop Max. Price doesn't matter."

I glanced at his trailer. It was nice but not especially pricey. "Why? Is he rich?"

"Not at all. He just steals what he wants. And if the owner gets in his face in the process, he breaks the owner's knees. Or head. Or maybe just shoots him."

I was beginning to get a picture of Max, someone who was more monster than man.

"What would be your guess as to which guns he'd bring on a horse camping trip?"

The man seemed to think about it. "Well, he couldn't really carry all his weapons on a horse, right? But he would certainly bring at least one rifle – probably the Kel-Tec – and a semi pistol and the sawed-off."

"Why so many weapons?"

"Well, first, he always brings a bunch in his truck. As he says, if you're prepared for any kind of war, you're more likely to survive. Second, his guns are like his masculine identity. For him, everything is about being masculine."

"They make him feel tough."

"Yeah. Ain't no one gonna mess with Max because he can shoot you full of holes, then blow you in two with the sawed-off. And if he has to, with his muscles, he could probably tear you limb from limb."

"To your knowledge, has he ever assaulted anyone?" I was thinking of the assault conviction Diamond told me about.

"Assault? Are you kidding? Of course. That's what Max does. He beats the crap out of people. Gets paid for it."

"Who pays for it?"

"Well, it's not like Reno's got the big city Mafia or anything. But word gets around that Max is a good enforcer. So he gets jobs. He even has a fee schedule."

"How do you know that?" I asked.

"I... Maybe I've said enough."

"I'm just asking for my own knowledge. I won't tell anyone."

The man looked skeptical.

"Consider this," I said. "Answer my questions, I go away and you'll likely never see me again. I'll never tell anyone where I learned what I know. But if you don't answer my questions, maybe I mention you to my law enforcement friends, they look up some of Max's adventures and decide to bring you in for questioning. In order to squeeze Max, they mention to him that you were in the station telling all you know and implicating him in multiple crimes. How will Max react to the news of..."

"Okay, okay! You promise you won't tell anyone where you got this info? Cross your heart and hope to die?"

"I won't tell anyone." I stared at the man. "You were telling me about his fee schedule."

"He told me about it. I remembered because it sounded like some kind of fast-food menu. One thousand to beat someone up. Two thousand to beat them up so they can't ever walk normal again. Five thousand to hurt them so bad they won't be able to remember any of the details and they'll spend the rest of their days in a wheel chair. Ten thousand if he went all the way."

"And you think he did this more than once?"

"Hell, yes. He bragged about it."

"Why would Max tell you this?"

"Why not? I might be able to refer business to him. I know some guys from my career at the prison... If they put the squeeze on me to give them a name of an enforcer, I'd have to name someone or face the consequences. Everyone who's been inside knows that guards have one foot in the cesspool. We can't work the job without acquiring knowledge of that world."

"Why wouldn't Max be worried that you'd tell the cops?"

"I suppose partly because Max ain't what you'd call a criminal mastermind. And partly because he never gave me any details or names. He always talked in generalities. But mostly because it's obvious that if I planned to testify against him, he'd go all the way with me, and my body would end up out in the desert, eyes bit out by lizards."

"Did Max ever have a regular job?"

"I just told you his job. He's an enforcer. And he does it regular."

"Can you give me any names of Max's friends?"

The man looked puzzled. "He doesn't have any friends. At least not any who come around here."

"You said he mentioned women he pursued. He must have mentioned some men now or then?"

The man shook his head. "Nope. Just women. He goes after them, makes them his conquests. It's his thing. Male friends aren't his thing."

TWENTY

Street's plane was due in late that evening. At the appropriate time, I was parked in her condo lot, leaning against the hood and trying to look cool like James Dean but not succeeding, because I didn't have a cigarette to complete my pose. The dogs were exploring in the forest.

When Street's VW bug pulled into the lot, Blondie streaked out of the woods and began leaping against Street's driver's door before she came to a full stop.

Street got out and administered to Blondie first, and then Spot who'd come on the run to get his share of attention. I was last, but Street saved her best for me, giving me a kiss that ran my heart rate up to the redline.

Some time later, we emerged from her bedroom, made some dinner, and opened a bottle of Madroña Malbec. We sat in her living room with the dogs at our feet and traded stories, hers of boring bug scientists and mine of Jade's disappearance.

Street was visibly upset when I told her. She wanted to know more about it. So I gave her some details, which I edited for comfort. I also told her about my inquiries with Jade's neighbors.

Eventually, I commented on Jade's neighbor Amy, the bottle blonde who had a problem with Chinese people. "Do you think this woman is far out there?" I asked. "Or is her attitude more common than I want to think?"

Street sipped some wine. "I suppose it's simple racism. She's suspicious and afraid of people who don't look like her."

"Based on her dark roots and blonde hair, she doesn't look like she used to, either."

Street didn't respond. She seemed to be looking into space. "Where'd you go?"

"Oh, sorry," she said. "I was thinking."

"About?"

"About if I should go blonde."

I leaned back to look at her face and imagine it surrounded by blonde.

"You think I should?" she said.

"I'm visualizing." I reached over and touched her locks. "I think I like it this way. Black. No, I guess this is auburnish. Or is this forest green? What do you call this color?"

"The name on the bottle is Midnight Love."

"You're kidding. What a name."

"You're supposed to say, 'What a woman.'"

"What a woman."

She slugged me on the shoulder. "You're supposed to trace my jawline with a fingertip when you say it."

We finished the bottle of wine, or, more accurately, I finished the wine, and I ended up sleeping over.

In the morning, I left with Spot. Blondie stood in the doorway, happy to be left home with Street. I drove to the South Shore and out Christmas Valley. I headed toward the Jaso Ranch, but parked in the street.

I wanted to walk the drive and see if I noticed anything that I wouldn't see when driving. I took Spot with me. I was walking past Sam and Andrew Garden's cabin when I saw a man coming through the forest on the narrow trail that went through the woods. He had a white face and a black sweatshirt, and he wore black gloves.

Sorin Lupu, the man with the sun allergy. Unlike the last time I saw him, he had his hood up.

I took hold of Spot's collar. Sorin saw me and stopped. He lifted his walking stick a bit as if to get ready. Even from a distance, he radiated fear.

"Don't worry," I called to him. "I'll hold onto my dog." I came a little closer.

"Thank you," he said. "Have you learned anything about

where Jade went?" Lupu had a strange look on his face. Probably worry and concern for Jade.

"I haven't found anything about her whereabouts. But I will."

Sorin looked past me toward the Garden cabin. "It looks like you've been at the Garden's house. Have you spoken to Sam?" Lupu seemed tense.

"Not today. The last time we spoke, he was very sweet, although it appears he's suffering the early stages of dementia."

Lupu frowned but didn't speak.

"You want to say something but are hesitant." I waited.

"I... I would be wary with Sam."

"Why?"

"It's just that one time I was speaking to Sam and Andrew when Jade approached us. Sam was making rhymes and telling stories and acting pleasantly confused. One of his little stories was somewhat wild. When Jade acted surprised and said something to Andrew, I happened to look at Sam. His eyes were narrow. He was watching Jade and Andrew as if to see whether they accepted his story." Sorin paused. "I've heard an American phrase about card games, how it sometimes seems that a person is only playing with a partial deck. But I got the sense that Sam has a full deck. Does that make sense?"

"You don't think he has dementia?"

Sorin shook his head. "I don't believe Sam is at all confused."

"You think it's an act."

"Yes."

I thought about it, then gestured at the forest. "Do you hike this trail often?"

"I try to get out once a day when the weather's okay. It helps clear my head of work details." Sorin stared at Spot with such intensity it was as if he expected Spot to charge and attack like a lion.

"I thought you were maybe retired."

He laughed. "That's funny. I'm no older than you. You're not retired, right?"

"Too many bills to retire. Maybe in twenty-five years. What line of business are you in?"

"I write informational articles for a website."

"Is it a site I know of?"

"I doubt it. But it's growing fast."

"What do they have you write?"

"They let me write about anything I want. Think of it like Wikipedia but take out the scholarly stuff and put in fun stuff. The site is supported by advertising. If an article I wrote is read by a bunch of readers, advertisers pay the website to put their ads next to the articles. Then the website pays a portion of their revenue to the writers whose stories drew the readers. It's only pennies a time. But after you get hundreds or even thousands of articles on their site and develop a following of readers who like your style, you can make a good living."

"What subjects do you write about?"

"I pick subjects that one doesn't see in the mainstream media, subjects that are often studied by scholars, but I write about them in – what's the phrase – easy-to-digest ways."

"Your neighbor Amy told me you talked about Chinese subjects. Is that something you write about?"

Sorin Lupu was frowning as if confused. "I don't understand. I don't think I've ever talked to Amy about anything Chinese. She must have confused me with… Oh, wait. I bet Amy heard me talking about the Chinese Room thought experiment."

"What's that?"

"I'm making it part of a series of articles I've written on the subject of the Philosophy Of Mind. Think of it as popular philosophy. Nothing intellectual. Just fun and intriguing."

"And that has to do with a Chinese room?"

"Not really. That's just a name. I can explain if you've got a minute."

"Sure." Spot turned his head around and stared toward the forest in the direction of the Jaso Ranch. I held on, waiting to see if anything appeared. There was no sound or movement that I could hear. Spot turned back toward Sorin Lupu.

"Philosophers have always wondered about the concept of

our mind," Lupu said. "The mind is not just our brains. It's something else, right?" He paused, thinking. "Have you ever heard of the Turing Test?"

"I think so," I said, trying to remember. "Something about the goal of artificial intelligence?"

"Exactly!" Sorin seemed very pleased. "Alan Turing was the British mathematician who broke the Nazi Enigma code during World War Two. His test idea was about communicating with a computer. He said that if a future computer would ever be smart enough that we think we're communicating with a human, then that would be a high level of artificial intelligence. That idea became the Turing Test, and it's become a fixture in the world of artificial intelligence."

I said, "So when you talk to one of those synthetic voices on the phone, and it doesn't understand you, it doesn't pass the Turing Test, right? You know you're talking to a computer."

Sorin was making an exaggerated nod. "Now imagine you can't tell. The voice on the phone is so good at communicating, you think it's a real person."

"Hard to imagine, but I get the concept. If you think the computer is a person, then it has a high level of intelligence. You write about that?"

"Actually, I'm writing about a fun refutation of that. There was a philosophy professor named John Searle at UC Berkeley back in the eighties. Searle invented his so-called Chinese Room thought experiment. Searle's question was this: What if you sent messages written in Chinese characters into a locked room? In the room is a guy who doesn't know Chinese. But he has an enormous instruction manual. The manual doesn't explain what the Chinese characters mean, only what characters to write in response. So the man follows the manual's instructions and painstakingly writes down other Chinese characters as a reply to the message. Outside of the locked room is a woman who is fluent in Chinese. When she gets the reply, she thinks, 'Wow, the person in the room is smart and even understands Chinese!'"

"I get it," I said. "The person in the room doesn't have any understanding at all. The human is just following instructions that make him appear smart. The instruction manual is kind of like a computer program. The implication is that a computer, or even a person, could pass the Turing Test by simply following instructions, but not having significant intelligence."

"Yes!" Lupu was excited and animated in an awkward way, moving his weight back and forth from one leg to the other. With his white sunblock face and his heavy drape of clothing, he looked like a crazy Gothic character in a strange play. Lupu gave me a big grin. "Searle's Chinese Room thought experiment has captivated philosophers for decades. It really gets to the heart of questions about our minds and our intelligence." Lupu beamed, demonstrating his dream smile as Jade Jaso had described it. "You could write my articles!" he said.

"No. But I'm glad to have a glimpse into what you're doing. Thought experiments are neat."

"Neat!" Lupu exclaimed. "Can I use that for my title? 'A Neat Way To Think About Artificial Intelligence.'"

I nodded. "Yes, of course. I'm happy to contribute. So what's the conclusion? Will computers ever acquire serious artificial intelligence? Or will they always just be clever, unthinking machines?"

"That's what's had philosophers and software engineers so bent out of shape, to use idiomatic English. They've spent enormous amounts of time on Searle's Chinese Room concept. Most seem to think we will eventually have computers with real high-level artificial intelligence. But they have a hard time explaining it. Anyway, that's how I earn my living. I do this with lots of subjects. I try to make complex ideas fun and easy to read about."

"You've succeeded with me."

"Thank you!"

"What's the next subject you're going to write about?"

Despite Sorin's white sunblock, his face seemed to light up further. "My earliest memories were about pretending I could fly. It has always been my grandest dream. So I'm going to write about flight!" He sounded very excited.

"Is Jade interested in this stuff? Or is she mostly focused on poetry?"

Lupu's face went from animated excitement to a kind of melancholy. "I don't think she would be interested in philosophy. To her, my interests are just more weirdness from the strange guy with the sun allergy." He looked at Spot, then at the forest. "It makes me very sad, not finding – what's the English phrase – common ground with Jade. I could be her friend, but she won't let me."

"You find it frustrating," I said.

"Very. But I should just focus on her needs. You need to find her. I should let you go."

"I'll let you know when I learn anything."

TWENTY-ONE

After I said goodbye to Sorin Lupu, he headed toward his house. As I walked away, I kept thinking about his look of frustration regarding Jade. How strong was that frustration? How much emotion did it cause him?

I walked past Sam and Andrew Garden's cabin. Maybe Sam Garden was inside thinking about his new empty life with Andrew gone in China. Or maybe he was out walking and dreaming up unusual rhymes. I wondered about Sorin's assessment of Sam's mind. Was it an act? If so, was it malicious, or was the old man simply amusing himself?

I continued on to Jade's ranch and let go of Spot's collar so he could run. He trotted around, nose to ground, sniffing out scents of the horses now gone. The hayrack still had what looked like most of a bale of hay in it. Both halves of the double door to the barn were propped open. The cavernous space that had seemed full of life before was now empty. Even the bright, welcoming sculpture lights above either side of the door looked strangely lonely. The forest beyond, with its birds and squirrels and bears, hummed with life. I was walking into the barn when I saw movement through one of the barn windows.

I ran back outside and around to the back side of the barn. A person was moving away through the forest, walking fast.

"You in the brown jacket, halt!" I started running.

The person stopped and turned back toward me. It was Jade's neighbor Amy, the physicist. Spot ran up to her.

She shrieked in alarm. When she realized Spot wouldn't hurt her, she was quick with words. "Why are you shouting at me?"

"Jade just disappeared, and her father died under suspicious circumstances. Now I find you on her property."

"I'm just out for a walk. All the neighbors enjoy the forest.

We don't worry about the exact position of property lines." She put her hands on her hips and made a good show of bluster.

"When I saw you walking before, you had your son and your dog. It was obvious that you take them out for exercise."

"My son is at school. There's nothing wrong with me walking alone."

"If we go to your house, we'll likely find your dog in the kennel. You would only leave him there because he makes noise, which makes it hard for you to go unnoticed."

The woman made a harumpf sound of exasperation.

"Tell me the truth or I'll call El Dorado Sergeant Bains and report you as a suspicious trespasser. He'll take you in for questioning. That can take most of a day. If your answers don't satisfy him, he can keep you overnight."

"Okay! Okay! You don't need to browbeat me."

"What is your real reason for being here?"

She took a deep breath and held it. Maybe it was to calm herself. Maybe she was buying time to make up a story. She exhaled and spoke.

"Years ago I gave Billy Jaso a gift."

"What kind of gift?"

"It was... A coat of arms. I embroidered it." She took another deep breath. "I thought..." She looked down at the ground. "I made it and gave it to him as a gift. Now that he's gone, I wanted it back."

"Why did you give it to him?"

"I told you how he was so kind. Clearing our driveway of snow. Doing other helpful things for us like planting trees. He was someone my husband and I could lean on in hard times. I wanted to give him something in return. So I incorporated images that were important to Billy. The Iberian Wolf, the most impressive animal in The Basque Country. I put in an F-One Hundred fighter jet. I used lots of, you know, red, the color of warriors."

Now she was on a roll, finding words easily.

My initial thought was that I could check the story by asking Jade. But she was gone, and Amy knew that.

"Where were you looking for it?"

She waggled her finger in a vague way. "The barn. I was looking for it in the barn."

"Why the barn?"

"Because that's where he hung it."

"It was in a picture frame?"

"No. It was just... He hung it on a nail in his glass shop."

"Did you find it?"

"No. Jade probably hid it so I couldn't find it."

There was no way for me to verify or dispute what Amy said.

I said, "If you want to avoid trouble with the law, you should stay off the Jaso property until after we find Jade and bring her home safely."

She walked away without saying anything. I watched until she disappeared through the woods toward her house.

I went over to the Jaso house. It wasn't especially sturdy in construction, but it had deadbolts. Breaking in would take more than a credit card slipped into the door latch. I didn't know if Sergeant Bains had sent out his team to search for evidence and if so, how they'd gotten in. Lock picks and search warrant?

A tire iron or a cat's claw are always easy tools to force open doors. But I didn't want to use such a destructive method. I walked back to the barn, went through the big double door, and looked around for burglary aids. Spot ran into the barn, followed me for a bit, then left to continue exploring. The utility room contained many tools of the broom-and-rake variety, but nothing good for breaking into houses. Same for the tack and grain room. I walked to the end of the barn where Jade had given Street and me a quick tour of her father's glass-blowing shop.

Once inside the door, I smelled, as much as saw, the world of glass. Everything was permeated with the not-unpleasant tinge of burning heat. Iron bars and tongs and shaping instruments that were constantly subjected to the blast furnace. Insulating gloves and pads. Fire brick that was heated to temperatures that burned anything combustible and turned everything else a glowing orange.

Even the glass seemed to radiate a scent. I'd never thought of glass as having a smell. And yet, like sand on a beach, there was a kind of stringent, clean aroma. Maybe it was the leftovers from dying fires. Hard and crisp. Edgy yet calming.

I picked up some of the tools. They all were dense and heavy. They would only be good for breaking through doors or even walls.

To the side was a wooden work bench with a dented, burn-scarred work surface. There were two shallow drawers just below the bench top. I pulled them open. More iron, glass-shaping tools. All were blackened with a coating of char. Pointed, rounded, curved. You get a ball of glass heated to a bendy, saggy blob of glowing orange, you'll want a wide range of heat-impervious devices to push the glass into a pleasing shape.

The two main work benches had metal surfaces. In a cradle near the metal surfaces were several metal tubes, blackened and charred. They were each six feet long. I thought they were the blow tubes. Nearby were wooden bins with the groups of multi-colored glass tubes that Jade had said were disturbed by an intruder. One of the tubes stuck out a few inches and hanging on it was a roll of duct tape.

It seemed like a dangerous pursuit. Depending on the type and size of the glass and the fiery temperature, you get an expanding ball, searing your face with its heat. Its orange glow reflects in your eyes, threatening to blow up if any impurities should combust. Shape the molten glass, add more pieces to it, and create a work that is colorful, functional, beautiful. It's as elemental an art as there is, with a history that reaches back thousands of years to the first time someone noticed fused and melted sand in the aftermath of a wind-fueled bonfire. Imagination meets fire. Mankind was never the same after that momentous epiphany. People finally had a way to create leak-proof containers to store food and water and wine.

I continued my search for any implements that would help me break into the house. I ended up finding the most nuanced tool of all.

At one end of Billy Jaso's glass workshop was a cork bulletin board. On it he'd pinned some drawings of art glass projects, sketched with pencil on paper. Just above the top of one drawing was the head of a small finishing nail, nearly invisible. I sensed a thickness beneath the paper. Hanging from the nail, down behind the drawing, was a key.

Even though the house was out of view from the road and other houses, the back door was the least visible to anyone who might come through the forest.

The key fit the lock of the back door. Jade's belief that someone had come into her house was looking more reasonable.

The door let me in to a small hallway with coat hooks and a bench where one could change out of boots, as evidenced by several pair of boots and shoes under the bench.

The inside of the house was as I remembered it from when Jade showed me what had been moved by an intruder. Scents of cooking mixed with hay and dust and dirt and even a hint of horse manure, which, unlike the waste production of many other animals, doesn't really smell bad at all, especially when dry. The floor didn't look dirty. Probably there were barnyard remnants on the soles of the boots by the door. I tried to kick the dust off my own shoes so that I didn't track it into the house. Being there alone, without Jade showing me in, made it easier to look around and assess the place.

The house, as Jade had pointed out, was not especially tidy. But neither was it a mess. It was lived in and had a standard assortment of qualities that indicated the personalities of Jade and her father Billy. Worn, comfy pillows on the chairs and the couch. One of those collections of intriguing words on refrigerator magnets for writing impromptu poetry on the freezer door. A collection of handmade ceramic coffee mugs hanging by their handles from a little metal counter rack.

In the living room was a small old-style TV, an old cassette tape player and a wooden box of tapes, a separate CD player and a stack of CDs. There was a bookcase with many volumes of poetry along with several Tahoe-related guide books. Hiking trails, cross-country ski trails, birds of Northern California, mountain wildflowers. There were several books of history, including three about Abraham Lincoln. America's wars were represented. The Civil War, World Wars I & II, the Korean War, the Vietnam War, the Mideast wars in Iran and Iraq and Afghanistan.

Next to the history books were four pilot log books, with leather-look covers, all held together with a heavy blue rubber band printed with 'Salinas Asparagus Farms.' I pulled one book out and opened it. It had lined columns for entering flight information, type of plane, date flown, and hours logged. It was similar to my logbook, although Billy Jaso, a pilot in Vietnam, had made uncountable entries in his logs, whereas mine barely got used every month or so. Billy's logbook was dense with numbers and information written with ballpoint pen and with a heavy hand that embossed any pages beneath the one he was writing on. I put the logbook back and turned to a book of Basque history, a book I'd seen elsewhere in Tahoe.

I remembered that Billy was Basque. I pulled the book off the shelf and flipped through it. It told of Basque men who came from Europe when gold was discovered in California. Like so many would-be miners who didn't find gold, the Basque had to fall back on earning a living in the way they knew best, which was herding sheep. They took sheep into the high country meadows around Tahoe in the summer and then brought them back down to the Central Valley in the fall. The sheepherders camped with the sheep, sleeping under the stars in whatever meadow they were staying in. What was unusual about these sheepherders was that they left pictographs by carving into the aspen trees. Now dubbed 'arborglyphs,' the carvings depicted the sheepherders' names, short poems, love notes to girls they knew and missed. The arborglyphs were a pictorial history of the sheepherders' lives. Because aspen trees don't live that long, the aspen trees are dying and the arborglyphs are disappearing. That history will soon be completely gone.

Billy Jaso probably had heard stories of his ancestors who herded sheep in Tahoe and maybe even back in the Basque Country in Europe.

On a wall in the dining area was an arrangement of four framed photos that were faded and wavy behind the glass. They were of a middle-aged man and a little girl who were riding bareback on a big brown horse with a white blaze on its forehead. The little girl sat in front of the man. She was solid of build, had shiny black hair, and she grinned like she was the primary source of sunshine to which the real sun had to play second fiddle. The man holding her from behind looked as content as a father in a fairy tale.

At the opposite end of the house from the living room and kitchen were three bedrooms and one bath. I'd already glimpsed Jade's and Billy's rooms when Jade had brought us inside before.

The third bedroom was used as an office. It had a large, dark-brown wooden desk that was 50 years old or more. It had built-in file drawers on the lower part of either side and shallow drawers above them. On the writing surface was a splotchy dark-green leather blotter and an old desk lamp with a shade to keep the light out of your eyes.

Back to back with the wood desk was a smaller desk with a laminate finish. The laminate was blonde. The desk light was a modern chrome spindle with one of those miniature, intense halogen bulbs. On the desks were two coffee mugs with pens, markers, and mechanical pencils. There was a calendar with scribbled notes.

I started searching the large, older desk first. In the upper drawers were standard desk items, stapler, paperclips, lined pads of paper, envelopes, a roll of stamps. In the file drawers were business records, bank statements, expense receipts, tax filings and the like. After that, I searched the newer desk.

What I was looking for but didn't find was something unexpected. When you're dealing with a missing person, you don't expect to find answers by going through utility bills. Instead, you look for a surprise, something that gives you new insight into the person who's gone missing, something that reveals things that were unknown if not outright secrets. There is no particular type of item that fills that bill. All that matters is the surprise, something you don't expect to see.

I turned my attention to the living room, the dining area, the kitchen, the closets. I looked in the flour and sugar jars, a cardboard container that held steel-cut oatmeal. I pulled everything out of the freezer and looked at the items up close to see if frozen goods might hide something revealing. In the bathroom, I opened the top to the shampoo bottle. I looked inside the top of the toilet tank and then got down to look at the tank's bottom in case someone had duct-taped anything out of sight. I pulled shoes off the top shelf in the closets and shook them to see if anything would fall out. I felt the lining of Billy's old bomber jacket to see if anything was sewn between the fabric layers. I slipped my hand into Jade's dresser drawers, feeling for anything that might lie beneath her clothes. I looked in the soap dispenser of the washing machine. I pulled out the lint screen of the dryer and looked underneath.

Eventually, I went back out to the barn and repeated the search process there. I reached a gardening scoop into the shiny metallic trash can that kept the grain rodent-proof to see if any container could hide near the bottom. Spot appeared next to me, sniffing.

"You want to try some grain? It's got a little molasses to sweeten it up."

He licked at it, got some on his tongue, made some chewing motions, then tried to spit it out, pushing his tongue out over and over.

I went through Billy's glass-blowing tool boxes. I searched all the riding tack, slipping my fingers into every pocket and crevice. I picked up a shovel and walked through the barn, poking the shovel into the dirt here and there just in case I should come upon an area with loose dirt, an area that might have been dug up in the last couple of years. I climbed up in the hayloft and moved bales around until I satisfied myself that no one had stashed secret goods and covered them with hay bales.

I had no luck, found no surprises.

I went back into the house. As I opened the door, Spot appeared at my side.

"While Jade's house is not pristine, it appears to be animal-free," I said. "Do you mind continuing your outdoor explorations?"

Spot realized he wasn't going to be invited in. He happily turned and headed back toward the barn.

I went in and sat down on the couch to think.

I played the private investigator puzzle in my mind. Imagine you have something intriguing. Something private. Something valuable that would drive a bad guy to extreme lengths to obtain. So you put it in a good hiding place. In the movies, there would be a secret catch at the back of a cabinet, and a hidden door would open and reveal a hiding place.

But in real life, you simply hide it in plain sight, someplace that anyone could find if only they had a year to go through every little part of your life. Because it's in plain sight, it doesn't draw attention the way an obvious hiding place would.

Without getting off the couch, I reconsidered everything I'd already seen in my previous search. Should I look once again in the kitchen, climbing up to see if anything had been put on top of the cupboards? Should I go back into the bedrooms, pull out all the furniture and peel back the carpet and look for a trapdoor into the crawl space? Should I start digging in the corral in case someone had buried a coffee can full of... what? Jewels? The key to a safe deposit box? It didn't matter to me so long as it was the surprise revelation that suggested why Jade had disappeared.

The answer was no. Those ideas violate the principle of access. All good hiding places have easy access. Without that, the hiding place is too hard to use and thus loses usefulness. The second principle of hiding places is that of emotional connection. If someone wants to hide a locket with a tiny photo of their mother, they don't attach it to the drain trap plumbing under the kitchen sink. They slip it into a little velvet bag and put it in with the pillow cases she hand-embroidered.

My mission, then, seemed to be looking for emotionally-important places in plain sight.

Without getting up off the couch, I looked across the living room and into the kitchen and dining area beyond. I let my eyes focus on wall surfaces, table tops, and counter tops. I looked at everything that was about decoration rather than function. I thought about smells and sounds, often the most important part of emotional importance.

As I scanned, I let my eyes linger for a moment on the bookcase. I'd already looked at it, pulled out books, considered how Billy and Jade Jaso valued them. Many of the books were emotionally valuable. They were conduits to important history like the Vietnam War. They connected to important experiences like hiking trails and the birds and flowers that sustained so many people in emotionally-hard times. I thought about Billy and Jade and the experiences that shaped them. Jade growing up with a loving father who introduced her to the world of horses. Billy trying to create a new life after the life-threatening experience of flying bombing missions. And then, after he was safe at home and rebuilding his life, his wife died a sudden, tragic death.

I looked across at the history of the Vietnam War.

If there was anything in this house that had the most emotional importance, it was that book of history, a tome that would help him make sense of those scarred years. The other items of critical importance, memorabilia of sorts that recorded that part of his life, were the pilot logbooks. I'd seen the dense notations, written with heavy hand, a daily record of events that no one would ever want to relive, yet experiences no participant could ever forget. Missions of war, missions that resulted in death and destruction. It was those logbooks that probably had the highest emotional temperature in the Jaso house.

I stood, stepped over to the bookcase, and pulled the group of logbooks out.

I sat back down, pulled off the heavy rubber band, and opened them up. Times, places, planes, hours logged. But he'd also made notes about the missions and fit them in here and there in the margins of the logbooks. Some of what Billy had written was prosaic. 'Fruitless search in the highlands.' Some of what he wrote was searing. 'The coordinates were off, but we still found the village with the tunnels. We got them all.'

The first, second, and third logbooks were similar. Dense writing, dense meaning.

The fourth logbook was different. In fact, it wasn't used as a logbook at all. It was a journal. Written in the same heavy hand, ballpoint pen. The surprise I was looking for.

Under the headings were dense prose. Notes, thoughts, quotes from books, diagrams, strings of numerals that appeared to make no sense.

I paged through the book, scanning here and there. There was an amazing amount of information.

First, was the history of the Chinese family of Billy's deceased wife Jade, the mother of the Jade Jaso, now missing. I already knew that family was held together by generations of women, all named Jade, all trained as jade carvers.

Another section was information about Billy Jaso's ancestors, who emigrated from the Basque Country and came to the new state of California.

The journal would take a good deal of time to read, but it might reveal many surprises.

As I flipped near to the end of the logbook, the back cover opened. There was a sheet of paper that folded around an envelope. I unfolded it. At the top of the sheet was printed: Steinerson Collectibles and below it an address in San Francisco.

It was a receipt made out to Billy Jaso for the sale of a letter. The sales date was twelve years ago. The description was 'A rare 1861 letter from Abraham Lincoln to California Governor Elect Leland Stanford, with an unusual double warning about ethics, the first involving racism against Chinese laborers, and the second involving the financial business practices of building the trans-continental railroad. This letter is a fine example of Lincoln's focus on ethical behavior in government, and it displays his customary exacting word choices and description. What makes this letter special is its unusual length – 3 pages – and its rare and delightful inclusion of a number code, something we believe to be unique among Lincoln memorabilia. A great addition to any collection. Please call for more information.'

There was a heading labeled 'Condition.' The description

stated, 'While this letter and its envelope have substantial rippling from water damage, the writing, while less crisp than normal, is clear and quite legible.'

Under that, it said 'Price $39,000.'

The envelope paper was old and yellowed and warped. It looked like the letter had been submerged for hours and then dried out without any effort to flatten the paper as it dried. Fortunately, the letter had been written with waterproof ink.

The address on the envelope was hand-lettered with a dip pen. The writing was done in cursive, not especially feminine or masculine.

The address was striking:
Hon. L. Stanford
Governor Elect
State of California

The return address was more striking:
President Abraham Lincoln
The White House
Pennsylvania Avenue
Washington D.C.

I was opening the flap to pull out the letter when I heard the sound of a vehicle pulling up outside.

Not wanting to stuff the letter and receipt into a pocket where they could get munched, I slipped the letter back into the rear cover of the logbook. I re-wrapped the rubber band around all four books and carried them out the back door.

I heard a car door shut on the other side of the house. I quickly slipped the key into the dead bolt, locked the door, and put the key in my pocket. I saw a shadowed gap between the back steps and the house siding. It was just wide enough to hold the books. I slid the four logbooks into the gap and walked around the house.

TWENTY-TWO

In the drive was a dull red pickup with a horse trailer in tow. The rear fender facing me had a big dent in it as if the driver had backed up the trailer, turned too sharp, and the trailer jack-knifed into the truck. A skinny man with stringy brown hair coming out from under an Oakland Raiders cap was standing near the driver's door. He wore faded blue jeans, a dirty white T-shirt, and over it a faded blue-jean jacket with metal buttons. The jacket hung open. The man held a piece of paper in his left hand. He was bending over and reaching down to his cowboy boot with his right hand. He straightened up and tugged on the hem of his jacket as if trying to get it to hang straight. Everything about him telegraphed trouble.

I decided it was best to act like I belonged here. "Afternoon," I said. "Can I help you?" I walked up to him, and leaned toward him, standing too close for his comfort.

"I'm here to see Billy Jaso," he said in a scratchy voice damaged by drink, or smoke, or inhaled drugs, or all three.

"Sorry, Jaso's out. Do you want me to pass on a message?"

He unfolded the piece of paper, and looked it over as if searching for particular information.

"No matter. I'll just do my business. I'm here to pick up a horse that Billy Jaso is holding for Dell Davis."

The name sounded familiar but I couldn't place it. "Sorry, I can't help you with that."

"Can't or won't?" he said.

"Ah, if only more men believed in the precision of words."

"What?" he said, looking confused.

"I won't help. You're not picking up a horse." I didn't add that the horses had all gone missing

"No matter if you won't help. This is the official repossession paper. I've got the legal right to take the horse. It's a palomino mare, name of Dixie." He thrust the paper toward me. "I'll just go about my business. You can go back to yours." He held out the paper to show me.

I took it and stuffed it in my pocket.

"Hey, you can't take that."

"I just did."

"That's mine. You don't want to get in a pissing match with me. Give it back or face the music, mister. I'm a legal repossessor. You get in the way of me, it's like getting in the way of the legal law. That piece of paper shows my authority."

"The legal law? Your authority is now in my pocket. I guess I'll have to face the music."

The man was fast. He had a .38 revolver out of the concealed-carry holster at the small of his back and pointed at my belly before I could react.

"Step away before I'm required to enforce my rights," he said.

I smiled at him.

"Mister, I'll give you one last warning. If you interfere with a legal repossession, that's like interfering with an officer of the law."

I put my thumb and forefinger in my mouth and whistled so loud the man flinched.

"What the..." he mumbled, shaking his head as if to clear his ears.

Spot came running up from the forest behind the horse trailer. The man saw him at the last moment. He turned, surprised.

I grabbed his hand that held the gun, both of my hands squeezing hard, pointing it away from me and Spot.

He pulled the trigger. The gunshot in the quiet forest was very loud.

Still gripping his hand with both of mine, I jerked it down onto my rising knee. His wrist snapped with a sharp, muffled crack.

The man screamed and dropped the gun. He reached down

with his remaining good arm and pulled a knife out of his cowboy boot. I kicked the hand as he straightened up. The knife skittered away into the dirt. The man bent down and reached for the knife. I stomped his hand.

He screamed a second time, then dropped down, kneeling in the dirt. I kicked his weapons away, bent down over him, and patted him down. I found no other weapons.

"Down," I said. "On your stomach."

He didn't move.

I walked behind him, put my boot on his back, and gave a big push forward.

He went down onto his chest and face with a big whoomph. His broken wrist was flopped to one side, his mashed hand to the other.

"You can't do this," he shouted. "I have rights!"

"You have the right to keep your mouth shut."

"When Dell finds out about this, you're gonna get so dead. You're gonna be dead meat. What's that called? You're gonna be carrion. Dead carrion."

"If you utter one more word without me asking you to speak, I'm going to take your belt buckle prong and use it to put a hole through your tongue and another through your nose and zip tie them together."

I now remembered that Jade had told me about Dell Davis and how he was a scammer who sold phony shares in a movie, and Jade's father Billy had bought Anne Gregory in an equine lien foreclosure. A horse that this man was calling Dixie.

I called Sergeant Bains. When he answered, I said, "I just stopped by the Jaso place to see if Jade had come back, and a charming gentleman arrived to steal a horse, one of the very horses that went missing with Jade. When I wasn't forthcoming, the man pulled a thirty-eight revolver and threatened me with it and fired it. I felt it appropriate to subdue him. His response was to pull a knife from his boot, which meant he required further subduing. He's presently waiting for you to come and ascertain the extent of his lawbreaking."

"I can be there in ten or fifteen minutes."

"Thanks." I clicked off. "Hang in there," I said to the whimpering form on the ground. "Help is on the way."

The man opened his mouth to respond, then thought better of it.

"I'm going to ask you a question," I said. "You can speak to answer it but not to say anything else. Where do I find Dell Davis?"

"I don't know." He was speaking into the dirt, his words mumbled.

"How do you contact him?"

"I don't. He contacts me. I can't breathe with my face in the dirt. Dust is getting into my nose! My legal law rights are being violated!"

"Do you remember what I said about the zip tie?"

He went silent.

"Where were you supposed to take the horse?"

"I was supposed to take her to Sacramento and wait for a call."

"A call on what phone?"

"My cell phone. In my truck."

"How do I find Dell Davis?"

"I already told you, I don't know!"

"I think you can remember a way."

"There is no way!"

I called Spot over. He came trotting, sniffed my hand, looked at the man lying on the ground, wagged, sniffed my hand again.

"Okay, I'll give you a half treat." I pulled out one of the little biscuits, held it in front of him as I broke it in half. He watched as I put half in my pocket, then fed him the other half.

I squatted down next to the man on the ground. His face was pointing away from me. I snapped my fingers and pointed to the man's back. "Lie down, Largeness."

Spot sat.

"Lie down. Here." I pointed. "Your head next to the back of this man's head."

Spot reluctantly got down, his nose right near the man's

head.

The man squirmed and got his head turned around to face Spot. When he saw Spot's head right next to him, he immediately gasped. His eyes seemed to develop a tremor, quivering left and right.

"No! No! Take him off of me! Don't let him bite!"

"I'll call him off if you answer my question."

"Okay! Okay! Hurry! I can't stand dogs. I'm going to have a reaction!"

I gave a little tug on Spot's collar, and we both stood up.

"Where do I find Dell Davis?"

"I don't know where he lives. But he goes to his favorite club most nights."

"What club is that?"

"The Flower Blossom Club."

"Never heard of it. Where is it?"

"I don't know. Sacramento someplace. I haven't been there. I think it's the back part of a bar. Disguised sort of. Ask around. It can't be that hard to find."

"Spot, stay here and watch him. If he moves, tear his arms off." With the man still lying on the ground, unable to see well, I took quiet steps over to his pickup. The driver's window was down. His cell phone was on the dash.

I heard the sound of car tires and turned to see Sergeant Bains pull up.

He got out, walked over, and looked at the suspect. "You have an interesting approach to subduing a suspect. No cuffs on his wrists. No rope hog-tying his ankles."

"Just words, officer. The sweet power of words."

"What you mean is you scared him to death."

"He was unruly until I told him that if he didn't shut up and lie still, I'd poke holes in his tongue and nose and zip-tie them together."

Bains frowned, then wrinkled his own nose, then rubbed it. "That's the real reason for going private, huh? Zip-tie creativity doesn't hold with the higher ups in the sheriff's office. But private... heck, creativity rules." Bains bent down toward the man and cuffed his hands behind his back. The man screamed when Bains touched the broken wrist.

"Can I get up now??!!" the man shouted.

"No," Bains said. He turned to me, "He's a whiner."

"He told me he was a champion of the legal law and if I got in the way I'd be dead carrion and that interfering with a legal horse repossessor was like interfering with a cop."

"Wow, sounds like you're in deep shit."

"He also gave me this." I pulled out the paper I'd taken from the man. "Said it was his legal law authorization."

Bains looked at the paper, started reading, and smiled. He walked over and squatted down next to the man.

"Let me read this," Bains said, "and you tell me if I get the words right. It says, 'This paper hereby authorizes Jim Bowie to repossess my horse Dixie. She's my horse. It's that simple.' It's signed 'Dell Davis.'" Bains looked at the man, then looked at me.

I said, "Such gravitas, it's practically like the Declaration of Independence. Jefferson couldn't have said it better."

"Okay, Jim Bowie," Bains said. "Let's see what the DMV calls you." Bains felt the man's pockets, pulled out a wallet, found a driver's license. "Oh, hello, you're called Jackie Willowisp, not Jim Bowie. That right? Jackie Willowisp?"

"Am I allowed to speak? 'Cause that man who assaulted me said I couldn't say a word."

Bains turned to me. "Did you say that?"

"Yeah, I confess. I can deal with guns and knives. But his constant babbling about legal law made me lose my composure."

"It's a good idea," Bains said.

"Losing my composure?"

"Zip-tying his tongue to his nose. That would be most effective subduing." He turned to the man. "C'mon, Mr. Willowisp, let's get you down to the office, book you for assault with deadly weapons, carrying concealed weapons without a license, attempted horse theft, and whatever else I think of during the drive to the station."

"I can't get up. You've cuffed me like an animal! My broken wrist will have to be amputated!"

Bains looked at Willowisp. "I agree. Handcuffs would only be appropriate for a very dangerous man. Someone armed with a gun or knife." Bains turned to me. "Did you make a proper citizen's arrest and Mirandize him?"

"Sorry, I forgot. You want me to do that now?"

Bains made a solemn nod.

I said, "Mr. Willowisp, I'm arresting you for assault with multiple deadly weapons and attempted horse theft. You have the right to remain silent and refuse to answer questions. If you can't afford an attorney, you might be screwed. And… lemme think, we'll use anything you say to keep you in the slammer for as long as possible. And if you don't say anything, we'll find other reasons to keep you in the slammer so our neighborhoods remain safe." I turned to Bains. "Sorry, I couldn't remember the exact words."

"Close enough. If some attorney uses that to get him off, we'll find another way. And you've still got the chance to find Dell Davis. Let's get him in the Sheriff's car."

The man refused to walk, so Bains picked up one arm, and I picked up the other. The man screamed as if we were tearing off his arms. We carried him, yelling, and put him in the back of Bains' vehicle.

Once in the back seat the man yelled. "I demand you turn on your dash cam so this is on the record. I'm being tortured! I've been assaulted. Dell Davis will have me out on bail in an hour. He'll have a team of lawyers shut down your entire department! I'm gonna sue you both for assault and false arrest. You two are gonna get your asses fired. I'm gonna be on Oprah for having my legal laws trampled. I know my rights!"

Bains shut the door and got an evidence bag out of the kit in the back of the patrol unit. He walked over to the weapons and turned the bag inside out to grab the gun and the knife. He sniffed the gun. "You touch either of these?"

"No. I just grabbed his hands as he held the gun, and I stomped the other hand that held the knife."

"Any idea where the missing round went?"

I gestured toward the forest. "Out there." I turned toward the red pickup. "If you'd like Jackie's phone, it's on the dash of his truck."

Bains glanced over toward the patrol vehicle where Willowisp was weaving back and forth in the rear seat. "Did our suspect indicate where Dell Davis might be found?"

"Yeah. Something called the Flower Blossom Club in Sacramento."

"Out of our county, so we won't be going there anytime soon. I assume you intend to go there."

"Just what I was thinking," I said.

Bains turned another evidence bag inside out, reached into the red pickup, and picked up Jackie's cell phone off the dash.

"You want to come down to the station and make your statement?"

"Sure."

Before we left, Bains said, "Let me call the impound lot." He dialed. A moment later, he said, "Sergeant Bains here, El Dorado Sheriff's office. I've got an abandoned truck and horse trailer at the Jaso Ranch in Christmas Valley." He recited the address. "Appreciate you bringing it in. Thanks."

Bains hung up, pulled out his book, wrote out a ticket, and stuck it under the wiper on the red pickup. Then he looked through the pickup. He saw nothing worth taking.

Jackie Willowisp saw him from the back seat of the patrol vehicle. He started emoting and thrashing, his opinions thankfully muffled by the windows of the vehicle.

I asked, "Has your team checked out the Jaso house?"

Bains nodded. "They didn't find anything useful."

"There's one thing I want to check," I said, "then I'll see you at the station."

Bains drove away with his prisoner. I trotted around to the back door, retrieved the bundle of logbooks, then went back to the Jeep.

TWENTY-THREE

That evening, I stopped by Street's condo before I headed up the mountain to my cabin. Her windows were dark. I remembered that she said she'd be late at her lab playing catch-up the next couple of nights.

I'd just been with Street the night before. Yet 24 hours later, I felt lonely as I drove up the winding road that I share with my vacation-home neighbors. There were no lights on at Mrs. Duchamp's place, the only neighbor of mine who lives there more than weekends when the neighborhood isn't buried in snow. Maybe she'd already gone to bed. Maybe she and her toy poodle Treasure were watching poodle videos on YouTube. The mountainside was black-dark.

I pulled onto the parking pad at my cabin. Normally, I let Spot run in the forest. But he'd spent the afternoon running at the Jaso Ranch. He wanted to come directly inside with me.

I drank a Sierra Nevada Pale Ale as I made dinner for both Spot and myself, a piece of grilled salmon brushed with olive oil and sprinkled with black pepper and lemon. I also cut up a head of broccoli, grilled it, and then I mixed it in with noodles tossed with more olive oil and more black pepper and more lemon juice. Maybe I should change my name to Tony Vicini and open a restaurant. Vicini's Olive Oil Grill. I stirred a portion of the dinner into Spot's sawdust-chunk dog food. He inhaled it with the same Shop Vac enthusiasm that he would have used with steak-on-sawdust chunks. "Is that a yes vote on the restaurant?" I asked.

He looked at me and ran the giant tongue around the substantial perimeter of his mouth. When he realized I wasn't dishing up seconds, he lay down on his big bed.

The air of approaching fall was getting chilly, so I made a

postprandial fire in the wood stove, small so it wouldn't toss embers out the chimney pipe. I sat in my rocker. Immediately, the heat from the wood stove combined with the sedative of a second beer, and I felt a powerful fatigue.

Despite my sleepiness, I turned on the reading light, pulled out the letter, and looked at it more closely.

The first thing I noticed was that the water damage to the envelope made the postage mark hard to read. But holding the envelope at an angle so that the light fell on it differently made the rubber stamp visible. It indicated that the letter had been mailed through the Pony Express in September of 1861. I didn't know much about the Pony Express other than it was an innovative way to get mail across the vast western part of the United States. It used a network of riders on galloping horses that moved mail much faster than the stagecoaches that previously hauled mail. I also knew that the Pony Express had gone through Tahoe. The business was short-lived, put out of business when the telegraph lines were stretched across the country.

But the Pony Express, even though short of duration, was important. And I held an example of why in my hands. A letter from President Abraham Lincoln to the new governor of California, Leland Stanford.

In some ways, it was a low-amplitude surprise that I'd found it in Jaso's house. It didn't stand out as if I'd found a weapon soaked with Jade Jaso's blood hiding under her bed. The letter didn't give me a clue as to where I might find Jade. But the letter's existence hidden in Billy Jaso's pilot's logbook was dramatic, regardless of what the letter said.

I opened up the flap of the envelope and pulled the letter out. It was three pages, each about 6 inches wide by 10 inches tall, folded in half.

The style of the flowing cursive handwriting was not easy to read, especially with the paper warped and rippled by water. But the letters and words were carefully formed. I read it through twice, the second time more slowly than the first. Much of the information seemed too detailed to grasp in my current state of brain fog. But I gathered that buried in Lincoln's careful prose were nuanced statements to Stanford. I further understood that while the significance of Billy Jaso's possession of the letter was not clear to me now, it would become clearer in the morning, especially if I could find a Lincoln or Stanford expert to go over it.

There was one other piece of paper tucked into Jaso's pilot logbook. I unfolded it. It was a map of the Tahoe Basin. In addition to all the standard stuff, names of all the small lakes, towns, and high mountains, there were two kinds of symbols that had been drawn by hand. One type of symbol was T-shape, like a Tesla logo. I realized it was meant to be a pickaxe. I'd seen it before. It was a symbol for a mine. There were a couple of dozen of them. The other symbol was a crude flower design, the way a little kid draws flowers, a vertical line with little loops at the top. The map didn't look significant in any way. But its location, hidden in a logbook with a letter from President Lincoln, gave it importance.

I slipped the letter into the "L" entries in my dictionary and went to bed.

TWENTY-FOUR

The next morning while I drank coffee, I did a little Googling about letters to and from Leland Stanford and Abe Lincoln, and I found something called The Stanford Archive Foundation in Sacramento. There was a phone number. I dialed and a woman answered.

"Brady Harper, Stanford Archive."

"Hello, my name is Owen McKenna. I'm a private investigator in Tahoe, and I have a question about a letter that President Lincoln sent to Governor Stanford in the fall of eighteen sixty-one. The letter…"

"Excuse me," she interrupted.

"Yes?"

"Stanford wasn't governor in the fall of eighteen sixty-one. He was governor-elect. Elected in the fall but not inaugurated until January tenth, eighteen sixty-two."

"Oh. Sorry. I'm not knowledgeable about the dates. You obviously are."

"My business," she said. "You were saying?" Her voice didn't sound brusque. But it was clear she would not tolerate any nonsense such as inaccurate statements.

"The letter was carried by the Pony Express," I said. "I'm wondering if I might come down, show it to you, and get your expert opinion."

"What is your question about it? If you're trying to sell it, I don't give that kind of advice." Her tone was calm, but there was a hint of stern in it that reminded me of my aunt when I was a little kid in Boston, the aunt who thought my mother didn't use appropriate discipline for a boy growing up without a father on the premises.

I said, "I have a client whose father owned the letter. The

father recently died in a fall that may or may not have been an accident. The man thought the letter was important. Now the man's daughter has just disappeared. I'm wondering if you might see something significant in the letter that wouldn't mean anything to me."

"Are you suggesting the man was murdered or the daughter disappeared because of the letter? Letters that Lincoln wrote can be worth many thousands, but I wouldn't think someone would kill for them. But I don't know anything about murder. Or kidnapping or whatever. I'm an archivist."

"May I make an appointment to talk to you?"

"Let me look at my schedule." There was a short pause. "Can you come by tomorrow morning at nine?"

"Nine is perfect. I'll see you then. Thanks very much."

After I hung up, I called Sergeant Bains and asked if he'd heard anything about Jade Jaso. He said he'd filled out a missing persons report but that there wasn't much more he could do. He added that the would-be horse thief Jackie Willowisp was still in jail and hadn't provided any other information.

The next morning I took my coffee mug on our morning walk. Spot ran around in the forest while I ambled and sipped. The sun hadn't yet come up over the peaks to the east. But the alpenglow was striking the mountains across the lake and turning them peach. The air was crisp and clear, the views grand. Despite many months since the previous winter, there were still snowfields on the Crystal Range.

We were in the Jeep by six-thirty.

Two hours after that, we were down the mountain and heading across the Central Valley to Sacramento.

I parked near the capitol building, under the shade of an enormous Redwood that, contrary to what one might expect in sunny hot Sacramento, obviously thrived. Because I expected the heavy redwood shade to remain over the Jeep for a couple of hours, I left Spot in the Jeep. I rolled all the windows down a foot. Spot was snoozing in the back seat. He lay on his back with his legs sticking up and leaning against the back of the seat.

The weight of his jowls pulled them away from his teeth. The overall look was an odd combination of harmless innocence and the carnivorous potential of his dramatic fangs.

"Be good," I said.

He ignored me, so tired was he from holding his giant head out the window and into the wind during the drive.

The Stanford Archive Foundation consisted of a single, large, high-ceilinged room in the old Dorchester building, a hundred-year-old brick box several streets over from the California State Capital in downtown Sacramento. The room was in the rear corner of the building, with the rest of the building's space being taken up by a busy coffee shop of the type that are finding success by positioning themselves as the anti-Starbucks yet offering the same range of sugary coffee drinks served up by hip young baristas with tattoos and metal piercings that were probably more aggressive than Starbucks would allow.

There was a small sign that said, 'Stanford Archives' next to a tall door. I opened it to the soft swoosh of air moving past weather stripping and stepped inside to a quiet square space that was about 30 feet on a side.

The room was well lit by large windows positioned at intervals wide enough to allow for capacious bookcases between the windows. The one wall without windows or a door was completely filled with bookcases that rose from the floor to a 12-foot-high ceiling made of copper-colored, pressed tin tiles. There was an angled ladder that rolled on wheels and was guided by a track near the ceiling. Attached to the ceiling were several bright track lights so that anyone up on the ladder looking at books could easily see the pages without taking the books down.

Near the north center of the room was an island grouping of an oak desk and a large oak flat-file cabinet in which one could store out-sized paper documents like maps. There was a computer on the desk and another on the flat file.

Near the south center of the room was another island comprised of two adjacent library tables with six reading lamps arranged across the wooden expanse. Tucked under the edge of the table were four heavy wooden chairs.

In the far corner of the room stood a podium-style desk. Attached to the desk was a bright light with a flexible metal gooseneck. Standing at the podium was a woman. She leaned in close over a group of yellowed papers. She held a magnifying glass and used it to scan the papers. She appeared transfixed by her project. A few moments after I walked in, perhaps alerted by the sound of the opening door or the warm coffee-flavored breeze blowing in from the coffee shop, she turned toward me.

Brady Harper wasn't as thin and tall as a street lamppost, but she was close. At 6' 3" or so, she didn't have to lift her gaze much to look me in the eye. The base of the Harper light pole was a pair of large clogs, the upper part of which was a gray metallic material that looked closer to chain mail than anything soft like leather. She wore narrow-cut black pants that were probably custom tailored for her height, yet still didn't quite reach the chain mail. Her shirt was black cotton, tucked in, which emphasized her thinness.

Harper had on heavy eyeglasses with metallic rims the same steely color as the chain mail. Above the glasses were short, black curls. The glasses were very thick, and they warped light like Mason jar bottoms, making her blue eyes look larger than life and, despite the scary sci-fi magnification, showed just how beautiful her eyes were. Deep blue irises like the Mediterranean Sea and bright whites like polished Thassos marble. Above her eyes were thin black eyebrows with dramatic arches. In spite of the dominant glasses, Brady Harper's eyes could convince landscape painters to become portrait artists. Competing with Harper's eyes in sheer drama was a purple bruise on the left side of her chin. There was a tiny track of stitches curving through the bruise. Judging by the bruise and a finger splint on the little finger of her left hand, it looked like she'd taken a nasty fall.

"I'm Owen McKenna. We spoke on the phone."

"Welcome."

"Thank you for seeing me on short notice."

She nodded and reached toward me, not to shake hands, but to give me a fist bump. "You said you had one of Lincoln's letters?"

"Yes. I'd like you to look at it, please."

I turned and looked up at the bookshelves. "I'm curious. You have as many books as a library. Is that what archives do? Collect books?"

"I suppose that's what some do. In this case, the Stanford Archive Foundation collects and catalogs items connected to Leland Stanford. Quite a few of them are books. Much of what is on these shelves is organized and entered into a computer."

"Books are your passion, no doubt."

"Books, yes. I don't know about passion for Stanford, but his life is my job. My masters thesis was on American history with a focus on Lincoln and the Civil War. There's a woman here in Sacramento who is distantly related to both Lincoln's wife and Stanford's wife. So she started the foundation."

"Ah." I nodded understanding. "She pays your salary. What a great job for an academic, to work for a person with such an interest in history."

"Technically, she provided the initial endowment. The endowment's earnings pay my salary along with our acquisitions budget. There is a board of directors. So I work for them. But I was hired at her request."

It seemed appropriate to show interest, so I said, "You said she was related to Stanford's wife. Who was his wife?"

"Jane Lathrop Stanford. More than anyone else, she was responsible for creating Stanford University. She funded the university, directed its development, made certain it included arts education, and she required that the university accept women, which was uncommon in the eighteen hundreds."

"I'm not surprised."

Harper frowned as if maybe I didn't understand the full importance of the situation. "It was a big deal," Harper said. "Most Ivy League colleges didn't begin accepting women to their undergraduate programs until the nineteen seventies."

"That surprises me," I said. "It seems very late."

The frown turned to a nod. "Jane Lathrop Stanford did a lot of important stuff. She was a good person. It was such a shame she was murdered."

TWENTY-FIVE

"Stanford's wife was murdered? How?"
"Strychnine poisoning."

"Whoa. How... dramatic," I finally said, surprised at feeling awkward, especially considering that I earn my living by investigating crime.

"It happened in nineteen oh five. She survived a previous poisoning attempt in San Francisco, which was part of her reason to sail to Hawaii to reduce stress in her life. But a second poisoning took place in Honolulu, and the second one was successful."

"Why don't I know about this?"

"Most people don't, and that traces back to a cover-up from the very beginning."

"By whom?"

"By her hand-picked university president, David Starr Jordan. Against all evidence, he immediately started saying that she died of a heart attack. He even went to Hawaii and intervened with doctors and the sheriff's office."

"Any idea why?" I asked.

Harper made a little nod. "Apparently Jordan spoke to Stanford's Board of Trustees and told them they should promote whichever report of Jane Stanford's death would be the least scandalous."

"So he was an early spin master, altering the truth to suit his own needs."

"Yes."

I paused, thinking about how narrow-minded my world was. The idea of rich, influential, university-founding women being murdered seemed like something from the theater, not real life.

Brady Harper was quiet, letting me process the thought.

"You said the Stanford Archive's benefactor is related to both Jane Stanford and Lincoln's wife. Lincoln's wife was Mary Todd, right?" I said, scraping long-unused trivia out of a dusty room in my memory cellar.

"Very good," she said. Harper made a big grin revealing teeth that were quite white but not perfectly straight. Which was only fair considering she'd won the beauty lottery in the eyes department.

"How unusual to discover that President Lincoln had a relative in Northern California," I said.

"I agree. Todd Valley, northeast of Auburn, was founded in eighteen fifty by a man named Dr. Francis Walton Todd, a cousin of Mary Todd."

"And that was before anyone could easily get here from the east," I said.

"Right. The transcontinental railroad wasn't completed until eighteen sixty-nine. Before that you had to come by horse-drawn stagecoach or by sea."

"By sea," I repeated. "People did that? From the East Coast?"

"Many people who were enticed by the discovery of California gold booked passage on sailing ships. The ships headed south down the Atlantic coast. The passengers would disembark at the isthmus of Panama, cross overland to the Pacific, then get on another ship to come north. That's how Leland Stanford commonly traveled to and from the East Coast. However, many people also sailed all the way down and around the tip of South America, then up the Pacific Coast to the San Francisco Bay. From there, they could come up the river to Sacramento."

I visualized the route as she explained it. "It's hard to grasp that one can sail from New York City to Sacramento without ever stepping out of a boat," I said.

"Yes, it is surprising," Harper said, "Anyway, you said you brought a letter."

"Yes." I handed her the manila envelope in which I had put the envelope from Lincoln.

She flexed it to widen the opening, peered inside, and set the large envelope on one of the two library tables. She pulled on white cotton gloves, struggling to get the left one over the splint on her little finger. I noticed that she'd cut the glove up the side to open up the fabric. She opened one of the flat file drawers and pulled out a large sheet of thin board. It was white and bendy. She lay the board on the table, picked up the manila envelope, and tipped it so the papers gently slid out onto the white board.

She first picked up the sales receipt from Steinerson Collectibles. She held it very close to her face while she read it.

Next, she looked at the envelope without touching it. Watching her careful movements, I immediately felt guilty about how I'd handled the letter. I hadn't even washed my hands.

"Why the large sheet of cardboard?" I asked.

"Archivists use cotton rag board, neutral PH. The kind of materials picture framers use."

"Why is it called rag board?"

"Because they make it from cotton. If you boil down cotton rags until they're pulp, then strain it through a screen and run the material through rollers, you get a board that is neutral PH. It makes a good work surface that will prevent the letter from coming into contact with any chemicals or skin oil."

"Then I've done lasting damage. That letter has my fingerprints all over it. Probably dog hair, too."

She turned and looked at me. I couldn't tell if she was surprised or not at my callous disregard for those things that were important to her world. There was no outward scorn, but she was probably thinking that I was an enemy of historical preservation.

Harper turned back to the envelope and looked at it up close without touching it. "It looks like your fingerprints are nothing compared to past water damage."

"Fortunately, the ink was waterproof," I said. "But because of the way the paper was rippled and abraded, it's still a little hard to read despite the waterproof ink."

Harper got out a camera and took several pictures of the

front and back of the envelope.

She gently eased open the envelope and slid out the letter. She unfolded the letter, set clear plastic weights over the letter's edges, then took more pictures. Front and back.

"As you can see by Lincoln's words and the post mark, it was sent via the Pony Express," I said. "Which is kind of cool."

Harper had pulled out a magnifying glass and was looking at the letter up close. "Yes, very cool," she said.

I didn't know if she actually thought that. Maybe she looked at Pony Express mail every day.

She pulled one of her tube lights over and looked at the letter up close, her nose nearly touching the paper. No doubt her sci-fi glasses magnified it to a dramatic degree.

"This is interesting," Harper said as she looked at it. "This letter was sent via Pony Express just a few weeks before the ponies stopped carrying mail."

"That was after the telegraph was connected across the country, right?"

"Yes. The telegraph immediately put the Pony Express out of business. Who would send a physical letter that took ten days to span the west part of the country and cost a lot of money when you could instead send an electronic message that arrived instantly and cost almost nothing?" She studied the letter. "Do you mind if I take the time to read it?"

"I would appreciate that."

"I should point out that the handwriting and style is very much like what I've seen on other letters written by Lincoln. So that initially makes the letter appear authentic."

Brady Harper leaned close to the letter and read aloud, slowly, her fingertip pointing at each of the words. Although I'd already read the letter, it seemed to have a new flavor as she put it into spoken words.

"'September twentieth, eighteen sixty-one.
Honorable L. Stanford
Governor Elect
State of California

My dear Sir:

I am sending you this letter via my agent in St. Joseph, Missouri, which, as you know, is the eastern terminus of the Pony Express. I expect those remarkable young riders should deliver this missive to you in California by the beginning of October.

First, I'd like to say that it was good to meet and talk with you in Washington this past summer. I am still appreciative of your support of me in my election as president a year ago.

I have just received the news that on September 4th, you were elected governor of the great state of California as well as being elected as president of the new Central Pacific Railroad. Congratulations on both accounts.

As you are no doubt aware, California, while small in population compared to our eastern states of New York, Pennsylvania, and Ohio, has grown fourfold since the previous census in 1850. This amazing growth is welcome news. And because of the enormous physical size of your state, I won't be surprised if, one day, California becomes a political and economic power in our country.

I am writing for two reasons.

First, like me, you joined with disaffected members of the Whig Party to create a new Republican Party in California. As you know, the new Republican Party was created as much to resist the spread of slavery as for any other reason. Our country is now being torn by this grave Civil War, and our Union soldiers fight in support of this very cause.

Embodied in this pursuit is the understanding that all races have rights under our constitution.

Yet I have learned of recent comments made by you to the effect that the Chinese immigrants who helped mine California's gold and are now building California's railroads belong to an inferior race and that they are causing degradation and have a deleterious influence on white people, which you refer to as the superior race.

I won't debate with you what I consider the lack of merit to your position. I will, however, point out that you are on tenuous ground considering that you and your companies employ many of the very Chinese immigrants that you disparage. To profit from the immigrants as you denigrate their character is beneath the ideals of our new Republican Party. I'm hoping you will see the error in your thinking. For justice to prevail in this Civil War, we need governors of the highest moral persuasion. I would hope that you adjust your thoughts accordingly.'"

Brady Harper paused and looked out one of the windows. The view was largely the green foliage of large trees with a filtered view of the building across the street. I couldn't tell if she was thinking about the nuances of Lincoln's letter or merely resting her overworked eyes.

After several seconds, she continued reading.

"'The second reason I write is that your position as the new president of the Central Pacific Railroad will present you with a very large financial responsibility. Having provided legal representation for the Illinois Central Railroad, I am aware of the complexities of railroad financing. Large amounts of money are involved in every aspect of this grand plan to span our continent with a rail line. I expect that, in the near future, I will be encouraging our Congress to move forward on funding this railway. Within a very few years, our nation is going to spend a sizable portion of its assets in pursuit of this goal.

Because of our civil war, our national oversight of the railroad building will be severely tested. So I am writing you with the request that you be as judicious in your governance of the railroad building as you will be in your governance of California.

When we met in Washington this last summer, we spoke of this very fiduciary duty. You assured me that you would be careful and conservative. You further added that you would acquire nothing from the railroad contracts beyond your normal salary and what you called the souvenirs of business.

Those last words, souvenirs of business, concern me. What

may be souvenirs to a governor and major businessman like yourself may seem substantially grander to persons of normal means, and thus inappropriate for a person making decisions with taxpayer dollars.

I trust you will keep this in mind and pursue your fiduciary duty with utmost seriousness. I know that you will honor the public trust as you spend our public money building the railroad that will move our country forward into a new era.

Yours truly,

A. Lincoln

P. S. You will recall that when you met Mrs. Lincoln and me in Washington last summer, you admired her Chinese necklace, and you mentioned your own acquisition of some art made from the same material. You added that this property was, despite its high value, an example of a business souvenir and that it cost you nothing. You further said that you no longer owned that art. But that comment and its implications have stayed with me and caused me no small concern.

We also discussed our mutual interest in a particular Greek scholar, which I imagine will come back to you as I append some numerals to this letter. I shall not apologize for my intimation appearing overly dramatic, for drama is my express intention.'"

I would have thought that Brady Harper could not lean any closer to the paper, and yet she did, her nose nearly touching the letter as she studied it.

"What did you make of this series of numbers at the bottom of the letter?" She pointed with her gloved finger.

I glanced again at the numbers I'd previously seen, trying to see them as a scholar would see them.

35212351124514 – 53211313 – 453225124531–351253 – 141222 – 2425442221453231 – 244331 – 312123113243233231 – 53215135 – 14122245 – 41243132

"I found the list of numbers baffling," I said after a moment. "Any idea what they could mean?"

Harper turned to look at me. Up close, her magnified blue eyes were startling enough to make me lose my train of thought. Her excitement was obvious and electric.

"It must be some kind of code!"

TWENTY-SIX

Brady Harper was so animated she shook. "The Greek scholar Lincoln mentions must have written stuff with number codes. And Lincoln and Stanford must have talked about that code."

"Did Lincoln do that often? Write with numbers?"

"Never, to my knowledge. However, he loved games and puzzles. So I'm not surprised that he and Stanford had this private communication. Although, given the serious tone of his letter, this wasn't any kind of amusement but simply what he said. That he intended it to be dramatic."

Harper looked again at the letter. "I can look up the Greek scholar." She glanced over toward the desk with a large computer screen. "Do you mind?"

"Not at all."

She walked to the desk, sat down and typed on the search page. Clicked. Read. Clicked some more.

A minute later, she said, "Here we are! There was a Greek historian named Polybius who lived a couple of hundred years before Christ. Among other things, Polybius invented a type of encryption device." She studied the computer screen. "You make a grid that is five squares by five squares. You write the letters of the alphabet in the squares. Then you can assign two numbers to each letter based on which horizontal row and which vertical column the letter's in. So A would be One, One, for row one and column one. B would be One, Two, for row one and column two. The device is called a Polybius Square. What fun! A cipher!" Harper said with enthusiasm. "Shall we try deciphering these numbers?"

"Have at it, please."

"Okay." She pulled out a pad of paper and drew a simple grid, five squares on a side. "I'll write the alphabet in the squares." She started writing and then turned back to the computer screen. "It says to put I and J in the same box. Of course. A five-by-five grid has twenty-five squares, and the alphabet has twenty-six letters. So we need to double up two letters. I and J are as good a pair as any other. Now, we'll take Lincoln's numbers and assign letters." She used her white-gloved fingertip to point at the numbers on Lincoln's letter, found the numbers and letter equivalent on the Polybius Square, then wrote the letters down.

"The cipher indicates that the letters that correspond to the numbers are…" She paused. "It's gibberish. It doesn't work. How disappointing!"

"Maybe there is another Greek dude who invented a different cipher."

"Maybe." Harper seemed dejected.

She stared at the letter for a minute. "Maybe Lincoln wrote it backward." She started at the last numbers and worked the other direction. "No, that doesn't work either. There's something else we're not thinking of."

"Aside from the number code, what do you make of the letter's content?" I asked.

"There's lots here to digest. But at the core, it seems that Lincoln knew that Stanford was a crook."

TWENTY-SEVEN

"Calling Stanford a crook is a strong statement," I said.

"Not to those of us who know him well," Harper said.

"Can you elaborate?"

"Well, it's obvious that Lincoln wanted to warn Stanford that people would be watching how he handled the railroad financing as he helped build the transcontinental railroad. What's not obvious is that it might be likely that Lincoln had heard negative things about Stanford. Things that, along with Stanford's comments about souvenirs of business, probably made Lincoln suspect that Stanford might help himself to public money."

"For a person who runs an archive of Stanford information, you don't have a very high opinion of him."

Harper looked around at the bookshelves. "The reason is that there's a lot of information available that informs my opinion. Lincoln's worries were later born out by many sources. Huge amounts of money from the railroad financing ended up in the pockets of Stanford and his cronies. The Pacific Railroad Commission in eighteen eighty-seven collected vast amounts of relevant information and produced several thousands of pages of documentation. They found that Stanford had lied and defrauded the American people of over sixty million dollars. And that's back when a million dollars was a great deal of money. It would be over a billion dollars in today's money. Simply stolen and hidden by reams of business paperwork. As governor, Stanford also defrauded the California taxpayers, funneling state dollars to his railroad and from there into his own pockets."

"What was his explanation?"

Harper shook her head. "He refused to testify. And two of

the judges who were ruling on a case relative to him were men he had appointed to their positions. He never commented on or acknowledged his theft, nor did he pay any price. He just walked into his dotage with an astonishing, ill-gotten fortune."

"Did the U.S. government just hand the railroads money?"

"The simple answer is, yes. Large quantities. Which Lincoln no doubt anticipated and which was likely the cause for his concern. The government made per-mile payments in three tiers. One price for level grade construction such as what we have here in the Central Valley. That base price was sixteen thousand dollars per mile. A second price for track laid on an incline in the foothills. Thirty-two thousand per mile. And the third and highest price paid for track constructed in the high Sierra. Sixty-four thousand per mile."

"Seems cheap, actually."

Harper shook her head. "Those amounts are eighteen sixty-one dollars. To get a rough idea of what that would be in today's dollars, multiply by about thirty."

"Let me think," I said. "Sixty-four thousand times thirty..." Harper was silent as I worked the numbers in my head... "would be about two million dollars. Two million to build a mile of track in the mountains. Even that doesn't seem like a big deal."

"I agree," Harper said. "But the base payments were just the beginning. On top of the base rate, the government paid all manner of other expenses."

"I don't understand."

"Railroad companies all across the country padded their expenses. Sometimes they laid track that went nowhere. In some cases, they built needless loops of track to increase the total mileage of track and billed the Federal government for it. In some places, two railroad companies each built a track next to one another, double tracks where there was only supposed to be one track. That meant the government was paying twice as much as intended."

"That seems like clear fraud."

"In effect, absolutely. But these railroad men were smart crooks. They buried their theft in paperwork."

"I always thought Stanford was a good guy, starting the university and such. Instead, you're saying he was stealing from the government. And earlier you said that his wife Jane was the main driver in starting the university. And to think your job is about preserving his legacy." I said it with a mocking tone.

"I care about the truth," Harper said. "There's no question that Stanford University is one of the world's greatest educational facilities. He and, even more, his wife Jane deserve credit for that. Leland Stanford was both good and bad."

"It sounds like you're not done with the bad."

"Taking excessive direct payments from the government was just the tip of the fraud."

"He stole more than the payments?"

"Much more. Railroad finance in the nineteenth century was even more complex than the physical building of the railroad." She stood up and walked over to the wall of bookshelves. There was a tall, square wooden box on the floor. In it were multiple rolls of paper standing on end. She pulled one out, brought it over to the big library table, and unrolled it, using long plastic bars to weigh down its edges and hold it flat.

It was a map of Northern California and Northern Nevada, vaguely similar to modern U.S. Geological Survey maps but much older, with yellowed paper and curly type fonts that looked Victorian in design.

"You know about checkerboarding, right?" she asked.

"No, I'm sorry, I don't."

The woman pointed with her fingertip. Across the map was a broad ribbon of yellowed squares that alternated with white squares.

"You've probably seen maps like these, divided into squares with every other square white and the other squares tinted."

"Yes. I have topographical maps like these, except the squares are variously white and green. Like a checkerboard. But I never knew what they represented."

"Each square is a mile on a side. The U.S. government worried that simply paying construction money to the railroads might give them an incentive to build cheap, bill high, and pocket the difference. So the government got the idea to make part of their payment in land. They gave the railroad the strip of land on which to build the tracks and then also gave them every other square mile for twenty miles on either side of the railroad. That was the checkerboarding. The railroad company would theoretically have an incentive to build higher quality tracks in order to raise the value of the land. Then the railroads could sell off this more valuable land to private parties who could build towns and other useful infrastructure. The land sales were supposed to help pay for railroad construction. The government planned to later sell the alternating squares they still owned. Thus the grand plan was to use land grants to both fund the transcontinental railroad and – down the road – raise cash for the federal government."

"Clever," I said.

"Yes, but full of problems. The worst was that the land grants put railroads in the business of selling land, and as you can imagine, this complexity created significant opportunities for graft and corruption. The federal government tried to retain some oversight of the process, but they pretty much lost control."

"Railroad executives taking the money for themselves instead of using it to build tracks?" I said.

"Yes, and on a huge scale. It was impossible for federal authorities to know how much money was involved and where the money was going. The railroad companies started separate financing companies to handle payments from the government and the money from land sales. The finance companies were used to pay construction companies to actually build the railway. The price gouging that resulted was huge."

I felt I was missing Harper's point. "I'm not understanding how this worked."

"It's a common way to make business dealings inscrutable to an outside viewer. Here's a simplified explanation. The government gave money to a company to build the railroad. The company took the payments from the government and the revenue from selling checkerboard land. They became a specialized finance company. This finance company hired a construction company to actually do the railroad construction."

When she talked of the finance company, she gestured to the right. When she spoke of the construction company, she gestured to the left. Her white-gloved hands were like a mime's. She used movements to clarify her words.

"But it turned out that the finance company and the construction company were both owned by the same men. So the construction company charged exorbitant construction prices to the finance company. The prices were much higher than the actual costs. That allowed the men who owned both companies to put a big chunk of that extra charge in their pockets and make it hard for anyone on the outside to know what was really happening."

"But wouldn't the government have had some kind of auditing role? So they could see what was really going on?" I asked.

"It's hard. A government auditor examining the finance company's books would find that the finance company paid what appeared to be legitimate construction bills submitted by the construction company. That same auditor might not have the authority or time or additional manpower to examine the construction company's books. But even if the auditor could examine the construction company's books, the additional layer of complexity would make it very hard to identify theft."

It started to make sense. I said, "And the construction company would have hired other contractors, and maybe those contractors paid kickbacks to get the job. And those contractors would pad their invoices in order to cover the kickbacks. And some of those contractors might be the same men who owned the finance company and the construction company. And maybe some of those contractors didn't actually do anything but skim money from the pot. It would be a nightmare for the auditor to uncover what really went on."

Brady Harper gave me a big grin. "You just explained the essence of graft and corruption in business and politics."

"You think this is what President Lincoln was referring to in his letter to Stanford."

She took a deep breath as if she were short of air. "Partly, yes."

"Is this supposition on your part? Or do other historians agree with you?"

"You've heard the term robber baron?" she asked.

"Yeah. It describes an unscrupulous businessman, right?"

"Yes. Stanford was one of the worst. Historians agree that much of his money was ill-gotten. That was corroborated by the Pacific Railroad Commission."

"You say Stanford was one of the worst. Implying there were other robber barons?"

"Many. Stanford's buddies who helped start the Central Pacific Railroad and made him its president were part of the same racket. We refer to these guys as The Big Four. Stanford's primary business partner, Mark Hopkins, was one."

"The man who built the Mark Hopkins Hotel in San Francisco," I said.

"Right. And Charles Crocker and Collis Huntington, who were both merchants who sold hardware, primarily to miners. They were all in tight business relationships with Stanford."

"I know the Crocker name because of the Crocker Museum in Sacramento. But I don't know Huntington. Is he connected to the Huntington Gardens in L.A.?"

"Yes. In addition to his role with the Central Pacific Railroad, he helped build the Southern Pacific Railroad, Southern California's electric system, the famous Huntington Library and Botanical Gardens, and gradually acquired one of the country's largest art collections, which he then donated to New York's Metropolitan Museum. He was also a benefactor of Yale University and built several hospitals."

"Is that all. So he was a charitable good guy?" I said.

"Actually, he might have been the worst robber baron of all. Like many of these guys, Huntington was caught with his hand in the cash drawer on significant occasions. And he was caught bribing politicians. People hated him."

"You have a bad attitude toward these guys."

"Anyone would, once you know what they really did. Certainly, they did some good stuff, but it's tempting to start universities and build hospitals when you want to put a little gloss on your life as one of the greatest thieves in American history."

"Another strong statement," I said.

"A true statement nevertheless. There's no question that the railroads transformed the country in many good ways. But they had many downsides."

"More than financial theft?"

"Yeah. But you didn't come here for my opinions on that."

"Sure, I did."

Brady Harper looked at me as if trying to see my interior. "Okay, I'll take you at your word. The downside that troubles me most is what happened to the Native Americans who lived on that land."

"The land the railroads went through," I said.

"Right. They'd been on that land for ten thousand years. No attempt was made to accommodate their needs or wishes. No one asked them what they thought. No one tried to pay them. They were considered to be savages, less than human. We accorded them no rights at all. Our ancestors just took their land and checkerboarded it, sold it off, and ran the railroad through. Then we forced them onto reservations and told them it was a favor for them. A gift."

TWENTY-EIGHT

As Brady Harper recounted the dark history of what happened to the Native Americans, I remembered some of the details I'd learned over the years. But, perhaps like most Americans, I had no idea how to respond. I had come into her archive thinking I was merely going to learn about a letter that Jade Jaso's father had acquired. A short time later I had learned that California's most famous men were up to their elbows in theft, and the railroads they built came at enormous costs to both indigenous people and the Chinese laborers, and the U.S. and California taxpayers.

As if reading my mind, Harper said, "I should let you know that there are revisionist historians who make the claim that Stanford and his cronies weren't so bad."

"You mean, they don't think Stanford and the other Big Four pocketed public monies?"

Harper shook her head. "No, they're not claiming those guys didn't steal. There's too much documentation about that. Instead, what they say is that these rich men did so much good for the country that it partially negated the corruption." As Harper said it, she pinched her lips and rolled her eyes like a school teacher who caught a kid stealing from the candy jar and then listened to the kid's justification that he stole to feed the hungry.

"In other words," I said, "because these guys donated money for schools and art museums, it made up for stealing from the public."

"Something like that. Morality is in the eye of the beholder."

"Or the revisionist historians," I said.

She smiled. "Anyway, that's the end of my rant. I always go

on too long." She turned and perched her hip on one of the library tables. "Earlier, you said you had a question about a guy who died in a fall, the person who had this letter," Harper said.

"The man's name was Billy Jaso."

"And the fall was suspicious?" she said. She touched her finger splint as she said it.

"Possibly. Most deadly falls are accidents. Especially when they involve an older person. This man was in his late seventies, so that could apply. However, he was apparently robust. Physically-fit people in their seventies do not commonly suffer falls so traumatic that they die. Speaking of which, it looks like you took a bad fall."

"Yes. I'm healing, but slowly. I try to remind myself that it could have been worse." She paused as if recalling a bad dream. "Do you have evidence to suggest that the death of this man who died in a fall was not accidental?" She frowned.

"Not direct evidence. Not even circumstantial evidence. Just questions."

"And they involve Leland Stanford?"

"Indirectly, yeah. Billy Jaso, the man who died, owned this letter from Lincoln to Stanford." I was thinking about how it had been effectively hidden. "When someone dies under questionable circumstances, we look at everything that was important to the person." I gestured at the letter under the plastic weights. "And now his daughter Jade Jaso has gone missing, which is always a strong indication that something is not right."

"Oh, no. I'm so sorry. That's terrible." Harper looked very distressed, almost on the verge of tears. It was a reaction I wouldn't have expected.

Harper said, "Do you think she's in danger? Or could she have just wanted to get away and not tell anyone where she was going?"

"Maybe. She seemed close to her father, and his death had a big effect on her."

Harper held my eyes for a long moment. I couldn't tell what she was thinking.

I continued, "I'm hoping that you, as a librarian, which is

to say keeper of literary and metaphoric stuff, would know what to look for as far as any possible connection between this letter from Lincoln and Jade Jaso going missing."

"Metaphoric stuff. Elegant phrasing," she said.

"Specialty of private eyes," I said.

She paused, seemed to look off into space, then said, "There is one thing that comes to mind. I should preface it by saying that I deal in documented fact. And what I'm about to say is mere speculation, a combination of rumors reinforced with odd thoughts that I've had now and then as I've cataloged the items in this archive."

"Such as..." I said.

"Such as a notion I have about Stanford's keepsake valuables."

TWENTY-NINE

At Harper's mention of Stanford's valuables, I said. "Ouch. It hurts when you pique my interest so hard it's like setting a hook."

Harper didn't grin, which showed that she took the rumor with complete seriousness. She walked over to one of the library tables, pulled out a chair, and sat down. She put one leg up on the table, her calf lying flat on the table surface. She pushed off with her other leg and leaned the chair back on its rear two legs until it was at a balance point. It was a common move that I used all the time to recline chairs not meant to recline. But from where I stood, it looked precarious. There was no soft rug or furniture behind her. If she fell over and hit her head, the fall could be potentially deadly. Maybe this was how she broke her finger and split open her chin. I wanted to protest, but that would seem condescending. This was her office. She could behave however she wanted.

Brady Harper stared off toward the wall of books. Her big blue eyes were unfocused behind the Mason jar glasses. It seemed she wasn't looking at the books but at something in her mind. She was trying to make a decision.

I waited, not wanting to interrupt her thoughts.

After a moment, she rocked forward on her chair so that all four legs were back on the floor.

She said, "When a journalist gets a glimmer of a story and finds evidence supporting her idea, she still has to corroborate the story from another source or two before deciding if the idea has any truth to it."

"Where are you on this spectrum?"

"I got the glimmer some time back and, since then, have found several bits of evidence that reinforce my idea. But I'm a long way from proving it true. But this letter and its intimations of something valuable – what did Stanford call it – souvenirs of business, puts my thought into sharper focus. But I will still have to do a lot of digging to be sure."

"The glimmer-to-truth passage is an arduous one," I said.

She made a single nod. "Are you familiar with Samuel Brannan?" she asked.

"Never heard of him."

She paused. "Where do I begin." Harper stood, walked over to her podium desk, picked up a thermos cup I hadn't seen, and sipped.

"Samuel Brannan is worth knowing about, so I'll give you a little background. Brannan was a contemporary of the Big Four, although he didn't know them early on. He was born in eighteen nineteen in Maine, so he was a few years older than Stanford, who was born in eighteen twenty-four. Brannan became an early convert to Mormonism. In eighteen forty-six, when Brannan was twenty-seven, he and a bunch of Mormons traveled by ship from the East Coast, taking the route I previously mentioned, around the tip of South America and back up our West Coast. He ended up in Yerba Buena, which, back then, was a little village in what was then Mexico but was destined to become the growing city of San Francisco. The Mexican-American War had begun during the six months the Mormons were on the ship. By the time they landed in July of eighteen forty-six, the U.S. had taken Yerba Buena, and it became part of the United States."

"Lotta stuff goin' on back then," I said.

"More elegant P.I. phrasing," she said with a smile. "Samuel Brannan started the first newspaper in Northern California, the California Star. His paper was the first to publicize the new gold rush. Conveniently, he started a hardware store at Sutter's Fort, which, as you probably know, is just a couple of miles from here in Sacramento. Like other merchants of the time, Brannan's store sold miner's supplies. But Brannan got there first. For a time, his was the only hardware store between San Francisco and Gold Country. And his customers were people who'd read about the discovery of gold in his newspaper. A classic case of cross promotion from one business to another. Brannan made big money and became California's first millionaire. Later, he founded the towns of Calistoga and Yuba City. During his business career, he'd gotten to know all of the Big Four railroad robber barons."

"Let me test my memory," I said. "Leland Stanford, Mark Hopkins, Charles Crocker, and Collis Huntington."

"Very good. You get an A." She sipped from the thermos cup.

"If these guys were all buddies, does that mean they shared Stanford's prejudice against the Chinese?"

Harper frowned. "I don't know. Maybe. I suppose it wasn't as bad as the prejudice against blacks. That was still the era when white men owned black people and controlled every aspect of their lives."

"A bleak indictment of my group."

Harper kept talking. "And when Lincoln made changes toward setting blacks free, the south went to war over it. Good heavens, how dare we say that whites can't own black people the same way they owned cattle. So whites killed each other over the issue. As you no doubt know, a huge percentage of all young American men died fighting for or against the right to own black people."

I nodded.

"And then John Wilkes Booth, a Confederate sympathizer, assassinated Lincoln for his crime of setting blacks free."

"Where was California on slavery?"

"Generally, California supported freedom for blacks. And that was a major reason the Whigs decided to form the new Republican Party. They wanted to make a clearer statement that blacks should be free."

"Why do you say California was generally pro freedom for blacks?" I said, getting used to Brady Harper's tendency to imply other meanings.

"Officially, California didn't want slavery in the state. However, many think that the real desire behind the anti-slavery stance was to simply keep blacks out of the state altogether. If word got out that you couldn't have slaves in California, then white slave owners wouldn't move with their slaves to California, and California wouldn't end up with so many blacks."

"This is an eye opener," I said.

Harper nodded. "At least California didn't go as far as Oregon, where blacks were simply outlawed in eighteen forty-four. If blacks tried to settle in Oregon, they were publicly whipped." Harper made a slow shake of her head as if she struggled to believe what she was saying. "I digressed again."

"No worries. I'm interested in this. But back to Samuel Brannan," I said. "Why did he matter?"

"Because the California Star, Brannan's newspaper, ran a story about Stanford's secret stash."

THIRTY

"Secret stash?" I repeated. "Is Brannan's story going to be exciting enough that I should be ordering in pizza and beer?"

Big grin. "I can't do pizza today." She looked at the time. "I have to leave for a couple of hours. But maybe we can lunch another day?"

"That'll have to do. When the time comes, can I bring my girlfriend?"

A cloud seemed to pass over the spectacular eyes. "What, um, does your girlfriend do? I suppose she's a Tahoe girl, all about skiing and hiking."

"Well, it's true she's an avid skier and hiker. Her name is Street Casey. She's an entomologist. Ph.D. from Berkeley."

Brady Harper's eyes widened. "A scientist! In Tahoe! How wonderful. Yes of course, bring her. Interesting name."

"Her mother didn't make it to the hospital in time. She was born in the street."

"Cool," Harper said. "We'll definitely do pizza and beer."

"Could we meet here in the hallowed archives? Street would love this place."

"Not only can we meet here, we can eat here. I even have a checkered table cloth."

"Checkerboarding extended from railroad land to the Stanford Archive tablecloths," I said. "I'll plan on it."

Brady Harper stood.

I said, "In the meantime, when can I get the story of Stanford's secret stash?"

"Can you come back at two o'clock? I should be back by then."

"I'll be here.

I left the Stanford Archive.

I'd previously looked up Dell Davis, the man who had scammed people on a movie investment, then lost his horse Dixie when he didn't pay the boarding farm and they sold the horse under the equine lien foreclosure law. Davis had spent some years in Folsom prison and was now out on parole. His flunky Jackie Willowisp had come to the Jaso Ranch in an attempt to steal back the horse that was now known as Anne Gregory. With some persuasion from me, Jackie revealed that Dell Davis liked to hang out at the Flower Blossom Club, a business name that sounded to me like a cover for a gambling operation. With some research, I'd found reference to the name in connection to a bar in a tacky neighborhood north of downtown Sacramento.

So I drove to the bar and parked. It was like a warehouse with no windows. But it had a little orange neon sign that flashed, "Bar Open." There were lots of cars in the lot.

"C'mon, Largeness, let's go check out a bar."

I took his collar and walked over to the door, a solid steel door with no window.

I pulled it open. Spot and I walked in.

The bar was small and boring. There was a metal bar along the left side, three pool tables on the right side, six booths in a row beyond the pool tables. The lighting was beer-brand signs, one of which flashed an irritating blue. The bottles behind the bar ran to cheap brands of vodka and tequila.

"No dogs," a long-haired bartender called out.

I ignored him. I paused to look around. Spot was hyper-alert for the simple reason that it was unusual territory. Spot and I walked past a couple of pool players who wore matching black cowboy hats, one of whom had a dramatic bulge under his shirt on the left side of his waist. One man was morbidly obese, the other morbidly skinny. The skinny one had a lit cigarette dangling from his lips. They glanced at us, looked for a long moment at Spot, and, with surprising calm, ignored him and went back to their game.

"I said no dogs," the bartender repeated.

I ignored him a second time. Despite all the cars in the lot, there were only the two pool players and a couple of solitary drinkers in the bar.

I walked back toward the rear of the bar, sensing a growing volume of music. There was another solid metal door.

"Hey, you can't go in there," the bartender called out behind me.

I pushed the door open. A huge, tall Hispanic man, fat but strong, suddenly stood up from a stool. He wore a black sport jacket over a black T-shirt, which was tucked into black jeans. Behind him was a stripper bar, lots of pink and red lighting, flashing orange neon, loud throbbing music, two young women naked on top and wearing only red thongs on the bottom, doing tricks on the poles. There were enough customers to explain the number of cars in the parking lot. Several of the customers were playing cards at two tables in the corner.

"Sorry dude," the bouncer said. "Members only."

"I'm Detective Owen McKenna." I flashed him the 19th century constable badge that I bought at a tourist shop in Virginia City. It's a golden shield with a glossy blue cloisonne design in the center, and it's attached to the front of my wallet's credit card slot. It looks surprisingly convincing.

"You gotta do a lot more than that to impress me," he said.

I lifted Spot's collar a bit, and he immediately responded by sniffing the man's crotch. "Then assume we're members, unless you want to pull your piece and see how fast this hound responds to my command."

The man was impressively stone-faced. He lifted his hands out from his sides just enough to worry me.

Maybe Spot had him quaking inside. Maybe not. I bent a little, tapped Spot's throat, and made a growling sound.

Spot looked at me and wagged.

"Go on, do it." I growled again.

Spot growled.

"Good boy, Show him you mean it." I growled in Spot's ear.

Spot lifted his lips, exposing the big fangs, and growled

louder.

The big man took a step back. His pink-brown face lost some of the brown and gained a little more pink.

I leaned in close to the man. "I'm only here to collar one of your customers. You're going to lend me your piece for a bit. Insurance, so to speak. Point it away from me and unload it. Don't worry, I'll give it back in a few minutes." The man looked down at Spot's jaws in front of important body parts, reached inside his jacket, and lifted a Glock out of its holster. Moving very slowly, he released the magazine and put it in his pocket. Then he ejected the round in the chamber and handed the empty gun to me. I hefted the gun, then did a simple sleight-of-hand that we used to practice at the SFPD. You pretend to pull a round out of your pocket and load the gun. The technique varies according to the pistol. It's never believable to anyone who's watching carefully. But it was a good surprise for the bouncer, because he thought he had the upper hand, and he wasn't paying attention. The fact that his weapon used a 9 mm bullet, the most common ammo, a bullet which I might realistically carry around in the coin pocket of my jeans, played into the believability of my charade. I could see the surprise in the bouncer's eyes. He'd been thinking about his backup weapon and how he'd use it to take me down. I pointed his Glock at his belly. "Now hand me your other piece," I said.

"There's no other piece."

"Yes there is. Probably on your ankle. Pull it out real slow." I tapped Spot on his throat, and he upped his growl for a moment, baring his fangs just inches from the man's belt.

The man slowly lifted his leg and hooked his heel on the cross rung of the stool. He bent down and reached to his ankle.

I pressed the muzzle of his gun into his belly flesh. "Slow," I said again.

The man lifted his backup, holding it by the barrel. It was a Beretta Pico.

I slid it and the Glock into my pockets. "You call anybody, make any noise, I keep these. If not, I return them soon, and you'll never see me again."

I palmed a dog biscuit and held my hand next to Spot's nose. No one could see the biscuit, but Spot could smell it. I pointed at the man. "Watch this man. If he moves, remember that farm we went to when the farmer was castrating young bulls and fed the cojones to you? You loved them!" I pointed at the man again and walked over toward the stage.

I recognized Dell Davis from a photo I got off the California Prison Roster website. I'd always thought the access fee wasn't worth it. But this time it was. Davis was on the far side of 55, with unwashed, longish gray hair that had been combed into place and held there by skin oil. He had on a Hawaiian shirt with a collar that was frayed and, despite the distracting color patterns, showed the brown of accumulated dirt. His pants were thin gray fabric stretched tight over flabby thighs.

He was sitting in a chair that he had pulled out from a table and turned around so that one of the dancers could give him a lap dance if she were sufficiently desperate to do it at a price he could afford.

I pulled out a chair and sat in front of him, close in, crowding his personal space.

"Looking for Jade Jaso," I said, leaning over toward him, speaking near his ear.

"Don't know what you mean."

"Yes, you do. Her father bought your horse Dixie for her. You sent Mr. Willowisp to steal Dixie, and that was a bad move. He gave you up."

Davis reached under his Hawaiian shirt and grabbed at something that sounded like Velcro.

"I'll take that," I said as I lifted his shirt and got hold of the hand that was pulling out a gun.

He tried to hang onto the piece. I made sure it was pointed away from people as I slammed his wrist down on the edge of the nearby table. I'd taken more guns off of men in the last few days than in the previous five years.

When Davis's wrist hit the table, he cried out and released his grip. The gun dropped to the table. It was a Colt 380 Mustang. I used a table napkin to pick it up and put it in the same pocket where I'd put the bouncer's Beretta. "Lots of pocket pistols in this joint."

He grabbed onto my arm with his uninjured hand.

I said, "Let go or I'll hit you so you can't breathe."

He pulled his hand away, farther than necessary, as if winding up for a home run.

I hit the man hard in the solar plexus. It knocked out his wind. His eyes went wide, and he bent over.

"Hang in there, buddy. Your breathing will come back in an hour or so. The soreness in your diaphragm will go away in two weeks."

I patted him down and found no other weapons.

I stood up and walked over near the bouncer who was still watching Spot. I gave Spot a pet and said, "Good boy, keep it up." I handed Spot a biscuit, pointed at the bouncer again, and turned to the nearby bar, which was much classier than the plain one in the front room.

"Bartender? That man over there is my prisoner, a convicted felon, illegally armed, AWOL from parole, a suspect in multiple crimes even including horse theft, if you can imagine that. Do you have some packing tape?"

The bartender nodded and glanced around at the bar and room, no doubt hoping there was no one else causing trouble. He reached down to a shelf under the bar, pulled out a hand-held tape dispenser, and set it on the bar.

I nodded at the bouncer as I took the tape back to Dell Davis, who was still bent over. I crossed his wrists behind his back and put tape around them.

I pulled out his wallet and flipped through his cards. He had five driver's licenses and about two dozen credit cards in a variety of names. I didn't bother taking a close look.

I put the wallet in with my growing weapons collection.

I lifted Davis so he was sitting up. "This is a one-way communication. I talk, you don't, except to answer my questions. If you try to say anything else, I hit you again, then I tape your mouth shut. Understand?"

He was beginning to get a little air in his lungs. It took all of his concentration.

"Back to Jade Jaso. You tell me where she is, I make your life sweet."

He shook his head, his mouth open a little. I didn't know if that meant he wouldn't or couldn't give me an answer.

"Last chance," I said. I pulled my arm back a bit, made a fist, and moved it enough that he could see it was aimed at his gut.

"No idea," he wheezed.

I called Sergeant Bains and explained that I'd found Dell Davis, the man who'd sent Jackie Willowisp to steal Anne Gregory.

"I'm wondering if you can look up the name of Davis's parole officer."

"Take me a minute," Bains said.

I waited.

Davis focused on breathing.

Spot was watching the bouncer, but he kept stealing glances toward me. No doubt thinking about another dog treat.

Two minutes later, Bains was back. "The PO is Jason Bradley," he said. He recited the phone number. Then he asked, "Does Davis know where Jade is?"

"Not that I can scare out of him. Thanks for the info."

I dialed the number Bains had given me.

"Jason Bradley."

"Are you Dell Davis's PO?" I asked.

"Who's this?"

"Owen McKenna, ex-Homicide Inspector with the SFPD, now private in Tahoe. I was tracking down a horse thief and potential murder and kidnapping suspect and learned about Dell Davis. Sergeant Bains of the El Dorado Sheriff's Office told me that he's your parolee."

"He absconded on his parole three months ago. He'll go back inside when I find him."

"I'm with him here in Sacramento."

"Let me talk to that SOB."

"He's having a little trouble breathing. He didn't like something I said, and he pulled on me. So I poked him in the gut. It'll be a few minutes before he's talkative."

"He was carrying?"

"A Colt Three-eighty Mustang, his sweaty hand prints all over it. It's now wrapped in a napkin and sitting in my pocket."

"He was sentenced to three years for grand theft, released after serving two. He's got enough restrictions on his parole that absconding parole means he'll go right back to prison. Carrying a weapon will get him more time. Where is he now?"

"At the Flower Blossom Club."

"Never heard of it."

"A gambling room and strip joint tucked in the back of a bar north of downtown." I gave him the address. "I'll hold Davis for you if you can send someone soon."

"I'm coming myself. Give me fifteen."

I clicked off and walked back to the bouncer. I spoke softly. "I appreciate your cooperation. So I'm going to give you back your sidearms if you agree to make a silent exit out the back door. That way you keep your pieces, and you avoid the coming uniforms. Capeesh?"

He nodded. I handed him his guns.

He walked toward a door that had a restroom sign over it. Before he walked through the door, he called over his shoulder, "If you want to play Italian, capisci is more accurate."

"Good to know," I said.

Jason Bradley came into the room ten minutes later. There was no bouncer to stop him. He walked over to me, reached for Dell Davis's arm, lifted him to his feet. I gave Bradford the Colt 380 wrapped in the napkin and Davis's wallet.

"His wallet has an interesting collection of cards you might want to look at," I said.

Bradley nodded, then looked around at the strip club. "These places float around, off the radar. Not paying their share of taxes. What would the church-going guvment types think?"

"Maybe a contradiction in terms?" I said.

"That guvment types go to church? Or that guvment types think?" he said.

"Good question."

THIRTY-ONE

I was standing outside the locked door to the Stanford Archive at two o'clock. It was ten minutes before Brady Harper showed up.

"Sorry I'm late," she said as she unlocked the door.

"No need. You didn't ask me to interrupt your day. I'm very grateful for your help."

She put her purse over by the podium desk, picked up a pencil, and made a note in what looked like a Dayplanner notebook even though she was young enough and tech-savvy enough to use her phone and computer for such tasks.

She straightened and turned to me. "Where were we?"

"You were going to tell me how this Samuel Brannan dude was the key to Stanford's secret stash."

"Oh, yes, of course. Back to Brannan." She paused to think about it. "On May fifteenth, eighteen fifty-seven, Brannan's newspaper the California Star published a story about an old Chinese man who approached Stanford with an offer. If Stanford would agree to give mining or railroad jobs to all five of the old man's sons, the man would give him a priceless artifact that he had brought from China. It was a no-lose situation for Stanford. After all, he was already employing thousands of Chinese laborers. This was merely fast-tracking the process to please one Chinese family. However, the article also said that Stanford denied that he'd taken a bribe."

"What was the priceless artifact being offered?"

Brady Harper grinned with the big jumble of white teeth. "That's the question to which we don't have an answer. But I found a clue."

"I bet you did."

Harper continued as if I hadn't said anything. "I was

going through a box of Stanford's papers. It was a jumble, no organization at all. I decided that many years ago, someone had dumped Stanford's paperwork as if to throw it away, then reconsidered and shoveled it all into a box. There were handwritten thank-you notes that people had written to Stanford. Tickets to plays. Old newspaper clippings, awards, letters, some early black-and-white photos, acknowledgments of charity donations. A couple of pieces of musical notepaper. A string-tied catalog from some kind of art auction. Scribbled reminder notes that Stanford had written to himself. Lists of legislators divided into good guys and bad guys. Shopping lists."

"Wait. Are you serious? Lists about who were the good guys and bad guys?"

Harper made a little sigh. "Stanford was clever smart, not intellectual smart. He had little erudition. His library was about appearances not information. So he didn't consider men in terms of their educated philosophical leanings. They were just good guys or bad guys, friends or foes."

"Was there something in that box of notes that mentioned Stanford's keepsake valuables?"

"Not specifically. But," she said, the Mediterranean Seas shimmering behind her glasses, "I found something that implies as much."

She stood up and walked over to one of the bookcases near the corner. On the bottom shelf were several fat binders of the type I'd seen used for scrapbooks. She pulled one out and brought it over to the library table. It was black, about 11 x 14, and 3 inches thick.

Harper sat down next to me and started flipping through it.

"Just curious," I said, "you catalog all this stuff and enter it into a computer database. But you don't consult the computer. You just pull it off the shelf. Do you know where everything is?"

She nodded. "Yup. I've got it all memorized. If a patron wants to see a bit of information, I email it to them, or I send them a link to a PDF. But if I want to see something, I prefer to get the actual piece of paper off the shelf." She flipped through the binder.

There were pages of items like she'd described. She came to a page with an off-white envelope. She opened the flap and pulled out a piece of paper that had been folded in thirds.

"This is a copy of the old piece of paper. This way we can see what it says without the stress of unfolding the original. The original is dated November first, eighteen fifty-eight. You'll no doubt remember that year as the one when Lincoln had his famous debates about slavery with Stephen Douglas, the senator from Illinois."

"I'm sorry, but you seriously overrate my knowledge."

She grinned. "Never too late to learn, right?"

I grinned back.

She lifted the paper she'd pulled out of the envelope and held it close to her face. "This is a work order with a description for work to be done and supplies required."

Once again, Brady Harper put her cotton-gloved fingertip under each word, no doubt to help with her bad vision. This time it was her left fingertip as she read aloud. I followed along. As with Lincoln's letter, her reading was halting and hesitant. Despite what looked like healthy eyes, the scholar had such bad vision that she could barely read. But she didn't seem self-conscious about it.

"At the top it has a business name: 'Tom's Woodworking, Sacramento.' Below that it says, 'Construction of boxes with internal custom support cradles to securely store and protect guardian lions.'"

"Any idea what that means?"

"I would guess it refers to the classic Chinese yin-and-yang guardian lions. They are a common sculpture subject, male and female lions that, in much of Chinese culture, are put at entrances to temples and tombs. You've probably seen some, even if you don't recall it. They've been in use for two thousand years, symbolically guarding the building from bad spirits. The concept has spread to much of the world, East Asia particularly. As you face a building, the female goes to the left of the entrance, and she has her paw on a cub, representing nurturing and protecting the inhabitants of the building. She is the yin. The male, the yang, goes to the right of the entrance, and he has his paw on a ball, which represents protecting the building and the physical world."

"What size are they?"

"They can be huge, many feet tall, made of stone or bronze. They can weigh thousands of pounds. But they can also be small figurines, like something you would put on a shelf."

"You think Stanford got a pair of these lions as a bribe to hire a man's sons, and he had a custom box built to hold them for safe keeping."

"That would be my guess, yes."

"How valuable are these guardian lions?"

"Like all art, it depends on who made them, the quality of the work, what they're made of, when they were made. Now you can buy fiberglass and plastic guardian lions cheap, even large ones. They are available in many places in Chinatown in San Francisco. But there are priceless guardian lion sculptures in museums that date back to ancient times."

"Are they ever made from jade?"

"Absolutely."

"The woman who went missing comes from a long history of jade carvers."

"That's perfect!"

"But the question remains," I said, "if Stanford did in fact get valuable carvings from the old Chinese guy, why were they secret? Why would he deny that the treasure existed?"

"Two reasons. One is that Stanford was concerned with his image. He wouldn't want people to think that he was so greedy that he'd take a bribe for hiring people when he was actively hiring hundreds of people anyway. The second reason was that, even though this was in the days of the wild west, it was still likely illegal to accept a bribe to hire someone."

I said, "Assuming the article in the California Star is true, Stanford got a valuable treasure, and he probably hid it to wait for the story to die down. So all we have to do is find it."

THIRTY-TWO

"Let's say you do find Stanford's treasure," Harper said. "Will that help you find the missing woman?"

"I don't know. But because I have no clues about where to look for her, I have to consider any related information as potentially valuable."

I gestured at the paper she held. "What are the other items on that work order?"

"I'll read it. 'Each cradle to be approximately twelve inches square by twelve inches deep. Cradle to be fitted with appropriate padding and lined with soft fabric.' Below that description is a list of supplies: Quarter-inch cedar boards, hinges, bracing, latches, locks, and pine tar. I have no idea what pine tar is. Or was. I have yet to look that up."

"I can save you the trouble. Pine tar is a black sticky goo you get when you put pine wood into a sealed metal container and bake it at high temperature. Baseball players use it on bats to make it easier to grip them. And it is used in some dandruff shampoos."

"Black goo," Harper said as if to verify the words I'd used.

"Yeah."

"It doesn't seem germane to making a custom box." She pointed at the words on the paper.

I sat back in my chair.

"Why are you looking at my gloves?" she asked.

"I was just noticing that you use both your hands interchangeably. Sometimes you point with your left finger, sometimes with your right. That's unusual."

"Detectives are very observant," she said.

"Our job."

"I'm ambidextrous. I write with either hand, too."

"Ah."

I walked over to the windows and looked out and up at the thick tree canopy that Sacramento was famous for, a few redwoods mixed in with hundreds of maples and elms and dozens of other species. I paced along the wall, under the shelves of books, turned, paced back, turned and paced another round.

"It's exciting to see how a private eye does his work," Brady Harper said.

I paced some more. "Here's a wild idea. Or maybe not so wild. I remember another thing about pine tar. It's used as a wood preservative. If you paint it on wood, it keeps the wood from rotting. Especially useful in preserving wood that might get wet."

"Okay," Harper said, frowning.

I continued to pace.

"That's it!" Harper suddenly said at high volume. "Sacramento was always flooding back before they built the levees to hold in the Sacramento and American rivers. Downtown Sacramento would flood. In fact, it's said that Stanford had to go by rowboat from his house to his inauguration in January of eighteen sixty-two. It was because of the floods that Stanford and his wife eventually remodeled his downtown mansion and raised it twelve feet."

"And," I said, filling in where I thought Harper was going, "if Stanford wanted to store the box down in some dark corner of his basement, he would expect it to periodically get wet when the floods came. A wet box would hold moisture for months. Pine tar would help it resist rotting."

Harper said, "If the guardian lions were carved from jade, that would work. Put pine tar on the wood, put in some drainage holes and air holes... That could protect the lions. They didn't have cardboard boxes back then, at least not the kind we think of now. So a pine-tar box makes perfect sense." Harper turned and looked at me head on. The Mediterranean was scintillating.

She continued, "Stanford would figure that almost no one would ever go down into the basement of his mansion because it would be dirty, musty, and mildewed from the periodic floods that plagued Sacramento in the mid-nineteenth century. It would be the perfect place to hide treasure."

"Right. You ever get tired of all this boring archive stuff, you could intern with me and learn the art of private investigation."

"Maybe I will. What does a P.I. intern earn?"

"Nothing."

"Hmm," she said. "A new career does sound enticing. Especially if I'm risking murder and its associated activities. But the pay scale is a little weak."

"Good point," I said. "You don't want to go into the murder business lightly."

I gestured at the paper. "Do you believe that this took place? That Stanford took possession of some valuable guardian lions?"

She shrugged. "Hard to know. But the work order for a custom box certainly makes it look like he did."

"Let me do some more detective work," I said as I paced some more. Over to one wall, back to the first. Right turn, around the library tables, over to the windows. I turned to Harper. "Does it make sense to you that a Chinese father would give Stanford priceless artifacts just for hiring his five sons?"

"Only sort of," she said. "Imagine that you've traveled for months on a sailing ship, living in the dark hold of the ship, desperate to get to a new country where the sun shines and there is gold in the soil and railroads to be built. Your greatest desire is for your sons to find good jobs in this new land. You speak no English. But you've brought a great treasure that will be recognized for its value, no matter the language of the recipient. If that treasure can buy jobs for your boys, you will feel you've succeeded as a father."

She paused, thinking, pursing her lips as if dissatisfied.

"That makes sense," I said. "But you've got a hesitation."

"I understand the desire and motivation of the father," she said. "But there were lots of Chinese people around, some of whom would probably speak his language, Mandarin or Cantonese or whatever it was. It's likely he would have found fellow Chinese countrymen who'd been in California for awhile. I would think they'd have told the father that Stanford and other employers were hiring everyone they could get their hands on. No bribes necessary."

"Good point. But the father might think a bribe would give his boys more job security. They wouldn't be the first to get laid off if jobs were cut back." I pointed at the binder. "Any other tidbits in your little black book?"

"Yes, actually. In some ways, the best is coming."

I raised my eyebrows.

"Five weeks after the date of this work order, Stanford wrote a note to his lawyer and he kept a carbon copy." Harper went back to the original binder, turned pages, stopped, and read, again leaning in very close and pointing to each word as she read.

"'Sir, in regards to our conversation about a wayward employee, I'm responding with details. I've done some searching of my records and I've learned that one of my builder's employees here in Sacramento, a man named Benat Mendoza, also worked for me in Port Washington, Wisconsin. Or rather, he worked for the builder who was constructing my new library in Wisconsin when it burned down. Mendoza was the main woodworker. The builder went bankrupt and some of his employees claimed they were never paid. Benat Mendoza was allegedly one of them. I believe the bankrupt builder owed Mendoza substantial wages. Mendoza claimed that, because the builder was contracted by me, I should have been ultimately responsible. But of course, by the letter of the law, I was not in any way responsible. It wasn't my fault that the builder went bankrupt. Unknown to me, Mendoza came out to Sacramento – no doubt following me with a nefarious purpose – contacted a builder who was doing work on my Sacramento house, and applied to that builder for work. As Mendoza was a talented woodworker, my builder hired him on the spot. My builder was unaware, as was I, that Mendoza had worked on my library in Wisconsin several years before.'

"'After two months in my builder's employ, Benat Mendoza

left. He gave no advance notice, nor did he make any comments to the other employees. He simply didn't show up one day. I accepted it as an unfortunate yet-all-too-common experience with workers.'"

Harper glanced at me, then looked back at the paper and continued reading.

"'Several days later, I noticed that a particularly important item of mine – a work of art I had actually hidden – was missing. When I asked all the other employees who were working on my remodeling project, two of them said that they'd seen Mendoza inspecting areas of my house where he had no purpose.'"

Harper took a breath, then continued reading.

"'I've come to the conclusion that there is a significant likelihood that Mendoza took my artwork and left with it. I'm asking that you contact the authorities and request that they go through the formal motions of declaring Benat Mendoza to be a suspect in the theft. It is imperative that he be caught and interrogated. If he has my art, he should face the maximum penalty allowed under the law.'"

Harper turned and looked at me. "Suggestive, no?" she said.

"Very," I agreed. "I wonder if there is any way to track Mendoza's movements all these years later."

"One hundred fifty or sixty years is a long time," Harper said. "I've thought about how he might be tracked. The only thing that could possibly be a clue is that Benat Mendoza is a Basque name. If someone maintained a Basque archive, so to speak, maybe someone could find references to Mendoza written in Basque."

"My client's father was Billy Jaso. Jaso is a Basque name."

"That's interesting. So if there were anyplace in the area where Basque people might have had connections in the nineteenth century…" she trailed off.

"There were quite a few Basque sheepherders in the Sierra," I said.

"Any idea where?" Harper turned the full force of the Mediterranean on me.

"Yeah," I said. "They were concentrated in the high meadows around Lake Tahoe."

Harper's eyes widened.

Her phone rang. She walked over to her podium desk, pulled her phone out of her purse, and answered it without looking at the screen.

"Hello?" There was a pause. "Oh. Zack." she said. Just those two words telegraphed a complete change of mood from engaged interest to depressed anxiety and fear. "No. I don't think so." Pause. "No, I won't. I should go. I have a client here. H… She's going to be awhile. I have to go."

Harper clicked off and put the phone back in her purse. After a moment, she pulled it back out, clicked a little switch that may have turned it to mute, then put her phone back in her purse.

"Everything okay?" I said.

"Yeah. Sure." Brady Harper turned away from me, walked over to a file cabinet, pulled it open, and flipped through some files. Aimless. No focus on me or the room. A lot of focus on the short phone conversation.

"I can go," I said. "I'll come back at a better time."

"No. It's okay. I just had a sort of brain cramp." She turned back toward me. Even from a distance it was easy to see that her face had colored and her eyes were suddenly red.

"Trouble with Zachary?" The words seemed flip, but I said them earnestly.

"Zackariah. No trouble. Just a thing we're going through."

"Is he your husband?" I hadn't seen a ring on her finger, but I'd learned that rings weren't fail-safe indications of relationships.

"Boyfriend," she said. "Ex-boyfriend." Her tone was heavy with distress and worry.

"I don't normally pry," I said, "but it looks and sounds like trouble from here. I've learned the signs. But if you tell me he had nothing to do with your broken finger or bruised face, I won't bring it up again."

Tears suddenly flowed in volume, and she made a sudden choking inhalation. Harper put her white-gloved-hands to her face, turned, and walked over to the wall, a movement that was an automatic attempt to put distance between one's self and the pain of the world. She turned sideways to the wall, leaned against it with her shoulder, then sagged down the wall until she'd collapsed onto the floor. Her six foot length transformed into a kind of pretzel. She buried her face in her hands and sobbed, her body jerking with spasms.

I've never been good at knowing when to get involved and when to leave someone alone. But when a woman is abused and desperate, something has to be done. I walked over, got down on the floor a few feet away from her, leaned against the wall and waited. I wanted to put a reassuring hand on her knee or shoulder. But I knew from my cop days that the touch from a stranger – no matter how well intended – could be a shock and even construed in the worst way. I waited.

Her crying was dramatic and a major contrast to the calm academic exterior that Harper had presented. She kept her face covered with her hands. The white gloves soon turned to moist gray with smudges of dark mascara. I waited for several minutes while she sobbed.

When her crying diminished, I spoke in a soft voice.

"How long has Zackariah been hitting you?"

She inhaled and choked and coughed anew. It was another long minute before she responded. "Eight months. When I first met him a year ago, he was very sweet and charming. In hindsight, I realize there were hints of insecurity, tensions at his work and such. But he was really nice to me. When we had our first real disagreement, it ended with him slapping my shoulder. A hard blow that really stung. I had a red blotch on my skin for a week. I thought it was my fault, that I'd been insensitive, and that I simply needed to do a better job at how I communicated. I thought that it was a one-time event. He even brought me flowers and a little card with hearts on it. He apologized and begged my forgiveness. But two weeks later it happened again and got worse. Instead of a slap, he used the heel of his fist. He hit me in places where my clothes would hide the bruising. When I told him I didn't want to see him again, he beat me up badly. Many blows. Very scary.

"He was arrested and charged, and I was willing to testify against him. But he had a very good attorney, and there were no witnesses. The charge was reduced to misdemeanor battery, and he paid a two thousand dollar fine."

"I'm so sorry," I said.

"I was able to get a restraining order. He was not to come within a half-mile of me or my apartment or my work, and he was not to call. But he keeps calling. I told the cops and they want me to make a recording of the calls. I was going to do that, but then he was outside my apartment a few mornings ago as I was leaving for work. He pushed me down and my face hit the ground. I split my chin and broke my finger. He said that he never wanted to hurt me, but that I was psychologically abusive to him, destroying his good attitude about life. He said the restraining order had been reported to his boss at work and it was ruining his career. He said if I ever did anything else he didn't like, my punishment would be severe."

"Did you tell that to the cops?"

"No. I was afraid. Terrified. And now I've told you. If that got back to him, he might kill me. I contacted a women's abuse shelter. They said that many times a restraining order simply doesn't work and that the safest thing is to take an assumed name, move to another city, and get a different job. But I can't do that without completely giving up my life and career. So I've been dragging my feet, hoping I can find another solution."

"What is this guy's job?"

"That's the thing. You'd think only lowlifes would abuse women. But Zackariah is an investment banker. Very successful. A vice president. He drives a shiny red BMW. Wears custom suits and polished black shoes. Lives in a fancy apartment in a high rise not too far from here."

"What bank does he work for?"

She lifted her head. Used both white gloves to wipe away tears. Shook her head. "I've already told you too much."

"What's his last name?"

She shook her head again. "I need you to forget that I said

any of this. I need you to stop asking questions. This is my problem, and I have to figure a way out of it."

"Okay. I won't ask any more questions. But may I comment?"

She nodded slowly.

"For twenty years, I was a cop in San Francisco. I know men like this. They are functional in many ways. But inside they are seriously sick. When they defy a restraining order and come to your home to threaten you, that is a big warning sign. Consider it a death threat. I encourage you to think about making an escape. If you want, I can help. I know of many resources that help women. Please think about it."

"I have. And I'm not going to run. Not yet, anyway."

We sat in silence for a few minutes, leaning against the wall of the Stanford Archive. It was awkward. More for her than for me. I tried to think of ways to make her feel better.

Eventually, I said, "New subject. Would you like to meet my dog before I go?"

Harper frowned. "Um… What kind of dog is she? Or he."

"He's a Great Dane. What makes you ask?"

"This is going to seem weird. But my sense of smell is very acute. I suppose I developed it as compensation for my bad vision. I smelled his scent when you walked in the door. But my first thought was that he's nowhere near as malodorous as some breeds."

"Malodorous. I'll be sure to tell him that." I smiled.

"I'm sorry. I didn't mean bad."

"You weren't far off. It's true. Some dogs are quite potent in the aroma department. Danes, not so much."

"I think my day is done here." She pulled off the tear-soaked gloves. "Yes, I'd like to meet your dog."

"Good. And it just so happens he really likes archivists."

"Really? What makes you think that?"

"Come, you'll see for yourself."

THIRTY-THREE

Spot was awake as we approached, facing sideways in the back seat, standing with two feet on the floor and two on the back seat, a one-sided crouch he'd perfected to accommodate the Jeep roof, which wasn't nearly high enough for a Great Dane.

"Oh, my," Harper said as we approached. "He's really tall. Not, of course, that I have a problem with tall. But, um… He won't…"

"No, he won't." I opened the door.

I reached in and took hold of his collar as he stepped out. Maybe my grip made him telegraph less exuberance than was his norm. Or maybe he picked up on her vulnerable state. Either way, he was acting as polite as a dog-show champion.

"Sit, Largeness," I said and gave a quick tug on his collar, up and back.

He sat.

"Oh, wow," Harper said. "I don't know what to say. Rarely does an animal render me, you know, speechless. I can't believe how… Right, well, he is large, that's for sure. Did you call him Largeness?"

"He also goes by Spot."

"Spot. Like the grammar school weekly reader my uncle told me about. Run, Spot, run."

As she said his name, his tail swept the sidewalk.

"He shakes, if you'd like to be formally introduced."

"I… sure. What do I do?"

"Just shake his paw. It works best if you use both hands. Spot, please meet Brady Harper. Give her a shake."

He ignored what I said and stretched his head toward her to get a good sniff.

"Spot, shake," I said more firmly and gave his collar a twitch.

He lifted his paw. She caught it with her two hands, gave it a pump, let go, then put her hands to her mouth and started giggling. "Oh, God, I think I just fell in love."

"You're not the first."

Spot stood up, taking an olfactory interest in her pants, sniffing her pockets for hidden treats, then sniffing the chain mail clogs, no doubt intrigued by scents he hadn't previously known to be associated with feet.

Harper reached out to pet him. Tentatively. When she saw that he liked it, she rubbed his head and neck with both hands. "He's beautiful!" Brady Harper had lost all traces of formality and seriousness. She even relaxed her posture into a kind of gentle S curve. The serious academic was melting like an ice cream cone in the sunshine.

"Shall we take him for a walk?" I said.

"Yes, of course, I insist," Harper said. "How do we do that?"

The question reminded me of the lonely rich kid, Joshua Kraytower, who'd never walked a dog until he met Spot a couple of weeks before.

"Just take hold of his collar," I said.

She tentatively reached out. "What side of him should I be on?"

"Doesn't matter. He's an ambidextrous walker."

Harper laughed.

I started down the sidewalk. Harper came up on my left, and Spot was on her left, which put Harper between us.

"This is new for me," Harper said. "Walking with males on either side of me, both of whom make me feel small. Well, smaller."

I nodded. We headed toward the capital.

"He's so tall you don't even need a leash," she said. "I grew up with dogs. It was a leash-centered world, the dogs always eagerly waiting for someone to pick up the leash. Or even just look at it." She was looking down at Spot, leaning a bit to get a side view of his head.

I nodded.

"Is he a good watchdog?" she asked.

"When he's awake."

"Does he keep bad guys away?"

"When he's awake."

"I suppose his growl or his bark would pretty much unnerve any bad guy."

"Pretty much," I said.

"When he's awake," Harper said, laughing.

"Yeah."

Harper pointed with her free hand. "This is the Stanford mansion coming up."

"The one he had remodeled because of the floods," I said.

"Right."

"I don't recall hearing much about floods since I came out to the West Coast. Is there still a danger of floods in Sacramento?"

Harper shrugged. "The Sacramento and American Rivers have been boxed in by levees. But if any of the upstream dams ever give way, then yes, all of Sacramento will be under water. The city is only a few feet above sea level. Back when this house was built, the floods were frequent."

"After Stanford raised the house, any water would have been confined to his basement."

She nodded.

We walked on by. I visualized a pine tar-preserved wooden box hiding in the corner of the basement until Benat Mendoza decided to steal it as payment for unpaid labor.

As Harper walked, she kept up a steady narrative about California history and Stanford-related trivia.

We walked through the capital park, around the capital building, and eventually circled back to the coffee shop building where the Stanford Archive occupied one corner.

"Your car must be nearby," I said.

"No, I take the bus partway and then light rail. Mass transit is the only low-impact way to efficiently move people."

"Something I haven't come to terms with, living in a place where there is almost no mass transit. His Largeness and I would be happy to walk you to your bus."

"No. No thanks." Her voice was firm. "I'll get my things from work and then catch my bus."

"Got it," I said.

We got to the Stanford Archive door, and said goodbye, Spot wagging as he soaked up Harper's gushing affection.

THIRTY-FOUR

Back in my Jeep, I thought about Harper's abusive boyfriend. Brady Harper's stress made me think about Max Miller Donovan's comments to his neighbor about showing the China girl what real men are like. And I remembered what Jade's workmate Vette said about Jade Jaso being pursued and persecuted and probably assaulted by two insecure men who couldn't abide a strong woman. The thoughts built to a kind of outrage. Maybe I was just imagining the knight-in-shining-armor-fantasy of righting wrongs. Or it could be that I was simply wishing for a straightforward approach to making the world a better place, where women could be safe from disgusting, predatory men.

I used my phone to search on bankers named Zackariah. It didn't take long to find him. Zackariah Willits Fairchild. Even though investigating people is my business, I was surprised at how fast I was able to learn all I wanted about Zackariah. Credit or blame social media, whichever is one's perspective. People post an astonishing amount of stuff about themselves online, often using public pages that anyone can see. It's as if everyone has become a narcissist wanting to show the world hundreds of selfies and other photos that reveal who their friends are, what groups they belong to, what their interests are, what kind of car they drive, where they vacation, what their schedule is, what books they read, what music they listen to, what movies and TV shows they watch. Perhaps there are still some people who are more interested in others than in themselves, and perhaps there are still people who are intensely private and don't want to share every little thing about their lives. But any private detective will tell you that those people are rare. It's a self-focused world. And the internet is filled with look-at-me bulletin boards.

On one public page, I learned that Zackariah Willits Fairchild was an only child born to a nondenominational minister father and a homemaker mother. They lived in Dubuque, Iowa.

I found an addiction website that gave people a forum to post about their traumas. The site let users choose a pseudonym for privacy. One poster's pseudonym was ZWFDubuque, a handle so transparent he was obviously hoping people would find and identify with his troubles. There was a link to his writing. I clicked on it, and it took me to his personal story.

Zackariah wrote, 'My father was a strict disciplinarian, so strict that my mother left us. Disappeared in the middle of the night. Dad always found Bible passages to justify whipping me. Five lashes for talking back to him. Ten lashes for lying. Fifteen lashes for anything he perceived as threatening or undermining his rule of law in the household. He was never interested in anything I did. When I made the A-squad hockey team, he never came to one of my games. Only when we went to the state championship, did he finally agree to attend. But he didn't show up. When I went home, I found him dead by suicide, hanging from the belt he used to whip me with. His suicide note, in its essence, blamed me and said I'd made his life intolerable.'

Zackariah went on to tell how he lived with a cousin in Iowa City, then ran away. He took a bus to California, got a job picking fruit in the orchards, and finished his GED. He went to a community college in Fresno, transferred to San Jose State, and graduated with honors. His degree was in economics. He got a job at a local bank, excelled at banking, transferred several times to bigger banks, and ended up in his current position in Sacramento.

I went to the website of an investigator service I subscribe to. They had his rapsheet details.

His first arrest was for domestic battery in Fresno, an incident that was reported by a neighbor. Charges were dropped when his girlfriend victim refused to cooperate with the prosecutor.

His second arrest came after a 911 call from a woman in San Jose who said she'd been beat up by her boyfriend Zackariah in her apartment. After his arrest, he refused to speak. They couldn't find any evidence – no DNA under her fingernails, none of his hair in her sink – and his attorney got the charges dropped.

His third arrest was when he beat up Brady Harper, resulting in a fine and a restraining order.

Under the identification tab, the website had his driver's license photo, birthdate, social security number, and recent phone number. The prefix looked like it belonged to a cell phone.

When I knew enough, I drove to the building that housed the bank where Zackariah Willits Fairchild worked. I got my white hard hat and orange vest out of the back of the Jeep. I put them on, grabbed my clipboard and my Kindle ebook reader, and walked over to Fairchild's building. I was sure but not positive I had the right man. I needed to see the red BMW that Brady Harper described.

I walked to the ramp that led down to the garage door and the underground parking garage. The door was shut. I waited for someone to activate the door and drive out. After ten minutes of no activity, I went around the building and walked in the front door. I entered a lobby that served a range of businesses including the bank, which occupied floors 2-5. There was a man in a uniform at the reception desk. He was keeping an eye on the lobby and the elevators while also gazing at three video screens in front of him.

I ran up in a hurry, trying to telegraph stress. "Guard, we're doing the impromptu seven-nine-three fire-access test, and your garage door is stuck!" I shook my clipboard at him. "Do you realize what that means?" I didn't give him time to think, never mind answer. "If your computer has locked out our codes and the fire department can't get into your garage, oh man, this building is gonna be locked down and shut out until those codes get cleared. Do you have the garage software APX update schedule?" I held up my little ebook reader and waved it through the air as if trying to catch a signal.

The man looked at me with a worried, blank face. "Sorry, mister, I don't know what that means."

"What? I can't believe this." I turned toward the elevators.

"Is there a garage code for the elevator?"

He shook his head. "No. Just hit G-one or G-two, depending on which garage level you want."

"Which is the level for the garage door?"

"G-one."

I trotted to the elevators, got in, and punched the G-two button. I called back toward him. "Maybe I can resolve this. Sit tight."

I rode the elevator down to G-two, then trotted through the garage. There was no red BMW. Either Fairchild was not at work, or he walked to work, or he was on the next level up.

I found the auto ramp and ran up to the next level. The red BMW was in a corner spot, parked at an angle to minimize the chance that someone might hit it by opening their car door.

I rode the elevator back up and walked to the reception desk. "Progress report," I said. "I was able to reset the computer update. Emergency averted. You don't know how glad you should be about that. You can go back to Code Green."

I touched the front edge of my helmet and walked out the door.

I fetched my Jeep and double parked it a block up from the bank. The street was a one-way, so Zackariah would pull out and drive away from me. The underground garage door wasn't visible from where I sat, but if anyone drove up the ramp to the street, I'd see it.

I waited two hours. At 7:30 p.m., as twilight was approaching, a red BMW came up the ramp and turned down the street.

I followed in my Jeep, keeping a good distance back.

Zackariah Fairchild didn't go to his high-rise condo, which was only a short walk away. Instead, he headed south to N, took a left, and drove east to the Midtown neighborhood. When he got to the crowded restaurant district, he drove around a block clockwise, then turned into a lot that fronted a busy restaurant. The restaurant entrance door was propped open and flanked by two men wearing black pants, starched white, long-sleeved shirts, and skinny black ties. They weren't big bouncers like at a biker bar. More like influencers, paid to look sharp, welcome the guests, and communicate that this was an upscale establishment. Men in dress pants and nice shoes and women in suits and dresses spilled out of the building holding wine and champagne glasses, enjoying one of those perfect, and common, temperate evenings that made up for Sacramento's hot end-of-summer days.

To one side of the door was an outdoor dining area set off by gold stanchions and red velvet theater ropes. Diners – mostly in their twenties and thirties – filled the tables, which were covered with white linen and sparkling wine glasses.

Everyone looked elegant and happy. The vibe was well-to-do-professionals, lawyers, doctors, bankers. No tawdry actor wannabes. No scruffy musicians or sculptors or writers typing on their laptops.

Jazz filled the air. From my open Jeep window, it sounded like a quartet. Piano, string bass, percussion, and a very muted, sophisticated trumpet. Like Miles Davis with Bill Evans setting up the chords on piano.

Instead of parking in the main lot out front where the hoi polloi might brush their gowns against his fenders, Zackariah Willits Fairchild drove his BMW around back, turned into an alley, and parked in one of two spaces that were outlined in white paint and had no-parking signs. He must have had privileges that came from knowing the restaurant owner. Or maybe he was the restaurant owner.

I turned off my lights, stopped at the entrance to the alley, and watched.

Fairchild got out. He was in his mid-thirties, and he moved and looked expensive. He was about the same height as Brady Harper. He had a solid build. Not show muscles but no doubt fit. He probably outweighed my 215.

During my cop years I'd seen many small guys who hit women. I'd often wondered if their small stature contributed to the insecurities that fueled their abuse.

But physically, at least, this guy looked like a woman's dream. Handsome, well-built, well-dressed, and with the indications of a substantial bank account. His demons didn't come from lack of attractiveness. They must have come from the deeper psychological fears indicated by the confession I'd read online.

The BMW lights flashed as he hit his key fob lock. Fairchild walked across the alley and up short stairs that were next to a tall dumpster. There was a steel door with a keypad to the side. As twilight descended, a security light had come on and illuminated the keypad. Fairchild pressed six buttons, opened the door, and went inside.

I paused to think how best to work my approach. There were two relatively easy ways to intimidate a man. Scare him with a threat or an implied threat, or scare him with physical abuse. Of course, the easiest way to scare is to have Spot growl in the man's face. But Spot is memorable, and I didn't want to make it easy for this man to figure out who Spot was or who I was. For my purposes, the non-canine approach was best.

I keep a Halloween monster mask in my catchall bag in the rear of the Jeep. Any ten-year-old knows that it's just a mask and might even hide a cute blonde cheerleader. But it can also create a terrifying countenance if the person wearing it acts like a monster. I didn't want to act like a monster. I aimed merely to frighten. I also keep a junior-sized maple baseball bat.

I left Spot in the Jeep. I took the mask and bat and walked over near the rear door of the restaurant. I stood behind and to the side of one of the dumpsters, pulled on the monster mask, and used my hard-to-trace burner phone to dial the number I got off the investigator website listing for Fairchild's criminal record.

"Who's this?" his deep voice barked into the phone. I heard the jazz quartet in the background on his phone. Another good facsimile of Evans and Miles, this time with the addition of Coltrane doing some counterpoint on the sax. They were on What Kind Of Fool Am I.

"You should know that someone is out back of the restaurant messing with your ride," I said and then clicked off.

The back door of the restaurant flew open with a bang 15 seconds later. Fairchild ran down the steps, peering through the dark toward his BMW.

The security light at the back of the building didn't provide much helpful illumination on the red car. Fairchild hit his key fob to unlock the car, which turned on the inside lights. He opened the door, stuck his head inside, pulled back out and shut the door. I got a clear view of his face in the security light. It was a positive ID.

I softly set the bat down. He looked down the alley toward the right. I came at him from the left.

It wasn't a hard blow. But it no doubt startled him that I grabbed his belt with one hand and the front of his shirt with the other hand, lifted him up onto his toes, and ran him sideways to a dark spot on the far side of the dumpster. I pushed him up against the dumpster hard enough to shock him but not hard enough to cause injury.

I leaned toward him, my monster mask just in front of his face.

"This can go easy or hard," I said in a harsh whisper.

"Show me your weapon," he said, "or I'm gonna kick your ass."

"My weapon is the Sacramento Vigilance Committee. There's seventeen of us. We got a report on you for abusing women."

"You SOB," he said in a low hiss as he swung at me with his left fist in an uncoordinated hook. I used my raised forearm to swipe the blow away and gave him two quick punches to the gut.

He made a big whoomphing exhalation and made another feeble attempt at hitting me.

I stepped back and sideways, took the wrist of his arcing arm with my hand, got my other hand on his forearm, and yanked his arm sideways. I jerked him off balance so hard he would have gone down but for me twisting him and his arm, stepping behind him, and bringing his arm up behind his back. I shoved him toward the brick wall. He turned his pretty face at the last moment but still made decent contact with his chin against the brick. He made a sharp grunt as I snapped the little finger on his left hand.

The combination of face impact and broken-finger pain made him go limp. He sagged down and collapsed as Brady Harper had, but with less grace. He went sideways as he fell, hit the dumpster, and made a thumping noise against the metal. He cradled the hand with the broken finger and made the distress sounds of panicked breathing. His chin was bleeding from the same spot where Brady Harper had her stitches.

I squatted down next to him and leaned in, my monster mask in his face. He cowered away from me.

"The Vigilance Committee got reports on you. We looked you up and have uncovered your secrets and your past. Including injuries to multiple women." I decided to use an incorrect name to obscure my relationship with Brady Harper. I didn't want him to think I'd met Harper. "Your most recent victim is named Betty Harder. Her injuries include a broken little finger on her left hand and a wound to her chin that required stitches. So we're giving you a simple ultimatum. Are you ready to hear it and agree to our terms? Or should I break some more fingers?"

He could barely get the words out. "No more fingers."

I pulled out my phone, punched up the icons that Street had shown me so that it would record video.

"Zackariah Fairchild, you have hit several women over the years, correct?"

"Women don't obey. They have to obey." Despite his pain and fear, his voice displayed anger.

"You've also struck Betty Harder on several occasions, correct?"

He mumbled.

"Speak up!" I said.

"Brady shows no respect. I had to teach her a lesson."

"You routinely hit her hard enough to cause bruises, but you aim your blows in places where those bruises would typically be covered by her clothes, correct?"

"Yes." His voice was tiny.

"You pushed her so hard she fell and broke the little finger of her left hand and cut open her chin, which required stitches, correct?"

Another mumbled word.

"Speak up!"

"Yes." Fairchild shook with fear. "She doesn't obey me. I had no choice."

"Despite the restraining order forbidding you to approach Harder or have any contact with her, you have called her repeatedly, and you showed up outside of her apartment and threatened her, correct?"

"I had to. She refused to do as I commanded."

"I'm going to give you the terms required," I said.

The man was shivering with stress and fear.

"You will never call Betty Harder again."

Fairchild didn't respond.

"Repeat what I said."

He said he'd never call her again.

"You will never go near her again. Not to her work or her home or anywhere else. Repeat it."

He repeated my words.

"You will never hit another woman again."

He repeated the words, but it sounded like he was on auto pilot. I had no doubt he was a serial beater. I only hoped that he would stay away from Harper.

"We are watching you, Fairchild. We know where you live. We know where you work. We know the car you drive. We know your relationship to this restaurant. If you break these terms, or if you ever hurt another woman or even go near Betty Harder, the Sacramento Vigilance Committee will come for you. First, we'll send this video confession to the bank president and CEO and all the board members. We'll also send it to the Sacramento Bee newspaper. One of our members is a tech guy who will post this video confession on social media and make it so whenever anyone Googles domestic abuse or your name, the first hit at the top of the Google search page will be you and your confession to assault. Your life as you know it will be over."

I turned off my phone recording.

I said, "If you touch another woman, we will abuse you in ways that will astonish. Do you understand me? You will be

amazed at what we will do. Just to be sure you get our meaning…"
I raised the bat high over his knee. He cowered.

"Do you understand?"

"Yes. Don't hit me, please."

"You hit women, but you don't want me to hit you. I don't think you understand." I swung the bat down with medium speed and hit his thigh muscle. He yelped and cried like a little boy. It wasn't hard enough to cause permanent injury, but he would have a hard time walking for the next week. Next I swung the bat at the pavement, this time faster. The blow was forceful enough that a chunk of asphalt broke off, shot up and hit him on his cheek hard enough to draw blood. He flinched and made a little whimpering cry.

"I'll never hit another woman again! I promise!"

"We'll be watching. There's seventeen of us and one of you."

From the shadows I watched as Fairchild struggled to stand, then limped into his little sports car and drove away.

As I walked back to the Jeep, I was surprised at my violent reaction to such a disgusting man. But I felt no guilt.

THIRTY-FIVE

The next day, I was catching up with Sergeant Diamond Martinez in his back yard down in Minden, Nevada, the little town in Carson Valley, east of Tahoe and 2000 feet below the lake.

Diamond opened two bottles of Peyote India Pale Ale and poured them into glasses.

I talked to Diamond about Brady Harper, the Stanford archivist who talked about a potential treasure that might have ended up in Billy Jaso's hands.

"Which could motivate someone to harm Jade Jaso in hopes she knew its location," he said.

"Yeah." I also told Diamond about my visit to Max Miller Donovan's trailer and what his neighbor told me about Donovan's gun porn fixation and his plan to take a woman he called China girl on a horseback camping trip.

"You're painting a dark picture. You think that's what happened to Jade?"

"That would be my guess. But I can't do anything until I find them."

"You got a plan for that?" he asked.

"Nope."

We sipped the deep bronze cerveza.

He turned toward Spot, who was lying on the small patch of grass that comprised Diamond's yard. Grass was a luxury Spot rarely found up in Tahoe.

"His Largeness watches every time I raise my glass to drink." Diamond picked up his beer and took a sip.

Spot's head lifted just a little as the glass went up, then went down a little as Diamond set it back down. His eyes and ears were focused on the action.

"Like a military fighter jet locking onto a target," I said.

"He drinks beer?"

"Only when he's got a designated driver," I said.

"Doesn't seem right that we're out here in the hot sun drinking a cool IPA and he gets nothing but water." Diamond stood, went inside, came out with a large glass bowl, set it on the ground, opened another beer, and poured it into the bowl. Spot watched.

Diamond sat down and looked at Spot.

Spot stared at Diamond. Glanced at the bowl of beer. Looked back at Diamond.

"Okay," Diamond said.

Spot jumped to his feet, took a fast step to the bowl, and drained it as fast as a high school kid sneaking a beer under the bleachers at a game.

Spot lay back down on the grass, belched, let out a big sigh, flopped over onto his side, and appeared to go to sleep.

I looked from Spot to Diamond.

"Thanks for making time to see me," I said.

"Nice the way you self-employed types can take off work whenever you want and make social calls in the afternoon," Diamond said. "I have to wait until I'm off shift."

"In some ways, self-employed people never get off shift."

One of Diamond's eyebrows twitched.

"Either we're shoveling coal, or we're thinking about where else we should look to shovel coal. Hard to escape work when there's no timeclock to punch out of and you always have to figure out how you're going to pay the next month's bills with no regular paycheck coming in."

"Wow, didn't know you shoveled coal," Diamond said with a straight face. "Seems you had a good job on the SFPD but you quit."

"True. Sorry, I didn't mean to sound snarky. I get stressed when clients disappear."

I looked over at the ancient, single-car garage with the swing-down door. The garage housed Diamond's Karmann Ghia. "Green Flame still running?"

"Not as well as the orange one you blew up. But your replacement ethic was appreciated."

"Least I could do." I didn't need to mention the bullets Diamond took while helping me take down a bad guy who was especially creative with explosives. If Diamond and I had kept track of favors, my debt to him would loom multiple times larger than his debt to me.

"You had a question," Diamond said. "Something about encryption."

"Yeah."

"Connected to the missing client you told me about," he said.

"Right."

"Were you supposed to protect her?"

"I told her I was an investigator, not a security guard. But she no doubt thought protection was implied to some degree. Not that it matters."

Diamond nodded. "She's gone. You care. Ergo, you need to find her. Is it possible she left voluntarily? Or do you think she was kidnapped?"

"Hard to know. Despite all the press it gets when it happens, kidnapping is rare. And the missing woman may not be the most stable person. She told me that when things get too stressful, she often disappears. Takes her horse, heads off into the wilderness. This time she went missing with all three of her horses and her pickup and horse trailer. We had an appointment. But she left no note or explanation."

"She usually take three horses when she skips town?"

"Doesn't seem so."

"So this ain't good."

I nodded.

"Complicated case," he said. "How did it unfold?"

"I talked to her co-worker at the Sac Fire Department. Found out there was another firefighter who didn't like her. They got into an ongoing disagreement. She may have also been assaulted by that firefighter and a guy he knew, the guy who I had you look up. Then her fellow firefighter died in a fall during a fire.

And her hand got mashed in the fire."

Diamond's brown face got very serious. "They wondered if she helped him fall."

"Yeah. They asked questions. She quit not long after."

"Then she gets the threatening voicemail, hires you to check on it, and goes missing."

"Yep. The last time I went out to her ranch to look around, a guy came to steal her horse under the guise that he was repossessing it."

Diamond nodded. "Which he couldn't do because she'd already disappeared with the whole barn."

"Right. So I searched her house and barn. I found a neighbor nosing around. Then I discovered that one of her late father's pilot logbooks from his service in Vietnam was used as a journal. Tucked inside the back cover of the logbook were some papers and an old envelope. The envelope contained a letter from Abraham Lincoln to Leland Stanford, sent by Pony Express in eighteen sixty-one."

"Curious."

"The letter was a warning of sorts for Stanford to be fiscally responsible while building the transcontinental railroad. It also had an oblique reference to what might be valuables that Stanford acquired."

"Treasure?"

I shrugged. "I took it to an archivist named Brady Harper in Sacramento and learned about the possibility that some valuables owned by Stanford were lifted by a woodworker named Benat Mendoza who wasn't paid when he worked on Stanford's library back in Wisconsin and the construction company there went bankrupt."

"Byzantine," Diamond said. He sipped beer. "So the Mendoza dude came to California from Wisconsin to attempt to find compensation for lost wages. Long way to travel for payment."

"I learned that Benat Mendoza was Basque. The missing woman's father who recently died, Billy Jaso, was also Basque. So it could be that Billy Jaso learned about Mendoza and Stanford's valuables from the Basque community."

"Basque insider stuff." Diamond said.

"They could pass along notebooks and journals, too."

"His logbook was actually a journal?"

"One of them was, yeah. There was also a map of the Tahoe Basin. On it were a range of penciled marks."

"Xs marking buried treasure?" Diamond sounded like he was joking.

"Pickaxes and flowers. Which I suspect are mines and something else."

"Curiouser." Diamond looked intrigued as evidenced by his eyebrow rising slightly.

"The most interesting thing is that Lincoln's letter had a series of numbers in it. The letter mentioned an ancient Greek historian named Polybius, a guy Lincoln and Stanford had apparently discussed when they met in DC a few months before. Harper got excited and immediately did some Googling on Polybius and found out that he invented an encryption device."

Diamond nodded. "I read about this once. A five-square grid, right?"

"Yeah. You assign row-and-column numbers to each letter of the alphabet."

"Cool to think ol' Honest Abe was into secret codes. What did the archivist's deciphering reveal?"

"That's just it. Nothing but gibberish."

"What's your next move?"

"Talking to a general smart guy who might think of what I'm missing."

"I know nothing about encryption beyond the basics."

"I didn't know there were basics."

"Maybe if I had a copy of the numbers…"

I reached into my pocket, pulled out a folded photocopy of the letter, and handed it to him.

He unfolded it, scanned it at high speed, which, despite English being his second language, probably meant he would remember every word. "Mind if I keep this copy? Maybe I'll have an idea."

"That's why I brought it. Take your time. It'll take me an hour to get home."

Diamond made a wry smile. "A whole hour? In an hour I could decipher the Voynich Manuscript."

"What does that mean?"

"I'm being sarcastic. The Voynich Manuscript probably dates from the Italian Renaissance. It hasn't ever been deciphered and even NSA cryptographers have tried. So take your hour. Live large, take two."

We finished our Peyote IPAs, I woke up Spot from his nap, and I pointed the Jeep back up the mountain.

The phone rang when I walked into my very little cabin made from very large logs.

"Owen McKenna," I said.

"The cipher for Honest Abe's message only needed a keyword."

"What's that?"

"Instead of starting with the letter A as you fill in the five-square grid, you start with a keyword. After the end of the keyword, you fill in the alphabet, except that if a letter is already in the keyword, you go to the next letter. In the end you still have a five-by-five grid with all the letters of the alphabet. But the letters are somewhat rearranged."

"What's the keyword?" I asked.

"In this case, Polybius."

"The name of the Greek dude who invented the cipher. That's too perfect."

"Sí," Diamond said.

"Did you figure out Lincoln's message?"

"Sí again. Ready?"

"Yeah."

"The message is, 'History will record how you acquired and dispensed with your jade.'"

"Jade! There's a gut punch."

"How so?" Diamond asked.

"The name of the missing woman is Jade Jaso. She comes from a long line of Chinese women named Jade. Jade was something her ancestors carved. And the Stanford archivist uncovered information about Stanford taking a bribe from a Chinese man in return for hiring the man's sons. The bribe was yin-and-yang guardian lions."

"The implication being," Diamond said, "that the guardian lions were very valuable. And now, ol' Abe's letter suggests they were made of jade."

"Looks like it," I said.

I thanked Diamond.

I dialed Brady Harper at her Stanford Archive address. It was early evening, so I figured she wouldn't be in. But I wanted to leave a message.

At the beep, I said, "Hi Ms. Harper. Owen McKenna calling to report that a friend figured out that the Polybius Square Lincoln used begins with a keyword. Please give me a..."

"I'm here," she interrupted.

"Oh, good. Is your recorder off?"

"Yes." There was a beep. "Off and erased."

"You're working late."

"A trait of archivists is that few of us have a social life. Books are, frankly, more interesting than most activities. You mentioned a keyword."

"Right. You start with the keyword. Then fill in the rest of the squares with the rest of the alphabet but don't repeat any letters that were in the keyword."

"The keyword is?"

"The name of the cipher inventor. Polybius. Deciphering the numbers Lincoln wrote gives the message, 'History will record how you acquired and dispensed with your jade.' Anyway, thought you'd want to know."

"Wow. This is so cool."

THIRTY-SIX

After calling Brady Harper, I called Street to see what her dinner plans were. She explained that she was working on an insect larva experiment that was time-sensitive, and she'd be staying late at her lab, and did I mind eating dinner alone with His Largeness. "I hope you still respect me despite my focus on work."

"Respect and admire. Only a rare few recognize the value of an evening with bug larva."

"Sarcastic?"

"I confess. But I'll survive a dinner alone with His Largeness."

I wished Street success with her creepy crawlies, got out the grilling pan with all the little holes in it, and used it to grill green beans, new potatoes, onions, and chicken breast fillets. After we ate, Spot lay down on his big bed next to the wood stove, and I poured myself a glass of wine. I once again pulled out Billy Jaso's pilot logbook journal.

I sat in the rocker. Jaso's handwriting was a small scrawl, dark blue ink in cursive. There were no dates, just well-written and earnest sentences. The journal provided the corroboration that Brady Harper desired. It reiterated much of what she had deduced from notes found with Stanford's possessions.

Taped in the front of the journal was a piece of paper that was an introduction to what would follow. I reread that introduction.

'This journal is the result of years of research into my wife's Chinese family history. I was very much in love with my wife. She was my light and my music, and I was looking forward to a promising life with her. She died young, when our daughter

Jade was only four years old. I was stricken by the loss, which was mitigated by having my daughter.

'After my wife's death, I studied Mandarin so that I could read the many letters and notes that were handed down from her ancestors. This journal is the summation of what I learned from those letters.

'I also studied my Basque ancestors. I put out notices on internet boards looking for Basque records in Northern California. I went to a cafe near the Golden Gate Fields horse racetrack near Berkeley, a cafe I knew to be frequented by Spanish and Basque immigrants. I put a handwritten card on their bulletin board asking for information about Basque sheepherders in Tahoe. I received an email from a young man. He said his Basque grandmother had a box full of Basque letters and even diaries that her family had kept. I was able to go through that trove with a Basque translator, and I found a note that suggests that a man named Benat Mendoza, an employee of Leland Stanford, stole property from Stanford in lieu of wages he had been denied.

'In an amazing confluence of family history, it appears that the property Benat Mendoza stole was jade carved by my wife's ancestors and used as a bribe to entice Stanford to hire relatives of my wife.

'Mendoza took the property to the mountains of Tahoe and joined some Basque sheepherders as a cover. Mendoza was said to have hidden the property in sheepherding territory.

'As of this writing, I've looked for this area and the treasure that may be hidden there. But I have not found it. Perhaps one day I will.'

There was so much dense writing in Jaso's logbook journal that it would take hours or even days to read it all. It was possible that Jade had already read it. It was also possible that she never knew what was in the last logbook. If I could find her and bring her back to safety, I would make certain to show her.

THIRTY-SEVEN

In the morning I tried to find the Pony Express reenactment group that Max Miller Donovan had been part of. There were endless listings, mostly of businesses using the Pony Express name to promote their services. Anything I might want to buy, from eyeglasses to auto repair to ski instruction, could be found with Pony Express branding.

As always, patience was the key to research. Eventually, I came to the Pony Express Future Champions of Life riding school in Carson City. The website proudly claimed that the school was run by Debbie Berrensen, an instructor who had "achieved full Future Champion Certification" just two years before. The website said they focused on teaching children to ride, and specialized in developing independence and self-reliance skills.

Even though I was no longer a child in several ways, the future champions concept sounded pretty good, so I dialed their number and got an overly-enthusiastic recorded message. Over soft background music of Willy Nelson singing Don't Fence Me In, the woman's voice promised to turn my child into an equine professional. Her pep-rally eagerness extended to a range of numbers I could press for such options as talking to the billing department, the lesson-scheduling department, making an appointment to visit and take a tour of the Future Champions of Life campus, and learning more about their horses, including show-champion Bella May!

Scheduling a campus visit seemed the next step, but my patience for the menu options had already run out. I hung up and drove to Carson City.

The address took me out Highway 50, east of the city. I got most of the way to the turnoff that climbs up the mountain to

Virginia City when I came to a small, rustic wooden sign that had the address number and the words "Future Champions of Life."

There was a split-rail fence around an area of sagebrush, and inside the fence was a small barn painted red and a lean-to shelter that was open on three sides. Standing in the shade under the roof of the lean-to were two sway-backed horses with large bellies. The horses were side-by-side and front-to-back so that their swishing tails would keep flies off the head of the other. I tried not to make comparisons, but these horses made Cyrano and de Bergerac look like medal winners. And if the Future Champions cheerleader lady ever got even a glimpse of Anne Gregory, she'd probably turn in her riding boots and decide to try a new career making sagebrush perfume or sagebrush tea.

On the far side of the fenced sagebrush pasture was a prefab home that was much larger and nicer than my own cabin. The side of the house was covered with a painted mural of full-sized cowboys with red kerchiefs riding chestnut-brown horses across a desert landscape with purple sagebrush. The artist was skillful, and the art covered every inch of the house siding except the window glass.

I parked near a Toyota Tacoma pickup that had been painted custom turquoise, walked past it and the horses to the house, and knocked on the door, my knuckles striking one of the galloping cowboys on his knee.

"Just a sec," a woman called out.

I waited a bunch of secs. The door eventually opened. The fiftyish woman standing there was wearing shiny turquoise cowboy boots with her tan jeans tucked into the tops. Her belt buckle was turquoise. She had on a leather vest with artful stitching and turquoise stones arranged in panels. The vest was held closed with just one button. She wore a Stetson cowboy hat with a turquoise hat band tipped rakishly on her head, and her long brown hair had been recently curled in wavy coils that danced to the side of her gray eyes. One delicate turquoise clip held a group of curls on just one side of her face, giving her an artful asymmetry. It was obvious she had prepped to look just so to a potential client who might want their child to be a Future Champion of Life. Or maybe a man who could be a Future Champion Date.

"Well, hello, mister," she said with a big grin as she looked up at me. "Aren't you a sight." She held a mug of steaming coffee in one hand and slid her other arm up the side of the door jamb and leaned against it. She had long, dramatic turquoise fingernails that made me wonder how she rode horses with them. Maybe they popped on and off. "Sorry to keep you waiting on the front porch," she said.

"I was happy to hang out with the Riders of the Purple Sage," I said.

"Huh? Oh, the cowboys on my house mural. Riders of the purple sage. That's good. I'll have to remember that."

I was surprised she hadn't thought of it before. I decided there was no point in mentioning how Zane Grey shaped my view of manhood when I was a boy growing up in Boston. "My name's Owen McKenna."

"And I'm Debbie Berrensen. Would you like some coffee? I've got a fresh pot going."

"No thanks. I'm a private investigator looking into a crime, and there may be a connection to a Pony Express reenactment group. Because your business uses the Pony Express name, I thought you might be a good resource for info. May I come in and ask you some questions?"

"Let's, uh, you and me go for a little walk and talk. I'll show you Bella May and the Future Champions campus, and then you can ask your questions."

I nodded and stepped back from the door. I understood the quid pro quo. She'd consider my questions as long as I would consider her sales pitch. For all she knew, I might have, or know, a whole passel of children in need of her Future Champion skills.

She came out the doorway with a kind of continuous head movement that made all her curls shimmer and shake.

"This way," she said. She started walking toward the horses, her hips doing such an exaggerated sway that I wondered if she'd been injured. Or maybe the cowboy boots were painful.

She stopped when she saw Spot with his head out the Jeep window. "Oh, Lord, who is this boy?" She called out with such enthusiasm that Spot started wagging. With no hesitation, she walked up to him, grabbed his head, and bent over so that her curls covered his head. He wagged harder.

"He goes by Spot."

"Spot, you gorgeous handsome hunk. Can you come out to play?"

I opened the Jeep's door, and Spot jumped out. Debbie Berrensen bent down and slapped her thighs and did little jumps this way and that, and Spot appeared to think she was the best thing that had happened to him since the archivist Brady Harper fell in love with him. He danced around her, dodging her, then submitted to her wishes as she smothered him with kisses and hugs. Eventually, she released him from her grip. He trotted off, slaloming around purple sage as he investigated the smells of the landscape.

Debbie Berrensen held her arm out toward the desert and swept it in a half circle. "What you see before you is the Future Champions campus. See that trail over there? That leads to an extensive network of the best riding in the entire country. From that single starting point, you can actually trace the history of the American West." She turned and looked at me, her curls bouncing. "Isn't that exciting?"

"Yes, it is."

"As our students learn to negotiate the twists and turns of those trails, they learn to negotiate all the twists and turns of life. It's a proven scientific correlation." She turned and looked at me as if to see whether I comprehended the concept or not.

"Horse riding befits life," I said. "Works for me. Do you know about these Pony Express groups?"

"Let me introduce you to Bella May," she said, ignoring my question as if sensing that, once I got the information I wanted, I would no longer be a captive audience.

She walked over to a low place on the split-rail fence, swung her leg over it with a practiced movement that showed she was still limber in ways that exceeded what was needed for serious hip sway, and then walked across the dirt toward the horses. Her boots kicked up little dust plumes. The turquoise would need polishing before her next potential customer arrived.

I followed her.

The woman stopped at the sway-backed horses. One was dusty white, the other dusty buckskin. Both were somnolent in the desert heat, eyes half shut against the day and their swishing tails.

Debbie Berrensen put her hand on the neck of the white one. "And this is Bella May. She won the blue ribbon for Children's Riding Confidence at the county fair. We are so proud to have her as our champion headliner here at the campus."

I patted the horse. Bella May closed her eyes even further. "Nice calm disposition," I said.

"Oh, I like that phrase. Calm disposition. I'm going to remember that."

"Back to the Pony Express groups," I said. "Do you know of any in Carson City?"

She turned from Bella May to me, put one hand on her hip, and gave her head just the tiniest shake, which made her curls shimmy. "I sure do. In fact, I write the newsletter for our local group. I call it the CC Pony News, and my motto is All The Mail That's Fit To Email. Isn't that cute?" She reached over and carefully pressed her open palm against my shoulder.

I nodded. "Yeah, that's cute. What exactly is the mission of your group?"

"The Carson City Pony Express Riders is a group for Pony Express fans. We're all about doing social stuff on horses."

"Horse socials?" I said.

"Yes! That's perfect!" This time her touch was more of a slap to my shoulder. "Calm disposition. Riders of the purple sage. Horse socials. You're kind of a word guy, huh?"

"Not really. I wonder if you could check your email list or your membership list for the name Max Miller Donovan?"

Her face colored. "I don't understand. Why are you asking about him?" All the cheerfulness was gone from her voice. She sounded instantly depressed.

"You know the name Donovan?"

She squinted at me. "I do. I took him off our list. I don't even want to think about him." Her voice had become venomous yet fearful.

"My client has disappeared. Donovan is a person of interest in the case."

"He shouldn't just be a person of interest. He should be your number one suspect."

"That's a strong reaction," I said.

"It is. With reason. I don't care if he sues me for slander. After what he did to me and…" She stopped.

"Did Donovan come to your group meetings?"

"Yes. At first, I thought he was like the other members, wanting to support Pony Express history. But then I learned otherwise. I should have been more suspicious when he didn't pay his membership fee."

"Can you tell me what happened?"

"I'd be too embarrassed. And disgusted. He's got this pattern. He comes on all friendly like. He can be sort of charming. And he's very – Lord, I hate to say it – very attractive in the manly ways. I was so stupid. I agreed to go on a date with him. But he took me to his place, and – can I be honest with you? – then he basically attacked me. He degraded me. He was brutal. It was like he hates women and wants to hurt us. It took me a week to recover physically. I'll probably never recover emotionally."

"Did you report the assault?"

"No. I'm embarrassed about that, too. But he scared me to death. He made a thing about showing me his guns and knives and these sharp star-shaped things you throw. When I said I'd call the cops on him, he said what we did was nothing more than a little rough lovemaking, and that I'm the one that seduced him, and that if I called the cops he would kill me. I still believe it. Talking to him, it's like you're looking into the eyes of death. Of the worst evil there is. So I chose to keep the attack to myself so I could stay alive. I know that sounds melodramatic. And I know it would be best for other women if I could somehow get him arrested and jailed. But I couldn't very well do that if I were dead, right? It was the same way for my friend. We were both just violent conquests. He figures out how to get a lady alone so there are no witnesses and then he goes sicko. He hurts. He's as brutal as can be. Three years later, I'm still trying to remember what normal life is. I try to put on an act. With you, for example. I keep testing myself just to see if I can still do normal."

"You can, Debbie. I'm very sorry about what happened. If there's anything I can do, please let me know."

She looked at me with steel in her gray eyes. "What you can do is figure out a way to put that psycho away and do it in a manner that he doesn't think any of his victims were involved in him being jailed. That way he might not come after us."

"Was the assault at his trailer outside of Reno?"

"Yes."

"Did he quit coming to meetings after he assaulted you?"

"Yeah. But if he comes to more meetings, I'm ready." She pulled back the upper part of her vest to reveal a holster with a small handgun.

"Is that a Kimber Micro?"

She nodded. "The Desert Night model. It's not accurate at any distance, but if I stick the barrel in his perfect abs, it'll put holes through him. The magazine holds seven rounds. That should get the job done."

"Do you know any friends of his?"

She shook her head. "He's not the kind of guy who has friends. All I remember is that he said he had family in Tahoe."

"Did he mention any of their names or where they live?"

"No."

"Have you seen Donovan since he attacked you?"

"No, thank God."

"Can you think of anything else I should know about him?"

"Only that if you go after him, bring a posse. He's as strong as he is mean. Big too. Not tall like you, but way more muscles. Sorry if that sounds judgmental on you."

"No apology necessary. It's a simple, helpful description. I'm wondering about another man named Billy Jaso. Was he part of your group?"

"Yes. Billy was a bright spot. What a terrible shame when he died. He was a real gentleman. Helpful and kind. He was our group historian. An expert's expert. He knew everything about Pony Express history and the history of the Civil War. That whole period. And all the stuff going on in California and Nevada back then."

"It was Billy's daughter that went missing."

Debbie put her palm to her mouth. "Oh, that's terrible! What was her name?"

"Jade Jaso. Did you ever meet her?"

She shook her head. "No. But if she takes after her father, she's got to be a real sweetheart. Do you think she'll be okay?"

"I don't know."

"Has there been a ransom note?" she asked.

"No. We haven't heard a thing. We don't know she was kidnapped. She just disappeared. Her horses, too."

"The kidnapper took her horses! That's weird."

"Did Billy Jaso know Max Donovan?"

She frowned. "I don't know if he knew him well. But I saw them talking to each other during our annual Meet 'n Greet."

"Any idea what they talked about?"

"No. Billy was a talker, though, I'll say that. Always going on about his horses and history. He even knew stuff about President Lincoln. He'd talk to anyone who showed an interest in history."

"How do the reenactment rides work?"

"Each year we pick a route from the Pony Express trail. We choose an eighty or hundred-mile segment, the amount the Pony Express riders did every single day. Of course, they would change horses every ten or twelve miles or so. Our members get to choose what part of the ride they'll take. Most just choose one ten-mile segment so they can go on their own horse. Some who can get a friend to trailer a fresh horse will ride two segments. One year we had a guy ride all one hundred miles, ten miles on each of ten horses. It was such a big deal when he made the whole route. He could barely walk afterward. But it just underscored how far those young kids rode every single day to deliver the mail."

"Did Max Donovan go on the reenactment rides?"

"I remember he took one eight-mile segment using another member's horse, because he didn't have his own horse. There'd been some discussion about it because Max is big, probably two thirty. You can't put that much weight on just any horse. But the horse he borrowed was a good-sized Mustang, and as you might know, Mustangs are as tough as horses come. Afterward, Max bragged about his ride like he'd just won a gold medal in the Olympics."

"From what you know of Max, if he kidnapped Jade Jaso and her horses, where do you think he'd go?"

"Well, I have no idea. But the thought really scares me. Him taking her captive and dragging her out into the mountains somewhere and degrading her like he did to me. It's horrible to think of, her being his – well I might as well say it – his sex prisoner."

I pulled out my card and handed it to her. "If you think of anything else I should know, please call me."

She held the card delicately so that the long turquoise nails wouldn't get damaged. "Definitely," she said. "And if I do think of something, maybe we could – you know – talk over coffee. Thinking about Max is the worst thing for my mood, but I can still recognize a real gentleman."

"Thanks." I whistled for Spot. He trotted up, sniffed the pocket where I keep the treats, and I pulled one out.

"Doesn't that spoil him?" Debbie said. "Giving him a treat just for coming when you whistle?"

"Yeah. He's pretty good about coming when I whistle. But a treat makes his response way more reliable."

I thanked her and turned to leave.

"I hope you catch that SOB," she said. "He's one hundred percent evil."

THIRTY-EIGHT

" **I** found the yellow pickup," Diamond said on the phone a few hours later. "Ford, F-One Fifty, nineteen eighty-six."

"Where?"

"At the top of the Spooner Summit pass is a parking area on the south side of the highway."

"Where people begin their hikes on the Tahoe Rim Trail," I said.

"Sí. It was parked at one end, under some trees, directly behind a horse trailer. Hard to spot."

"Is the trailer big enough for three horses?"

"Maybe. I'm not horse trailer-fluent. The trailer's hitched to a two thousand eight silver Dodge Ram pickup belonging to Billy Jaso."

"You got an insider at the California DMV?"

"I called Bains at the El Dorado Sheriff's Office," Diamond said.

"So it's looking more like Max Donovan could have kidnapped Jade and her horses too. I wonder how he forced her to drive to Spooner while he was driving his own pickup?"

"Good question."

"Any indication which way they went?" I asked. "North or south?"

"I'm just a cop. Don't know anything about tracking. Maybe you know a Washoe or Paiute tracker. Or we could get a dog. If only we knew someone with a dog. Oh, wait, you've got a dog."

"Funny guy. I'll go over to Jade's barn tonight and get some horse items. I could use them to scent Spot on. Maybe Street can bring Blondie. If we can establish which way they went, we could get some horses to follow."

"Not to be a buzzkill," Diamond said, "but they could be anywhere. Even if they stayed on the Tahoe Rim Trail, that's most of two hundred miles long, right? You could be out there for weeks searching."

"Good point. I should do an aerial search, first. If I can find them, then I can go after them on the ground."

"We can," Diamond said. "I've got vacation days saved up."

"Big of you to offer. But I was planning on going alone. This isn't your job."

"Yes, it is. Turns out one of our deputies was off duty and visiting a Carson City bar maybe ten days ago. A rowdy patron who turned out to be Max Donovan got in his face. The deputy asked him to settle down. Donovan took a sudden swing at him, knocked him to the floor. By the time our deputy came around, the guy was gone. Our deputy's lady friend saw Donovan get into an old yellow pickup and leave. She wrote down the plate. It was Donovan's."

"Okay. That gets you a trail ride invitation."

"You said all three of Jade's horses were gone. You got a reason why someone would take all three?"

"He probably wanted a pack horse to haul food and gear."

"And weapons," Diamond added.

"Yeah. A lovely picture. I talked to Max Donovan's neighbor. He says the man rarely goes anywhere without a rifle, a semi-auto pistol, and his sawed-off."

"What's your guess on why Max Donovan would want to kidnap Jade Jaso?"

"I met a riding instructor outside of Carson City. She said she was assaulted by Donovan. She described him as a brutal sexual predator. It reinforces what his neighbor said about him forcing Jade to go with him on a camping trip."

"How did Donovan even know Jade Jaso?" Diamond asked.

"According to the riding instructor, Jade's father Billy talked to Max Donovan at a meeting of a Pony Express group. I think Donovan learned about Jade from her father Billy. I'm guessing

Donovan went to the fire station in Sacramento in search of Jade. He met a firefighter named Barry at the same fire station where Jade Jaso worked. According to a woman who worked with Jade, Donovan came by the fire station to visit with Barry. When Jade saw Donovan, she had a big negative reaction. Her colleague thought that Jade had seen Barry and Donovan the night before and had probably been assaulted by them."

I took a breath and continued. "Right after Max Donovan visited Barry at the station, the crew was called out to a fire, and Barry was killed in the fire."

I heard Diamond inhale over the phone. "You think she might have pushed him to his death?"

"Could be. And the mention of it on the voicemail threat could be telling."

Diamond took his time responding. "Donovan lives in Reno and goes to bars in Carson City. It's not obvious how he would find out that the Jasos lived in Christmas Valley."

"The riding instructor said Billy Jaso was a talker. He probably told Donovan."

"It still seems improbable, a gun freak like Donovan mixing with horses," Diamond said. "That was a nineteenth century association. These days, gun guys are into pickups and toys with engines. Not so much horse stuff."

"I agree. Max Donovan's neighbor in Reno said Donovan pursues women who wear cowboy boots. Donovan probably has no interest in the Pony Express and only went to the meetings because he's into women who wear cowboy boots."

"I've heard of boot fetishes, but that's extreme." Diamond sounded disgusted. I heard him breathing on the phone. "Meaning what? This stalker cruises events with horses, meets a man who talks about his daughter and her horses, and so the stalker goes after her because she might wear cowboy boots?"

"Who knows?"

"I'm eager to meet up with this lowlife."

"You and me both," I said.

"So Max Donovan kidnaps Jade Jaso because he's a sexual predator who's into cowboy boots. You think this is an open-ended thing? He keeps her prisoner for days? Then what? Kills her after he gets tired of her?"

"The archivist in Sacramento showed me evidence that Stanford had a jade sculpture that may have been carved by one of Jade Jaso's ancestors. The archivist also had evidence that suggested a Basque woodworker may have stolen it and taken it to Tahoe where he hid it in sheepherding country. Billy Jaso's journal corroborates this. If Jaso had told Max Donovan about that, it could be that Donovan was motivated by that valuable item and Jade was an added enticement. He might think that Jade knows the location of the hidden carving."

"You couldn't make this up if you tried." Diamond's disbelief was obvious.

"No, I couldn't."

"So it ain't your basic kidnapping," Diamond said. "How hard do you think it will be to find them by air?"

"Somewhere between quite and very. When you search mountains and valleys, canyons and crags and cliffs, it starts to seem pretty overwhelming. And most of the territory is covered with forests that you can't see through. Even if they stayed on the Tahoe Rim Trail, that's a lot to search. And if they are under the forest canopy, then there's almost no way to find them."

It was a moment before Diamond spoke. "I'm hoping you have an idea that could increase our odds of finding them."

"I do," I said. "I've got a map that Billy Jaso had stashed in his journal along with the letter from Lincoln."

"The letter you showed me."

"Yeah. On the map, Billy marked a bunch of mine locations."

"This is sounding better already. You think Jaso would have hid stuff in a mine?"

"Not normally. But when mines are marked on a map, it is suggestive."

"Can you still rent that plane at the South Tahoe airport?"

"I hope so."

"I'd like to come along and help be a spotter," Diamond said. "But I'm buried for the next few hours."

I couldn't remember ever flying with Diamond. Like all pilots, I wondered if he was really buried or if he was uncomfortable with flying in small planes.

"I'll search by myself," I said. "Unless Street wants to take a plane ride."

"Let me know when you find them and get back on the ground. If I'm unburied by then, I'll come along. I know you won't bring a weapon, so it would be good for me to make up for that."

"My weapon is a razor-sharp mind."

"Wow." Diamond said.

"I knew you'd be impressed. One more thing. As best I can tell, Max Donovan doesn't know about me. If I find him by air, then I could approach on the ground as if I'm just a hiker exploring the Tahoe Rim Trail. I don't want Street to hike with me because this jerk is dangerous. But if you and I are together, Max might get nervous. And if he senses that you're..."

"A cop," Diamond filled in, understanding where I was going, "he'll probably shoot sooner rather than later."

"I'd worry about that, yeah."

"So I go in my civvies. I wear my dude ranch cowboy hat. All my weapons are stowed in concealed-carry holsters or hidden on my steed. I'll practice up on my ah-shucks-demeanor and remark about how we got no lakes like this in Arizona."

"That should do it," I said. "One last question. Do you think we're nuts to track this guy and attempt to take him into custody without backup?"

"A little," Diamond said. "There's five counties that make up the Tahoe Basin. Depending on whose jurisdiction we're in when we find him, I could call for appropriate reinforcements. But we probably won't be in a position to wait long. But the basic principle of law enforcement still applies."

"What's that?" I asked. "Impartial adherence to the law and dedication to Sir Robert Peel's policing principles?"

"No. Bob ain't out on the trail with us. The principle I was referring to is, 'Find the dirtball and lock him up.'"

"Good attitude," I said. "Talk to you soon."

THIRTY-NINE

Over the last year, I'd been periodically going out for a quick Cessna hop around Lake Tahoe, maintaining the required 3 takeoffs and 3 landings every 90-days so I can carry passengers if needed. Staying current meant I could rent a plane on short notice.

I called the one-man aviation company I rent from at the South Lake Tahoe airport and spoke to the instructor I'd gotten to know a little.

"I've got the Skyhawk and the One-Fifty," he said when I asked what was available immediately.

"The One-Fifty will be perfect," I said, thinking about the poetic coincidence of hunting a bad guy who drove an old Ford truck that shared a name with the Cessna.

"Lemme guess," he said. "You're doing an air search, and you want to float your way real slow between the mountain peaks, so a forty-eight mile-per-hour stall speed is the goal. Slow is the objective, right?"

"Yeah. I know guys who can bicycle a level highway faster than that."

"You looking for a body, or what?"

"Bodies. Alive. And horses."

"Where you gonna look?"

"The TRT," I said.

"The Tahoe Rim Trail pushes two hundred miles in length," he said. "You do some sightseeing on your way, the miles will add up."

"A One-Fifty has a range of five hundred miles, right?"

"Four hundred fifty, give or take."

"Great. I'll be back before the tanks run dry. Does that fit your schedule today?"

"I have to watch you do your run-up. It's in the contract. But the moment you rotate and are in the air, I'm hitting the links. Got a buddy with a deal at Edgewood. Then lunch at the Red Hut Cafe. Then I go home for a nap 'cuz Missy my cat was sick last night and I was up comforting her for hours. She's better now so I'm thinking I can get in a snooze. Bring your cell and call my office when you got an ETA on your return. I'll be there for your landing. That's in the contract, too."

"I wonder why," I said.

"Lawyer stuff. If you crash, there's less liability to me if I can testify that I saw your approach, and that the plane was perfect, and that it was obviously pilot error that caused you to stall and pancake and flip over." He paused, then added, "'Course, my only real concern is that you are safe and happy."

"Of course. Even so, it's so reassuring to know that everyone wants to cover their ass. See you soon."

I hung up and called Street. "Diamond called to say they found Jade Jaso's truck and horse trailer on the south side of Highway Fifty at Spooner Summit."

"She's in the Tahoe Basin? That's great!"

"Yes and no. A pickup belonging to Max Donovan was also there. More evidence that he kidnapped her and her horses. My best guess is that Max is forcing her to look for the place where her father thought the Stanford valuables might have been stashed. I'm renting a plane so I can fly the TRT, search for the mines on the map, and see if I can find Jade and her horses. Would you like to come along to help me look?"

"I'd love to. Give me a sec to check something."

I waited while Street looked at her calendar or journal or her lab experiments with maggots or some other lovely critters. I'd learned that timing was critical in the entomology business. Wouldn't want to miss a pupation or molting or hatching or whatever excitement was about to transpire with the tiny six-legged animals that, by all measures, will likely inherit the Earth when we destroy it.

"Would we be back by evening?" she said in my ear. "I'm monitoring an online forum, and I'll need to check the results by eight p.m."

"Yeah, if Jade and the bad guy can be found, we'll be done before dark. I don't like to fly at night in the mountains, anyway."

"Okay. You want to pick me up? Maybe leave Spot here with Blondie?"

"Be there soon."

I drove to Street's condo. Street grabbed her binoculars, we left the dogs, headed to the south end of the lake, and turned into the airport. My aviation guy was there.

He gestured out toward the little red-and-white plane on the tarmac. "That bird's engine was overhauled just last spring. I've got her gassed and washed and spit-polished. Once you're up checking out the scenery, you'll be forgiven if you find yourself thinking she's brand new."

It was a good observation for a plane built in the mid '60s. Unlike with cars, pilots don't just revere 60-year-old planes for their classic designs, but also for their still useful function.

I signed the paperwork, he gave me the key, and we walked out to the plane ten minutes later. I opened the door, pulled out the checklist card, and started going down the items that I could recite from memory. I was thorough about the process, not just because Street was watching, but because there is value in the thoroughness. Check the wings and flaps and ailerons, the elevator, rudder, and fuselage surfaces. Drain a sample of gas from the tank sump and inspect it for stuff that shouldn't be there, contamination, water, or anything else. Feel the propeller, looking for dings and nicks or anything that might suggest that the prop couldn't handle an RPM of 2750 for hours at a time. Kick the tires and verify they have air and tread. Check all the leading edges, the tiedown, the lights, static port, the front strut, the engine, air filter, oil level.

I helped Street into the right seat, I got into the left, and we fastened our belts. I started in on the cabin and cockpit checklist, which is much longer. I checked all the flight controls and instruments, adjusted the altimeter, turned on the radio, transponder, and lights.

"Everything looks good?" Street said, tension in her voice. She'd been up with me several times. But passengers in small aircraft are often wary, even if they've flown before. We get into an airliner and we take it for granted that it will reliably fly us across the oceans. We walk onto a ship, we assume it will float and deliver us to distant ports of call and not hit a rocky reef and sink. But a small plane is different.

"Everything looks good," I said.

"This is an old plane," she said.

"Which means it's demonstrated its airworthiness a thousand times. It's been well maintained. The mechanics have given it their approval. And just to be sure, I'm always thorough with the checklist routine."

She nodded. I noticed her hands were clenched into fists in her lap. "Are we at the right weight or temperature for the plane? What's that other thing called?"

"Density altitude?" I said.

"Yeah."

"You are light weight, so it's easier for the plane to climb into the sky. The temperature is cool and the barometric pressure is high. That all adds up to good flying conditions."

"Nothing can go wrong?"

"Well, technically, something can always go wrong. But it's unlikely. You can relax."

When I was done with the routine, I started the engine, taxied out to the end of the runway, and began the run-up procedure, which basically means setting the brakes while you throttle up the engine and verify that the instruments show that everything is working properly.

When I'd checked everything and throttled back to idle, I said, "Ready?"

"Ready."

"Comfortable?" I said. "As always, you don't have to do this."

"I want to do this."

I nodded, picked up the radio, announced my departure, and released the brakes. While still idling, I rolled forward and turned onto the runway. Once we were pointed down the runway, I pushed the throttle all the way forward.

Flying a little plane is not unlike heading out on a little boat. You give it gas, it jumps forward, there is some shake and rattle, and it wavers a bit side-to-side as it goes down the runway. Then, like a boat hitting planing speed and stabilizing, you hit what's called rotation speed, which in a Cessna 150, is a little over 50 miles per hour. I eased the yoke back, the tail lowered a bit, and we lifted off.

FORTY

We climbed into the air with most of the runway still in front of us. The shimmy and sway went away, and we were left with the steady drone of engine and prop vibration as we gained altitude.

We'd taken off on a north heading. With just a few hundred feet of altitude, the panorama of the lake opened up before us. We were 500 feet or more above ground level when we crossed over the shore and the edge of the vast blue water. I set a northeast course, angling to cross back over land near Cave Rock on the East Shore, not far from my cabin.

"It never gets old, does it?" Street said, speaking loudly to be heard over the roar of the engine. "The view, the excitement."

I turned to look at her. She was grinning. Any tension about flying was gone.

"Never," I said.

We continued to climb at a gentle rate. Our speed was 70 miles per hour. As we crossed back over land, we were at 8000 feet, which was 1800 feet above the water. We cruised above Glenbrook, still climbing, heading toward Spooner Summit.

"There it is," Street called out, pointing. "Jade's horse trailer. And the old yellow pickup is tucked under the trees behind it. That's the one we're looking for, right?"

"Max Miller Donovan's," I said. "They could have walked the horses across the highway and ridden north. But I'm guessing they followed the Tahoe Rim Trail heading south. You have an opinion?"

"Works for me."

I nodded and banked the plane to the south.

I checked my altimeter. We were now at 9000 feet. I continued a gradual climb. I wanted to be high enough to stay well clear of the mountaintops. Genoa Peak, directly east of my cabin, was at 9150. Despite calm wind, the rule in flying near the mountains is to always assume that the altimeter can be off, the weather can change, and there can be downdrafts. Your assumed safe above-ground clearance can quickly evaporate. In addition to that, I didn't want to startle Street by skimming too close to the rock, whether intentionally or not.

"Anything specific I should watch for?" she asked.

"Horses. Jade Jaso. A gun freak who's holding her captive."

"What does a gun freak look like?" Street asked only somewhat facetiously.

"Big guy with guns. His neighbor says he's a handsome guy who thinks he's magic with women. From what the neighbor said, he's likely got a rifle hanging from a gun sling across his shoulder, a sawed-off shotgun strapped to his chest, and a pistol in a hip holster."

"Is that all," Street said. "Why would he need all those weapons?"

"He doesn't. A gun guy doesn't carry multiple weapons because he needs them. He carries them because they make him feel more potent. More masculine."

"You don't carry any gun. Do you feel masculine?" she asked.

"Enough, I guess," I said.

"You're masculine enough to have me."

"And you'll have me even without guns. I appreciate that."

"Do you suppose that gun freaks have trouble attracting girls? Is there a connection there? Or are there women who are drawn to men with guns?"

"I'm guessing the answer to all three questions is yes. But there are exceptions. Women are often attracted to Diamond, but they usually don't know he carries a sidearm."

"But Diamond's a cop. Would he carry a gun if he weren't a cop?"

"Probably not."

"You were a cop." Street was craning her head to look down and back. If she saw anything, it didn't cause her any worry.

"Did you feel you needed weapons back then?"

"Yeah. I carried my sidearm but no backup weapon."

"And then you had to use your gun to kill, and it caused you so much stress that you quit your career and moved out of San Francisco."

"Killing will do that. But if I hadn't been a cop, I wouldn't have carried. So that takes both Diamond and me out of the realm of gun freaks."

"Don't most ex-cops carry a gun?"

"Yeah. But that doesn't make them gun freaks. Ex-cops carry because it's sensible. Some people carry a grudge against cops. And some of those people are nuts."

"And now you're never armed."

"Armed, but not with a gun," I said.

"Oh, what, armed with your wits?" Street giggled.

"Wits and brawn," I said.

She laughed harder.

"This gun freak we're looking for," she said. "You referred to him as a big guy. Does that mean he's got brawn like you?"

"Way more. I saw his weight bench. This guy is a gorilla. No contest between us."

"So if he's got more brawn than you, and he's also got guns, how are you going to deal with him if we find him?"

"Wits, I guess."

Street didn't respond. Maybe she thought she was glad to be connected to a guy who didn't want to make his way in the world by relying on brawn and guns.

Or maybe she thought I was naive and foolish.

We flew farther south. "Check it out," I said, pointing down to the right.

"What?" Street seemed to scan back and forth. "Oh, my God, that's your cabin! From up here it looks so… Tiny."

"That's because it is tiny."

"No brawn, no guns, and tiny cabin, too," she said. "You must be really secure."

"Did you say no brawn?"

"I didn't mean no brawn like, you know, no brawn. You've

got enough brawn to, um, impress a girl."

I nodded and didn't reply.

"Really," she said, slugging me on the shoulder. "I wouldn't want you all muscle-bound. Those steroid muscles don't do anything for me."

"Me neither," I said.

"Where's that mine map?"

I pulled it out of my pocket and handed it to her.

Street unfolded it and held it open on her lap. "This is an unusual combo. It's a basic map of the Tahoe Basin, but it's got all these hand-drawn components. Groups of flowers to make it look decorative. And these other little marks look like Tesla logos."

"Funny. I thought the same thing. I believe that's Billy Jaso's symbol for a pickaxe."

"Oh, of course. Mine locations," she said. "There's quite a few of them spread all over the basin. How do you suppose he found out their locations?"

"It isn't hard to research. There are websites that show active mining claims all across the country. I even have old topographical maps that show mine locations, marks that were removed when they came out with the new editions."

Street frowned. "I bet they took the locations off so they wouldn't have so many problems with people searching out mines, falling into shafts, suing the government for publicizing an attractive hazard."

"You're probably right. But because Billy Jaso did the research, Jade might have had a copy of the map. Which means her kidnapper could be using the exact same map that you have in your lap."

Street looked down at the map with intensity. "How long would it take for us to fly over every mine?"

"My rough guess is that we could inspect them all in about three hours. You can navigate."

Street looked out the window on the right as we went by Cave Rock. She turned and looked forward and to the left. "We'll use the clock navigation reference. This plane is the center of the dial. Noon is straight ahead. Six o'clock is directly behind us. The first mine is at about eleven o'clock." She pointed ahead to the left.

I banked slightly to the left, and the plane went into a gentle curve. After a slight change of heading, I straightened out. Our altitude was 9200 feet, roughly 500 feet above the ground at our current location. We both stared ahead. I continued climbing and leveled out when we got to 10,000 feet. That would be sufficient to clear the nearby mountains. I would only have to fly higher when we got to the taller mountains south of us.

"I'm thinking we're about to go straight above the mine right now." She turned and looked out her side window, straining to look straight down. "I don't see anything."

"I realize my strategy is faulty," I said. "I shouldn't fly directly over the mine. It's too hard to see anything right below us. I should fly a clockwise circle around it. That way we'll be in a bank to the right. You can look out to your side. If you see any possibilities for horses or people, you can look through your binoculars."

I flew past the area I thought had the mine. When we were a few hundred yards past it, I put the plane into a steep bank to the right. We came around back toward the mine location and then made a clockwise circle around it. We were about a quarter mile out from where I thought it might be. Street stared out her side window as we went around at a medium bank. Periodically, she raised her binoculars and studied the area.

When we'd completed a circle, she said, "Nothing. No horses, no people, nothing that looks like a mine. There aren't even enough trees to hide under if one wanted to."

"Okay, we'll head to the next one."

"But if there had been someone there, they'd know we were onto them with us tracing circles above."

"Got it. This time I'll plan the circle route in advance. I'll plan a partial circle, high enough and far enough out that someone below wouldn't be convinced we were trying to find them."

Street glanced at the map. "The next one is just past

Kingsbury Grade, to the east side of Heavenly Ski Resort." She looked off toward the vast blue plate of the lake. She said, "And with less repetitive flying around any given site, we're less likely to spook the muscle guy with the guns."

"Now you're thinking of him as the muscle guy."

"That's how you described him," she said. "Or maybe it was brawny guy. You said he was handsome and had lots of muscles. You said there was no contest between him and you."

"Yeah. But I didn't think you'd catalog him that way."

"How did you think I would catalog him?"

"I thought you'd think of him as a pea-brained idiot who can barely speak English and who drools out of the corner of his mouth every time he uses a word with more than two syllables."

"You obviously have a bad attitude toward men who kidnap women." Street's sense of irony was always in fine tune. Now it seemed to have moved toward serious sarcasm.

"You got that right."

"What will you do to him if you can get past the muscles and drool?"

"I'll hog-tie him."

"Against his will." She looked at me. "And we're in a plane. How will we meet this drooling guy on the ground?"

"Depends on where he is. If he's close, I hike in. If he and Jade are very far up in the mountains, I could even go after him on horseback."

"We'll hike in or ride horseback."

"You shouldn't be in such a dangerous situation."

"Don't give me the 'protect the little woman' excuse."

"I just want you alive and healthy." It sounded lame even as I said it.

"That goes for you as well. I don't want you going alone to meet a gun freak."

"Diamond will come with me."

"You just assume that Diamond will come along to join in the fun?" Street said.

"We discussed it. He's got a thing about catching

criminals."

"And he carries a gun," Street said.

"Two, when he's feeling a sense of threat."

She looked down at the map. "This next mine coming up is southeast of Monument Peak."

"That's ten thousand feet. And Job's Sister and Freel Peak are almost eleven thousand. So I better coax this baby up a bunch higher." I eased back on the yoke, and the Cessna slowly climbed into the deep blue sky.

We flew to the side of Genoa Peak, then over Kingsbury Grade and the Summit Village hotels and condos. I went to the east of Heavenly and the East Peak lake, then banked in a gentle turn to the right. Heavenly spans part of California and Nevada. The ski runs on Heavenly's Nevada side sprawled below us, a mixture of green grass, viridian shrubbery, and gray rocks, waiting for the heavy snows of winter.

"This next mine isn't near any landmarks," Street said, "so I don't know an easy way to find its location. The little Tesla pickaxe is on a steep slope but with no identifying landmarks."

"I can see the Mott Canyon chairlift." I pointed.

"Good landmark. I see the canyon on my map, but the chairlift isn't marked. Judging by the topo lines, we should go over Mott, then curve just a little bit clockwise around Monument Peak and then go straight south toward Job's Sister."

I did as she said.

"There's Star Lake in the distance," Street said. "That's a mine shaft I don't need to revisit." There was a tightness in her voice as she said it.

"No kidding." Several years before, Street had been held prisoner by a psycho in a mine near Star Lake.

Street pointed down. "See this ridge almost below us? The next mine is just to the south of it, below the ridge about – I don't know – a quarter mile or so. Long before we get to Star Lake."

"Got it." I took a course that put the mine location at about two o'clock. As I got close, I put the plane into a right bank.

Street stared out her side window. She held the binoculars,

and briefly raised them to her eyes now and then.

We'd flown most of a circle when she said, "Nothing. I see nothing that looks like a mine."

"Okay, point me toward the next one."

"That would be the Star Lake mine."

"Will do."

I pulled out of my banking turn and headed south to Star Lake. Job's Sister, Tahoe's second highest mountain, loomed above the lake. But I'd brought the plane up to 11,000 feet and was still climbing. We'd be safely above the summit in another minute, assuming, that is, that there were no significant winds aloft to create wind shear or other invisible hazards. The Cessna claimed a service ceiling of 14,000 feet. I'd never flown that high in a Cessna before, and I didn't plan to go that high. But I'd need to go to 12,000 feet to be safe going over the mountaintops.

I didn't worry about oxygen levels because we would still be below the threshold for requiring supplemental oxygen. And Street and I lived and hiked at high altitude and were adapted to lower oxygen levels. So conditions that might bother sea-level dwellers wouldn't bother us.

We came near Star Lake. The cabin that had been over the mine entrance was just a pile of burnt wood, left over from the forest fire that nearly killed us. Nevertheless, I made the clockwise circle. Street looked with her binoculars and said she saw nothing.

We continued our trek, looking at the mine symbols on the map, flying to where we thought they might still be, and inspecting them from the air, looking for any sign of people or horses. We went from Job's Sister across South Lake Tahoe to Emerald Bay. From there, we headed to the high country of Desolation Wilderness.

"How many mines have we looked at?" I asked. "Six? Seven? And how many are left to go?"

Street moved her fingertip to count. "We've been to eight of the places on Billy's map. And of those eight, we saw what clearly looked like five mines. Or at least piles of rubble that weren't natural and so probably had once been mines. And now we've got, one, two… Six more to go. Speaking of which, the next one is coming up. Just beyond Jack's and Dick's peaks."

She held up the map so I could see and pointed.

I looked out at the panorama of mountains and got a visual fix on the location she had indicated. I did as before, putting the plane into a banking, clockwise turn with the mine location at the approximate center of my circle.

Street scanned the area below. It was so rocky, there were only a few, lonely trees, mostly dwarf examples of their species, plants hardy enough to establish some type of root structure in the cracks of the barren, rock landscape but not capable of growing into robust trees. After a minute, Street said, "Nothing. No mine location. No mining debris. No sign of people or horses."

As we flew, I glanced over at the map Street held. She had placed her thumb on one pickaxe mark and her little finger on another, spanning the distance between them, then moving her hand to compare it to another pair of mines.

"You're trying to figure out the most efficient way to visit all the remaining mine locations," I said.

"Yes. The remaining mines require us to go nearly all the way around Lake Tahoe. From here in Desolation Wilderness and Rockbound Valley to Granite Chief Wilderness. And there are three more up by Truckee."

"Does what we're doing still make sense to you? I feel like the whole plan is questionable."

Street turned to look at me. She glanced down at the map, then looked out her side window toward Lake Tahoe below. "I'm wondering about the flower drawings," she said as she stared down at the mountains and lake.

"I wondered about it, too. Billy Jaso was a bit of a romantic. He raised a daughter who was focused on poetry. But I haven't seen or heard anything about flowers."

Street nodded. "I agree. Jade Jaso is the only person I've ever known who named a horse after a Yeats poem. But she never mentioned flowers. And there were no flower beds at her house or barn. And for that matter, these flower drawings don't look poetic, if that makes sense."

"What do they look like?"

"I don't know how to describe it," she said. "They look decorative. Like Billy Jaso was prettying up his map. But they're too regular. It's like they're informational. More like the Tesla pickaxes."

"The pickaxes are there to convey locations. Is it possible the flowers do the same thing?"

"But locations of what, I wonder." Street looked at the map again. "Maybe these hand-drawn flowers mark wildflower locations. You and I have been to at least two of these places because they have terrific wildflower displays in July and August."

"That's intriguing. If the little flower symbols are about wildflowers, then we have to connect wildflowers to the Stanford treasure."

"Or..." Street said, drawing out the word. "We have to connect the flowers to the guy who stole the Stanford treasure and then hid it."

"The Basque sheepherder. Billy Jaso was Basque. The Basque came to Tahoe to herd sheep. Maybe sheep like to eat wildflowers. Maybe... Wait." I startled myself with a sudden thought.

"What?" Street said.

"Look at how those flower symbols were made."

She was quiet a moment. "Well, the drawings are actually quite abstract. He drew a vertical line and then did a puffy kind of circle shape around the top. Like a little cumulus cloud perched at the top of the vertical line."

"Right." I reached over and pointed. "Most really bad drawers like me would draw individual petals. Six or eight of them at the top of a vertical line. The puffy cumulus cloud approach is more abstract and sophisticated than a beginner like me would draw."

"What are you saying?"

"I'm saying, maybe those little marks aren't flower symbols at all."

"If not flowers, what would they be?" she asked.

"What about sheep? Or trees?"

"Owen, I think you're right! But why would Billy Jaso put trees in different places on the map?"

"Look at the topo lines. I bet the little plant symbols are in places that aren't very steep. I'm guessing they are mostly flat areas."

Street held the map up close to her face. "Yes. Close topographic lines show steep slopes. But these topo lines are very far apart, which means the lay of the land is mostly level."

I said, "A hundred and sixty years ago, sheepherders brought their sheep to graze at high meadows. Meadows form where the soil doesn't have good drainage, right? If the land stays very moist for long periods of time, most trees don't grow, but grasses do grow."

Street was still looking at the map. "But these symbols look even less like meadow grass than they do like wildflowers."

"I'm guessing that's because there is one tree that grows in wet meadow areas. aspen trees."

"Of course! Billy Jaso was marking aspen groves, which were at or near good grazing areas."

I said, "And the aspen trees were where the Basque sheepherders carved their drawings into tree bark."

FORTY-ONE

At the realization that the symbols were aspen trees, not flowers, Street nearly shouted, "I've seen the book with the Basque arborglyphs. Pictures and poems and drawings."

"In the journal that Jade's father Billy wrote, he mentioned going to a Basque woman and having her read old Basque letters. Just like the archivist Brady Harper, he learned about the Basque sheepherder Benat Mendoza, who may have stolen a treasure from Stanford and carried it up to Tahoe. We know that Basque sheepherders took their sheep to the meadow areas near aspen groves. So we have a strong suggestion that Stanford's treasure might have ended up near one of Tahoe's meadow areas."

Street looked at the map. "Before we fly all the way to Truckee to check out the rest of the mines on the map, maybe we should visit the aspen groves that are on the south end of the basin."

"Worth a try, I think."

Street oriented the map on her lap to fit with the area below us. "Okay, Mr. Pilot, take us just south of Emerald Bay and Cascade Lake. There are tree symbols right on Highway Eighty-nine. They're near Baldwin Beach."

"I know that meadow and aspen grove," I said. "On the highway near the Spring Creek turnoff."

She nodded and looked out the window.

We came near the aspen grove, I did the clockwise banking turn, and Street studied the trees below.

"No horses, no people, no ancient sheepherder shack. Of course, I wouldn't expect they would be so close to a busy road."

We flew on to check an aspen grove where the Upper Truckee River wound its way through meadows near the lake shore and emptied into the lake. As that meadow and grove were in the city limits of South Lake Tahoe, we didn't expect it to yield any results, either. And it didn't.

Billy Jaso had put several of his flower/aspen grove markers near Washoe Meadows State Park, a rare park that had no signage or access road announcing its existence. The park is just south of the Upper Truckee River, and features a long meadow up its center with adjacent aspen groves. I remembered from past hikes it was often used by horseback riders.

We flew over it. Again, there were no horses or people.

Street directed me to other groves. It began to seem futile.

"The next batch of groves are out Christmas Valley."

"Where the Jaso ranch is. That would be ironic if Max Donovan kidnapped Jade and her horses, forced her to park all the way over at Spooner Summit, only to end up riding back to Christmas Valley."

"Ironic?" Street said. "Or good obfuscation?"

"Good point. From what I've heard about Donovan, he isn't the obfuscating type. His neighbor told of how he gets drunk and shoots his beer cans for fun. Not much obfuscation there."

The airport we'd taken off from was to our left as we cruised out to the far south end of the Tahoe Basin. We were far enough above ground that horses would be hard to see. But I didn't want to go lower as we inspected the Christmas Valley aspen groves. The valley is hemmed in by cliffs on both sides. For safety, I wanted to stay above the closest mountains.

Street used her binoculars to study the ground.

"Nothing," she eventually said. "This is proving to be a bust."

"Where to next?"

"All that's left are the groves up near Steven's Peak." She gestured toward the huge mountain that loomed to the south. "There are multiple groves in Meiss Meadows to the west and north of the peak, and there are some on the higher flanks of the mountain."

"Okay, time to go back up high. Steven's Peak is ten thousand feet." I pulled back on the yoke, nudged the throttle forward, and put us into a steady climb. I knew the Cessna wouldn't gain altitude fast enough to clear the mountains on a straight-line flight, so I put the plane into a steep, climbing bank. My turning radius was short enough to stay away from the cliffs. We went round and round twice. I straightened out heading south, then leveled off as we got to 11,000 feet.

Street pointed at the area to the west of Steven's Peak. Meiss Meadows was shaped a little like a three-sided baking pan, relatively flat and surrounded by steep mountains on three sides. It channeled snowmelt into the headwaters of the Upper Truckee River, Lake Tahoe's largest inflow.

"Meiss Meadows would have been a sheepherder's paradise," I said. "Forests and lakes and lots of grassy areas."

"And lots of aspen groves," Street said. She pointed at the large, bold cliffs on the side of Steven's Peak. "More up on the mountain under the palisades."

"Shall we fly over Meiss Meadows first?"

She nodded.

"The groves are numerous enough that it doesn't make sense to circle each one," I said. "Okay if I treat the group of them as a single extensive grove?"

"Makes sense," she said. "I should be able to scan the area with my binoculars."

We flew a large clockwise circle over the area. Street studied the ground, with and without the binoculars.

"Can you go any lower?"

"Only if I shift my pattern to the west. I don't want to get too close to the cliffs of Steven's Peak."

She nodded.

I put the plane into a slight descent and moved my search pattern away from the cliffs.

Her gaze was intent. She raised her binoculars, scanned left to right, lowered them, frowned, raised them again. As I began my second trip in a large circle, she shook her head. "I don't think anyone is down there. Or if there is, I can't see them, horses or not. Let's shift back toward the palisades."

"Gotta go back up," I said.

"Right."

Once again, I climbed back to a safe altitude and began a banking circle that had as its focus a large aspen grove at the base of the cliffs. I'd completed most of a circle when Street spoke.

"I think I see something. Yes, I do! Horses. One, no, two of them! I want to ask you to stop, but that's absurd. Just ignore me. Continue what you're doing." She was quiet, still holding the binoculars to her eyes. Then, "There's a third! A third horse!"

"Where?"

"Look at the base of the cliffs, then shift your gaze a little bit toward the aspen trees. There are some evergreens, Jeffrey pine, I think, judging by the warm color of green. Where the pines meet the aspens are two horses. And in the middle of the aspens is the third horse."

"Still no people?"

"No." Her head and hands and binoculars moved as one as she looked back and forth. "There he is!"

"What do you see?"

"A man, holding a gun. A rifle. He's pointing it at something. I can't tell what from up this high. It looks like a boulder. There's something bright on the boulder. A few of them. One of them just flew away. It must have been a bird. Another just moved. Now it's on the ground. I think he's shooting beer cans!"

"Can you see what he looks like? Clothes? Hair?"

"He's hard to see because he blends into the background. He's wearing camouflage clothing. Pants anyway. He's got long hair. Medium brown."

"Camo shirt?"

"I can't tell. Maybe. But his arms are bare. I think he's got on a shirt, but the sleeves are rolled up. His arms look smudged blue. Tattoos."

"A lot of musclebound guys roll up their sleeves. It's part of the display."

"He's holding the rifle in his left hand and moving his right arm. I can't tell… Yes, I can. He's drinking beer. He just tossed the can on the ground. It's bright like the ones on the boulder. There are other cans on the ground. He just aimed again at the boulder. He's kind of wavering. Like he's drunk. Another can just flew. Now he's turning. I can't see why. Maybe someone's coming. Maybe he's looking at Jade, wherever she is. No he's not. He's looking up. Oh, my God, Owen, he's looking at us. And he's raising his rifle!"

I immediately turned the yoke, increasing the bank of the plane. Our turning circle tightened.

"Owen! I just saw a flash of light. I don't understand. Does he have a light attached to the rifle?"

"I doubt it. You just saw a muzzle flash."

"He's shooting at us!"

FORTY-TWO

Few things focus a person like being shot at.
We were now flying north. I banked the plane a little the other way, then back. We were making S-curves through the sky as we flew away.

"Another muzzle flash! And another! And there's something else. There's a long streak of light over the pine trees. Like a shooting star."

He was shooting tracer bullets, but I didn't say so. I didn't want to alarm Street any more than necessary.

Because of Street's commentary, I knew the shooter hadn't taken time to reload, so he'd probably loaded a tracer bullet for every four or five regular bullets. It was a standard way to help a shooter see where his bullets were going, a way to increase accuracy. Street had described the streak of light as being visible against the pine trees. Because we were so far above the shooter, I didn't think she'd be able to see a tracer if it had been shot level across the ground. But if it had come far up into the sky toward us, it would stand out.

I focused on flying a curving, evasive path, trying to gain altitude, trying to put as much distance as possible between us and the shooter.

"Another muzzle flash!" Street sounded very tense.

"We're on our way out of his range." As I said it, I sensed an unusual sound that I couldn't identify. A plinking sound, not especially metallic. But higher and sharper than a thud. And then came another similar sound. Then a third.

"Ouch," Street said. Not a loud exclamation but like what one says when bitten by a horse fly. She reached down to her right hip and rubbed it.

"You okay?" I said.

"Yeah. Maybe I put a toothpick in my pocket and I just poked myself with it."

I made another banking S-turn. The yoke felt normal as I turned. Same for the rudder and the elevator. I listened to the engine. Nothing seemed out of place.

"No more muzzle flashes," Street said. She was still rubbing her hip.

"We're now almost a mile away from the shooter. Out of range." I looked around the cockpit, checking the windows. I looked out and up at the left wing, checking all of the surfaces.

"What are you looking for?"

"Just checking to see that everything is normal. Maybe you can look out the right side, up at the wing." As I said it, I sensed some darkness toward the blurred circle of the prop. I lifted up in my seat so that my head was touching the plane's ceiling. The darkness was a stream of black smoke coming out from the cowling over the engine. A bullet had struck some part of the oil system. The roar of the engine still sounded normal, and the prop still turned. But I had no doubt we'd been hit and we'd face serious consequences soon.

"What do I look for?" Street said, unaware of what I'd seen. Her face was against the passenger's side window.

"It's very hard to hit a moving target like us, especially one so far away as we are. But just to be sure, look for any variation on the surface of the wing, the ailerons, the flaps."

"Which are which? Oh, I suppose it doesn't matter. No, I don't see any variation. The surfaces are smooth. No dents or bullet holes. No…" she paused. "There is something strange. I can't really tell what I'm seeing. Nothing on the wing. But behind the wing. It almost looks like spray of some kind."

That was a shock.

"I'll lean across you and look," I said. I shifted in my seat, leaned over Street, my shoulder coming across her chest. "Where do you see it?"

"There." She struggled to pull her arm out from where I'd pinned it. She pointed. "See? Back there. Behind the wing. Almost like an optical illusion."

Except it wasn't an illusion. It was spray. Gasoline. Streaming from a bullet hole that was just barely visible.

"Can you see it?" she asked.

"Yeah. We've been hit, and we're leaking gas."

Despite the loud rush of air and the engine noise of flight, I could hear Street inhale. She put her hand to her mouth, then inhaled more deeply. She pulled her hand away from her face, moving her fingers as if something was on her fingertips.

Her hand, and now her face, were smeared with blood.

FORTY-THREE

"Street, you've been hit."

She stared at her hand and said, "It's not that much blood, so I'm probably okay." It was an impressively cool reaction to being shot in a plane. She reached her hand down between her hip and the door of the plane. She palpated the area, winced, touched some more. She shifted in her seat, angling her right hip up, ran her fingertips along her pants. "I think I've only been grazed. I can see where the door is splintered. It probably slowed the bullet." She unbuckled her belt, lifted up to pull her pants down a bit, then examined her wound. "It's a superficial wound. Like a scrape. Why it's bleeding so much, I don't know. One of those vascular areas, I guess. I'll be fine."

She looked back out the window toward the wing. "Owen, when you said we're leaking gas, you sounded so calm. Like it's no big deal. Tell me if it's no big deal, so I don't worry about the gas, too."

"I'm sorry, hon, it is a big deal. We're leaking gas at a good rate." I paused, thinking it was important to be honest about all aspects of our situation. "The engine has also been hit. We're streaming black smoke. Probably an oil leak is running over the hot engine and burning."

It was a moment before Street reacted. "What do we do?" Her voice was lower in pitch and calmer still.

"All we can do is try to make it back to the airport."

"Is there anything to do about the engine being hit?"

"No. Maybe it's a slow oil leak. Maybe the gas leak is slow, too. Maybe not. All we can do is try to make it to the runway."

"Is there a way to shut off the gas flow or something? Because the tank is in the wing, then doesn't that imply there's another tank in the other wing? We could fly using that tank's gas."

"There is another tank." I was looking ahead toward the airport, which was visible about eight miles distant.

"Then can't you just run the engine with gas from that other tank?"

"Yes and no. The other tank doesn't appear to be leaking, which is good. And the engine will continue to run as long as it gets gas and enough oil to provide lubrication. But this particular model Cessna has a cross linkage from one gas tank to the other, with no way to shut off the cross flow."

"Which means?"

"As the gas leaks out of the right tank, the gas in the left tank will flow into the leaking tank. The two tanks will equalize."

Street was unfamiliar with planes. But she was smart about all things, familiar or not. "Meaning that a leak in either tank will cause gas to eventually drain out of both tanks."

"Right."

"Is there no valve to shut off the leaky tank?"

"Most planes have that. Even many Cessnas. But not this particular model."

"Is there anything else you can do?"

"Yes, but I don't know if it will help or not. I can bank the airplane to the left and apply the right rudder to keep the plane flying straight, more or less. It sets up what's called a slip. That's a very inefficient way to fly. But it makes it so the left wing and its tank will be lower than the right. We normally only do a slip when we're trying to land in a cross wind."

"If the left tank is lower, the gas won't be able to flow up and over to the right tank because the right tank is above it," she said.

I nodded.

"But less efficient flying means you will burn up more gas. Do we have enough to make it to the airport?"

"I think so," I said. It was partially true. But there was also a bit of hope in the statement. "Conserving gas by flying at an angle seems a higher priority than flying more efficiently. But I'm not sure."

"I can't believe this," Street said through clenched teeth.

Her hands were fists in her lap, knuckles white, bloody streaks obvious across the skin. "Getting shot out of the sky in Tahoe of all places."

"I've got some Kleenex in my day pack," I said. "Maybe you can use a wad of it as a pressure compress on your wound."

I banked the plane a little to the left and pushed down on the right rudder pedal with my foot. The plane immediately tilted and started "slipping" to the left. We were no longer flying to where the plane was pointing. To compensate for our change in flight direction, I pointed the plane a little to the right, crabbing to make up for the slip. As soon as I started the process, I started to doubt the sense of it. I had no idea if reducing gas leakage was worth the loss in efficiency from slipping the plane.

I pulled out my phone and handed it to Street. "Can you please dial nine, one, one?"

"You want me to explain?"

"As pilot, I should probably give them the details."

Street dialed and handed me the phone. When the dispatcher answered and asked for name and address, I said, "Owen McKenna calling from a Cessna One Fifty flying at..." – I made a quick glance at the altimeter – "ten thousand five hundred feet. I'm on a north heading, coming up Christmas Valley from Steven's Peak." I gave her the aircraft details. "We've taken rifle fire from the ground and have a fuel leak and engine damage. I'd like to request fire department presence on the taxiway at the SLT airport, as I'm hoping to make it there. I'd also like you to patch me through to Sargent Bains, El Dorado Sheriff's Office."

"I'll have the fire department en route in a minute. Regulations require me to keep you on the line, sir."

"Thanks. But I can't stay on the line. I'm flying a damaged plane." I clicked off and handed the phone back to Street. "Sergeant Bains should be in my contact list."

Street found it, dialed, and handed the phone back.

Bains answered. I repeated my situation to him.

"You're leaking fuel and oil?" Bains said. "Not what you want."

"If we make the runway, I'd like you to coordinate some interference. We'll want to head to the shooter's location very quickly."

"Got it," he said. "No time to pause for Q and A with the firefighters. I'll make it clear everyone lets you go. Assuming you land okay, that is. If you think you can't make the runway, we can close the highway."

"I'll try for the runway. There are power lines and utility poles on that highway. I'd rather put down on the meadow just south of the runway. But if I lose power soon and my choice is the highway or the trees, I'll call you back."

"Okay, I'm going to have a patrol unit go to Meyers to be ready to stop northbound traffic. And I'll put another unit on the highway near the airport. You call if you want me to have them close it down."

"Will do. In case we don't make it, we believe the shooter is Max Miller Donovan."

"The man who took Jade Jaso," he said. "Douglas County Sergeant Martinez told me."

"He's on the west side of Steven's Peak, near the base of the palisades. In addition to taking Jade prisoner, he has her three horses, which will help identify him. He's armed and also drunk."

"Great combo," Bains said.

"He was using tracer rounds when he shot at us." In my peripheral vision, I saw Street jerk her head.

"Were you able to verify that Jade is okay?" Bains asked.

"No. We didn't see her. But I assume she's being held nearby."

"Did you get his location? GPS coordinates?"

"No. But he was near an aspen grove near the base of the palisades to the west of Steven's Peak. Not too far from Meiss Lake and Round Lake."

"You think he was on the Pacific Crest Trail?"

"No. I think he was northeast of the PCT. But he may be heading that direction."

"Sounds like he's close enough to Steven's Peak that he's in

Alpine County. No matter. We're closer than Alpine's guys and we've got more manpower. You got an idea of where this guy would go?" Bains asked. "Hope Valley?"

"No idea. Does El Dorado County still have those volunteers who use their own chopper?"

"The Jet Ranger. I haven't heard the latest. I'll find out. But CHP might have one a lot closer, anyway. I'll do what I can. In the meantime, I can get deputies to hustle up the trail from South Upper Truckee Road. Your plan is what?"

"Not sure, yet. Street's been shot."

"What?!"

"She says it's just a scrape. But there's a fair amount of blood."

"A bullet groove will do that."

"If we make it back to the airport, we need to make an assessment of her condition, maybe get her to a doctor."

"NO," Street said firmly, her voice loud enough that Bains could probably hear it over the phone. "I'll let the fire department paramedic take a look at it. If he or she says a bandage will get me through the next few hours, then that's what I do. As long as I'm conscious, I'm in charge of where I go and how I'm treated."

"You hear that?" I said into the phone.

"Loud and clear. I knew your lady had a strong personality. Better do what she says, huh?"

I glanced over at Street. "Right. Anyway, I – or we – will drive from the airport back to Christmas Valley and hike up toward Meiss Meadows as well."

I sensed his hesitation.

"We'll be spotters and stay out of your way," I said. "You can use every pair of eyes you can get."

More hesitation. "Okay," he finally said, likely realizing that there was no point in trying to change our behavior. "Good luck with your plane." Bains clicked off.

I looked at Street. "You still feel okay? You're not light-headed?"

"I'm fine. It's just a scratch."

"A lot of blood for a scratch." I handed my phone back to her. "This call to Diamond, please."

She didn't speak as she tapped the screen.

I focused on my gauges, trying to estimate – based on our gas supply – if we would make the airport or not. As for the oil leak, I had no way to judge the impact.

Street handed the phone to me after it started ringing.

"Sí, McKenna," Diamond said in my ear.

"Street and I are still in the air. We found Max Donovan."

"That was fast."

"Street spotted him drunk in an aspen grove on the side of Steven's Peak, shooting at our plane."

"How do you know he is drunk?"

"Even from the air, Street could see him wavering. One of his rounds punctured Street's hip."

"Jesus!" Diamond said it with the Mexican 'Hay soos' pronunciation. "How bad's she hit?"

"She claims it's just a scrape."

"Knowing her," Diamond said, "it's probably serious. You want me to arrange a medivac helicopter to be waiting at the airport?"

"No. She was adamant that the fire department paramedic can treat her."

"You called them why? Fire danger?"

"Maybe. Another round punctured our starboard gas tank and we're spraying gas over the landscape. A third hit something up front. We're trailing a black smoke trail like we're in an aerobatic show."

"You're leaking gas," he said. Diamond's statement was a 'just the facts,' conclusion with no emotion. "You're attempting to make it to the airport?"

"Yeah."

"I'm off duty, and I'm on the South Shore. I can be at the airport in ten minutes. Fifteen max."

"We might not make it."

"Then I'll be there to help clean up the mess. You want me to scare up troops?"

"Not necessary. I just spoke to Bains. His official territory and all. He says he will have deputies hiking up toward Meiss Meadows in a short time. Assuming we nail our landing, I'd like you to come with Street and me. Bains'll be cool with you helping."

"Okay. Put that crate down gently, buddy," Diamond said. "Keep that girl of yours in one piece." He clicked off.

I handed my phone back to Street. "One more call please, to our poor aviation rental company."

Street found the number, dialed, and once again handed me the phone.

I explained our situation to the man. Then I added, "So sorry about your plane."

"You're trying not to auger in, and you think I'm worried about the plane? Just put that boat down where the wheels can roll. If you can't make the runway, take the highway. If you've got binoculars, you can see where overhead lines cross the road and pick a good place to get to the pavement."

"Thanks. I already called Sergeant Bains. He's ready to close the highway if necessary."

I hung up and put the phone in my pocket.

"What should I do?" Street said. She was staring out at the distant runway which, though miles ahead, was easy to see. It didn't seem to be getting any closer.

"Nothing much to do," I said. "Hold your hand on your bullet wound to slow the bleeding.

She glanced out at the wing that was still spraying gas, even though we were flying at an angle.

"What happens if we run out of gas?"

"The engine will quit."

"What about the oil leak? Does that kill the engine, too?"

"Maybe. If so, we'll try to glide to the runway."

Street looked out at the spraying gas then turned to stare at the runway in the distance. "Does that work? Gliding a plane without power?"

"It works pretty well," I said. "Once the propeller quits turning, we can still glide almost a mile and a half for every thousand feet we're above the ground. Right now, we're down to a little over nine thousand feet, which means we're about three thousand feet above the ground."

"So we can glide about four and a half miles," she said. "How far do you think we are from the airport?"

"Six or seven miles."

"Are we screwed?"

"Not at all. We haven't run out of gas yet."

Street's hands were white. The pale color made the smears of blood look even more red. Her jaw was still clenched.

"Let's hope the engine keeps running for another three miles," I said. "If it goes four, we should make it easy." I glanced at the gas gauges. The needle on the leaky right tank was on empty. The left was on ⅛. Complicating the stress was the knowledge that up to a gallon of gas per tank was unusable, the quirks of a design such that the gravity-feed system doesn't draw all of the gas out of the tanks. And I was purposely flying at a banked angle, which would make fuel flow worse.

Street was shaking her head. "We might die," she said. "And you're cheerfully saying that if we can go another three miles before the engine kills, we'll glide in easy. How do you glide a plane without power?"

"The main thing is to keep pointing down at enough of an angle that the plane goes fast enough and doesn't stall."

"What exactly happens when a plane stalls?"

I didn't want to say that the plane falls out of the sky. "It means you don't have enough control to keep it going the way you want."

"It sounds like you're saying it's better to crash with some control than to crash with no control."

"Something like that." I turned to Street and tried to give her a reassuring smile. I gave her thigh a gentle touch. "As long as your wound isn't severe, I'm sure we'll be okay." As I said it, the engine quit.

FORTY-FOUR

It's an eerie and distressing feeling when the engine noise goes away, and the blur of the spinning prop is replaced by a stationary propeller. The prop was frozen in position in front of us, pointing at eight o'clock on the left and two o'clock on the right. The only sound was the whoosh of air going past the plane.

To prevent a stall, I pushed in the yoke a bit, tipping us forward and down, keeping up our airspeed, hearing Street's words echo in my head. 'Better to crash with control than crash with no control.'

I watched the airspeed indicator. I didn't know what the best glide speed was to maintain control. I guessed I needed to stay around 60 or 65 knots, which meant 65 to 70 miles per hour.

As I watched the gauges, I quickly realized that the stationary prop was creating drag and slowing us down. I had to pitch the plane down at an uncomfortable angle to keep my airspeed up around 65. It seemed like I was diving down toward the ground.

The South Lake Tahoe airport sits on a meadow where the Upper Truckee River approaches the big lake. It makes for a wide-open approach when the wind is out of the north and landings are to the north. I got on the radio. I was rusty on the routine. I fumbled it as best I could remember.

"Mayday, Mayday, Mayday. Cessna One Fifty, out of gas, on glide to enter the pattern on final leg at KTVL runway three six." I glanced again at the altimeter. "I'm at one thousand feet AGL, coming straight in from the south."

I hoped that any other aircraft would give me plenty of room.

I kept up my steep descent.

We came down fast. The runway seemed far away. There was lots of dried meadow between us and the tarmac. I resisted the universal urge among pilots to try to stretch the glide, which has led to uncountable stalls and the resultant deadly crashes. Keep up the airspeed. A controlled crash is better than an uncontrolled crash.

Because I was no longer trying to prevent gas from flowing out of one tank and into the other, I released my rudder pressure and straightened my ailerons to come out of the slip. That would produce less drag. The plane's position evened out, no longer leaning to the left. I treated it like a normal landing except I didn't pull the flaps, as they would create more drag. I would save the flaps for the last moment. I stayed with my descent approach. As I got very close to the ground, I set the flaps, which would give me a little more control as my speed dropped.

I waited to flare until I was about to touch down. I ignored the painted bars at the threshold of the runway, which still seemed far in front of us.

With just feet to go before impact, I turned off the electrical master switch. I didn't need electrical power, and reducing any chance of spark seemed a good idea with gas leaking out of the tank.

At the point where I would normally have cut the engine power, I pulled back on the yoke, flaring the plane, making the plane angle back, slowing our speed and letting the plane settle down into the cushioning ground effect of air compressed between the wings and the ground.

The threshold of the runway approached and flashed beneath us as we touched down. Home safely. Alive. No crash. Fantastic luck.

But something was amiss. The right wheel dragged dramatically. A flat tire. Probably shot out by the rifleman.

The drag on the right made the plane swerve to the right. As we careened, the plane leaned to the left. The left wing tip went down and hit the tarmac. That created a drag worse than the pull of the flat tire. It caused the plane to skid around to the left.

We bumped and skipped and jerked as I applied the brakes. The plane came to a stop on the runway, and the left wingtip lifted back off the ground. We were damaged but still upright.

I did a maneuver I had practiced in my mind as we were coming down to our potential deaths. I immediately reached over and unhooked Street's safety belt as I also unlatched my own belt. I got my door open, leaped out, and sprinted around the plane. I jerked open Street's door, grabbed her by the arm and pulled. As she started to tumble out the door, I got my other arm around her body, lifted her, wrapped my arms around her, and ran away from the plane, away from the smell of leaking gas, away toward the meadow. Never know when gas fumes touch something hot and the whole thing explodes in a fireball.

In the distance, a red firetruck, lights flashing, rushed down the taxiway toward us.

I stopped and held Street upright in front of me and kissed her. She was trembling.

"Are you okay?" I said. "I'm so sorry you had to go through that. Is there anything I can do? Anything at all."

Street looked up at me, tears in her eyes. "What I want is to go get that guy!" Her voice was a hiss of anger. "That's what I want. We have to save Jade!"

FORTY-FIVE

The firetruck stopped when it was close to the plane. Men jumped out. They unwound hoses. I didn't know if they were going to spray water or foam or wait and see if the plane caught fire.

I took Street's hand and ran away from the plane. She was moving well despite the bullet wound on her hip.

In the distance came an El Dorado Sheriff's SUV. Behind it was an old pickup. Diamond Martinez.

The SUV pulled to a stop. Its windows were down. There were two deputies, male and female, the woman driving.

"Are you Owen McKenna?" the driver asked.

"Yes."

"Good to see you made your landing." Her tone was dry, her understatement notable.

"Probably could have made it another twelve inches if I wanted to."

Street shot me a look. My tendency is to joke in times of stress.

I looked at the plane askew on the runway, damaged, both doors open. Beneath the right wing was a dark circle on the tarmac, eight inches across. The plane was still dripping gas. The firefighters were poised with their hose, holding off on blasting the water cannon, which would probably destroy the plane that could otherwise be repaired. It was a sensible restraint that probably went against the rules. Like when a cop, contrary to the shoot-to-kill rule, doesn't.

The deputy cracked a smile at my weak joke. "Sergeant Bains said we're to follow your request."

"Thanks. Street Casey, here, sustained a bullet wound. She needs a paramedic to take a look at it."

The cop nodded, reached out her window, and made a waving motion. A fire department paramedic hustled forward. She carried a large black bag.

"We got a report that one of you is wounded?"

I gestured at Street. "Grooved by a bullet while we were flying. Please take a look."

The paramedic went to Street and set down her bag. I gave them some distance as they talked. Street dropped her pants a bit. The two women were fully exposed on the tarmac. No other options seemed reasonable. I got a glimpse of Street's bare thighs and slim hips in lacy white undies that were smeared with blood.

The paramedic looked and probed. She got out a pad – maybe some kind of antiseptic – and washed the wound. Then she applied some butterfly tabs to pull the skin together. She put a wide bandage over the area. Street pulled her pants back up.

I approached. "Okay?"

"Okay," Street said. "She says I need stitches. I said that can wait."

I turned to the deputies. "I can talk to the fire department later. Behind you is Sergeant Martinez from Douglas County. We'll ride with him. You guys can head out to Christmas Valley and meet Bains. We'll be right behind. We're searching for a man named Max Donovan who has kidnapped Jade Jaso. He's armed and dangerous. They're on horseback in the vicinity of the palisades on the west side of Steven's Peak. Near Meiss Lake."

"Got it," the woman said.

We got into Diamond's ancient pickup. Street winced with pain as she scooted into the middle of the seat. I got in on the outside.

"What's your plan?" Diamond asked.

"From what Bains said, I think the El Dorado deputies are heading out South Upper Truckee Road and hiking up the trail toward Dardenelles Lake and beyond."

"So we will take a different route," Diamond said it like it was obvious.

"I'm thinking we head up eighty-nine and park near the

trailhead that leads to Big Meadows."

"The back way in," Diamond said. "Smart."

Diamond drove fast. He careened out of the airport.

He headed out to the little town of Meyers. He went around the new roundabout and exited heading south on 89.

"You're not wearing your hiking boots," I said to Street. "Will you be okay?"

"I'm wearing my parkour shoes. They're good as long as I pay attention to foot placement."

"You don't have a jacket. If we hike up into weather, you could get very cold."

"My anger will keep me warm. And yes, we have no extra food. We're breaking all the rules."

I picked up on her attitude. "Your sense of injustice will give you fuel."

"Exactly," she said. "I've known guys like this. Angry guys who take out their masculine insecurities and anger on women."

"Guys like your father."

"Yeah. This guy kidnapped Jade and nearly killed us. He's going down!"

The intensity of Street's anger was understandable. But it was also frightening. I didn't know if her emotion would cloud her judgment.

Highway 89 goes south a few miles and then begins climbing up toward Luther Pass and Hope Valley beyond. Diamond slowed at the trailhead, turned in, and parked. We got out, Street grabbing her binoculars. I held my topo map. The three of us moved fast. Diamond put his hand on Street's shoulder. "You okay?"

"I will be when we catch this jerk."

Her voice was nearly a hiss. I'd never heard her so angry.

We ran across the highway, Street limping. There was a wooden Forest Service sign that said 'Big Meadow Trailhead.' The path behind it was part of the Tahoe Rim Trail. It went up a slope next to the Big Meadow Creek. In a quarter mile or so, we came out of the forest and onto the broad, open meadow.

Waterhouse Peak loomed above us. Not far away was Steven's Peak, higher than Waterhouse, looking more ominous than it did from when we were up in the sky less than an hour ago. There were two other hikers coming toward us as we crossed the meadow. They chatted and laughed, unaware that a drunken, airplane-shooting gun freak was not far away.

Street was leading us fast, nearly jogging, drawn by the pull of knowing that Jade was somewhere near. The trail was double in places and single track in others. To make it easier, Diamond stayed directly behind Street. I brought up the rear.

The trail we were on was a portion of the Tahoe Rim Trail. Hence, it was well graded and well worn. It went into the forest, over rocks, and then up a broad slope and over a shoulder before descending down toward Round Lake. Steven's Peak was ahead of us to the left.

Diamond spoke in a low voice as we hiked. Although he was in front of me, it was easy to hear him.

"You got a take on this shooter? Where he might be?"

I had my map out and folded to show our current area. "It's not clear to me," I said, perusing the map. "But we can make some deductions. If you look up at Steven's Peak, there are a series of three palisades just to the right and out of our sight. They are tall, broad cliffs 400 to 600 feet tall. You can go around them above or below. But they form a rampart that is difficult to go over."

We paused and looked at the map.

"The Tahoe Rim Trail – this trail – goes around them to the right. Because we saw Max Donovan and the horses below the cliffs, he might still be where we saw him, maybe sleeping off his beer or maybe digging for treasure. If not, he'd probably move north or south, staying on the trail for ease of horse travel. The Meiss Meadows territory to the west of him is mixed, partly rolling, partly steep, but without many good trails. I think he'll stay on the trails if he moves." I raised my voice a bit. "Street, do you agree?"

"Yeah." She was still radiating anger.

Diamond said, "So one choice is to walk toward him on the

trail. If he and Jade and the horses come toward us, it's a sudden surprise. Maybe he gets an itchy trigger finger. But if he moves away from us, we'd never see where he went unless we're moving substantially faster."

"There's another choice," I said. "We go above the palisades. If we veer off this trail to the left and go up the drainage basin that curves up toward Steven's Peak, there's a ridge we can intersect on our right. It provides a few different routes to observation points above the cliffs. It might take some exploring and climbing, but we might get to a place where we can look down from above."

Neither Diamond nor Street responded immediately.

I waited.

Eventually, Diamond spoke. "Bains and his guys will go up the trail from the end of South Upper Truckee Road. So we've already got multiple law officers heading to the area below the cliffs. Makes sense we take a different route."

Street added, "When the kidnapper senses Bains' men, he'll probably try to escape. If we're above him, we can maybe see where he goes."

"Sounds like we have a consensus. Street, feel free to head left off this trail at any point that looks like good footing. Let's aim for the sharp edge on that ridge at one o'clock."

One hundred yards farther, Street left the trail. She began walking through tall meadow grass that was turning brown, a sign that our footing might not be as wet as if we'd come in mid-summer.

Neither Diamond nor I said anything. We knew Street would choose a route that was as good as any.

After most of a mile of bushwhacking through the meadow, Street turned right and headed up a rocky ridge. The boulders and trees and other obstacles were larger and more numerous than on the meadow. But we no longer had to high step our way through grass and brush. As we rose up, we were coming up the back side of the palisades. In another five minutes of hiking, Street paused.

"From this point, I can't visualize the shape of the cliffs that will appear below us." She pointed. "It looks like this narrow finger of rock projects out from the mountain. We might get a view looking down. So I'm inclined to go that way. But we might also come up short, unable to see anything but a few rocky crags. Input?"

Diamond and I studied the landscape. I compared the ground in front of us to my map. That didn't help.

"I'll go with your impulse," Diamond said.

"I second that," I said.

Street walked out the narrow rock that began as a separate ridge but grew to be a tongue of rock that got narrower and rose higher. The ground on either side fell away. Soon, we were on a rock pier of sorts, ten feet wide, that stuck out into the air. The ground on either side dropped off 200 feet or more. Street paused, took two steps to the side, and looked down.

I resisted the urge to caution her. She had good judgment about her balance and physical abilities. For that matter, she could run parkour-style through the forest with far more skill than I ever could.

"I don't see anything," she said.

Diamond stepped the other direction and looked down. "Me neither."

Street said, "We need a place that projects out farther and is higher up."

"Lead on, guide," I said.

As Street about-faced, I saw that blood had soaked through her pants, coloring the side of her hip dark red-brown.

She backtracked down the finger of rock. When she got back to the ridge, she turned upslope, hiked another quarter mile, then started out another projection. This one went farther and higher. But the end provided no more useful view. We could see the beautiful lakes and forests and meadows of Meiss Meadows. But we couldn't see the base of the cliffs where we'd seen Max Donovan and the horses.

"Same situation here," Street said. "Suggestions?"

"I think the concept is good," I said. "Maybe one of these knife-edge fingers of rock will provide a good view. Or maybe not. But I think it's better to keep looking than go back to the main trail and simply end up where Bains and his men will be. Diamond?"

"Sí." He turned to Street. "Carry on, intrepid leader."

Street nodded and hiked farther up the ridge.

On the third narrow pier of rock, we found a view. It wasn't partial or tepid or somewhat useful. It was grand. We could look down and even back at the cliffs that were now mostly behind us. The entire expanse of the Meiss Meadows territory stretched out before us. We could even see the Tahoe Rim Trail, a beige-colored line that looked penciled in through the forests and around the edges of the lakes.

Street walked near the edge of the drop-off. She got down on her butt and scooted forward until she was sitting near the edge. I'm not afraid of heights in any significant way. But seeing her perched on the edge of a 500-foot drop-off, however strong the rock was, gave me butterflies in my gut. I always think of earthquake scenarios in such situations. Even when a person is sitting on something solid, what happens if the Earth has indigestion and suddenly bucks you off?

Street raised her binoculars and started scanning the territory below.

Diamond did like Street, sitting where he had a good view in a slightly different direction. He was a bit farther from the edge, which meant his position didn't look as precarious as Street's. He also used his binoculars.

I opened the map and compared the surrounding terrain to the topo lines on the paper until I had a good idea of our location.

After a minute of quiet, Street said, "Found them."

FORTY-SIX

I got up and walked closer to the edge of the cliff. "Where are they?" I asked Street.

She was looking through her binoculars. "Look at Round Lake. It's the biggest lake in the area and the one that's closest to us, right?"

"Right."

"So you see where the Tahoe Rim Trail comes from the north and follows the shore for a ways?"

"Check."

"Start at the south end of the lake and move away from the lake going – let me think – southwest. There's a string of small lakes. Six or eight in a kind of row. Near one of the middle ones are three horses."

"I don't see them. Probably just need binoculars."

Street handed her glasses to me.

"I see them," Diamond said.

"Now I do," I said. I handed the glasses back to Street.

"It's a great location for them to hide," Street said. "The TRT leads everyone away from that area. The Pacific Crest Trail, too. The forest on the small rise at six o'clock blocks the view of them."

"Do you see Donovan or Jade?" I asked.

"No. No people. No movement."

"Diamond?"

"I don't see them either," he said.

Street put down her glasses as if to think better. "I think Donovan moved there after he shot at our plane because he realized that we would report his location. Now he's practically hidden from all directions."

Diamond said, "Could be Donovan thinks he can hide there

until dark. But if he senses Bains and crew coming, he might leave. Especially if Bains has a search dog that barks."

"I'll phone Bains and give him the location." I pulled out my phone and dialed. When Bains answered, I told him what we knew.

"We're north of Round Lake," Bains said. "We'll be on him in fifteen or twenty minutes. Maybe less. Where are you now?"

"There's a cliff on the shoulder of Steven's Peak. We're up there looking down at Round Lake."

"Good place for you to be a spotter. Let us know when you see him move."

I didn't want to say that we wouldn't be staying in place. "I'll be in touch."

After I hung up, Street glanced at the map in my hand and said, "What do you think is the best way down?"

I hesitated. Accosting a gunman who'd kidnapped a woman and shot at airplanes was, by any normal measure, excessively dangerous.

"There's no point in telling me you don't think I should go," Street said, anticipating my thoughts. "That poor woman is being held captive by a monster. Who knows what he's already done to her. I will do whatever I can."

I realized that some part of Street's fury came from her residual anger about her father and his abuse of her. Psychologists probably had a name for it. Soft words that would describe transference of murderous impulses from one evildoer to another. For that matter, I knew that my anger about Jade's abuse by her colleague and her subsequent kidnapping had factored into my anger at Brady Harper's abusive boyfriend. Had I not already been inflamed, I might have gone easier on him. Then again, I was glad I'd scared him. And, right or wrong, there'd been a few times since the incident when I wished I'd been more forceful with him.

I pointed at the mountain behind us. "There's a slope that leads southwest off this mountain. It's steep, but taking a kind of traverse path might allow us to get down." I looked again at the map.

Street turned. "Diamond? Input?"

He glanced at me. "I'm with you, Street. I want to kick this guy's ass. But to puncture your plane's gas tank means he's armed with a serious rifle. Probably has other weapons, too. Either we need to sneak up on him, or we have to act like hiking tourists so that he doesn't suspect anything."

FORTY-SEVEN

With a little bit of directional information from my map, Street led the way. She limped but soldiered on. I knew better than to suggest she might rest. At times, the mountain was merely steep and only required careful attention not to twist our ankles as we hiked down and across the slope. At other times, we came to small forests of manzanita that we could not hike through without chainsaws and backhoes. So Street angled around, tried different paths, retreated, chose new approaches. At one point, she came to a scree slide that was hemmed in by impenetrable manzanita except at the bottom. Facing the only option, she got down on her butt and slid down the scree slope, a small avalanche of sliding stones gathering around her. Diamond went next. I took up the rear, my butt pummeled by bruising rock chips.

We got down the mountain fast.

Once on level ground, Street's impatience was palpable. "Where to next?"

"Dare I ask what you envision for your role in this mission?"

"I help. I distract. I grab Jade and hustle her out of this psycho's clutches."

It was a good answer that I couldn't fault. "I worry," I said.

"Me too," she said. "Which way?" she asked again.

I looked at the map, compared it to the surrounding terrain, and pointed. "That way."

Street led the way. Again, Diamond was in the middle, and I took up the rear. We hiked through forest and over rocks.

As we hiked, I said, "Diamond, you know warfare history and strategy. Maybe it doesn't apply to this situation, but what's your recommendation for our approach?"

He thought about it. "Surprise him. Surprise is worth a musket and a cannon."

"Maybe you could expand on that answer?" I said, knowing that it might mean that Diamond would launch into a history lesson. But we had some distance to hike. Street was limping with pain, and blood was soaking through her pants. A distraction would be good.

"You asked me about the code that Lincoln used in his letter to Stanford," Diamond said, "the cipher invented by the Greek dude Polybius. Turns out that Polybius's main gig was writing history. And one of the most interesting subjects he wrote about was the great general Hannibal from Carthage."

"The guy with the elephants," Street said. "A couple of hundred years before Christ, right?"

"Sí. Back in the day, the Roman Republic was basically taking over the Mediterranean. The guys across the sea in Carthage, the present location of Tunisia, didn't like that. So Hannibal led them in a fight against the massive Roman Army, and he scored victories that no one would have thought possible."

"Using surprise as a tactic?"

"Exactly. One of Hannibal's timeless strategies was to surprise them by showing up in a manner that the opposing forces hadn't considered. In one of his most famous battles at the Italian town of Cannae, Roman forces assembled tens of thousands of soldiers in a huge group. Their idea was that their opponents would come at them head-on and find that no attackers could fight through such a mass as they had. But Hannibal didn't attack them head on. He surprised them from behind and encircled them with a much smaller army. Then he picked them off with arrows and javelins from the outside before charging with their swords. The Romans were devastated. An even bigger surprise was when he came down from the Alps with elephants. He'd brought them across the Mediterranean from North Africa, marched them through Spain up into Europe and then down south through the Alps. No sane Roman could have envisioned that an army with war elephants that had swords attached to their tusks would descend down from the glaciers to the north.

It was a brilliant surprise, and the elephants terrified everyone they encountered."

Diamond stopped and turned his head as if listening to the forest. He returned to hiking. Eventually, he said, "In our case, only we know we're here. This bad guy, Max Donovan, has no idea. That's a huge advantage."

"How do you see surprise playing out for us?" Street said from in front of Diamond. She sounded impatient.

Diamond said, "As we get close, let's go very quietly. Soft footfalls. Whispers. We'll hope to spy this bad boy from a distance. Probably, we'll see or hear the horses first. Once we know where he is, I'll circle around and get on the far side of them."

"That's where Bains will probably come from," I said.

"If Bains gets there first, that makes it easier. More soldiers. But I don't think we should wait for them because their noise will probably scare Donovan off. After I leave, you two hang back. When you hear my cricket clicker, you both whistle back."

"Whistle?" Street said.

"Sorry. I forgot to tell you." Diamond reached into his pocket and pulled out three little devices. "This one is my clicker." He squeezed it. It made a very realistic cricket sound. "These are the bird whistles." He handed one to each of us. "Twist the end."

We each gave them a turn. Street's made a strong warble. Mine was a softer, higher, trilling scale. I had no idea what kind of bird they mimicked. But I was confident that our target would be fooled.

"When you hear my cricket, sing like birds. We'll start moving toward each other, closing ranks. Our boy might be anticipating company, but he probably won't think we're coming from two opposite directions."

"We close in. Then what?" I asked.

"You two distract him, I arrest him."

"That simple," I said.

"That simple," he repeated. "We're not in my county. But I can still make an arrest, and I've got the weapons to enforce it."

As we continued hiking, I wondered where Diamond's

concealed weapons were. He was wearing a loose windbreaker jacket. He probably had one gun under his arm and another in an ankle holster.

Street led us through a forest that was open enough to allow easy walking but was too dense for running. She'd regained a trail but came to a dead tree that lay horizontally in front of us. The trunk bridged from a boulder to a mound of dirt so that it was about three or four feet above the ground. Most of its branches had fallen away. Street decided the easiest route was to climb over it. I heard her grunt in pain.

Diamond followed, with me last.

Diamond spoke in a softer voice. "One of Hannibal's other strategies was to strike fast and hard. He demonstrated that there's no point in delaying a battle you have to fight."

As he said it, it seemed like Street cocked her head a bit. She didn't look back at Diamond. Maybe she was just trying to be sure she caught his words.

I was looking at a rise in front of us. "Hold up," I said. I unfolded my map. By comparing the lay of the land to the map's topo lines, I thought we were close.

I whispered to both of them. "I'd guess that Donovan and the horses are just over that rise. He would park on high ground with tree cover, and I can see the tops of trees from here."

This time I led the way, forcing Street and Diamond to go slower than they otherwise might. The trail curved as it approached the rise. I stepped carefully, making sure I didn't stumble and create noise. The slope increased with each step, seeming like a shallow staircase. As I got higher, my view expanded. I could sense a perfect campsite about to appear, with a view of the next lake and the surrounding mountains, and the cover of trees that a scumbag would want.

I slowed to a creeping pace. Then stopped.

In the distance were two horses. The mustangs. Cyrano and de Bergerac. Mostly obscured by trees.

Beyond the mustangs was Max Miller Donovan. I recognized the big guy from the Nevada DMV photo Diamond had emailed me.

FORTY-EIGHT

Donovan stood in a spot of sun. He held a can of beer. His sleeves were rolled up. On his back hung a rifle from a sling that went over one shoulder and across his chest. On his hip was a holster that hung from a low belt, cowboy gunslinger style. He didn't have a big revolver as one might expect, but instead a smaller automatic. Probably a 17-round magazine instead of a revolver's six bullets. Enough bullets to kill all of us and Bains' men twice over. Max lifted the beer to his mouth. The can flashed in the sunlight.

Diamond came up close behind me. He whispered, "I'll circle around. Give me five minutes."

I nodded. Diamond headed off into the forest.

Street and I hunkered down, me kneeling in the dirt at the edge of the trail. She sat.

Street looked though her binoculars. "I don't see Jade or Anne Gregory," she whispered.

"Me neither."

We watched as Max finished his beer.

I realized something sharp was poking into my knee. I reached down, scraped at it with a fingernail, and scooped it out of the dirt. A little chunk of granite.

I had one of those moments where my mind wandered. I thought of the granite chunk in the dirt under my knee and the granite piece that was found in Billy Jaso's brain. Billy Jaso's death had been ruled an accident. He'd apparently fallen, hit his head on a rock, and died. As I pondered that, I thought of how Diamond had just mentioned javelins and arrows.

So I played the game, What If?

What if someone used a sharp chunk of granite as a point on a javelin and threw it at Billy Jaso? Tahoe was full of rock. The ground was covered with sharp pieces of granite. As for javelins, Billy Jaso had a bin full of potential javelins in the form of heavy colored tubes of glass in his glass shop, ready for melting in the blast furnace. The weight of a single glass tube would make for a powerful weapon, thrown or thrusted. A piece of granite could be taped to the end of the tube. The tubes were short, but if feathers or streamers were taped to the rear end, they would fly like arrows. I'd seen a roll of duct tape hanging off one of the glass tubes. And if someone wanted to destroy evidence, the javelin tube could be tossed into the blast furnace, which may have been going or had been recently fired up. It took hours to cool down a furnace, which, at 2,500 degrees, would destroy anything.

If the location where Jaso died had been treated as a crime scene, maybe there would have been other evidence, incriminating fibers and such. But Jade Jaso had discovered her father in the dark. The first responders had treated it like any accidental fall. Get the victim on a gurney and rush him off to the hospital. Without cause to investigate further, there would be no evidence to analyze. It would be hard to even find the place where the man had fallen.

I raised up a bit and looked off toward the horses and Max Donovan. The horses were still there, but Max was no longer in sight. I dared not move. Wait until Diamond's cricket sound.

When I realized how easy it would have been to kill Billy Jaso and make it look like an accident, I thought of people with opportunity. I couldn't fit Jade into the role of murderer.

But what about Amy, the physicist? She'd been sneaking around the Jaso barn, supposedly looking to recover a gift she had given Billy. And she freely admitted her disdain for Billy's daughter Jade, who was half Chinese.

And what of Jade and Billy's neighbors, Sam Garden and his grandson Andrew? I thought about old man Sam's wandering mind, heading into dementia, making up verbal rhymes that were almost like riddles and Sorin Lupu's thought that Sam Garden was faking his dementia. In one of Sam's rambling episodes, Sam had referred to Andrew as Anders. At the time, it seemed like a typical brain cramp. Now, crouching in the forest in Meiss Meadows, watching a kidnapper through the trees, I wondered.

I got out my phone and Googled the name Anders. It was common in several countries. It was also a Basque name. Like the last name Garden. Was it possible Andrew's name was actually Anders? Why would that matter? Billy Jaso was Basque. The unpaid woodworker, Benat Mendoza, who had supposedly taken Governor Stanford's valuables as compensation for unpaid work, was Basque. According to Billy Jaso's journal, Mendoza had taken the valuables out of Stanford's basement and carried them up to Tahoe where many Basque sheepherders had gone.

If Billy had known other Basque people – especially if they were neighbors – would he have been inclined to reveal bits of his story? Would he have told Sam and Andrew/Anders? Would Benat Mendoza's story about the treasure filter down through the generations? When I'd asked Sam if Billy Jaso had any secrets, Sam referred to secret treasure.

So what, McKenna? I asked myself.

I looked out toward the horses, then glanced at Street. Diamond's cricket was still silent. I went back to my Google explorations. I was slow with my phone skills. My cell connection, so often absent in the mountains, was slow as well. It took me some time to find the Buddhist monastery in China where Andrew Garden had gone on his spiritual journey. When I finally loaded the website, it had links for past attendees and current attendees. The names were listed. The list of current attendees included Andrew Garden. Even though they had a no-photo policy, it was still obvious he was on the other side of the world studying the Four Noble Truths.

Or was he?

What if Andrew had searched on his name and found that someone with the same name had signed up for a retreat at a no-photo Buddhist monastery? It would be easy to put out the story that he was going there, knowing that anyone who happened to check would see his name as evidence that he had signed up and planned to attend. Except that it wasn't evidence.

It was barely an indication.

That got me thinking about my other conversations. I'd talked to Debbie Berrensen, the woman in the Pony Express group in Carson City. She said Max Miller Donovan told her he had family in Tahoe. What if Max was related to Andrew? If they had different fathers, then their last names would be different. Andrew had told me about a big guy talking to Billy at the ranch. Could Andrew have been referring to a half-brother and brought him up to mess with my investigation?

It was a stretch to even consider it.

But it was possible.

One of the first times I'd visited Jade Jaso at her ranch, Andrew had surprised me at the edge of the Jaso corral, appearing at my side with no sound revealing his approach. I'd commented. He'd said he'd always been picked on by bullies as a child, so he learned to sit with his back to the wall and walk silently when he was around others who might be predators. Bullies like a half-brother named Max Donovan?

I raised up again and peered through the forest. Nothing had changed.

I whispered in Street's ear. "I'm going to shift about ten feet to the right. I think I'll have a better view."

She nodded.

I moved like I was stuck in molasses, slow and deliberate. As I stepped off the hard-dirt trail, I watched for dry sticks that might snap and make noise. I came to a group of trees that grew from a place a few feet higher than where we were crouched.

When I had gotten into position and steadied myself and was confident I wouldn't make noise, I looked out from behind a large Red fir.

Max Donovan was visible over to the side. He was standing over Jade Jaso, who sat on the ground leaning against a tree. Max was leaning forward and had his arm up, gesturing in a threatening way as if to strike her.

She leaned away, cowering from him.

Words filtered through the trees. I strained to hear them.

"... the truth, China girl... your old man... couldn't stop

talking. Way back... meeting in Carson... Billy was talking... history stuff. Family histories. ...was him who tol' me about you being a fireman. Proud of how tough you were. So I had to see if you were as tough as he said... met that guy Barry and found out he was hot under the collar about you... had our fun. And now I showed you again. This time I'm gonna let my brother... "

Jade started yelling. She was facing away, and I couldn't make out the words. Her voice was wrenching, a howl of protest. She screamed and cried.

I could barely breathe. I wanted to charge out toward him. But he had a pistol on his belt and a rifle across his back.

I changed my position to see better. All three horses were now visible, Cyrano and de Bergerac where they were before. But I could now see Anne Gregory in the trees to the side.

A lonely cricket, unwilling to wait until dark, sounded through the forest. I waved at Street and pointed to the bird whistle she held in her hand.

She twisted the end, and a warbler erupted in song.

Max Donovan had lifted his head and was facing toward the cricket sound, where Diamond was hiding in the forest. Max put his hand on the butt of the pistol in his hip holster.

I twisted my bird whistle. The imaginary feathered creature made a sweet, soft trill.

I realized my view would be even better if I could simply rise up another foot.

There was a root projecting out of the dirt at my feet. I put my boot on the root, grabbed the huge tree trunk with my arms, and stepped up, getting a better look at the three horses.

The root broke with a sharp snap.

I quickly dropped back down as Donovan turned toward the sound of the breaking wood.

I stayed crouched as I duck-walked toward Street. She looked alarmed at the noise I'd made. But I was focused on something else. Something I'd seen as I looked toward the horses. It took me a moment to realize what it was.

All three horses had saddles.

FORTY-NINE

There was a third, unseen, person.

Diamond didn't know. He was walking into a trap of sorts, thinking that as long as he took control of Donovan, he was safe.

I stepped back to Street, bent down, and whispered. "There's a third person. We have to go now. We'll make like we're ordinary hikers. We have to warn Diamond."

She nodded and stood.

We began walking toward Donovan and Jade and the unknown third person. With the three of us, it made at least six people total.

I thought about Diamond's one-through-four social hierarchy based on the number of people. One person was good for contemplation, two, companionship, three, community, and four, cacophony. When I had asked him about five people, he said 'five or more meant it was time to rock 'n roll!'

I put on my best drunken cowboy yeehaw falsetto and started singing a disjointed, out-of-tune version of the Springsteen anthem. "We might be broken heroes, baby, but we were born to run! C'mon, hon, let's hit the highway. We're born to run! " I sang loud enough for Diamond and everyone else in the area to hear me.

Diamond appeared on the far side of the horses. He had his weapon out and was sneaking up on Donovan, who'd turned toward me.

I stopped and yelled, "Hey, baby, it's time to rock 'n roll!"

A moment after I said it, Diamond dropped to the dirt and rolled as a bright blue, glass javelin shot through the air from the side. The javelin flew where Diamond had been standing. It landed on the dirt.

Diamond jumped up. His gun was leveled on Andrew Garden, who held another of the heavy glass tubes, this one green. I couldn't see it clearly. But it had some kind of point like a sharp rock and homemade feather fletching attached to the rear end to keep it flying straight.

"One move," Diamond said. "One twitch…"

But Andrew was running, weaving back and forth. He arced around in a half circle and hurled the second javelin. Diamond dove away.

Donovan had his pistol out. He turned toward Diamond and Andrew, stepped around a large boulder, then raised his gun and took aim at Diamond.

Street came from behind Donovan, a flash of movement, running as if she hadn't been shot. She leaped up, hit the boulder near Donovan, and lifted off it in classic parkour fashion. Her left foot kicked Donovan just below where his rifle hung, her foot hitting the small of his back. It was a serious blow. But more impressive was that she pushed down as her foot struck him, raising herself higher like a tic tac climb. Her right foot struck the back of his head. His head snapped forward.

He staggered, off balance. It was amazing that he didn't plunge to the ground.

I took my cue from Street and started running myself. I hit Donovan as he was still making large running steps, trying to keep from falling forward. My bent arm and shoulder hit the rifle that hung between his shoulder blades. He bounced forward so fast and hard that he couldn't get his feet under him. He went down face first, sprawling on the dirt.

I thought Street's and my blows together would shock him into submission.

Instead, he immediately jumped up as if he had only stumbled and Street and I hadn't touched him. His Glock was still in his hand. I lunged toward him as he came to his feet. I got his gun arm under my arm. I clamped down my arm and rotated hard as I dropped, pulling him to the ground with me. It was a lucky move, catching him just so. Donovan grunted as his right elbow broke. The Glock fell to the ground. I rolled over his body and grabbed the Glock as I jumped to my feet.

Donovan threw a wild kick from the ground. His boot hit my hand as if to crush all my bones. The Glock flew away into the woods.

Before I realized what had happened, Donovan was back on his feet. The broken elbow rendered his right arm useless. I would have expected him to succumb to what would be excruciating pain. But he ignored it. He reached his left arm over his shoulder and pulled the rifle over his head. I knew I was dead if he could point the rifle toward me, so I couldn't back away. I once again launched myself at him. I grabbed the rifle with my two good hands, which was a giant advantage over a man with one arm.

Donovan was a big guy, not as tall as me but heavier and much more muscular. I didn't realize just how much stronger he was until he jerked the rifle away from me with his one hand. I had a moment of panic as he swung the gun around. I again grabbed the rifle, this time with both hands on the barrel. I knew he'd expect me to pull it away. So instead, I pushed it toward him as I ran at him with the full body charge of a linebacker driving to sack the quarterback. My blow didn't move him very quickly, but I got a foot behind his as he trotted backward, and he went down. I turned sideways and fell hard on him, my elbow to his body.

He gasped, not because of my blow to his middle but because it tweaked his broken elbow. His rifle was crosswise between us. I still had one hand on the rifle barrel and the other on the stock.

Beyond me, I saw Andrew Garden on his stomach. Diamond had his knee on Garden's back as he cuffed Garden's wrists. Street was on the other side cutting a zip tie off of Jade's wrists.

Donovan did a bucking maneuver that was so intense I was pushed over on my side. I still gripped the rifle, but Donovan was already on his feet. As I stood, he kicked the rifle out of my hands. The rifle hit the dirt. The shock in my hands was as sharp as if he'd hit the rifle with a baseball bat.

We stood facing each other, both panting. Donovan had

his left fist – his good arm – up. I moved forward, both of my fists up. He threw a punch. I dodged. He threw another. I tried to swat it away with my forearm. His fist glanced off my arm, a numbing blow. I threw a jab. He dodged. I moved in closer. He hit me with a gut punch that nearly knocked out my wind. I was winded, sloppy, feeling off guard. I tried a looping hook. He stepped away from it, then hit me with another gut punch.

I reeled, stepping away, gasping for breath.

He snapped a front kick at my abdomen. I bent forward to minimize the blow, but still, it was worse than the gut punches. I nearly fainted from pain and oxygen deprivation and nausea.

I was being beaten to a pulp by a man with a broken elbow. I had no professional boxing or kickboxing training. He'd obviously had a great deal of both. I realized he was going to kill me. I made two quick jabs, then rushed him. I got him in a clinch. He pummeled my back with his fist.

His broken arm was inside of my clinch. I got my hands over that elbow and torqued it hard.

He screamed. His body jerked as if under electric shock. I rotated, stomped one of his feet, and did a loose throw. I bent a little, got my hip into him, straightened my legs, forcing him up with my hip, and threw him to the ground. I stayed with him as he went down, landing on his body for the second time. He made a sound that was half grunt, half scream. I got his right wrist in my hand and jerked, flexing his broken elbow the wrong way. He howled as if he were being ripped in two. I thought that would end the fight.

But Max Donovan had superhuman reserves. The moment I relaxed, he slammed the heel of his left hand up and hit my jaw, jamming my teeth, stunning me. Then he rolled out from under me as if his elbow weren't even hurting.

We both got to our feet at the same time. I saw Diamond walking over slowly, his gun in his hand.

"Give it up, Donovan," I said, panting, gasping for air. "Or Diamond will shoot you."

Donovan didn't even look at Diamond. He came toward me. His good hand was clenched in a tight fist. He had fire in his eyes.

"Last chance, Donovan."

Donovan continued to advance. "Last chance or what?" He reached down, unclasped his belt buckle, pulled the belt out, and held it by the light end. He kept coming.

A belt with a metallic buckle at the end is a devastating weapon. So simple, yet if it connects, it's almost as disabling as a bullet.

I thought of pulling out my own belt. But it had always been a handicap for me that I can't bear to be merciless even if someone is trying to kill me. It was the same reason Diamond hadn't already shot him. Neither of us was sufficiently feral to contend with someone like Max Donovan.

Donovan brought his hand back like a pitcher about to unleash a fastball. I tried to take two fast steps back, but I wasn't fast enough. The belt buckle flashed like a gold lightning bolt.

In my peripheral vision, I sensed Diamond grab a branch off the ground and sweep it into the air in front of Donovan.

The belt wrapped around the branch. I leaped toward the branch, driving it back into Donovan. He yelped as I hit his elbow. I tried to grab him as I went down, but he jumped back. His foot caught on something and he sat down on the ground, his legs outstretched like a little kid's.

I was so out of breath I could barely get up off the ground.

Donovan was panting hard. "Okay," he finally said in a rough whisper. "I give up." We waited while Donovan slowly got to his feet. He moved slowly, favoring the broken elbow. Diamond had his gun out and leveled at Donovan. Donovan turned slowly, then shot his good arm out toward Diamond, releasing a fist full of gravel at Diamond's face. Diamond staggered back as Donovan ran toward Jade and Street.

Jade was up in the saddle on Anne Gregory, her body bent underneath a nearby tree branch. Street was rubbing Jade's wrists where the zip tie had cut and bloodied her skin. They both turned, alarmed, as Donovan ran toward them.

Street reached up and slapped Jade on her thigh. "Run! Get out of here!"

Jade gave her reins a shake, and Anne Gregory ran forward.

Max Donovan ran straight to Cyrano, who stood eating grass, his bridle on, the reins draped over the saddle's pommel. Donovan put a foot on a nearby fallen tree and leaped onto Cyrano. Donovan used his one good hand to grab the reins and urged Cyrano forward. The horse took off running.

Jade put Anne Gregory into a tight loop through the area and then headed out a trail.

Donovan kicked Cyrano and got him to follow Anne Gregory.

Horses are herd animals, and they naturally follow each other. It took no skill for Donovan to get Cyrano to gallop after the big palomino. The two horses and riders went out the trail.

From where we stood, we had a good view as Jade took Anne Gregory into a big curve at high speed. Jade was up and forward on her saddle, like a jockey, leaning into the curve.

Donovan was following fast, urging Cyrano to go faster. Maybe Max was just trying desperately to escape. Or maybe he wanted to catch Jade and force her to come with him yet again. But he had to catch her first.

"Do you think I should go after them on de Bergerac?" Street said, her voice shaking with fear and worry.

"No. That would be dangerous. And Jade is in her element. I think she will escape."

I stepped up onto a rise to better see them as they galloped away from us. Street followed me.

We watched as Jade took Anne Gregory around yet another curve in the trail. They were moving at full speed, 30 miles per hour or more. Then Jade steered Anne Gregory off the trail and into the forest.

"I just remembered that downed tree over where Jade is going!" Street said. "If Jade doesn't see it in time, that could prevent her escape!"

"I think Jade is purposely aiming for it. She knows what to do."

As I said it, Jade seemed to adjust her position, rising slightly off the saddle, imperceptibly changing Anne Gregory's rhythm.

Jade steered Anne Gregory off onto a different trail and headed toward the downed tree. Donovan was directly behind her, urging Cyrano on.

Jade seemed to have an invisible communication with Anne Gregory, slightly adjusting her gait, controlling how the horse ran. It was a kind of equine ballet, beautiful and sublime as woman and horse streaked through the forest, an almost poetic motion that aimed toward a violent climax.

Anne Gregory didn't pause, didn't slow, didn't make any obvious moves. She just galloped like a thoroughbred race horse going smoother as she ran faster. She launched up into the air and over the downed tree like it was something she did a dozen times a day.

Donovan was following as close as he could. He kept Cyrano galloping at full speed.

I remembered Jade explaining to me that Cyrano didn't do jumps. She said he always tries to run around any obstacle. And if that's not possible, he stops dead.

There was no way for the horse to run around the downed tree, so Cyrano made an astonishing, quick stop in front of it. All four legs and hooves were angled out in front of the mustang as Cyrano came to a jerking halt.

Max Miller Donovan shot forward, over Cyrano's head, over the downed tree, and off to the side of the trail. He reached his one good hand forward as if to cushion his collision with the ground. But before his hand hit the ground, his head hit a boulder, full face against the rock. At that speed he would be dead before his heart could finish the next beat.

Jade turned to look behind her. Then she slowed Anne Gregory and came to a stop.

Diamond kept his hand on Andrew Garden's cuffed arms as Street and I ran to Jade. Jade slid off of Anne Gregory and was walking back down the trail toward Cyrano who still stood where he'd done his quick stop. Jade stared at Donovan's body as Street ran to her. Street touched Jade's shoulder. Jade's eyes were wet with tears. It was clear they weren't tears of sympathy for the monster Donovan who'd kept her prisoner and assaulted and tormented her. Just tears of emotional release.

Jade spoke in a small voice. "Now they're both gone."

I said, "Max Donovan and Barry Whaler?"

"Yes. Andrew Garden is a scheming, devious, lying, vile human who disgusts me." She looked over to where Diamond stood with his hand on Garden's arm. "I hope he goes to prison for a long time. But Max and Barry were much worse. The essence of evil."

The words reminded me of Debbie Berensen, the children's riding instructor, who'd said the same thing about Donovan.

Jade continued, her voice shaking, "When they attacked me, I prayed I could one day kill them both. And I prayed that if I couldn't, they would die anyway. I desperately wanted to make certain they couldn't do to any other woman what they did to me. Imagine the tragedy if they'd taken some teenage girl instead of an older, hardened person like me. I managed to push Barry to his death. Now Donovan has caved in his own head." She gasped and choked as she said it.

Jade ducked under the downed tree, walked over to Cyrano, and hugged his head.

Then she looked as if she had a new realization. She reached up and touched the base of her neck where her father's dog tags had hung. "Dad's tags… They're gone! Where did they go? It's too much. It's too much…"

She dropped to her knees, bent her face down to her hands, and sobbed.

FIFTY

It took many long minutes for Jade to calm. Street sat on the ground next to her. Diamond stayed back with Andrew Garden and talked to Bains when he and his men came up the trail.

When Jade was able to talk, I said, "I think it's over, Jade."

She looked numb with shock. She turned and stared at Max Donovan's body.

I said, "It will take some time for the cops to close this case. You will have to answer a lot of questions. In the process, you might not want to volunteer that you wanted to kill Barry and Donovan."

Jade turned and looked at me. Her eyes were still filled with tears and more pain than any person should ever have to face.

"It's too late," she said. "I already told the Sacramento DA that when Barry attacked me during the fire, I pushed him into the flaming light shaft."

Two days later, I was at my office early. I was paying bills when the landline rang. The readout said No Caller ID.

I answered, "Owen McKenna."

"Good morning." A woman's voice. "I'm calling from the District Attorney's Office in Sacramento in regard to your information request about an assault that took place in Sacramento several months ago. I understand you are a former Homicide Inspector with the SFPD."

"Correct."

"To verify your ID, may I have your badge number during your employment?"

I was hoping for this phone call, and she sounded legitimate. She would have the badge information available, so it was a reasonable request to verify my identity. I gave it to her. I added, "I'm sorry, I didn't get your name."

"Instead of names, let's just say I'm a supervising criminal investigator. If you can meet me, I will give you the info you requested."

"You want me to come to the DA's office?"

"I'd like to meet at the public library just down the street. I have an opening at three o'clock this afternoon."

"That would be fine."

She gave me directions.

I took Spot and drove down the mountain. I found room in the ramp on L Street. Spot had his head out the window as I shut the door. He looked eager and then, when I didn't open his door, disappointed.

"What?" I said as I gave him a rough head rub. "You're looking for the tall, blue-eyed archivist who fell in love with you? Brady Harper? Sorry. Different kind of appointment."

He gave me his droopy-eyed look of disappointment.

Inside the library, I pulled out the Post-it note on which I'd written what the woman said. She'd told me to ask the librarian to take me to the conference room the DA used. Which I did. The man escorted me to a glass-walled room about 12 by 15 feet. The windows had blinds that were down. The man made a soft double knock, then turned the doorknob. He held the door open for me.

I walked in. Sitting in an upholstered chair at a long table was a woman with frizzy gray hair, gray-rimmed glasses, and wearing a gray wool pant suit. On the table in front of her was a mahogany-colored leather briefcase, an eye-catching contrast to the gray. It probably garnered her more respect than if it had been gray. And it went with her thin gold necklace from which hung a polished mahogany-colored agate. The briefcase was closed but bulged enough that it looked like it might burst open.

The woman stood but didn't reach to shake hands. "Owen McKenna?"

"Yes. Thanks for seeing me, Ms…" I hesitated, then filled in, "supervising criminal investigator."

She gave me a soft, pleasant smile.

She was sitting in a chair at the end of the table. I sat near her at the table corner, turned 90 degrees from her.

"Please forgive me for not introducing myself," she said. "We'd like this meeting to remain anonymous. This is a sensitive matter."

"Because it involves the death of a fire department employee? Or because it involves a murder that was never prosecuted?"

The woman looked startled. She calmed and said, "To call it a murder is speculation."

"I'm just guessing based on what Jade Jaso told me."

The woman made a single nod. "In her police interview, Ms. Jaso confessed to pushing Barry Whaler down the light shaft. She said she argued with the man about how to save the employees in the burning building. She said he slammed her into a wall that was on fire. To stop her fall, she reached out to catch herself. But her hand got stuck in a crack in the burning boards. The burning was severe enough that she lost three fingers. She screamed at the man, and he came over, grabbed onto her, and tried to pull her into the adjacent light shaft. She kicked out, and he fell into the light shaft instead."

"You believe her as I do."

"Yes. In addition, her confession was made under mental duress. She said he'd attacked her for the second time in twenty-four hours. The first was a sexual assault the night before. Her confession is probably inadmissible. And, of course, confessions are only one part of a murder case."

I was only slightly bewildered. In an effort at clarification, I said, "A case where she had motive, means, and opportunity. Add to that a confession, and it looks like a slam dunk. Please know, I don't want her prosecuted. I believe that if she pushed the firefighter to his death, it was justifiable homicide."

The woman made another single nod. "Technically, justifiable homicide applies to self defense situations or when one is attempting to prevent a deadly attack. So, yes, based on her statement, it was justifiable homicide. However, we have no witness, no evidence of the attack during the fire. But we do have evidence of sexual assault the night before. And juries are becoming more accepting of killings that were triggered by assault or domestic abuse. These situations bend to a new era."

"A violent double rape shares characteristics with domestic abuse?"

"So you know about the double rape?"

"No. I surmise. Jade Jaso's work colleague said that Jaso was terrified when she saw the perpetrators the next day after a traumatic experience that Jade wouldn't talk about."

It was a moment before the attorney replied. "DNA from the fireman Barry Whaler was found during the doctor's examination of Jade Jaso. As was the DNA of his friend, Max Miller Donovan. The doctor's examination took place less than eighteen hours before Whaler fell to his death during the warehouse fire. A defense attorney could argue that the circumstances were sufficiently distressing that the rape victim might be destabilized for many hours. Another possible defense would be Jaso's statement that Barry Whaler had attacked her and was going to compound his previous assault from the night before by pushing her into the light shaft. He wouldn't worry about her claiming rape if she were dead. Maybe, as she said, he tried to throw her into the light shaft. Maybe, as she said, she fought back and he fell instead. In that case, his death would absolutely be justifiable homicide."

I thought about what she'd said. "From what you're saying, if Jade Jaso had been charged with murder, she might have been acquitted for reason of justifiable homicide. Why wasn't Barry Whaler brought in immediately? How was he able to report for work the next day?"

"He was brought in. The police had him in for questioning much of that night. Of course, they didn't get the DNA test results until much later. He wasn't charged that night. He certainly would have been charged when the police got the DNA results. Nevertheless, as with Jaso, it was surprising that he went to work a few hours later."

"What about the other man? Was he charged?"

"The other man was Max Miller Donovan, a felon who had three friends and a bartender testify that he was at a bar in Reno when the rape took place here in Sacramento. One hundred thirty miles away. Five years ago, Donovan was convicted of assault. Two years ago, after he got out of prison, Donovan was tried in Las Vegas for sexual assault, and the charges were dismissed when the woman declined to testify. In addition, Donovan has been linked to threats and intimidation in several past cases. Just two days after the rape of Ms. Jaso, she said she had changed her mind and was unwilling to testify against Donovan. In my opinion, it is clear that she was threatened."

"So regrettable."

"And not uncommon," the woman said. "When a woman is raped and beaten and is then so terrified that she refuses to testify about it, the full picture of that crime is revolting beyond description."

"The bottom line is, the DA didn't prosecute Jade Jaso for murder even though the case against her was technically strong. Your office decided not to prosecute for other reasons."

"Yes."

"Would you care to elaborate? As someone who has gotten to know Ms. Jaso, I'm concerned. There is no statute of limitations on murder in California. What is the likelihood that she will never be charged and that the details of the fireman's death will be forgotten?"

The woman spoke slowly. "As you know, all District Attorneys pursue cases solely at their discretion. Our office puts enormous energy, financial resources, and emotional effort into our pursuit of justice. But there are many aspects to justice. There is the crime itself, and the people involved. There is society's reaction and society's needs. With each case, we try to look past the basics and consider it in relation to a larger picture. Contrary to what people think, we don't care exclusively about whether or not a case is winnable, although that is, of course, important. The other impacts on justice are more important."

"You're saying the DA is activist," I said.

"By some measure, all DAs are. They're like judges. Most of the time, they want to faithfully respond to the law. But they choose which cases to pursue based on many factors. And many cases are not just black and white. Often there is a substantial gray area. Like judges, DAs want to provide an unbiased interpretation of the law. But the larger picture compels us to adjust and fine tune. Laws are written by politicians. As a former police officer, you know politicians create laws as much for how the laws impact whether voters will keep them in office as for whether or not the law is good or just."

"Yeah, I've come up against a lot of questionable laws. Some of them are really stupid."

"We'd like everyone to remember that."

"Are you saying you won't ever prosecute Jade Jaso for murder?"

The woman took her time answering. "I can't promise that we would never charge this woman with murder. But we..." She stopped her sentence and looked across the room.

I waited.

"We have a kind of filing system," she said. "You might consider it primitive, but it's effective. Think of it as triage. Cases that are viable and useful by every measure get filed in one room. Cases that we deem iffy, either in terms of usefulness to society or our likelihood of success go in a second room."

"Are you speaking metaphorically, or is there really another room?"

"There are three rooms." The way she said it, I couldn't tell if she was being literal or not. "Cases where we don't perceive a good purpose by any measure go in the third room. This is regardless of our chances of winning them. We call it the dead-docket room. Ms. Jaso's case is filed in that room. We even go so far as to take the computer files, transfer them to a memory stick, and file those in with the papers. So the case is no longer in our computers. It would be very unlikely that anything about that case is ever brought into daylight again. And with the passage of time, the principals will have moved away, or died. Witnesses' memories will become less clear. While I can't promise the case will never be reconsidered, you can know that it's extremely unlikely that any action will ever be taken against Jade Jaso."

"Are you aware that the other rapist, Max Donovan, kidnapped Jaso, hauled her into the mountains in a misguided attempt to dig for treasure, and then died when he tried to chase her on horseback?"

"Yes." The woman slowly shook her head as if amazed at the depravity. "I understood he fell from the horse, and you were a witness to that death."

"Yes, I was, along with my girlfriend, and a sergeant from Douglas County, Nevada."

She looked at me.

I said, "I'm wondering if the fact that Jade Jaso was involved in the death of another man who assaulted her would affect your opinion that the DA won't come after her on the Barry Whaler death."

"No, it won't. The only effect that death had on me and another woman in my office who worked with me on the case was that we toasted Jade Jaso's survival with a glass of fine wine. That poor woman has been through so much, we salute her tenacity."

I stood. "Thank you for that assessment. I've taken enough of your time. I should let you get back to work."

EPILOGUE

"Typical American backyard party," Diamond said, "the guys hanging out, eating chips, drinking beer, while the women do all the work."

Our lounge chairs were grouped around a fire pit on Jade Jaso's ranch, midway between the house and the barn. We had a small fire going in the fire pit, three Jeffrey pine splits arranged in a little teepee. The corral fence was just twenty feet from us. Anne Gregory had her big head over the top rail. Periodically, she tossed her head, and her golden mane rippled, a super model fluffing up her hair. Back by the barn, Cyrano and de Bergerac were pulling hay from the hayrack, demonstrating their work ethic for eating.

"Parties aren't like that in Mexico?" I said. I was watching as Street and Brady Harper played sous-chef to Jade Jaso's pizza cooking extravaganza. Jade's former work colleague Vette was holding a beer and watching, leaning against the picnic table.

From my time with Street, I knew the look of the scientist's observation. Vette was observing how Jade adjusted to this kind of social interaction, something, no doubt, unusual for Jade and probably Vette, as well. There was no hierarchy of social order, no sense of rank or military precision, no carefully-prescribed job descriptions, no admittance test, no jockeying for position, no tiny adjustments of everything because the boss was nearby, no inhibitions of behavior to avoid antagonizing someone who was naturally evil. Just a group of people being friendly, telling jokes, laughing, coordinating the group activity of cooking pizza in an outdoor, wood-fired oven.

Jade was holding a firewood tongs. She nodded at Harper. Harper, who towered over Jade like a giraffe over a Shetland pony, slid a narrow split of pine into the brick pizza oven. Smoke billowed out and sparks popped. Harper made a squawking sound and jumped back in surprise. The little embers fell onto the large brick patio that surrounded the oven. They were rendered harmless by the brick and by the rain we'd had two days before. Jade reached in with the tongs to adjust the position of the split. Blondie sat on the brick patio and watched. Polite. Reserved.

Earlier, Spot had taken up his flirtation with Brady Harper, performing and wagging and doing the thing where he walks his front paws out until his chest hits the ground and his rear legs are still straight and his back is impossibly arched and his tail is working as if keeping time to a Louis Armstrong and Ella Fitzgerald duet. Harper had clapped and pet him, and when he jumped up, she spun and dodged, laughing and shouting, "Oh, my God, I think I have to get a big dog!"

Now Spot lay on the dirt between Bains and Diamond. I was on Diamond's other side. Beyond me was Sorin Lupu, sitting but not relaxed. He had on the full sun gear, sun hat with wrap-around neck shade, long-sleeved shirt, light black fabric gloves on his hands. His only visible skin was his face, which was white with sunblock cream. He didn't seem tense with the presence of the others. But he kept glancing at Spot, wary, but acting a little more accepting. Sorin's main focus was Jade. His worry about whether she'd be comfortable with his presence was palpable.

"Mexicans party like Americans," Diamond said, answering my question. "We just do it more often, talk louder, and have more fun."

"I've never been to a party that played this kind of music," Sergeant Bains said, as he looked over at a small boom box. "What is this?"

"Bach's Brandenburg Concertos," Diamond said. "And, no, it ain't what we listen to in Mexico. Great music, but Bach's more about musical beauty than fun."

"Probably mariachi music is the preferred Mexican entertainment?" Bains said.

"That's more for ritualistic occasions. Weddings, festivals, Mexican cultural events."

"What about backyard parties?" Bains said.

Diamond shrugged. "Rock 'n Roll pretty much dominates everywhere." He looked across at Jade. "Except when the hostess is a sophisticated, poetry-loving, Baroque aficionado."

Sorin glanced at Diamond as he said it, then focused again on Jade.

"What exactly qualifies as Baroque?" Bains asked.

"Got me," Diamond said. "Bach, I guess. Maybe Handel. I suppose there's a formal, processional quality to it." Diamond leaned forward so he could look over toward Sorin. "What do you play at parties in Romania?"

Sorin made a little jerk in surprise. He turned away from Jade and looked at the rest of us. "Romania is pretty western. The young people listen to hip hop and rock. But older people still listen to Romanian folk music, with pan pipes."

"Pan pipes?" I asked.

Sorin picked up his beer bottle and blew across the top to make the pipe organ sound. "Like that. Only several pipes of different lengths, thus different pitches."

"Pan..." Diamond said, then stopped.

"The Greek god of nature, of life," Sorin said. "The inspiration for Peter Pan."

"The boy who can fly," I said. I remembered that Sorin had mentioned his next series of articles was about flying. He'd said he always dreamed of flying.

Bains was watching Street. "Who woulda thunk you could dance to Bach?"

Street was swaying and nodding her head, one of her feet tapping with the rhythm. She held out her right hand and was snapping her fingers. Jade and Brady made fainter movements that still underscored the concerto rhythm. Vette was nodding her head.

"Street could dance to a funeral dirge," I said. "Finding joy in any music is her antidote to darkness. Maybe it's the same for Jade and Brady and Vette, too."

Bains said, "You mean dark moods?"

"Any darkness."

Brady Harper said something we couldn't hear over the

music. The four women all laughed.

Jade spoke and gestured. It was nice to watch her. The woman who was so tense and edgy looked calm, if not relaxed. The tightness was gone from her mouth. Her eyes had stopped squinting as if being under an interrogation lamp. Some antic Brady Harper did made Jade's mouth hint at a smile. No teeth showed. There was no crinkling around her eyes. But the worry lines seemed less long or deep. And it no longer looked like she held her head tense as if to absorb a blow. Her hair seemed less stiff and even waved a bit, its blue-black shine catching the sun and looking as dramatic in its dark sheen as Anne Gregory's blonde locks looked in their yellow sheen. Jade's hands, which normally oscillated between rigid fists and tense extension, seemed to soften. At one point, she gestured with her bad hand. Her ring and little finger drooped. Just like a gesture of comfort and inquiry and interest. Just like the gesture of a woman who was focused on an interesting thought and was no longer wondering if an attacker was about to leap out and haul her away, kicking and screaming.

Jade wasn't jovial or funny or effervescent or ebullient. She still didn't smile, and she didn't dance. But her pull-back from the chasm of darkness was a transformation I savored. She was no longer imploring anyone to think she wasn't crazy. She wasn't checking behind her to assess the threats. Her voice wasn't strident. Her shoulder muscles weren't bunched.

I knew she would regress now and then. I knew she'd wake up with night sweats and shivers. I knew she'd stare at the phone with momentary terror when it rang.

But the healing had begun. Street had already talked to Jade about getting together to ride. And Brady Harper and Vette had made plans to come up from the valley and stay at the ranch with Jade. They would hike and have a picnic lunch on the Upper Truckee River just 300 yards away.

Jade murmured something, and Street grabbed a long metal fire poker next to the brick wall that made up the side of the oven, slid it into the narrow opening, and pushed some of the burning wood around.

Jade picked up a 6-foot pole with a large metal paddle at the end. She angled the paddle onto the picnic table where there was another metal sheet with a large, homemade pizza on it, heavy with fresh veggies, peppers and cherry tomatoes, and excessive amounts of cheese. Moving slowly and holding steady, she slid the pizza onto the metal paddle, and transferred it into the pizza oven.

Sorin Lupu was looking at Jade so intently it was as if he was studying her. Bains was still watching Street dance.

"Those women seem to have more differences from each other than us guys do," Bains said. "Very different occupations, styles, interests, physicality. And yet something unites them. I wonder what it is."

In my peripheral vision, I saw Diamond glance at me. He was probably looking to see if, and how, I would respond.

I said, "One thing that unites them is they've all been abused by men. Jade, Street, Brady. Vette hasn't spoken of it, but I would wager she's spent some time coping with the same problem."

Bains nodded. "The darkness," he said.

Anne Gregory pawed the ground.

Diamond drank beer. "Our half of the species is now more insecure. It used to be our physical strength made it so we could rule the world. But over the last hundred years, physical strength lost its value. Now, more women than men graduate from college. More women get graduate degrees, become doctors and lawyers. And even in occupations where strength still makes a difference, there are women like Jade and Vette who can haul the load like any man. So insecure men lash out. We can still beat up women. So we do. It's hard to find words to describe how wrong and stupid and vile that is."

Bains and I were quiet. Sorin was still watching Jade. His frown was a mix of worry and hope.

Diamond continued. "These women who are so different find common ground in their oppression. Makes them dance to Bach."

"Women helping women," Bains said. "I wonder if there are women composers they could dance to."

"There are several important women composers, and more women joining their ranks every year," Diamond said. "Women writers sell more books than male writers. The all-time best-selling writer is a woman. Women are directing movies, writing plays, choreographing Broadway shows, painting major paintings. There are women running Fortune Five Hundred companies. Women holding major political power."

Bains was frowning. "Things could be equal if we could just find the men who hurt women and take them out."

"And then get out of the women's way." Diamond drank more beer.

Anne Gregory nickered.

"I'll show you a trick that Street taught Blondie," I said. I walked over near the entrance to the barn. There was a barrel where Jade kept some apples. It was sitting next to the barn beneath one of the hanging light sculptures that Billy Jaso had made out of hand-blown glass. I pulled an apple out.

"Blondie," I called out, patting my thigh.

Blondie jumped to attention and ran to me.

Street saw Blondie run, watched for a moment, realized that it was me getting her attention and all was well. Street turned back to Jade and Brady. Vette still leaned against the picnic table, keeping a little distance, watching how the social mechanism worked.

I saw Spot lift his head off the ground and look at Blondie as if wondering what she was doing. But he wasn't motivated enough to get up.

I walked with Blondie over to Anne Gregory. I rubbed the side of the horse's neck, then lowered my hand for Blondie to sniff.

Blondie and I walked some distance away. I had Blondie sit. I pointed at Anne Gregory while I put my hand at Blondie's nose. "Do you have the scent?" I handed the apple to Blondie. She took it in her mouth. It stretched her jaws wide. Her look was intense. She understood there was a task at hand. I dropped my hand in a pointing maneuver toward Anne Gregory.

"Take her the apple, Blondie." I gave her a little pat.

Blondie didn't run but, instead, trotted over to Anne Gregory. It was as if she knew it was smart to telegraph calm around a half ton of horse. Blondie went to the fence and dropped the apple. It rolled just far enough to stop directly under the bottom rail of the fence.

Anne Gregory walked over and lowered her head, sniffing the ground. Puffs of dust lofted into the air. The horse turned her head a little sideways, reached her lips under the fence, and got a grip on the apple. She knew that apples roll away. So she used her lips to press the apple down against the dirt and hold it in place while she got it in her teeth. Then she backed away a step, chewed up the apple, and swallowed it.

"Good job, Blondie!" I said. I rubbed her.

When I sat back down on my chair, Bains and Diamond and Sorin were smiling.

Jade's voice called out over the concertos. "Any of you guys want pizza?"

We all stood. Spot jumped to attention. Brady Harper was at the picnic table working the pizza cutter. Street was sliding pieces onto plates. Vette was handing out beers. Jade was already tending the second pizza in the oven.

We stepped into an informal line to receive our pieces. Sorin Lupu made a point of staying last in line, moving slowly, being excessively polite.

We ate ravenously. The pizza had more ingredients than I could count.

"This is spectacularly good," I said.

Diamond and Bains mumbled and nodded their agreement. Lupu stood to the side, the odd man who didn't feel he fit in, culturally, experience-wise, sun-wise. But he ate and seemed to enjoy it.

"You said this was vegetarian?" Bains said to me.

I nodded.

"I can't believe that."

"That's what happens with a brick, wood-fired pizza oven," Jade said.

"We know better," I said. "Brick oven helps. But the chef

makes the food."

"Do Spot and Blondie want some?"

"After it cools," I said.

We all crowded around the picnic table. The first pizza lasted two minutes. The second pizza not much longer. Vette popped the tops on more beer. She handed one to me, one to Diamond. "Sorin?" she said. He smiled and shook his head and pointed to his first beer, which was still two-thirds full.

Brady Harper sidled over next to me. "Because you witnessed my breakdown over my ex-boyfriend, I thought you should know he hasn't contacted me again. No calls, no visits, no threats. Life is hugely better."

"Really? I'm so glad to hear that."

"You wouldn't have anything to do with that, would you?" The pools of the Mediterranean stared out through the Mason jars.

"No, not at all," I said.

Harper looked at me long and hard as if trying to see through me. She made a fist, kissed one of her knuckles, and, as if in a slow-motion punch, gradually arced her fist toward me so that the knuckle gently touched my jawline.

"My checkered tablecloth is ready for when you bring Street to visit the archive," she said.

Jade looked at Spot. "He's lying on the only good patch of grass. Hogging it all. Meanwhile, Blondie is lying on the hard dirt."

"He does that," I said.

"I'll get Blondie something to lie on." She stood and walked into the barn. After a minute, she came out with a cloth.

Jade was spreading it on the ground when Harper said, "What is that cloth?"

"Just an old cloth Dad had in his glass shop."

Brady stood up and walked over. "This looks familiar." She picked up the cloth and felt it with her hands. It was tan in color, with a coarse weave. She sniffed it. "Do you know where he got this?"

"No. It's just some old cloth he found. Why?"

"Our archive was given a box filled with miscellaneous stuff from Leland Stanford's house. In it was a small piece of similar cloth. I wondered why it was in with his stuff. I spent some time thinking about it and then brought it to a seamstress. She said it was woven from unbleached, unwashed wool. Like if someone had spun yarn out of leftover wool that was discarded for being of poor quality. Apparently weavers have often utilized inferior wool. They make yarn and then weave it into rough cloth for use as mats or horse blankets. The seamstress thought the cloth was quite old. Anyway, this cloth of yours looks just like it."

I walked over to look at the cloth. I picked it up, turned it over, felt it, smelled it. "Is this the only piece of this cloth?" I asked.

"As far as I know," Jade said.

I called out, "Hey, Spot."

He looked at me with an intensity that could only come from anticipating pizza.

"Come here." He jumped to his feet and trotted over. "You, too, Blondie." She'd already been watching Spot. She jumped up. The two of them crowded me, hoping for pizza.

I broke off two small pieces and fed one to each dog. The pieces instantly disappeared. No chewing. No savoring.

"Want more?" I said. Both dogs were wagging with enthusiasm. "You gotta earn it. First, sit."

They both sat so fast, it betrayed their complete understanding of the command. It was one of those things dog owners quickly realize. When it comes to basic commands, the dog knows exactly what you want. Any hesitation has nothing to do with lack of understanding, only lack of motivation. Give a dog some pizza motivation, they will swing from a trapeze.

I squatted down next to them and held out the cloth. "Do you want more pizza? Smell this cloth. Take a good whiff." I put the cloth over Spot's nose, then over Blondie's. "Do you have the scent?" I put the cloth on Spot's nose a second time, then Blondie's. I put my hand on each dog, vibrated them, and put some enthusiasm in my voice. "Find the scent!" I dropped my hand in a pointing motion. I wasn't pointing at anything in particular. "Find the scent and you'll get more pizza!"

The dogs raced off. Spot knew the routine. Blondie was learning fast. Spot knew my command indicated there was a matching scent somewhere nearby. He had no idea that I was just fishing. But he knew that if he could find a matching scent, there would be a pizza reward.

Spot ran in a circle, head high, air-scenting. Blondie watched him, then ran off on her own, exploring the fence around the corral. Anne Gregory stood watching, her ears alert. Cyrano and de Bergerac ignored the dogs, so focused were they on eating that delicious dried hay.

Spot ran over to the barn. He didn't have the focused search pattern of a professional rescue dog. Instead, he sniffed a little here, sniffed a little there. He trotted through the open barn door and disappeared in the shadows. Blondie saw him and sprinted to join him.

Still holding the cloth, I walked into the barn after them. The dogs were both over in Billy Jaso's glass shop, sniffing a wooden shelf.

I called out. "Jade, can you come in here?"

She must have been moving toward the barn already, as she appeared in the door in a moment.

I pointed to the dogs. "Is this where that cloth was stored?"

"Yeah. It's been on that shelf for months."

"Okay, Spot, Blondie, good job!" I pet them vigorously. "Come get your treat."

They ran around me with excitement as I went back to the picnic table and broke off more pieces of pizza. I tossed the pieces to them. They each snatched them out of the air. A string of saliva flew from Spot's mouth as he caught his piece. The string lofted into the air, then arced to the dirt of the corral.

"Want more pizza? Sit."

The dogs eagerly sat.

"I want you to find more scent." I repeated the scenting routine, the same cloth over their noses, and sent them on another mission.

Dogs understand that if they're sent out on a scenting mission a second time, it can only be because you want them to find another source of scent. They ignore the first source. Blondie ran around the far side of the barn. Spot ran back into the barn. Blondie appeared over by our cars, trotting with her nose to the ground. Spot came back out the barn door and stopped for a moment. He held his head high, his nostrils flexing as he looked around. He glanced up toward the sky like he does when a soaring raptor calls. Then he headed off to the house. He made a circuit of the house. Blondie went into the corral and over by the hayrack. She seemed oblivious to Cyrano and de Bergerac, and they were oblivious to her.

Spot joined her in the corral. He looked skyward again.

I walked over. I stood where Spot had stood and looked skyward. From that perspective, I thought maybe he wasn't looking at planes or trees. Maybe he was looking at the top of the barn door.

"What are you looking at, Largeness?"

He wagged, then continued to look around.

"Jade," I said, "I noticed that there are a pair of light sculptures above all the doors including the barn door. Do they all light up? Even these big ones above the barn doors?"

Jade was over at the picnic table. She held a piece of pizza. A string of cheese arced from the piece to her mouth. She was reeling it in with her lips.

"Yes, they all light up."

"They mark the entrances in a similar way that Chinese guardian lions are used to mark entrances. Only your dad put them above the door instead of at the bottom of the threshold." I stared at the two large sculptures above the barn door. When I turned to look at Jade, she was staring at me. Then she stared at the light sculptures above the barn door.

She walked toward the barn. "Spot," she said. "Were you looking at the light sculptures?"

We all, dogs and Anne Gregory included, had stopped what we were doing and watched Jade. Only Cyrano and de Bergerac maintained their focus, eating hay.

Jade reached inside the barn door and flipped a switch.

The sculptures glowed the beautiful soft blue of the sky near the horizon on a sunny day. The glass was translucent. Nothing but light showed from inside the sculptures.

Jade stood beneath them and looked up at them. They both had some type of thick hooks at the top, which were hanging from heavy-duty screw hooks that went into the barn wood at the top of the door. Near the hooks were outlet boxes with cords and plugs that came from the top of the glass.

After several seconds, Jade flipped off the switch, then went into the barn and came out with a large, aluminum stepladder, probably ten feet tall. I was about to ask if she wanted help, then thought better of it. She'd worked as a firefighter. She knew about ladders. She carried this one as if it were as light as a cardboard ladder, her good hand gripped the ladder rail, her bad hand hooked through the ladder.

Jade spread the legs of the stepladder and wiggled it to stabilize its feet in the dirt. She climbed up the ladder until she was standing on the highest step, just below the top. She leaned her knees against the top for balance. Then she reached up, unplugged the light, cradled one arm around the big bulbous sculpture, and unhooked it. She held the ball to her chest. She was small, and the sculpture was large. She looked like a little kid trying to hold a beach ball.

With perfect balance as both of her arms gripped the blue ball, Jade walked back down the ladder. At the bottom, she set it in the dirt. Now that it was closer to us, it looked even bigger. Once again, Jade went into the barn. This time she came out with a tarp. She went to spread it out on the dirt of the corral, but the breeze folded the tarp.

Sorin was standing nearby.

"Sorin, would you help me, please?"

His face lit up as if the sun were shining on it.

"Of course," he said. His pleasure at being able to help Jade was obvious.

"I'll hold the tarp on this end," he said.

Jade said, "I've got this end. Owen, maybe you can set the sculpture in the middle of the tarp. That will keep it from blowing."

I picked up the sculpture carefully, cradling it next to me.

"This thing is very heavy," I said. "I haven't worked much with glass, but I can't believe a hollow glass sculpture would weigh this much." I gently lowered the sculpture to the tarp.

Jade set some pieces of wood on the perimeter of the tarp.

Anne Gregory walked over. She didn't step on the tarp. But she stretched her nose forward over the fabric and sniffed the sculpture that she'd, no doubt, been aware of as it hung above her barn for much of the time she'd lived with Billy and Jade Jaso.

Jade made one more trip into the barn and came out with a horseshoe.

"This has been hanging up for decades, but I don't think it's ever done its job of bringing us good luck. Maybe that's about to change."

Jade knelt down next to the sculpture. She leaned it this way and that, then made a decision. She tapped the horseshoe against the glass. Nothing happened. She tapped harder. Still nothing. She held the horseshoe several inches higher, then brought it down like a hammer.

The big blue sculpture cracked like a fantasy egg, with one half of the bulbous shape tipping to the left and the other half to the right.

There were gasps from the others.

What was revealed was a complicated wood structure that cradled and supported a guardian lion that was sculpted from jade. The jade lion was about eight inches tall. It was highly polished on most of its surface, yet had elaborate engravings and inlaid gold in various places. It was easy for even a non-expert viewer to see that it had been created by a sculptor with the highest level of skill. A truly spectacular work of art.

"The lion has its left paw on a cub," I said. "This would be the female. The Yin, right?"

Jade nodded but uttered no word. She looked up at the other sculpture light that hung above the other side of the barn door. She re-positioned the ladder and began climbing up.

A half hour later, Jade had freed both jade lions and their wooden cradles from the glass balls.

Brady Harper suggested that we shouldn't touch the sculptures and should only touch the wood cradles. She said she knew a sculpture archivist at the Crocker Museum who would explain what we should do next.

We all got down near the tarp, some of us cross-legged, some with legs stretched out in front of us and leaning back on our outstretched arms. Diamond squatted as he often did, rocking forward so his weight was on his toes, then back so he teetered on his heels. We stared at the the guardian lions up close.

"If I remember the records at the Stanford Archive, the wooden cradles were probably made in the eighteen fifties," Harper said. "But the sculptures... Wow, they could be many hundreds of years old. I have no expertise in this area. But I know that Chinese lapidary artists were exceptionally proficient by the Shang Dynasty. I'm not saying these date to that point. But jade-carving skills go back that far."

"When was the Shang Dynasty?" Street asked.

"The second millennium BC," Sorin said. Everyone turned and looked at him.

"More than a thousand years before Christ." Street's awe was pronounced.

"In other words," I said, clarifying, "quality jade carving in China goes back over three thousand years. A thousand years before the Roman Empire."

Harper stared at me. "Jade sculptures from that long ago are usually very damaged and found in pieces. But these lions could nevertheless be very old. Hundreds of years, certainly. Maybe more."

Sergeant Bains was looking from the sculptures to Harper and back. "It sounds like these babies are priceless."

"That'd be my guess," Harper said. She turned to Jade. "You said that the women in your family were named Jade going back many generations."

"Yeah. At least to the fourteenth century from what I've heard from relatives and from what my dad learned reading the family notes that were in Mandarin." Jade was staring at the sculptures. Her eyes seemed glazed over as if she was visualizing a very long history that stretched from ancient times to her. "My mother died when I was a little girl. But I remember her telling me that each mother before her related the story of how our distant grandmothers learned the art of sculpting jade but that they always had to pretend it was their brothers who did the sculpting. The women would make the art, and the men would sell it as their own creations."

Vette looked riveted. "Your maternal ancestors were all jade carvers?"

"Some more than others," Jade said. "Apparently, many of them had an unusual aptitude for carving."

"And so," Harper said, "one of the brothers ended up with these sculptures and brought them with him when he and his family sailed to California during the Gold Rush. He had no money, but he had sculptures that were valuable enough to entice Stanford to hire all of his sons."

Harper got onto her hands and knees and crawled over to the sculptures. She leaned in so close that her nose was almost touching one of the wooden cradles. Her head turned left and right as if she were finding the best angle to see through her glasses.

Harper inhaled.

"What, dear archivist, are you seeing?" I asked.

"My God, now I know why Lincoln's letter to Stanford had the number code. At least I think I know. This sculpture has a rebus!" She leaned over to look at the other sculpture. "This one, also!"

"What's a rebus?" I asked.

"A puzzle," Street said.

Sorin spoke. "Words and pictures, combined to make a hidden message."

Several of us again turned to stare at Sorin.

"My father told me about them," Jade said. "He had learned that accomplished Chinese sculptors always carved little pictograms and arranged them so they had special meaning to anyone who understood them. Usually the message brings good fortune to the person who understands it."

Harper was nodding. "The symbols and their order can be deciphered if you know them and their history."

I said, "You're basically saying that these guardian lions have a code?"

Harper turned toward us. The Mediterranean flashed behind the glasses.

"Yes! If you're skilled and perceptive enough, you can read the hidden message!" Harper's enthusiasm was contagious.

"You were connecting this to Lincoln," I said.

"Yes, this is so exciting," she said. "I can barely stand it! According to Lincoln's letter, he met Leland Stanford in the summer of eighteen sixty-one in Washington. The letter states that Stanford noticed the necklace Mary Todd Lincoln was wearing. Stanford mentioned that he, too, had some Chinese art made of the same material. Now that we've seen these jade sculptures with a carved rebus, it probably explains why Lincoln used the Polybius code to refer to the jade that Stanford had told him about. It wasn't just that Lincoln and Stanford both knew about Polybius."

"It was because," Diamond said slowly, figuring out where she was going, "Stanford probably told Lincoln that his jade guardian lions had a rebus carved in them."

I turned to Jade. "Did you suspect that they were here at the barn all along?"

Spot had walked over to the edge of the tarp, tentatively reached out and put one paw on the fabric. He looked around as if to see if people would object. When we didn't, he carefully stepped over near Jade and lay down next to her.

Jade put her hand on his head, then said, "For many years, Dad talked incessantly about where they might be hidden. He'd learned Mandarin so he could read my mother's journals and her mother's journals about her jade-carving ancestors. And he'd practically memorized notes that were written by a Basque sheepherder who'd claimed to have stolen jade from Governor Stanford, jade that the sheepherder claimed was payment for unpaid work."

Harper said, "Do you know where he got those notes?"

"He got some stuff on eBay," Jade said. "And he met a Basque woman in the East Bay who had a bunch of stuff from the Basque community. He scoured the internet for historical artifacts and bought everything he thought sounded interesting." She stretched out her legs on the tarp and gazed at the two guardian lion sculptures. She sipped some beer.

Jade continued, "There was apparently some newspaper article I haven't seen, published by the California Star back in the late eighteen fifties. The article talked about a Chinese man who approached Stanford with the sculptures. The man's name was mentioned. The name was a possible connection to my mother's ancestors."

Harper was nodding. "I've got a copy. I'll show you sometime."

Jade continued, "When Dad saw that, he became more convinced about the original source of the art. He focused on legal questions about Stanford's claim of ownership. He determined that even by nineteenth century law, the jade was basically acquired in an illegal bribery-for-jobs claim. Add to that my dad's belief that the guardian lions were carved by my maternal ancestors, and he was pretty much fixated on the jade sculptures. He felt he could prove that I had the strongest claim to the sculptures."

"So you knew about them all along," I said.

"Let's just say I knew about the possibility of their existence. But I certainly didn't know that Dad had already found them and hidden them in his glass work. This is a complete surprise."

We all stared at the sculptures as if they might get up and start moving around.

Brady Harper looked at Jade. "You told us about how you wanted to start a horse-riding camp for women? Disappearing and Rebuilding on Horseback."

Jade nodded. She looked at Harper, then glanced at Street and Vette.

"You said that it would take money."

Jade nodded again.

"I don't know what these guardian lions are worth, but I'm pretty sure they will bring far more money than you would need."

Jade's eyes moistened. She spoke in a very quiet voice. "That would be so great."

Diamond spoke up. "Sorin, my man, don't forget the chains."

"Oh, yes," Lupu said. "I almost forgot." He leaned back on one arm and stretched out his legs so he could reach into his front pocket. He felt around, finding nothing. He then stood up, looking embarrassed.

"Sorry, I'm absent-minded. They're here someplace. He reached into his other pockets, then pulled out a small bundle of chains with little metal tags. He held them in his open palm, then used his other index finger to stir them a bit as if to check that all the components were there. "Looks good," he said.

He walked over toward Jade, who was staring with wide eyes and the severe frown I'd learned wasn't judgment, but instead was intense focus.

Lupu said, "When I found out that you'd lost your father's dog tags in Meiss Meadows, I asked your friends to take me up there, for I'm very good at searching." He waved his arm as if to include all of us. "We went yesterday. Owen and Sergeant Bains couldn't come. But Street and Sergeant Diamond Martinez showed me the area where you got on Anne Gregory to make your escape. Sure enough, I found them stuck on a tree branch. Apparently they'd gotten caught and were broken as you galloped away. Both tags swung over and up onto another little branch and were caught in a way that made them almost invisible and impossible to see from the ground. I used a needle-nose pliers to reattach the chains where they broke. It's not a perfect repair, but it holds them together." Lupu reached out his hand and held them out to Jade.

Jade stood up and took them, her eyes wet with tears. She looked at them, gripped them in her good fist for a long time as if squeezing memories out of the metal. Then she looped them over her head and pulled the tags around so they were at the base of her throat. She grabbed Lupu hard and hugged him as if to prevent him from breathing. He was tall and she was short, so her head was turned sideways at the lower part of his chest. He held his arms and gloved hands out at his sides, floating in the air, awkward as a scarecrow, not knowing what to do. But she kept holding on, and he eventually lowered his arms to her and gently caressed her shoulders and back and then stroked her thick black hair.

In time, Jade leaned her head back and looked up at his face. "I know you can't be out in the sun. But maybe sometime you and I could pour some mugs of coffee and go for a walk in the moonlight."

Sorin Lupu made his dream smile, white teeth in the white sunblock face. "It would mean the world to me, Jade Jaso. The world."

Jade took hold of Sorin's hand and pulled him down to sit next to her on the tarp. Spot was on her other side, lying in the ready position, elbows propped out like outriggers. His eyes briefly glanced up at Anne Gregory who stood nearby. Then Spot did the slow lean toward Jade, flopping over on his side so that his back and head pushed against her leg. Jade put her hand on him, and he made a huge sigh and shut his eyes in blissful sleep.

About The Author

Todd Borg and his wife live in Lake Tahoe, where they write and paint. To contact Todd or learn more about the Owen McKenna mysteries, please visit toddborg.com.

A message from the author:

Dear Reader,

If you enjoyed this novel, please consider posting a short review on any book website you like to use. Reviews help authors a great deal, and that in turn allows us to write more stories for you.

Thank you very much for your interest and support!

Todd